The Face at the Window

Ruby Speechley

First published in the United Kingdom in 2021 by

Hera Books
Unit 9 (Canelo), 5th Floor
Cargo Works, 1–2 Hatfields
London, SE1 9PG
United Kingdom

A CIP catalogue record for this book is available from the British Library.

Print ISBN 978 1 80032 613 2
Ebook ISBN 978 1 91297 371 2

Look for more great books at www.herabooks.com

Printed and bound in Great Britain by Clays Ltd, Elcograf S.p.A.

The Face at the Window

For my dearest son Charlie,

with all my love.

Prologue

The sour yellow streetlight illuminates the landing as she creeps down the stairs fully clothed. The clock in the kitchen shines blue numbers in the darkness: 1.11 a.m. She slips her coat and boots on then checks her pockets for the last time – passport, mobile, cash, keys. Another minute and she'll be out of there. For good.

Was that a sound on the landing, a footfall? She strains to hear in the near silence above the hum of the fridge. Something clicks. What was that? Hurry, before he wakes up.

As she turns the back-door handle, the kitchen light flickers on and he is striding towards her in his dressing gown. She pulls the door with both hands, but he twists them away and pushes her to the ground, towering astride her.

'Going somewhere?' he booms and reaches down to empty her pockets onto the cold hard floor. The mobile slides across the tiles. Her fingers stretch to reach it. He stamps hard on her hand and she howls, the agony ricochets up her arm. He picks it up, showing one of her messages, then he smashes the screen against the side of the counter. Shattered fragments shower over her as she rolls on her side protecting her bump. His satisfied grin morphs into a grimace. She's trying to do everything in her power to protect her baby, but what if it's not enough?

Chapter One

I can't be late. I manoeuvre the pram one-handed round the corner, past the neatly stacked sacks of barbecue charcoals towards the tills. If I can get this lot packed away and dinner on by the time Nick comes home, I can be at the restaurant by four. I stop at the sight of the queue in front of me. Thomas starts grizzling. I stand behind a tall man whose trolley is piled high with trays of marinated meat and burger buns. I rock the pram back and forward but Thomas isn't fooled and bursts into a continuous cry. Sweat trickles down my neck, prickles under my arms.

My shopping basket hangs lopsided by my side, against my bare leg, handles pressing red angry lines into my arm. I tug the hem of my shorts trying to ignore the pain of metal biting into my skin and curse myself for not wearing something longer, more sensible. For the tenth time the packet of coffee balanced on the top slides onto the floor. I put the basket down heavily to reach for it. If it were for me, I'd happily leave it behind, but it's one of Nick's staples. He needs his caffeine fix every morning. Running out of Colombian medium ground is not an option.

Thomas's cries grow louder and more desperate. Everyone's judging eyes pierce into me. I reach into the pram, softly calling his name, and hold his smooth little fingers, but instead of grasping mine back, they pull away and open wide, emphasizing the escalating wave of crying. I try making clicking noises with my tongue against the roof of my mouth, a sound that is curious to him and usually makes him stop and listen. But not today. Why not today? Please!

I wipe my forehead with his muslin cloth and straighten up, hand on my back, lengthening my spine. I let out a breath and when I look up, it's as though my prayers have been answered. She's like an angel standing in front of me, smiling; her bright violet-blue eyes, slightly cocked inquisitive face, silky blonde hair and long side fringe.

'Hello, Rosie, it's so good to see you,' I gush, tears forming instantly in my eyes.

'Are you okay?' A concerned frown passes over her. We both wince as Thomas's cries rise in pitch.

'A bit frazzled. He hates it when the buggy stops moving.' I pull my face into a smile, but I honestly think I'm going to cry. 'Would help if this queue wasn't so bloody slow.' A few people turn to see who spoke. The man in front nods. I cross my arms, willing it to move forward an inch at least. 'I need to get home and sort out my husband's dinner in time to get to the restaurant.'

Rosie's frown is back again, but this time it's accompanied by the slightest hint of a smile. She still lives at home with her mum so I'm probably like some old married woman to her. She leans into the pram and touches Thomas's palm. He curls his fingers around her thumb and grips tightly, pausing for a few moments to examine her face and catch his breath. She'd probably be surprised if she knew I was twenty-two, only two years older than her. I don't wear all the young fashions like she does, the crop tops and trousers, the little skirts and strappy dresses. They suit her. They'd look awful on me. Nick says he doesn't want me looking what he calls slutty. He prefers me in classy classics he calls them, like these thick cotton nautical shorts, sailor's style ribbon blouse and canvas lace-up deck shoes. As soon as Rosie takes her hand away, Thomas screws his eyes tight and lets out a high-pitched scream which shakes me to the core.

'Can I help at all? I could push him round for you, if you like?' Rosie gathers her hair in one hand and drapes it over one shoulder, then she dips her head again and smiles at Thomas. He stops crying and gasps back tears as he watches her with wide wet eyes.

'Oh God, could you? Would you mind?' I say, grateful beyond belief for her kindness. She shows the same calmness at work, sorting out difficult customers with her charming smile and understanding words. Helping people, making them feel special seems to come naturally to her. It's like she can tap into their wavelength in an instant. Nothing is too much trouble for her.

'Honestly, I'd love to. You finish up here while I wheel him up and down out the front. I'll wait near the bench.'

'Goodness, you're a lifesaver, Rosie, thank you. I've got your mobile number, haven't I? In case this takes even longer, or you need to call me if he's not calming down.'

'Yeah, course. Don't worry, he'll be fine with me; we're going people watching, aren't we, Thomas?' She pulls smiley faces at Thomas, finishing with a laugh and a wink. Already his cries are slowing into steady chugs. I peel my handbag off the pram handle. Rosie takes hold of it.

'See you soon.' I kiss his hand and touch his warm flushed cheek. I wish I could be a better mum for him. No one tells you how hard it is to comfort your own baby, keep them happy all the time.

Rosie presses down on the handle and the pram tips up jolting Thomas forwards. A little more heavy-handed than I'd like, but I smile to reassure her it's okay. She looks too young to be in charge of a baby, but I know from work how capable she is.

The further she pushes him away from me towards the exit, the more my body tightens. I fight the urge to run after them. They're only out the front, I tell myself, but it's torture being separated from him.

The crowd is moving in all directions. Rosie half turns and waves at me above people's heads. I glimpse her blonde hair briefly once more, then she's gone.

The queue finally starts moving. At last I reach the conveyer belt and can rest my basket on the edge and empty it. The freedom of being able to use both hands is ridiculous. I can't see the bench outside from here, but I keep checking anyway, expecting them to bob into my line of vision at any time. I send Rosie a quick text to say I'm third in the line now, so shouldn't be too long, and I hope Thomas has calmed down. I wait for a reply, but my phone stays silent. I expect she's seen my message but daren't stop and text back in case Thomas starts up again.

It's almost ten past three by the time I carry the shopping outside. I head straight over to the bench and dump my bags on the seat next to a woman with a pushchair carrying twins. I sit down and we smile briefly at one another. It's the second time today; we've already seen each other going into the shop. I explain about Rosie looking after Thomas for me. She says that's a kind thing of her to do. I scan the square. I can't spot Rosie, but then it's full of market tents today and she could easily have popped into one of the small shops round the outside or further up to the merry-go-round. She may be in the coffee shop. The thought of resting for a few moments with a creamy cappuccino is bliss, but I really need to get moving. I text her to say I'm waiting on the bench, then I lean back and shut my eyes for a few moments. I feel the bruise on my hip where it caught the corner of the table.

My eyes flicker open. I stand up. Is that Thomas's cry? I strain to hear, but to me it could be any baby; it's not distinct enough. Nick says mothers instinctively know their own baby's cry, so why don't I? I check my phone. Still no message. Have I made a mistake? Did she mean another bench? My eyes dart around me. She could be waiting somewhere completely different. But I can't see any other benches close to the supermarket. I'll wait another five minutes, I don't want to badger her when she's been so kind to me. I stare at the screen clock, counting down every painfully slow second in my head.

The moment five minutes has passed, I call Rosie's number. It goes straight to answerphone. '*Hi, I can't get to the phone right now, please leave a message after the beep.*'

'Oh, hi, Rosie, it's only me. Gemma, that is. Just to say I'm ready to go. Sorry it took so long. I'm on the bench outside Sainsbury's like we said. I can't see you, so thought I'd better call as I really need to get going. I hope Thomas has calmed down. I'm so grateful to you for looking after him. Could you call me straight back, or come and meet me, please, whichever is quickest? Thank you.' I click the 'end call' button. My hand is shaking. I sit again, looking left then right, picturing Rosie waving and smiling as she approaches, a little out of breath.

I wait another five minutes and she still hasn't come. I keep checking my phone for texts and voice messages. I wonder if she's emailed me but nothing's come through. I must have made a mistake. I wasn't listening properly. Nick's always saying I never listen. Did I give the impression I wanted her to take him straight to Papa's Pizza? She understands how behind I'll be with tonight's prep. I imagine explaining to Nick why I'm late home. Why his dinner isn't ready. He'll know it's all my fault. Tears roll down my face. I sniff and rub them away with my fingers and try calling Rosie's mobile again. But this time it says in a very clear voice, '*This mobile is switched off.*' What can this mean exactly? Has she turned it off deliberately or has the battery died?

'Are you okay, love?' An old man with a walking stick and one orange bag of shopping is sitting where the mother was earlier. I don't remember her leaving or him arriving. A few other shoppers gather round as I explain what's wrong. The man's watery red-rimmed eyes look sad.

'I think we need to call the police, love.'

Panic floods through me. 'Don't you think they'll have been held up somewhere?' I stand up and he stands too.

'I'll tell security, they'll know what to do,' he says. He walks lopsidedly towards the doors, his stick clicking on the ground like it's counting down the seconds.

'What do they look like?' asks a woman with a small dog on a lead. I describe Rosie and the pram and the woman leads a small group into the market, calling their names.

I climb up on the bench in an attempt to view the whole square and shout at the top of my voice. 'Rosie, Rosie, Thomas, Thomas!' A few people stop what they're doing and stare. The mother with twins from earlier comes over and looks up at me.

'No sign of your baby yet?' Her face is creased with anguish. Is that what I look like?

'I don't know where they could have got to.'

'How long's it been?'

'About fifteen minutes since she left the shop.'

She sucks air in through her teeth, her face hitching up on one side.

I step down, blinking at the ground, then into her eyes. 'Oh my God, my baby is missing!'

Chapter Two

Twenty-Three Days Before
Gemma

A magpie is chattering on the low picket fence outside our front garden. Becca and Ben are arm in arm crossing the road, heading our way. I grab my phone and I hurry down the stairs, glancing at the screen. A notification flashes up. I can't see who it's from, but there are lots of exclamation marks and swear words. The doorbell rings as I reach the bottom stair.

'Come in, come in! So good to see you.' I wave them through and kiss Becca and Ben on both cheeks. Becca hands me a bottle of alcohol-free fizz and Ben passes a bottle of red to Nick who appears behind me.

'How are you guys?' Nick leads the way into the living room where the patio doors are wide open. 'Long journey?'

I slip my phone onto the sideboard. Everyone laughs at our standing joke. It's so silly, it's hard not to. I met Becca at the yoga classes in the village hall about five months after we moved in and we hit it off straight away – we walked home together, chatting all the way. We couldn't believe it when we stopped in our road, realizing we lived opposite each other.

'Who's having what?' Nick claps his hands together. He's already had a cheeky first glass or two while cooking dinner.

'I don't mind joining you in an alcohol-free night, Gemma.' Becca follows me out onto the patio and puts a Waitrose bag on the table. She looks glamorous as ever in a turquoise backless dress and kitten heels. She's pinned up a section of her gorgeous curly red hair with a sparkly clip.

'Are you sure? You don't have to.'

'Yeah, honestly. I don't want you to be the odd one out.'

'Red for me, mate,' Ben says.

Nick takes both bottles into the kitchen followed by Ben, who is already asking him 20 questions about his new motorbike. I step inside for a new pack of serviettes and glance at my phone. The message has gone.

'Are you okay?' Becca asks.

'Yeah, sorry.' I press the button to switch my mobile off.

'So how are you feeling?' Becca pats my arm. 'Not long to go now.'

'Really well. A bit tired in the evenings. Hard to believe in two weeks or so I'll have my baby in my arms.'

'Can I?' Becca puts her hand out.

'Of course, although I think he's asleep.' I swirl my palm over my bump. Then Becca lays a hand gently on one side of it. 'Everything okay at your last appointment?'

'All good thanks.'

'I'm hoping I'll be on duty when you go in. Just drop me a text when you go into labour.'

'I will. It'll be good to see a friendly face.'

'No more thoughts about leaving then?' She whispers as she takes a box of fresh cakes out of the bag on the table.

'Not since Christmas. He's been better, really trying.'

'I hope so. You know if you ever need me…'

'I know, and thank you, but this baby is going to change him.'

'Do you really think so?'

'He's normally down the pub on a Friday, but he stayed here last night. He didn't even make a fuss about it.'

'That is a good sign.'

'We wouldn't even be here if it weren't for you,' I whisper near her ear and cover her hand with mine. She looks up. My face is a tight ball, trying not to cry. I place her hand back on my bump and the baby moves, his head pushing out against my skin. 'He says thank you.'

'Here we are, alcohol-free, ladies.' Nick hands us both a flute of fizz. Ben's carrying their larger glasses of red. He passes one to Nick and raises his glass.

'A toast to the safe arrival of your bouncing baby boy. May the labour be short and painless.' Ben dips his head to me; his smile is warm and reassuring. He and Becca work at the local hospital where they met. She's a midwife and he's a knee surgeon.

'God, I hope so.' I laugh.

'Cheers!' Becca cries and everyone clinks their glasses.

'Dinner will be served in approximately two minutes.' Nick hurries off to the buzzing oven.

'Go and give him a hand.' Becca strokes Ben's arm. 'And could you put these in the fridge, please?'

'Got him well trained at last.' Ben winks at me and takes the box of cakes to the kitchen.

Dinner is a success and Nick is on top form telling jokes and sharing work anecdotes with Ben. I wish he could be like this – good-humoured – all the time.

Later in bed, Nick is gentle with me. Every position is uncomfortable, but he insists a strong orgasm can trigger labour. I want to ask why he's in a hurry for our baby to arrive, but I don't want to spoil his good mood. I'm convinced he's as excited as I am.

Once he's asleep, I take my phone into the en-suite and switch it on. In a few moments I'm scrolling through my social media, trying to find the message I glimpsed earlier. I find it on Instagram. A reply to an old post from a week ago from someone called Magnifique. It's the picture of us in the back garden in front of the pink camellia bush, me with my bare bump and Nick's arms around me, fingers curled into a heart shape.

All right for some, isn't it? Thanks for rubbing it in!!
Look at my perfect life, perfect baby and perfect fucking
husband!!

Bloody cheek. Who is this person? Is it a friend of a friend,
but which one? I click on their photo of a skull studded with
diamonds. There are no posts on their feed and no details about
them. I'm tempted to leave a reply, but why should I have to
justify myself to someone I don't know?

That's assuming it is a stranger.

Chapter Three

'Scarlett, come down, your dinner's ready,' Mum calls up the stairs.

I finish applying a second coat of mascara then put my satin dressing gown on to protect my lacy dress. The gown material is soft against my shoulders, and I imagine it is real silk, not Tesco's finest polyester.

'I told you I wasn't eating until later.' I sit at the table and give my plate of pasta a little push in protest.

'I've not given you much. I don't want you drinking on an empty stomach.'

'Who says I'm drinking?'

Mum's newly micro-bladed eyebrows shoot up.

'So are you going to tell me about this bloke you're meeting?'

'Not much to say. His name is Cole and he's totally gorgeous.'

'How old is he, what does he do?'

'He's twenty-eight,' I lie, 'and he works in an office, some agency to do with the environment.' I'm getting good at airbrushing the truth. I twirl spaghetti carbonara around my fork and take a bite. Anyway, Mum isn't exactly honest with me so why should I be with her?

'Sounds respectable. Is it serious?'

'Yeah, course. Been with him six months already.'

'Really? I thought he was new.' Her eyelashes flutter.

He's the first proper man I've dated. Nothing like the silly immature boys that I usually end up with. This is the real thing.

'Yeah, and by the way, when we get married, I want *both* my parents there, especially as I don't have any grandparents, that I know of.' I take another mouthful, rest my fork on the side of the plate and watch for her reaction while I chew. Gran died a month before I was born. I think it's sad I didn't get to know her.

'Not again, Scarlett, please.' Mum pours a glug of white wine into her glass.

'Cole says I've got a right to know who my dad is.'

'Oh, does he now? And when did it become any of his business?'

'He cares about me, is that all right? He says fathers should have equal rights, so legally you can't stop Dad and me from seeing each other.'

Mum knocks back a mouthful of wine and pours out another glug. 'He hasn't got a clue, so I suggest he minds his own bloody business.' She turns her head and grinds her teeth together.

I glance at her profile, high cheekbones, smooth skin, worried eyes.

'Look, all I'm saying is you must have loved him once. You had me, didn't you?' I try to picture their happy faces the first time they saw me. 'Presumably, you loved him while I was being conceived, when I was born, so tell me what went so wrong?'

Mum's eyes redden. 'It's not that simple. It's all a bit of a blur.'

'Why are you making excuses? You must remember something. Why won't you tell me?' I stand up, and my chair goes flying backwards. 'Or maybe that's it, you're telling the truth – because you don't know who he is. So, tell me *all* their names and I'll find out for myself.' My voice is strangled. I can't believe I said that.

'How dare you insinuate…? I'm doing this for your own good.' Mum stands too. Her face is flushed, eyes wet.

'My own good or yours?' I yell. This has gone on too long all because I'm too scared of upsetting her, of her rejecting me.

13

Like when I was fourteen and she found out I'd borrowed three pounds to go into town with some girlfriends; she didn't speak to me for three days after. Stealing, she called it. She came after me and demanded I empty my pockets in front of my friends. I was mortified. I'd intended to pay her back. I'd wanted to buy her three bunches of daffodils from the supermarket for Mother's Day.

Mum doesn't answer. She stares down at the table, her fingers spread, pressed into the gingham cloth.

'I'm not a bloody child any more.' I storm out of the room and run upstairs. She should have told me years ago. I'm twenty-one next month, old enough to decide if I want to see my own bloody father or not. It's not up to her. I wish I could picture his face. I remember my hand being held in a warm palm and when I looked up his smile was obscured by sunlight. No one said he was my daddy though, so I suppose it could have been any of Mum's boyfriends.

I can't wait to move out, live in my own place with my own rules. Cole says as soon as his divorce comes through, he wants us to get married. We'll live in a lovely modern house on the new estate, not a poky old place like this one. Somewhere we can bring up our own little family. All my life I've yearned to know what it would be like to have a daddy, be his special little girl. One of those dads who lifts you up in the air in his big strong hands and loves and hugs you like no one else on earth.

A memory slides into my mind of coming home from school, showing Mum the Father's Day card I'd had to make.

'Why don't I have a daddy like everyone else?' I'd asked her.

'Oh sweetheart, not everyone has a daddy. Sometimes things happen to people that we can't do anything about.'

'Did something happen to my daddy?'

'Yes, darling, it did.' She'd cried and tried to hide it from me. And I know how upset it still makes her when I ask about him, but she refuses to give me one single clue about who he is.

A few minutes later, I hear the doorbell ring. Mum answers it and I'm grateful to hear Amy's voice.

'Hi, Kelly, is Scarlett there, please?'

Mum invites Amy in and tells her to go on upstairs. A moment later there's a light tap, tap on my bedroom door.

'Hey, are you okay?' Amy comes straight over and hugs me. I wipe my eyes and explain to her what happened with Mum. How I've never confronted her like that before. How can I move on with my life, not knowing who my dad is? I need to know the truth.

'Sometimes it's better not knowing,' Amy says.

'Whose side are you on?' I pull away from her. She sticks her bottom lip out like a small child. As if I'd ever doubt her loyalty.

'Mum told me about my dad when I was little, but I wished she hadn't,' Amy says. 'I'd built up this idea of what he was like in my head, how kind he was, how much he missed me and she completely burst my bubble.'

'But Cole says mothers use any old excuse to cut dads out of their kids' lives because it's easier for them. He could be out there looking for me right now.'

'Then if he is, he'll find you, won't he?'

'Will he, though? All I've ever wanted is a dad.' I stand at the mirror.

'I know, I was like that too.' She reaches for my hand and we touch fingertips.

'All my life I've wondered what part of me looks like him. If we have the same eyes or ears. Maybe he loves reading as much as I do. Although Mum's a bookworm, too. Is that what they had in common? But why does she get so upset whenever I mention him?'

'Perhaps he met someone else, ran off with her best friend and broke her heart.'

I nod. 'That could be it. It would explain why it's so painful for her.' I blot my skin with a tissue. 'Oh God, I was so mean to her. I said that maybe she didn't know because it could have been anyone.'

'Scarlett!'

'I know. Why did I open my big mouth?' I peer closer at myself. 'Look at the state of me. I'll have to re-do my face now.'

'What time are you meeting Cole?'

'Eight.'

'Are you sure you want me to come?'

'Yeah, of course.' I smooth on foundation with my fingertips.

'You know he doesn't like me, right?'

'He does really.' I look in the mirror. But it's true, he doesn't, and what's worse is she doesn't like him either.

–

We take a bus into Bedford town centre and walk up past Debenhams to The King's Arms. The usual Friday night crowd are there and as soon as I spot Cole, my spirits lift. He gives me the biggest, warmest hug. He smells so good I could stay in his arms all night.

'Hey, babes, how's it going?' He plants a kiss on my lips before I can reply. 'I got you a beer.' He reaches out to the bar and grabs two bottles and takes a swig from one and hands me the other.

'What about Amy?' I take it and knock back a mouthful.

'Oh, sorry. Do you want mine?' He holds it out to her by the neck, the rim shiny with his saliva. Is he serious?

'I'll get my own, thanks.' Amy lowers her eyes and eases past my back to the bar.

'Suit yourself.'

'Do you want me to wait with you?' I whisper in her ear.

'It's okay.' She doesn't look at me.

'I'll wait. Let me get them.' I touch her shoulder and flick a glance at Cole. He could try and make an effort with her, she is my best friend. His phone lights up. He taps on it, reads and then frowns.

'What's up?'

'It's nothing. See you in a sec?' He points at his mates with his thumb and heads over to them. I lean on the bar. The barman catches my eye and comes straight over. A woman further up gives me the death stare. *Sorry, love,* I say with my best sad face.

'What can I get you, beautiful?' The barman has a cheeky smile.

'Wasn't that woman first?'

He glances at her and shakes his head.

'Okay, well two bottles of Bud, please.' I finish my first and push it towards him.

The live band start playing Martika 'I Feel The Earth Move'. The guitar and synth intro ricochets through my body and I can't help but sway with the music.

I hand Amy her bottle and dance with mine towards Cole, using it as a microphone. I know all the words as well as the moves. Amy follows close behind, very much not dancing.

Cole reaches out to me and his hand weaves through my hair to the back of my neck. He gently draws me to him and we kiss passionately. Amy sits at a table nearby not looking at us.

'Why are you still being like that with her?'

He arches one of his eyebrows, as if the answer is obvious. I play-punch his arm. I'd have thought they'd be getting along by now. I hope Mum's not like this when she eventually meets him. He is 'the one' so they'll have to get used to it. I know what Mum will say. *But he's a married man.* He assured me he'd separated from his wife before we met. When we get married, I'll do whatever it takes to make sure my dad is there to walk me down the aisle.

Chapter Four

Where are you, Rosie? I keep looking around, hoping that she's been delayed somewhere and is coming back any moment now. I can't think about the alternative. It doesn't make any sense. I'll have to call Nick, but how will I tell him? He'll never forgive me. I shiver. The mum with twins, Jade, takes a multicoloured crochet blanket from the back of her pushchair and wraps it around my shoulders. Its softness and the clean baby smell make me weep all over again.

The old guy with the stick totters out of the supermarket accompanied by a woman in a suit with a name badge on her lapel. She is about my mother's age, with cropped brown hair and round glasses. My heartbeat pounds in my ears. Within seconds of me confirming that Thomas has not been returned to me, Cynthia Bryan, security manager has introduced herself and is straight on her two-way radio asking the customer service manager to call the local police station urgently.

I cover my ears. The ground seems to tilt away from me. This can't be happening. It's not real. Is it? I stagger around, hoping to bump into them. Maybe that's them by the greetings card stall, there's a girl crouched down choosing a roll of wrapping paper, one hand still on her buggy. But no, when she stands, she's not as tall and slim as Rosie.

My baby isn't missing, they've got lost somewhere, that's all. Taken a turn down a residential road that goes on and on and looks like all the other roads in this part of Bedford. Rosie can't work out her way back. I check my phone again, silently pleading with her to call me, tell me where they are so I can go and get them. I don't mind how far it is. I'll understand. She was doing me a favour, being her usual practical and thoughtful self. I won't be mad at her, I'll be relieved. So, so relieved. Tears choke me. I'm kidding myself. They'd have been back by now. It's been almost twenty minutes. Something's not right. Something has happened to them.

'The police are on their way,' Cynthia says, gently guiding me back to the front of the shop. People are staring at us, at me. I squint back at them. What do they know, did they see something I missed?

The woman with the dog and the small group come back solemnly shaking their heads. I thank them and they hang around looking helpless.

Panic strikes my chest. 'Does anyone know where they are?' I shout to no one in particular. 'A girl with mid-length blonde hair pushing a green BABYZEN pram… my newborn baby, Thomas, inside.' How many girls around here are pushing prams, have blonde hair like Rosie? There is nothing that makes them stand out. Several people shake their heads then carry on walking by, back to their normal lives.

I turn to Cynthia. 'What if they've been hit by a car while they were crossing the road or someone has abducted them?'

'Whatever has happened, we will find them, Gemma, there's CCTV all round here, and we're already checking the cameras in the shop.' She passes me a cup of milky tea one of her team has brought out.

'It's on Twitter and the BBC.' A teenage boy from the small group holds up his phone. 'Baby snatched from Bedford super-market.'

'Oh God, this can't be happening.' I sit on the bench and curl over, arms holding myself.

A few minutes later police sirens fill the air.

'Shall we wait inside?' Cynthia sits next to me and touches my arm gently.

'No, I can't. What if she turns up and I'm not here?'

'I think she would call you?'

'We'll let you know, love,' says the woman with the dog.

I stare at my phone which is practically glued to my hand. I must have tried Rosie's number thirty or forty times.

'Her phone is off. Someone must have switched it off. I think they've been taken.'

'You don't think she might have turned it off herself?' Cynthia says quietly.

'Why would she do that?' I frown at her.

'I don't know, it's something we need to find out.'

A tendril of doubt creeps into my mind. Could Rosie have switched her phone off deliberately? But why? Was she a tiny bit jealous of me? I'm aware that from the outside it looks like I have it all – a house, a business, a husband and a baby. But she wouldn't take my baby because of that, would she?

'I need to call my husband.'

Cynthia nods and moves away. My fingers tremble as I tap in his name.

'Where the hell are you?' Nick asks before I can even speak.

'I'm sorry I'm… I'm still at the shops.'

'How long are you going to be?'

He's shouting down the phone at me to get a move on, except the noise becomes one big blur I can't decipher. My mind replays everything Rosie said to me, every look, every gesture in case I missed a clue. *I'll look after him. He's safe with me.* I search the square from left to right, right to left, backwards and forwards until I'm dizzy. I think I see a green pram near the crossing on the left, opposite the primary school gates over the road. Yes, it's definitely blonde hair, if a little messy. I stride towards them and my hand drops to my side, still gripping the mobile.

'Rosie, Rosie!' I shout until my lungs burn.

'Come back, come back, Rosie.' I break into a run and I catch up with her in the middle of the road, but she doesn't stop. I call her name again and stretch my hand out to tap her arm. She half turns towards me and frowns. Her skin is wrinkled, eyes confused. She's holding a small straggly dog in her arms. The pram isn't quite so green close up, it is more of a murky blue. The pram is empty. There is no baby.

'Sorry, I'm so sorry,' I say and cover my mouth with my hand, watching her continue to the other side of the road.

I can hear Nick's voice calling my name. The lights change to green. Cars rev their engines; one driver hoots at me. I run back the way I came and once I'm on the pavement, I bring the phone up to my face. My head feels suddenly light, my hands a little shaky.

'Something terrible has happened.' Tears are running down my face.

'Tell me what the bloody hell is going on,' Nick yells, blasting my eardrum.

Blood rushes to my head. My chin trembles as I speak. 'Thomas has been taken.'

'What…' His voice is muffled, distant.

Sparks of light fly at my eyes. I think I'm going to faint.

Chapter Five

21 Days Before
Gemma

The temperature is already climbing by the time I park the car in the multi-storey at 6 a.m. The short walk to the restaurant through an avenue of lime trees is a mini meditation every day, especially as there's hardly anyone else around. Except this morning. I glance over my shoulder for the third time. Sometimes I'm unaware of early morning joggers until they glide past, startling me. They are so silent you can only sense someone approaching if you're paying full attention. Today I could swear someone is behind me, eyes boring into the back of my head, but each time I look there's no one there.

I pull my bag up higher on my shoulder and grip it tight to my hip. Just in case. Nick's always reading out the latest crime headlines from the *Bedford Echo*. Drug dealing, burglaries, even murders. When we moved to St Marys in Biddenham three years ago, the sales blurb had called it 'a desirable village location on the outskirts of Bedford with parks, scenic river walks, bike trails and golf courses nearby'. And it is lovely to look at. But is it safe?

I find myself considering all sorts of questions I've never thought about before I became pregnant. Life has become one danger zone after another, nothing like I expected. Will I stop all this worrying when it's born?

I walk faster, checking around me, across the street and behind me again. A road sweeper looks up from his broom momentarily. My heart is pounding so hard my chest hurts. I'm very lucky. I know that. We have a beautiful four-bedroom new-build, just like the show home. Nick wanted us to copy the décor of the marketing suite, so many of the pieces are the same. Opposite us lives my best friend Becca. She has literally been my lifesaver. But in the last couple of years there seems to be a new crime every week. Boy racers, cars broken into and groups of youths from outside the estate coming in at night and wrecking the play equipment at the park.

Usually I walk to work or cycle, but this baby has become so heavy I have to rely on the car. I stop against a wall by the card shop to catch my breath. If there really is someone following me and they try to rob me, what could I even do to defend myself? I'm eight and a half months pregnant.

I walk on and when the restaurant is in sight, I reach in my bag for the key and hold my mobile in my other hand.

As soon as I reach the door, I shove the key in and turn it. One last glance over my shoulder. A young girl is hurrying away towards the station. She's wearing black all over except on her feet. Her trainers are bright yellow. Is that who I heard? Hardly a threat, is she?

I shut the door and bolt it behind me. A few minutes later Georgio arrives to start the prep. Sometimes I only feel safe when I'm here alone.

Chapter Six

Amy comes to mine after work at 6.30 p.m. the next day. Still living at home at twenty, in a small two-bed semi on the assisted housing side of the old Manor Park estate, is not my idea of fun. I'm saving up to move out, house share with her and maybe a couple of other friends but ideally move in with Cole. I long for a detached house so I can turn music up without wondering if it will be met with a thump on the wall. A house that is always clean, *really* clean, without things falling apart, would be heaven. No cracks around the windows or creaky floorboards, just everywhere freshly painted white and brand new thick bouncy carpets. I've seen walk-in wardrobes on Rightmove bigger than our living room.

Mum sleeps in the main bedroom so I can have the bigger loft space. She uses the box room as her hobby craft area where she keeps bits and pieces she's collected from the tip, boot sales and markets like cracked, broken and odd pieces of crockery and coloured glass. She makes colourful mosaics out of it for the house and garden and has sold a few at craft fayres. She says it's about making something beautiful out of damaged pieces.

Amy and I sit on bar stools in the kitchen eating mini jam doughnuts and sipping strawberry milkshakes through curly straws like we're still at school.

'Cheese toasties?' Mum asks. We both nod, yesterday's argument swept aside. Except I've not forgotten.

Mum's gone blonde again. Jane who works in her salon has done it for her this afternoon. It always leaves Mum in a better mood. She says it makes her feel attractive again. Light brown made her invisible, apparently. I notice she makes an extra effort, putting on lipstick and checking her appearance in the hall mirror, before she opens the door to the delivery man. I imagine her Facebook marital status: *Seeking replacement husband* – for the last however many years. She agreed to never friend request me.

'It's less than a month until your birthday. If this weather holds up, I thought we could have a barbecue. What do you think?' Mum switches on the sandwich toaster and takes a block of cheddar out of the fridge.

'Yeah, sounds good.' That's something Mum always does well. Her parties are legendary.

'I can help,' Amy says. She came here straight from work in the pop-up shop in Bedford town centre. It used to be British Home Stores. Now it's just a huge space with mobile racks of odd clothes, 1950s-style dresses, rocker jackets and Doc Marten rip-offs, all against a backdrop of scuffed-up BHS signage. Sleazy-looking place with low flickering lighting and a bucket full of discount lacy knickers in lurid acid colours. I told her to come and work with me at Warehouse.

Mum is humming to a tune on the radio as she passes across our steaming hot cheese toasties on her way out to the yard. I wait a moment to see if she's coming back in. She clatters about with the watering can.

'How am I going to find out my dad's name then?' I whisper.

'Isn't it on your birth certificate?' Amy frowns.

'What? There's only my name.'

'You've only got the short version then.'

'Oh. Mum's never said.'

'Order the full one, his name should be on it unless...'

'As easy as that? Where do I get it from?'

'I think you can order it on the government website.'

'Why don't I know this?'

Amy shrugs. 'I guess she doesn't want you to see it.' We finish our toasties and slurp up the froth from the bottom of our glasses, seeing who can be the noisiest.

In my bedroom, Pixi has made herself comfortable on my pillow. I stroke her back and her eyes close as she purrs. Amy falls in a star shape onto the spare mattress on the floor. She's pretty much a permanent fixture at the moment. Mum won't hear of her being left at home alone while Tina works at the club every night. They had a massive fight last week. After that Mum's barely spoken to her. Hard to believe they used to be best friends. From right back when me and Amy were babes in arms, Mum says. Not sure exactly what happened between them. Still, as long as Tina doesn't stop Amy from staying here. No disrespect, but we look after her better than she does.

'Don't you have any other family or old friends you can ask about your dad?'

'No one I know about. All Mum told me is we moved away from Brighton before I was a month old. She says she needed a completely fresh start. I guess that's when they split up. As far as I know she hasn't kept in touch with anyone from back then.'

'What – no one at all? That's a bit extreme, isn't it?'

'She lived close to her mum, but she died and then there was the break-up, so I suppose there was nothing else keeping her there.'

'Must be someone, a neighbour or a friend, maybe one of her mum's friends?'

'She doesn't tell me anything.'

'What about Christmas cards? Are there any you get every year, but she doesn't say who they're from?'

'I think there are a couple, but I can't think of any names.'

'Does your mum have an address book?'

'You mean a paper one? Yeah, she does, actually, it's pretty old too.'

'I bet there are some old addresses in it. You might find one for Brighton, someone who knew your parents when they lived together.'

'I never thought of that. There could be all sorts of information in there about where they used to live, people they used to know. By the way, I forgot to ask. Can you cover for me again tonight? Cole is taking me to that posh hotel in Hertfordshire.'

'Okay.' She sucks her bottom lip in.

'You can stay here. Sleep in my bed if you want.'

'But what if your mum comes up asking for you?'

'She won't, she's going out soon,' I laugh. 'She didn't last time, did she?'

Amy shakes her head.

'Anyway, if she does, you can tell her I'm with my boyfriend, she can't do anything about it. I'm not a child. I just don't need her 20 questions right now.'

After a shower, I pull my rucksack out of the wardrobe and pack a few essentials like sexy lingerie, smart clothes, toiletries and make-up. I curl my hair and slip into a strappy silver dress and heels. Mum shouts up the stairs that she's off out and we both shout, 'See you later!' I grin at Amy and open my laptop. She goes on Snapchat.

'Is he waiting for you?' I tease.

The biggest smile lightens her face. I know it's not kind, but it's the only time she really manages to look attractive. She has brains I'd kill for and is more caring than most. To be honest looks can be deceiving. Blonde hair and violet-blue eyes like mine can hide a dark heart.

I imagine this bloke of hers is massively overweight, has spots and greasy head-banger hair. Sounds like he doesn't go out much either which makes me wonder if he has a job. What car does he drive? That usually tells you lots about a man. She slips her headphones in. I can tell when they are chatting because her face softens, head tips to the side and in between fast typing, her hands attempt to smooth down her frizzy hair.

I type in gov.uk and find the page for ordering birth certificates. I scan through the page, answer their questions, then simple as anything I pay eleven pounds and order a full copy. In approximately a weeks' time, I'll find out who my dad is.

Chapter Seven

There are police searching everywhere for Thomas. Detective Sergeant Helen Seymour and Detective Inspector Rachel Read tell me that all media outlets have been briefed. I gave them the best description I could of Rosie, and I've texted my head chef, Georgio, to tell him what's happened, that I won't be in today, but could he and all the staff please cooperate as fully as they can with the police.

When Nick arrives, he's ushered in to join us in the security manager's office, a small indistinct room with a table bolted to the floor, four plastic chairs and a metal grille across the window. There's a water cooler in the corner. My paper cup in front of me is empty.

Nick's eyes burn into mine with questions until I'm forced to look away. He leans down and hugs me then sits next to me, arms crossed, body tense, a solid mass of muscle radiating anger. I'm shaky and cold. I wish I still had Jade's baby blanket around my shoulders. Worry about what he might say and do stirs the sickness already churning in my stomach.

'There's no sign of where Rosie and Thomas have gone and not one definite sighting,' Inspector Read says. It's as though they've completely vanished. My mind skips ahead to what might have happened to them. Rosie falling in a ditch and Thomas being thrown from the pram. Then she's running across a busy road and the pram's wheel buckles as she tries to push it up the kerb, a van speeding towards them.

Inspector Read coughs and I look up. She runs through everything with me again. From the moment Rosie came up to me in the supermarket to when she left with Thomas. Nick doesn't sit still the whole way through my explanation. He tuts and shakes his head, stares at me frowning, incredulous at everything I say. He holds my hand and tilts his head at the inspector. I wonder how much notice they're taking of him. If they believe I'm as incompetent as he is making out. All that matters to me is that Thomas is found unharmed. Rosie wouldn't hurt him, would she? I don't think so, but how well do I really know her? What if someone did snatch them from the street and has both of them locked away in a van somewhere, or a basement where no one can hear them calling for help? She mentioned a boyfriend, but not his name or anything concrete about him that I remember. Is this about pretending to him that Thomas is her baby?

'And Nick, can you confirm where you were between 3 p.m. and 3.30 p.m.?' Detective Sergeant Seymour leans across the table towards him.

'I was at home working. In the office before that, for the local council in the town centre.'

'I see, and can anyone corroborate that for us?'

'I haven't seen or spoken to anyone since I left the office at midday, so no. Hang on, you don't think I've taken my own kid, do you?' He plants his hand flat on the desk. 'Some woman we barely know has taken him, you should be out there looking for her, not trying to pin this on me.'

'We simply need to confirm your whereabouts for the time around 3 p.m. when Thomas was last seen.'

Nick shifts back in his chair, arms crossed.

'Did you know Rosie Symonds to speak to?' The inspector dips her head so slightly it's almost hard to spot.

'No and I wouldn't have a clue what she looks like either.'

'But you know she works at your wife's restaurant?'

'I've heard Gemma mention the name once or twice. Unfortunately, my wife can be naively trusting sometimes.' He touches my leg as though he feels sorry for me.

'Do you think that's true, Gemma? How well would you say you know Rosie?'

'I know she has a boyfriend she's completely smitten with, she lives with her mum, is a good worker, diplomatic, trustworthy and hard-working. She fitted in with the rest of the team straight away. I trusted her enough to feed our cat when we went away for the weekend, and she really took a shine to Thomas when I took him into work. Asked all sorts of questions. She was really good with him, not like some girls her age who only seem to be interested in drinking.'

'What sort of questions?'

'About how often I feed him, if it's breast or bottle. How many nappies he uses in a day, how often I change him. I wondered if she was planning on having one herself.' I cover my mouth with my fingers. 'Oh my God.'

Inspector Read nods slowly. 'I think we can safely assume that Thomas is still in Rosie's care and hope that she is looking after him.'

'Okay, well, we're running a nationwide search for her name so a match should throw up information about her ASAP and hopefully a lead,' Sergeant Seymour adds.

I swallow the lump in my throat. 'You don't think they could they have been... taken?' I keep my eyes on her and ignore the groan from Nick.

'Not from what you've just told us, darling,' he says. 'She's probably been sitting on another bench somewhere playing mummy and is on her way back right now.'

Inspector Read looks at Nick then at me. 'Anything is possible at this stage, especially as there have been no positive sightings yet, nothing solid to go on. We're keeping all lines of enquiry open.' She glances at the sergeant, then back at us.

'We've checked the home address you gave us for Rosie and unfortunately, it cancels out our initial theory that she's taken Thomas there.'

'Why's that?' Nick asks. There's a moment's silence before Read answers.

'Because Rosie gave Gemma a false address.'

'What?' I feel fresh tears building. 'I can't believe it. Why would she do that?' I think I'm going to be sick.

Chapter Eight

21 Days Before

Gemma

As soon as I wake I check my Instagram account. Since that first comment two days ago there have been others, more angry, more intense, questioning why I deserve to be pregnant, have a beautiful house and a nice life. Scary to think it could be anyone in the world passing judgement when they know nothing about me or what living my life is really like.

By the time I get home from work, Nick's almost finished decorating the nursery. There are scuffs of paint on his jeans and hands, but he looks pleased with himself. His stubble has grown and he's letting his hair grow longer. This scruffy look is sexy on him. I'm pleased he decided to have some time off to make sure the nursery is ready.

'One more coat tomorrow and it's done. Do you like it?' Nick stands back and admires his work.

'It's perfect. Much better than marigold.' I take a few snaps with my phone to add to Instagram. My account is a catalogue of our lives together in our perfect home, with our beautiful things and our journey to becoming a happy family of three. A small part of me thinks it's good to look through them, remind myself what I should feel grateful for, that I really am as lucky as it seems.

We picked pale blue for the walls and freshened up the white gloss on the door, window sill and skirting boards. I ordered some navy blue and white alphabet curtains and a handmade wooden rocking crib and furniture.

'The little surprise I was telling you about has arrived.' He grins and dashes into our bedroom. I can't think what it can be.

'Open it.' He hands me a cardboard box.

I pull up the tabs and take out a pile of tissue paper. There's something carefully wrapped in more tissue paper underneath. I lift it out and glance at him.

'Keep going,' he says, rubbing his palms together.

I carefully unwrap it. Inside are six beautifully carved wooden letters. I can't believe he's done this. Well, I can. Heat surges through me. I clench my teeth, holding in the urge to shout at him.

'Don't you like them? They're all handcrafted and we can paint them if you want to?'

I pin on my best smile. He's been trying really hard lately.

'All one colour, or different colours, it's up to you.' He picks up the letter T and smooths his fingers over the rounded polished edges, then holds it out to me between his thumb and forefinger.

'I thought we hadn't decided yet.' My voice is steady, considering.

'I know but Thomas was the only name we both liked.'

'What if they're wrong and it's a girl?'

'Thomasina is nice.'

'Is it?' I take the letter T from him. The wood is cool and smooth. Tom, Thomas, Tommy. It's a solid name with a softness to it.

'Thomas was top of our list and you knew I really wanted to name him after my grandad.'

'The baby's not even born yet. What if you've jinxed it?'

'Don't give me that crap.'

'I wish you'd checked with me first.' I'm careful not to raise my voice.

'Well, I'm sorry for doing something nice. I thought you'd like it. I wanted to surprise you.'

'You have, honestly, it's beautiful, but I wasn't sure if I liked the name Thomas enough.'

'What, you want me to send it back and call him something modern like Tyson or Tyler?' His face reddens and the vein on his forehead is bulging. I should have kept quiet.

'No, no, it's okay. Honestly, it's fine. You're right, it was one of our favourite. And I do like it. I like it a lot. We'll call our baby Thomas.' I place the letter T on the window sill and he lines up the rest of them next to it.

'Hello, Thomas,' he says stroking my bump.

After dinner, I hear Nick go out while I'm running a bath. I watch from the bedroom window. He hurries across the road, phone lit up in his hand. He seems to be heading in the direction of the park at the edge of the estate. I wonder if he's meeting someone. If he is, I ought to feel devastated. Instead, a tiny part of me is relieved.

Chapter Nine

I drive through Ashridge Forest and cruise slowly up the sweeping gravel drive to the country hotel in Aldbury. The white stone front is flood-lit with red lights. I pull up right outside, parking my old Fiesta next to a handful of Porches and Ferraris. A butler answers the door, takes my overnight bag from me and escorts me to the room at the top of the stairs, the one with the four-poster bed and luxury en-suite.

Once I've freshened up, I wait for Cole on a gilt-edged chaise longue in the lounge. The chandelier reflects glittering light across the white-pillared room. A man in a tuxedo plays softly on the grand piano accompanied by the low murmur of intimate conversations coming from the other guests. I order a Sex on the Beach cocktail from the waiter and when it arrives I take a photo of it and add it to my Instagram page with the hashtag #livingthelife and #luxuryhotel. I Snapchat the same to Cole followed by a selfie of me holding the glass. I'd never have imagined being invited somewhere like this when we first met in the pub all those months ago.

I'd gone in The King's Arms that night by pure chance. I was supposed to be going to a house party, but I'd stopped there on the way for a couple of tequila shots with friends. Turned out the live band and the atmosphere was too good for any of us to leave.

He was standing at the other side of the bar. His gaze kept sliding in my direction and our eyes met a couple of times. He exaggerated surprise at realizing it was me, apparently not quite believing it; he pointed at himself, at me and then the line-up of bottles behind the barman. I nodded, followed by a nonchalant shrug but inside I was screaming with utter, utter joy. It was as if the whole room fell away into a blur. I couldn't believe it was really him. He was rock-star sexy in black jeans and white T-shirt with a fit body to match. He navigated his way over to me and his eyes were sparkling.

'Is it really you?' he'd said with a smile that ended me. He pretended he couldn't remember my name. I was wearing calf-high boots, short tartan skirt and a black lacy top. I was no longer out of bounds.

We'd leaned in at the same time and I let him kiss me on both cheeks. It merged into a half embrace which lingered with the side of his face in my hair, his hands gently on my arms. I took in a deep lungful of him mixed with Acqua Di Gio, setting off sparks all over my body. If I'd died in that moment, I'd have been happy.

'So what have you been doing with yourself?' He took a swig of beer, leaning on the bar. Even the way he held the bottle between his thumb and forefinger was sexy and cool.

'I'm a shop assistant at Warehouse, saving up to do a journalism course. Trouble is I'm trying to save up for a flat too.'

'You'll get there, I know you will. You're a hard worker.' He'd looked me deep in the eyes and my pulse flew off the scale. Then he looked away abruptly as though he'd only just realized he was staring at me.

'Where do you work now?' I asked.

'Local council's environment department.'

'Oh. Really? I would never have guessed you'd do something like that.'

'I like it. Feel like I'm doing some good in the world.'

'I thought you were before.'

'Always good to try something different.' He turned to the bar, making it clear that subject was closed. 'What can I get you?'

'Another Bud, please.'

There were flecks of grey in the dark hair above his ears, he was at least ten years older than me, but his maturity added to his sexiness. He handed me a bottle and clinked his against it.

'I watched some of those old films you were always banging on about. *Rebel Without A Cause*, *Giant*, *North By Northwest*, *Rear Window*, and yeah, I totally loved them.' I put the beer bottle to my mouth and tipped it up. He seemed to be watching me intently.

'Banging on, was I?' He nodded his head slowly, a smile emerging on his lips. I laughed and he joined in, his eyes lingering on mine again.

'I want to see more,' I said.

'Do you now?' One eyebrow went up and we laughed again.

'Seriously, I do. Got any other recommendations?'

'I've got loads more I can suggest. But tell me about Hemingway?'

'What about him?' I tipped my head to one side and gently snagged my bottom lip with my teeth.

'Did you ever?' He pouted and waggled his beer bottle between us. 'You and him?'

'Yeah, actually. Several times. Fell for him completely. As soon as I read *White Hills*, then *Francis Macomber*, I was utterly smitten.'

'Glad to hear it. So tell me what you made of the subtext in *White Hills*?'

'That the man is an arse thinking an abortion is so easy.'

'Ah, but you've got to remember when it was written.'

'Still an arse.'

He laughed heartily. 'You've not changed a bit, Scarlett.'

We chatted for the rest of the evening and I soon found out he was drowning his sorrows because he'd not long split up with his wife. And I was there ready to pick him up.

It wasn't every day I was in the company of someone as gorgeous and intelligent as him. He genuinely seemed interested to hear what I had to say. I had no idea if he had feelings for me or simply admired me like other men did, but it felt like it was about more than that, a real rekindling of minds. He wanted to know everything about me, what I liked, where I wanted to travel to, what I dreamed of doing with my life. We discussed our favourite American writers and all the countries and places we wanted to visit and found we both longed to tour Russia and Japan. I was in awe of us liking so many of the same things. Boys my age were usually into football and computer games and not many read books.

'Will you come with me to the theatre one night?' he'd asked, touching my palm with his fingertips.

Was he asking me out on a date? The age gap didn't bother me. He probably just wanted a bit of friendly company while he got over his wife.

'I'd like that a lot. And one night you must let me take you to the Comedy Store.'

I mentioned I was writing poetry again and he offered to read some for me if I wanted his opinion. He said he was writing too, a TV drama series he hoped to pitch to the BBC. He said I was the first person he'd told.

'What's it about?' I'd asked him. We'd moved to a booth near the back of the pub by then, away from the live music down the front. No one else existed when we were talking, we were so focused on each other.

'I suppose you could call it an up-to-date *Waterloo Road*,' he said, 'but based in a college rather than a secondary school. It covers all the subjects you'd expect: sex, drugs and bullying. The first episode is about a student who appears to be on drugs because they look so tired and dirty, but it turns out they're caring for a sick parent whilst trying to study for their A levels. So far I've got a teacher love triangle and a student-teacher crush.'

'Oh I see.' I laughed and prodded his arm playfully.

The smile in his eyes buoyed my heart. He took my hand and lifted it to his mouth, keeping his gaze fixed on me as he brushed each finger gently against his lips and tongue. From that moment on, I'd craved him with every inch of my mind and body.

The butler opens the door and Cole strolls in like he's James Bond, wearing a slim-fit suit and dicky bow. I come over all light-headed; I think I'm actually swooning. I wriggle my body, easing my tight dress into place before I stand up. He strides over and pulls me to him and kisses my lips.

'You look amazing,' he whispers in my ear and nibbles my lobe gently.

After dinner, we're all over each other as soon as we close our bedroom door.

Later, we're sitting on the bed in our fluffy bathrobes sipping chilled champagne.

'Can't we go to your house next time?' I ask him, running the back of my fingers along the stubble on his face.

'What – don't you like it here?' He reaches around my neck and guides me towards him. 'I like spoiling you.' He kisses me passionately, pressing his body against mine.

I break away and gaze down at his chest, working my fingers through the hair covering his smooth skin. 'I love it, I just wondered why you've not taken me there.'

'It would be weird for you, upsetting maybe.'

'Because her stuff is still in the house?'

'Partly, although she's moved most of it out. She's not lived there for months.'

'So let me come over, I want to see what it's like so I can picture you there when you're not with me.'

'It could compromise the divorce if one of the neighbours saw you. She could accuse me of adultery.'

'Okay, but once your divorce comes through, you want us to be together properly, don't you?'

'That's the plan, but you wouldn't want to live with another woman's choice of décor, would you?'

'I don't mind.'

'You say that now but I don't think you'd like it. You're so wildly different from her. You have a much more eclectic taste and hers is so... bland.'

'Do you think so?'

'Better for me to sell up and choose somewhere new together.'

'Can we?'

'Of course. Anything for you, you know that.' He throws off his robe and stretches his long athletic body out on the bed.

'Does she have to agree to the sale?'

'It'll be part of the divorce agreement.'

'So she'll get half?'

'Not necessarily. It's me who's been paying most of the mortgage and I put the deposit down.' He tucks his hands behind his head and starts doing sit-ups. I caress his taut biceps with my fingers every time his head touches the pillow.

'By the way, I've sent off for my full birth certificate. Mum made sure I only had the short one which doesn't have parents' names on it.'

'See, didn't I tell you women have cunning ways of deleting fathers out of their children's lives?' He sits and tops up our glasses.

'Well, not any more. As soon as I know his name, I'm going to find out where he lives and go and see him.'

'Good for you. You can find out the truth behind why she stopped him seeing you in the first place.'

'That's exactly what I'm hoping, Sir.' I salute him and he smiles, pulling me towards him. When he speaks to me in his teacher voice it takes me straight back to being in his classroom, and wanting to do anything to please him.

Chapter Ten

Monday 13 August 2018
Gemma

'Are you telling me you didn't check a new employee's address?' Nick's eyebrows shoot up, there's fire in his eyes.

'I checked it was genuine and was satisfied with that. There was no reason for me to question it.' I picture Rosie walking into the cloakroom that day. How she'd comforted me and really listened. That wasn't false. She'd genuinely cared.

'But you checked her references, didn't you?' Nick clicks his jaw from side to side.

'We'll ask the questions here, thank you,' says Seymour.

There's a knock on the door.

'Excuse me, ma'am. Have you got a minute?' a policeman asks, looking round the door at Seymour and Read. They both excuse themselves and leave the room.

As soon as the door clicks shut, Nick reaches over and spreads his hand out on my thigh, caressing my bare skin where my long shorts have ridden up. He holds me with his eyes, those eyes that first captured me, the dark rims around sea-green pupils.

'How could you let someone walk off with our baby?' His hand moves further up, under the hem and pinches my skin, pressing his fingers deep until I quietly yelp.

'You're hurting me,' I whimper, trying to pull away from him.

'My son could be dead in a ditch by now, all thanks to you.' He growls the words in my face through clenched teeth, his face screwed up close to mine, spit flying from his lips.

'I didn't know this would happen. She offered to help.'

'She could be anywhere by now.'

'It might not be her fault.'

'Don't be so fucking naïve. Palming him off on someone you barely know. What kind of mother does that?' His fingers press my skin even harder, deeper. I try to move away, but he jabs the heel of his shoe down onto my toes.

I squeal and reach down to press the throbbing pain. Blood seeps through my white canvas trainer.

Then he lets go of me, sits upright in his chair and crosses his arms as though he's not even spoken to me. The skin on my leg stings. The muscle feels bruised.

The sergeant and inspector come back in and sit down, their faces solemn.

'We've done a nationwide check on Rosie Symonds,' Seymour says and glances at Read. 'And there's no one of that name living within a hundred miles of Bedford.'

'What?' I jump forward in my chair, trying to take in what she's said.

'How's that possible?' Nick drags his hand over his forehead.

'It's looking more and more like the woman who's been calling herself Rosie Symonds has taken Thomas deliberately, befriending you, Gemma, for this very reason.'

'I trusted her with my newborn baby.'

'It's okay, you weren't to know, we'll find him, I know we will.' Nick takes my hands in his. I flinch, squinting up at him.

'Why has she done this to me?'

'I'm sorry, Gemma. If you can think of anything else she said to you that might be a clue...' Inspector Read takes a sip of water, her eyes still on me.

'Time is of the essence in cases such as this,' Sergeant Seymour adds.

'Which is why we'd like you both to do a TV appeal for information as soon as possible.'

Nick nods, still holding my hand. But I'm not really listening, I'm thinking back to the day Rosie walked into the restaurant. Bright and friendly, full of enthusiasm. Something about it has been niggling me and suddenly, I remember.

'There is one little thing.'

'Yes?' Read says.

'The day Rosie came in for the waitressing job, there'd been another girl standing out on the pavement peering in through the glass. Something about her was familiar but I was distracted by Rosie speaking to me and I've only just thought of it now.'

'Go on.' Read finishes her water, exchanges a glance with Seymour and picks up a pencil.

'The other girl had bright yellow trainers on. A few mornings before that I was opening up and felt someone following me. All the way from home pretty much. I'd glanced round a few times and all I'd seen behind me was this flash of yellow and black. I thought I was being paranoid because it was just a young girl, not a man who might have been a genuine threat.'

'This could prove Rosie had already targeted you before she worked for you.'

'Exactly what I was thinking. I mean, she came in off the street, she didn't apply in the usual way and I was completely taken in by her experience and enthusiasm. One of the staff had let me down and she was there to help out. It seemed a good opportunity to give her a trial. She made me believe she really needed that job.'

'We'll have to see if this other girl helped her in any way...'

'But I don't understand,' I say, leaning forward, pressing my hand to my chest, 'if her name's not Rosie, then who is she? Who's taken our baby?'

Nick gently squeezes my hand.

I pull away and run to the toilet next door and throw up.

Chapter Eleven

Nineteen Days Before
Gemma

Lunchtime trade today is busier than ever, but I'm desperate to sit down. I drag a stool over to the reception podium and ask Bonnie to show people to their tables for me. I rub my bump with the heel of my hand. Maybe the baby has shifted into its engaged position because it feels like it's dragging down, so much heavier than last week. I'm not ready to become a mum yet. I'm terrified. I'd like to have waited a few more years but Nick was so desperate to become a dad, it was impossible to say no.

There's a lull around 4 p.m. so I pick up my phone and check for messages. I keep hoping there'll be a voicemail from Mum and Dad but there never is. I thought they might make an effort when I told them I was expecting their first grandchild, but it seems to have pushed them further away. If a baby doesn't help them change their minds and forgive me, I don't know what will.

I open Instagram and check the likes and comments. I blocked the person who was making crude remarks and put up a new set of photos of the redecorated nursery before the crib and furniture arrive. Now it's finished it's so fresh and airy. I took a photo of the wooden block letters on the window sill too. No harm sharing the baby's name now we've decided, is there? If Nick doesn't think it's jinxing it then I shouldn't either.

Nick's already in bed when I get home. I stayed at work later than I intended but I need to make sure I've got all the rotas and supply orders in place in case the baby comes early.

I switch the kitchen light on and open the fridge. Nick has left me some chicken wings and salad. There's a note stuck to the top of the cling film in a heart shape with 'I love you xx' written on it. He's been different these last few days. More into the pregnancy and reading up on what to expect during childbirth, how he can prepare, what he can do during labour, rubbing my back, passing me drinks. He wasn't sure he wanted to be in the delivery room at first and I didn't push him because I knew Becca would be there for me if he wasn't. But he's researched it, talked to other dads, and he thinks he'll regret it if he stays in the waiting room.

I turn the kitchen TV on low and catch up on the news while I eat. It's so uncomfortable lying in any position now, I put off going to bed. But then I'm so tired in the mornings, I'm struggling to get up early. Some nights I seem to lay there tossing and turning until daylight.

I put Missy out and go upstairs. The nursery door is open. I go in, switch the light on and imagine carrying my baby to bed or coming in to check on him. I don't want to be a stay-at-home-mum, though. I enjoy my job too much. Why should I give it up? Working after the baby's born is going to be a challenge though because Nick thinks I should employ a manager to take over so I can have a year's maternity leave, but I know that once that happens, he won't want me to go back full time. He'll make it as difficult as possible. My parents started a trust fund for me as soon as I was born, and that money helped me start my business three years ago. I'm grateful they didn't change their minds about letting me have it. It gives me hope that they've not turned their backs on me completely. I named the restaurant Papa's Pizza after my dad, as he's the one who showed me how to make the best pizzas. Sometimes it feels like it's the only bit of independence I have left although the profits go into our joint account.

I stand at the window looking out over the new estate. From here rooftops can be seen in all directions and skinny young trees that barely cast a shadow. Nick chose this house before it was built, months before we met, and by the time we came home from our honeymoon it was ready to move in to. We're lucky to live in such a beautiful house that's so perfect and pristine. But it's not really me. If I had the choice, I'd live in the country in a house with a bit of space around it and character features like old fireplaces and alcoves, somewhere that needed renovating with a bit of TLC.

Something moves across the road, giving me a start. Someone is standing there in a baseball cap and tracksuit looking this way. I step back from the window, switch off the light. There's a car parked half up on the pavement not far from them. I'm not sure of the make but it's one of those old cars that teenagers race up and down in. What if they're checking the place out to burgle later tonight? I creep downstairs and make sure all the doors are bolted.

When I check out of the nursery window again, the car and the person have gone.

Chapter Twelve

20 July 2018
Scarlett

I wonder what Cole is so desperate to tell me. After our night at the hotel last Saturday, I'm wondering if he's going to ask me to move in with him. Anxiety dances in my stomach as I check his message again on my mobile. I stand at the corner of Bridge Street, out of sight. A black cat meows and rubs around my ankles. He looks a bit like Pixi. I shoo it away with a gentle swipe of my hand. Cole strolls up to the Co-op in his white T-shirt, jeans and Ray Bans. The doors swish open as though he has commanded them to.

Five minutes later, he's out again, gripping a bottle of red by the neck in a see-through bag as though it's a chicken he's caught for dinner.

I haul my bag up higher on my shoulder and hurry after him. He rounds another corner, the bottle swinging low by his side.

I stop at the cafe, eye up the queue to check he's there, then sit at a table set out on the pavement. A minute later he sits opposite me with a cappuccino and a black coffee, a bubble floating in the centre like an all-seeing eye. I cross my bare legs and turn sideways, as though he's intruding on my space and I've never seen him before in my life.

He leans in close, grazing the side of my cheek with stubble and in his deep chocolatey voice come the words, 'Fancy seeing you here.' Sharp minty breath mixed with sexy aftershave. He momentarily pulls down his sunglasses and gazes at me. His eyes crease his tanned skin, the smile is surprisingly coy. A shimmer runs through my body. I want to touch him, kiss him but the rules are clear. No shows of affection in public. He can't afford to compromise the divorce proceedings, I understand that. He doesn't want me to be named as the reason his marriage has ended. Thoughtful of him. It was broken before I came along, though. I'm not a marriage wrecker.

He tips down a mouthful of coffee, eyeing me again over the top of his glasses. 'Shouldn't you be getting off to work?'

'I've been laid off.' The job at Warehouse was only temporary but it stings. I needed the money.

'You'll find something better.' He taps a cigarette out of a packet from his shirt pocket. 'I always said you were a rising star.' He sticks one in his mouth and lights it, blows smoke away from my face then looks over his shoulders before he continues. 'There's something I need to tell you.'

I shrug as though I'm not bothered, but I'm desperate to hear what he has to say. 'You texted, so here I am.' My voice comes out in a strange undulating wave. Nothing like the confident way I usually sound.

And then his hand is on my knee, and my entire body melts to his warm touch, smoothing higher up my bare thigh and reaching all the way down to my ankles. I'm tingling all over. I want him so bad.

He checks around then leans in close again, his lips then teeth skimming my ear lobe, hot breath on my skin. Under the table his fingers caress between mine. I take in a lungful of his aftershave and float away on a fantasy.

'It's over, honey,' he whispers in that sexy tone of his, so I'm not sure at first if he's serious. He could be suggesting I strip off, his delivery is so steamy.

'You what?'

'We're done.' He draws his hands away and sits back as if that's it, he's had enough of me. The look on his face is that of someone who'd never contemplate going near someone like me.

Pins prick my eyes. I blink them away. Maybe I conjured his words up in my head and he didn't say that at all, so I stay silent. But then he slams me hard with:

'I mean it, Scarlett.' It's his superior tone now. Always goes back to that. He shifts further back in his seat so he's sitting poker straight.

'I don't understand—' I cross my legs. My ditsy print skirt fans out either side of the chair. He can't help glancing up and down, then straight at me, swallowing me up.

'It's complicated. You understand, don't you.' It's not a question. He touches my shoulder lightly. A miniature version of me is reflected in his shades.

'You mean the divorce is?' I probably sound naïve but I don't understand the ins and outs of it. Am I meant to know what it means to be stuck in a loveless marriage?

'It's just not possible.' He presses his forehead.

'I don't understand… you said—'

'I know, honey, I know.' He gives my arm a gentle pinch as if to say he was stupid enough to believe it too.

'But the other night at the hotel, I thought—'

'I had an amazing time too, but things have changed.'

'What has? I don't understand.'

His phone rings, an old-fashioned trill and he stands abruptly, shifts his sunglasses onto his head. He holds a hand up to me which I guess is goodbye, then he weaves around tables to one as far away as possible and sits.

And just like that, I'm forgotten.

I stare into space, zone into the easy chatter around me. The clatter of cups on saucers and bursts of laughter. I'm dizzy with disbelief, trying to catch his eye but he's still talking on his phone, checking his watch, then swinging back on the chair, scanning around everywhere, at everyone, except me.

Minutes later a woman joins him. She has mousy features, tiny eyes made bigger with smudged black kohl, beaming at him with her thin lip-gloss smile, fake honey-tanned skin, caramel balayage hair which snakes sleek and shiny halfway down her back. She raises two hands full of shopping bags. There's a gold band round her ring finger. Cole stands, takes the bags from her and she holds his face, pausing a moment before kissing his lips.

This is his wife.

I am suddenly made of stone, unable to move. His arms wrap around her, face nestling in her hair – *she is mine*, he is saying to me, *you don't matter*. Nausea pushes a lump into my throat. All our months together. All his promises. Now he's back with her just like that?

She sits with him, unbuttons her coat and in slow motion it falls away. My mouth drops open at her undeniable bump. I'm such a fool. Always the fool. He's hidden it well from me. I'll give him complicated. He was fobbing me off.

We belong together, Cole, don't you know that? I want to scream at them. A rage deep inside me threatens to erupt. I want to leap at him, tear him to shreds. But no. Far wiser to bide my time.

So I pretend to leave, scoop a stack of coins left for a tip into my palm and slope away without passing their table, but I know he's seen me go. Her back is to me, the swathe of hair perfectly in place. Two innocent shopping bags packed with baby clothes nestle under the table by her legs.

I stride to the pavement at the front of the cafe and stop at the feet of a man sitting against the wall. He's probably not as old as he looks, bowed over a plastic cup in front of his crossed legs. Grubby trousers full of holes. I drop the coins in with a satisfying clunk, half filling it. The man's bearded face and earnest eyes tip up to meet mine. The question that springs to mind is: *Is he old enough to be my dad?* Mum's voice pipes up in my head: *I've told you not to ask me. I don't want to talk about him.*

In the car park behind the cafe, a honeysuckle bush gives off its thick sweet scent. I rub my eyes and wish I'd taken my hayfever tablet.

I wait in my Fiesta and watch them return to their flashy motor. A VW people carrier with fancy wheels. We've done it on the back seat. I feel stupidly melancholic and wonder for a moment if he's thinking about us too. How special we are together. He promised me they were over long ago. What an idiot I was to believe him.

I have a sudden urge to pick up a handful of stones and chuck them, shatter the windscreen all over their smug faces. I'd love to get hold of his phone, scroll through all our sexy text messages and show her. I bet he's deleted them now they're back together. I wonder what she said to persuade him, apart from, *I'm having our baby*. What does he see in her? She's nothing more than a mouse.

They get back to their car and Cole helps her into the passenger seat. If he spots my car, he doesn't let on. She is seriously humongous. He must have known about it for months and kept it from me.

I follow them all the way back to a posh new estate on the other side of Bedford. I cannot believe he lives here. They pull onto the drive of their detached house, the size of about three of our semis. The front garden is full of flowers and exotic-looking shrubs, set back from the road. Pots of conifers perfectly lined up either side of the front door and there are even hanging fucking baskets. *Kept me well away from all this, didn't you, Cole?*

Why does *she* deserve this life? Why should she have him? She's got a fight on her hands because I'm going to get him back. Even if it kills me.

Chapter Thirteen

Monday 13 August 2018
Gemma

The police whisk us off to Millennium TV studios about ten miles away in Thurleigh. In the back of the car, Nick clicks the BBC news on his phone, and turns it up so we can both hear it.

'*Gemma Adams, a new mother from Bedford, left her newborn baby in the care of her employee outside Sainsbury's supermarket this afternoon. Both employee and baby have since been reported missing. The young woman, Rosie Symonds, which is not believed to be her real name, offered to look after the crying infant while Gemma finished her shopping.*

'*Baby Thomas, who went missing in his pram around 2.55 p.m., is just five days old. The police are concerned for the welfare of both baby Thomas and Rosie Symonds, and are asking the public to come forward with any information that may lead to their whereabouts.*

'*Police have released CCTV footage of Rosie Symonds walking at pace, pushing Thomas in the pram towards the exit and out of the supermarket. Detective Inspector Rachel Read is with me now. What can the public do to help?*

'"*Although we can't see her face clearly in the footage, partly because of the large sunglasses she's wearing, we're asking for anyone who recognizes anything about this woman to come forward. She is aged 21, with mid-length blonde hair, slim build and approximately 5' 7" tall. Any members of the public who saw her pushing a distinctive green BABYZEN pram should contact the police as soon as possible. Time* is of the essence in cases such as this. We're in what we call 'the golden hour', the first hour after anyone goes missing, which is when we're most likely to find the person, child or in this case, baby, alive and well."

'Thank you, Inspector Read. Let's go over live to our reporter who is outside the Adams' family home in Bedford.

"'Hello, yes, this is where Gemma Adams set off just a few short hours ago for what she thought would be a normal everyday shopping trip in the sunshine, enjoying being a new mum about town with her new baby. There was nothing to indicate that today she wouldn't be bringing her baby home.

"'Within the next half hour, the parents are to make an appeal for Thomas's safe return. Police are asking for Rosie to give herself up and bring this little boy back to his distraught parents. Back to you in the studio.'"

Nick closes it and opens Facebook. He types in a post on his page in capital letters then shows it to me:

> OUR NEWBORN BABY THOMAS WAS TAKEN FROM GEMMA THIS AFTERNOON WHILE SHE WAS IN THE SHOPS!!! CAN YOU FUCKING BELIEVE IT? PLEASE, IF ANY OF YOU KNOW WHO THIS WOMAN IS – ROSIE SYMONDS – THEN PLEASE TELL ME OR GEMMA OR THE POLICE AS SOON AS POSSIBLE SO WE CAN GET THOMAS BACK SAFELY. IF THIS SICKO IS READING THIS MESSAGE, YOU'RE TEARING US UP HERE, PLEASE BRING HIM BACK SAFE AND SOUND. (Please share this message far and wide. Link below to news story).

I open my bag, and take out Thomas's small blue rabbit, clutching it to my face which is wet with tears. *Please come back to me, my darling boy.*

Chapter Fourteen

Eighteen Days Before

Gemma

I've taken the morning off because I have a check-up with the midwife at 10.30. The delivery van bringing the new furniture arrives just after 9 a.m. I'm upstairs but can't rush to the door as easily as I used to, so I call Nick in case he hasn't heard. He comes out of the kitchen drying his hands on a towel which he promptly slings over his shoulder and opens the door.

'Could you bring them up to the nursery, please?' Nick says when one of the deliverymen asks where we want them. He gives him two pairs of elasticated plastic shoe coverings.

The two of them open the back of the van and carry every box inside and up the stairs. They carefully unpack the hand-crafted pieces and move them into place under my direction then take the packaging back out with them. The room looks exquisite. *It's almost ready for you, Thomas.* I glide my hand over my bump and I can't stop my mind flashing back to Christmas, the pain and blood and how I never thought I would reach this day. I'm so close to welcoming my baby into the world. He will be so loved.

One of the men hands Nick an electronic reader to sign. My gaze is drawn away from them to something moving across the road. There's that person hanging around again. Baseball cap and hoodie. It's probably one of the kids from the estate. I shouldn't assume they're all trouble just because of the hoodie. Maybe they live in this road or are waiting for someone they know. But the same car is parked further up so maybe they're not from round here. I can't see the number plate. They could be watching all the houses. See who's coming and going. Should I call the police? I'll mention it to Becca. Ben's Neighbourhood Watch secretary for another month. He can email everyone about it.

I take a few photos of the new crib and all the matching furniture and post them up on Instagram. Someone I've not heard of before has left a comment about my photo of the wooden letters spelling Thomas's name.

Tom-arse. Who'd call their kid such a crap name? 😊

What a spiteful thing to say. I hate these trolls hiding behind their silly little profile pictures. This one is of a cartoon carrot, of all things. They're a bunch of cowards. I've decided not to block anyone else. Instead, I take a screenshot. From now on, I'm going to save any trolls' comments and when I've collected a few, I'm going to report them to Instagram. Becca said it could be the same person changing their handle every time and by blocking them, I'm letting them get away with abusing me. But I don't understand who would be targeting me. I don't have any enemies that I know of.

Nick's phone pings as he comes up but he ignores it.

'Are you happy with it all?' He takes my hands.

'It's so beautiful, thank you.'

We move into each other's arms. This is the Nick I fell in love with. As long as the other side of him doesn't make an appearance again, we can be like a normal happy family.

That youth is still hanging around across the road. Now they're looking down at their phone just as Nick's pings again. It's either a strange coincidence or the person down there is trying to contact my husband.

Chapter Fifteen

Amy can tell something's up with me. She's asked me twice what's wrong, but I'm not in the mood to tell her.

'I hate seeing you like this – is it to do with your birth certificate?' She reaches across my bed to hug me and then I'm crying again.

'Is it something to do with Cole?'

'*She's* pregnant,' I whisper through my teeth.

'What, his wife?' Amy frowns. Her wayward Nanny McPhee tooth in her top set slips through her lips.

'It's not funny.' I smack her arm.

'I'm not laughing, I just wondered if he has a death wish.' She shakes her head. 'Are you sure, though?'

'I saw her.'

'I thought she left months ago.'

'That's what he told me, but he's kept me well away from their house, hasn't he, so who knows?' Another wave of tears builds in my eyes. I swallow. 'She's bloody out here, about to drop.' I attempt to recreate the size of her bump with my arms.

'Wow, not recent then.' Amy frowns, looking genuinely shocked.

'Exactly. So how long has he been hiding this from me?'

'Total bastard. What are you going to do?'

'All that stuff about finding a house together once the divorce has come through was utter bullshit. He must have been lying to me the whole time.'

'Scarlett, why didn't you text me?' Amy's face animates the pain churning in my guts.

'I may as well tell you. Surprise, surprise, he's finished with me.' My chin wobbles as I speak. 'And I've lost my job.' I throw myself face down on the bed sobbing. I didn't know love could cause this level of physical pain; a broadsword twisted between my ribs. I've always made sure it's me that finishes it first. If I ever get a whiff of a boyfriend straying, I pre-empt the ending as swiftly and as painlessly as I can because I can't allow myself to hurt this much. It's unbearable.

'I'm so sorry.' Amy is tearing up too as she reaches for me. She's bought into this romance as much as I have. I thought it was meant to be. Apparently not for him so much.

'But I still love him and want him back. That cow is not going to have him just because she got pregnant.'

'Didn't he tell you why?' Amy's voice has a whiny edge like it's her who's been dumped.

'I'm guessing they're back together because of it.' I point to my stomach. 'It's obvious, isn't it?'

'Could she have tricked him into having a baby?' Amy wipes her tears on her sleeve. She cares what happens to me and I am grateful. I don't mean to snap.

'Possibly. Although he told me they were separated before I came on the scene.'

'Were they, though?'

'I don't know now.' I ponder her question. 'She must have already been pregnant before they separated. So, not that long before we hooked up, they made a baby together. I need to know dates. I need to know if he's been lying to me.' I thought he'd want me now more than ever if she has duped him, or am I the stupid one here? He says I do things she would never dream of.

'He has to come to his senses, realize he can't stay with her because of a baby. It's you he loves.' Amy shakes her head, her wispy hair barely moves. 'I'm going to come up with a plan to get him back to you. You wait and see.'

'Thank you.' I lean over and give her a tight hug.

–

Later, at 8 p.m. we take a taxi to The King's Arms in the high street to meet our usual gang. It used to mainly be made up of friends from school, but it's evolved over the last couple of years as new people have joined us and a few have gone off in serious relationships.

It's already heaving by the time we get there. The live band by the entrance is playing Daft Punk's 'Get Lucky' and a small group of older women are gathered at the front, dancing like they're twenty-five not fifty-five. I head straight for the bar, scanning faces as I steam through the crowd, dragging Amy by the hand behind me. I'm aware of heads turning and men eyeing me up and I use it to politely muscle my way into a gap at the bar on the side nearest the band. I wave my twenty-pound note with the rest of them and a cute guy with curly hair next to me offers to buy me a drink. 'I'm meeting someone,' I tell him. He's a bit put out.

Trouble is, I can't see Cole anywhere. I could really do with him coming over right now and explaining himself. I was so sure he'd be here, despite what he's done. Friday nights at The King's Arms are like a religion to him.

'You okay?' Amy asks.

'Yeah.' The band play a rendition of 'Happy Birthday' for one of the women dancing in front of them. Maybe that will be me one day trying to hang on to my youth, dancing round my handbag. What if I never feel this way about anyone again?

'What can I get you?' the barman asks, snapping me out of my daydream. I order two bottles of Bud each to save going up again.

'Can you see him yet?' I ask loudly in Amy's ear. She shakes her head. We squeeze our way to the back and find a small table someone has just vacated. 'I'm going to text him.' I wait a moment to see what she thinks.

'It's up to you.' She swigs her beer straight from the bottle.

I take my phone out and stare at the screen, willing it to light up with his name. If I start Snapchatting him, I won't be able to stop. Especially if he ignores me.

The guy from the bar is leaning towards another bloke and laughing as they glance over at us.

'I'm going outside to ring him. Will you be okay in here?'

Amy nods and finishes one bottle, starting on the next straight away. I press the 'call' button and hold the phone to my ear as I find my way out of the main door. Outside, couples are huddled up together along the front window and a group of rowdy men are hanging near the road holding their pint glasses. I turn left and wander down the little pathway into the graveyard next door. This was where Cole led me that first evening. Away from the crowds and the music. Into the darkness. I'd trusted him. I sank into his arms and we kissed passionately. I honestly couldn't believe my luck. This gorgeous older man who I'd lusted after was telling me I was beautiful and funny. He made me feel so special.

The answerphone kicks in. I cancel the call and try again. Could he be driving here? As I'm standing in the shadows, I catch sight of his mates strutting across the road towards the pub. Smart shirts and trousers, confident swagger and loud banter. I search for Cole amongst them, but he's not there. I hurry into the pub after them and tap Kyle on the shoulder. All six feet of him turns around and he grins as soon as he sees me, swamping me in a big bear hug.

'How are doing?' he asks.

'I'm okay,' I say, shyly. I've always had a soft spot for Kyle. He smells clean and spicy.

'You looking for Cole?'

I'm so grateful he's the one to say it. Maybe he's already heard.

'Yeah, he's normally here by now, isn't he?'

'Ah, I don't think he's coming. Didn't he tell you?'

'Is he okay?'

'Nah, nothing like that. His missus is expecting their first child and I think she had to go to hospital.'

'At this time of night?' I bite my tongue.

'Are you okay?'

'Yeah.' I try to smile.

'Can I get you a drink?'

'I'm fine, thanks. I'm with a friend. Great to see you, though.'

'You too.' His gaze lingers on me a few seconds too long but gorgeous as he is, I'm not ready to move on. I turn away to hide the pain. What does Kyle think I was to Cole? Just a plaything while his wife was away? He saw us kissing, cuddling and dancing together almost every Friday night for months. Or maybe he and his mates think it's normal to have more than one woman on the go?

When I sit back down with Amy, I stare at my bottle and pick at the label. My face can't even remember what a smile feels like. What the hell am I going to do?

I tap my phone and open Facebook, see if he's posted anything about why he's not come out. I chuck my phone in my bag in disgust. Amy looks up.

'What's happened?'

'Cole's only gone and blocked me.'

Chapter Sixteen

At the Millennium TV studios we're met by Chief Inspector Rich Blackmore. He strides with purpose towards us and shakes our hands firmly. He's tall, over six feet, so he can't help looking down at us, but his blue eyes are kind. We follow him into a side room where he briefs us on how the appeal will be orchestrated and what we need to do.

'Once I've done the introductions, just read out your statement we've prepared, Gemma. It's always more powerful coming from the mother, but if you get stuck, Nick can take over. Okay?' Blackmore looks from me to Nick and back again until he's sure both of us understand and agree. 'You'll be fine.' He glances at the blue rabbit in my hand and touches my elbow. 'Remember, Thomas needs both of you to be strong.'

The terror of speaking live on television creeps up my throat and into my mouth. I swallow the knot of fear back down. I'm not sure I can do this. I grab hold of Nick's wrist and his heavy frowning eyes show he's frightened too. I picture Mum and Dad sitting down to their tea, switching on the news and seeing me. To my shame, they've not met Thomas yet. In fact, I've barely spoken to them since Nick and I got married.

Blackmore leads us into a studio set up with a long table and microphones. A dazzling array of cameras flash at us as we're ushered into our seats by the man in charge of PR. I hold my arm up to cover my face. Behind us is a wall of pop-up screens.

One with the police logo and another is a blown-up image of Rosie in the supermarket. My sharp intake of breath is audible as I pass the last one, a blown-up image of Thomas taken on my phone at home only this morning. Nick grabs my hand and guides me into a chair. The cameras continue flashing and even when they've stopped, I'm blinking circular shapes of bright light. Beyond the table are rows of expectant faces, notepads and pencils poised.

Blackmore speaks first, outlining the facts and most up-to-date information about the search. Or as I see it, listing my incompetencies as a mother. He talks about the urgency of the situation given Thomas's age and the added difficulties given the current heatwave. Then he hands over to me and I'm frozen to my seat. A murmur circulates throughout the room. I stare at the piece of paper in front of me, my face growing hotter and hotter, every word on the page is spaced out so I can read it easily, yet it's a jumble to my bleary eyes.

'You can do this,' Nick whispers into my hair and pats my hand. 'These people are here to spread the word and help us find our baby.'

I stand up, glance at Thomas's picture behind me, then take a deep breath.

'*Our darling baby boy…*' My voice breaks. I clear my throat and start again. '*Our darling baby boy Thomas was taken from me…*' My chin trembles and I falter, unable to read any more of what they've written for me. I'm surprised when Nick touches my elbow and gently helps me to sit down. He stands up and takes the piece of paper from me and continues reading.

'*Our son Thomas is out there somewhere with a girl called Rosie, except that's not her real name. I don't know why she tricked Gemma and didn't bring him back when she promised to. Gemma made the mistake of trusting her.*'

I need to be strong and brave for Thomas. This is my chance to help him. I stand again and nod at Nick who hands the paper back to me. I place it on the table, take in a breath and say what I want to say.

'Wherever you are, Rosie, whatever the reason for taking our baby, please, please bring him back to us, please just bring him home, safe and… unharmed,' I sob, covering my mouth with the back of my hand. The truth of my words leaves me breathless, the final words more mouthed than spoken. I glance down at the piece of paper then up at the hard-nosed journalists, now saddened or embarrassed at my outburst. There's a strange reversed Mexican wave as they lower their heads in succession, maybe moved by a shared devastation that anyone could take a newborn baby from its mother.

I try again, taking another deep breath, tears running down my face.

'I'm begging you, Rosie, please bring our baby back.' My pitch escalates with the thought that every second we're sitting here Thomas could be moving further and further away from us. 'We miss him so much. We love you, Thomas.' I bury my face in my hands.

Nick stands again and links his arm through mine. He passes me a hanky from his pocket and we sit down together. A long moment passes before Blackmore speaks. He points to the pixilated blown-up photo of Rosie, her large sunglasses obscuring her face.

'As we've already said, Rosie Symonds is not this woman's real name. So, what is it? Someone out there must know. We're asking members of the public to come forward if you recognize her. If you know her true identity, call us immediately. Time is of the essence. And let me remind you, it's hot out there and this infant is only five days old. Does anyone have any questions?'

Hands shoot up around the room. Blackmore picks a man from the back row with white hair.

'Is that the best photo you have of her?'

A murmur of agreement trickles around the room.

'That's all we've got at the moment.'

The man continues. 'Is there a possibility both have been abducted by a third party?'

'Anything is possible, but we have no reason to believe that is the case. Until we've checked the CCTV in the area, we're keeping all lines of enquiry open. If anyone saw them leave the shopping area, where did they go, which direction were they heading in, did they meet someone else?' He points to a woman in the middle row holding her pen in the air.

'Chief Inspector, could baby Thomas have been passed to child traffickers? Maybe taken to order? What I mean is, do the public need to be vigilant? Is it possible this woman is back out there right now looking for another baby to abduct? Could there be a whole gang behind this?' She holds the pen against her lips as the room erupts in a collective, outraged gasp. Fear and nausea rise to my throat. I can't stop the tears falling from my eyes. Nick swears under his breath, fists forming in his lap. My body won't stop shaking.

'All I'm saying is, this Rosie or whatever her name is, seems to have taken a lot of care in gaining Gemma's trust before walking off with her newborn in plain sight, easy as pie, *and* with the mother's consent so she had plenty of time to get away.'

Blackmore coughs nervously into his hand. 'We have no evidence whatsoever to indicate this is an organized abduction on a scale you describe, or that any such gang is operating in Bedford.'

'But could there be a third party involved?'

I shiver. Third party?

'What I mean is, a man or men who might hurt them both?'

'We don't know. I'd rather not speculate.'

The room is silent. There are no more questions.

'Thanks all for coming,' Blackmore says, 'contact details are on the hand-out, please take one on your way out.'

I stand up but my legs wobble, so I sit down again. As the room empties, Blackmore comes over.

'That seemed to go quite well.' He rubs his hands together. 'I'm confident we'll find out who this woman is by close of play today.'

'Where do you think this Rosie could have gone?' Nick asks. 'I'm guessing you've ruled out the possibility that she's simply got lost.'

Blackmore crosses his arms. 'That's why we need to identify her as soon as we can.'

'Do you think Thomas is still with her?' I ask, standing again. Nick's arm pushes through mine, clamping me to him.

'I do, yes. You say she's a caring girl, so there's no reason to assume she would harm him.'

'But what if someone else is involved?' Nick asks. He's on the same wavelength as me for a change.

'Let's stay positive, shall we?' Blackmore rubs his palms together and catches someone's eye behind us.

I'm trying as hard as I can to believe that Thomas is safe and well.

'Greg Clark, the Family Liaison Officer for this area, will be calling round to see you in a couple of hours.' Blackmore allows himself to be dragged away by one of the producers.

Hours? In the meantime, Rosie could be taking Thomas further and further away from us, making it even harder for the police to find him.

What if he forgets my face, my smell, the feel of me holding him in my arms?

What if he forgets I'm his mummy?

'Please, please find him,' I call after him.

Chapter Seventeen

Seventeen Days Before
Gemma

I smooth out the piece of A4 paper and stick it to the window nearest the front door. Someone's bound to want a summer job, aren't they? If there's no interest after a couple of days, I'll have to advertise online.

Half the restaurant is full already and early lunchers are going to start arriving soon. We started offering a breakfast menu up to 11.30 a.m. and it's become more popular than I expected, probably because of the American-style breakfasts. I pull the stool up to the reception podium. I have to sit sideways now the bump is so big. Looks like we're going to be packed out until 3 p.m., according to the lunchtime bookings. Can't complain. I glance up. A couple of girls are standing outside reading my poster. I check the rota then my watch. Simon should be here any minute. I've warned him twice this month about lateness. He's a good worker, so I don't want to have to let him go. One of the girls is coming in. She bowls straight up to me, no hesitation. There's an effortless beauty about her, tousled blonde hair, flawless smooth skin, like she's rolled out of bed looking perfect. I've always envied girls like this. Everything seems so easy for them.

'Hi,' she smiles at me, 'I'm really interested in the waitressing job you're advertising.' She points to the window.

'You're keen, I've literally just put that up there.'

'I am.' The smile grows wider and it's hard not to like her.

'Could you tell me a bit about the job, please?'

'Yes, of course. Would you like to come through and we can have a chat?' I take her to one of the back booths and nod at Bonnie to let her know I'm busy. She comes over and takes a coffee order from us.

'What would you like?' I ask the girl as she sits opposite me.

'Cappuccino, please.' She goes to take her purse out.

'It's okay, it's on the house.'

'Oh, thanks.' She puts her bag down.

'Nasty scratches you've got there.' I point to her hand. They look horribly familiar.

'That's my cat, she didn't like me moving her off the sofa last night.' She laughs.

'Ah, what kind is she?'

'A gorgeous tabby who thinks she's in charge.'

'Don't they all?' I show her the faded scratches on my arm thanks to Missy. 'Tried to grab a piece of loose thread in my top. That'll teach me.' We laugh.

I tell her about the main duties of the role and she tells me what experience she's had. She's so easy to chat to, I almost forget the time. Bonnie comes over and asks to speak to me.

'Excuse me a moment,' I say, standing up.

The girl smiles and I follow Bonnie to the till.

'Simon's called in sick. He's hurt his back,' Bonnie says.

'Couldn't he have phoned in sooner?' I check my watch. 'He should have been here twenty minutes ago.' I shake my head.

'I'm rushed off my feet as it is,' Bonnie says.

'Don't worry, I'll sort it out. You get back.' I look out at the girl sitting at the table sipping her coffee and wonder if she'd be up for a try-out. I haven't got any other options right now. She seems experienced enough. Says she's worked in bars in London.

'Sorry about that, can I get you another coffee?' I ask sitting down.

'I'm good, thanks.'

'One of my waiters just phoned in sick and I was wondering if you're interested in a trial straight away?'

'Oh right, well, yeah, I'm free all afternoon. I'd be happy to.'

'That's great, you'd be really helping me out. I must warn you, though, we're expecting a full house.'

'Fine with me. I'm up for the challenge.'

'Excellent, let me show you to the cloakroom and I'll bring your uniform.'

I point her in the right direction and take a clean tabard out of the store cupboard and a clipboard, info sheet and pen from the drawer. God, I don't even know the girl's name, how embarrassing. I can't blame everything on baby-brain.

'Here you are, if you could wear this and fill in your contact and bank details.' I hand them to her. 'I'm so sorry, I didn't ask your name, we were so busy chatting about cats and everything else.'

'Ha, yes. My name is Rosie.'

Chapter Eighteen

It's gone midnight by the time we curl up in our beds. The darkness is interrupted by the flickering streetlight right outside my window. Amy is laid out on the mattress, covered up to her shoulders in a thin sheet. We waited in the pub until last orders, but Cole never turned up.

'What am I going to do about him?' I ask.

'You really want him back?'

I nod and turn away, so she doesn't see that I'm struggling to hold in the hurt burning in my eyes. I wish I had a dad to talk to about these things.

'What do you know about this wife of his?' Amy props herself up on an elbow. I love that she doesn't tell me this is all my problem, that I should sort it out myself. I know I can count on her. She's the most loyal person I've ever known.

'Nothing. I've only seen her once.' Shadows of passing cars leave light trails along the wall and across the ceiling. 'You should have seen the smug look on her face. So manipulative and clichéd getting pregnant to win him back. Makes me sick.'

'So you think she knows about you?'

'I don't know.' I tap my phone and scroll through Cole's Instagram. He's not blocked me there yet. Like his Facebook page, he uses the pseudonym Truman Fitzgerald. 'I wonder what her name is. He'd never tell me the few times I asked.

Said I didn't need to know. If he told me, she'd become a real person in my head.'

'Look at the comments on his posts, it might give you a clue.'

It could be any of these people. He doesn't use it much.

'How does he know it's his baby anyway?'

'I've actually no idea.' I sit bolt upright.

'What if she's lying to him?' Amy sits up too and points her finger at me.

'Oh yes!'

'Tell me what she looks like.' Amy crosses her legs.

'Mousy, plain but covers herself in thick make-up, spray tan, hair extensions, nails, the lot. I don't know what he sees in her. All that fakery.' I shudder. 'Silly cow.'

'How old is she?'

'I don't know, pushing thirty maybe.'

'So, it's easy. You're twenty, beautiful, available. Everything she isn't. She's old, pregnant and getting fatter by the day. All we need to do is convince him it's not his baby, that she's been seeing someone else.'

There's a glint in Amy's eye. It doesn't appear often. The last time was when she put poison down for Mr Willis' rats – he called them his pets, but they were filthy vermin coming up from the gutters, terrorizing our lives, attracted by the bird seed and bread crusts he scattered on his lawn every day.

'We can send him an anonymous letter telling him it's not his baby.'

'But if he believes it, won't he just get a DNA test?'

'He can't do that until it's born, which will buy you time to get him back. Can you imagine the rift it will cause between them? *Sorry, honey, I just need to check this is actually my baby, make sure you're not lying to me about sleeping with someone else.*'

'He knows my handwriting.'

'We can cut letters out of a newspaper.'

'You're joking now, right?' I stutter a laugh, not quite sure if she's being serious.

'No, really.'

'He will guess it's me.' I point out in words of one syllable. She's being stupid now, saying anything to impress me.

'Why would he? Anyway, you only have to deny it.'

I slowly shake my head.

'We could push her down a flight of stairs?'

'Amy, don't be crazy. We can't do anything like that, okay?'

'All right.' She shrugs and goes back to her laptop.

'There has to be another way. I don't want him to hate me, I want him to come back to me.' I'd willingly given myself to him, I was looking forward to our lives together. We agreed we were soul mates, so how can he treat me like this? He said his wife had moved back with her parents. All those times we spent together in fancy hotels. He said he loved me, not her. We planned our future, moving to a farm in the country with two dogs and a horse, maybe children one day. But all that time his wife was already pregnant. What if it really wasn't his, and she was cheating him?

'Does he use the same name on all his social media?' Amy pulls up Facebook and Instagram.

'Yeah, Truman Fitzgerald.' I point to the profile picture he uses of the author Truman Capote. 'That's him. He's not blocked you on Facebook then.'

'I never comment, so he's probably forgotten I'm there.' Amy twists her laptop around to face me. 'And I think this is her. She's on Facebook and Instagram.' She points to an Instagram page called @HappyWife. The posts are all perfect images. Pastel-coloured lights draped outside a summerhouse, the door teasingly pushed open to show a chaise longue and a pom-pom throw carefully angled across it. There are a few selfies, one's a side-view of her looking down at her bump, posted a week ago.

'Yeah, that's her. Mousy without all the make-up on.'

'She's liked every single one of Cole's posts and always comments something anodyne like, *How lovely! Ooh my favourite! Can't wait to see this. Didn't we have the best day ever?*

'Happy wife, eh? Is that meant to be funny?'

'So the first part of the plan is trolling her on social media.'

'Nice.'

'Don't use your own account to comment, obvs,' Amy says, opening a new window, 'set up a new one with different made-up names every couple of days. And if you switch to different devices, she won't have a clue who you are or how to trace you.'

'Genius. Thanks, Amy.' It's so nice that she's looking out for me. Was always the other way round back in the day. But when the bullies realized she was with me, they soon kept their distance, even Chantelle stopped pranking her. That poster thing she did of superimposing Amy's face on a squirrel was so low. But Chantelle's Mummy and Daddy were not best pleased to find out their little angel was a serial bully, especially as Mummy dear had been one of the school governors.

Amy sets an account up straight away and I drop a few choice remarks. Now I've regained some control I dial Cole's number on my mobile yet again, but it goes to answerphone. His smooth deep voice invites me to leave him a message, so I do.

'Call me. I need to talk to you.' I need to play this carefully if I want to get back at him and break them up, without him hating me as a result. I'll show him I'm the one he wants – that he can have the perfect life with me, not her.

Chapter Nineteen

Monday 13 August 2018

Gemma

The police take us home. For the first few minutes of the journey I keep picturing Thomas's empty baby seat in my car. I bat away my tears and runny nose with the back of my hand, hoping he will miraculously appear next to me and prove this is all a nightmare I'm about to wake up from.

What is left for me at home without Thomas? I draw in a sharp breath at how angry Nick will be with me once we're on our own. I'm not sure how much longer I can carry on living this life. But I have to go back, I need to be there for when Thomas is found. I can't abandon my business, everything I've worked for. My staff don't deserve it.

We finally turn into the road that leads to our new estate. I take out my phone. I should call Mum and Dad, let them know about Thomas before they see it on the news. But what do I say? They'll be worried sick. I'm not ready for all their questions. I could start by telling them how well my little pizza place is thriving and thank them a million more times for the money they gave me to get it started. How focusing on it has kept me going, given me a bit of independence to keep me sane. I'll promise to take Thomas to see them, as soon as he's found. I can explain exactly what happened. They'll understand. I'll tell them all about Rosie, how kind she's been, what a lovely girl she is, and why I trusted her. She meant to bring him back to me, I know she did, but something must have happened, and she can't contact me. Maybe if I tell them the whole truth, they'll help me. But what if they don't? What do I do then?

I look up and see part of my face in the rear-view mirror. My eyes are puffy and red. They might think it's all my fault, that it's because I'm not a good wife, I should have tried harder and now I've proved I'm a terrible mother too. They'll be so ashamed of me. And I can't... I can't let them down again. The phone drops from my hand into my lap. I lean forward and let the tears come again.

The police pull up right outside our house.

There's a reporter across the road speaking into a camera.

We get out and Nick unlocks the front door. He turns away down the hall, leaving the door wide open for me, an invitation into its hungry mouth, ready to swallow me whole once more.

As soon as the front door clicks shut, he's right behind me, breathing on me, pulling me round to face him. His hand goes to my throat, pushing my head back, slamming me up against the door. I can't swallow. My eyes flicker at the spotless white ceiling.

'You're a useless little bitch,' he growls, centimetres from my face, his spit landing on my cheek. He punches my side and when he lets go of me, I fall in a heap at his feet, curling into a ball, trying to catch my breath at the pain on top of the bruising from giving birth. He grabs my hair and drags me up the stairs. I stumble all the way, grazing my knees on the carpet. I want to scream at him to stop but it will only make it worse. He throws me on the bed and slams the door shut.

–

Later, I'm hunched over my drawn-up knees in the bath, rocking backwards and forwards, letting the hot tap run beneath me to wash away the blood and its offensive iron smell. The gushing water hides the sound of me weeping. My hand is shaking as I push the plug in and add a scoop of bath crystals. They slowly melt and give off a healing sea-salt aroma.

The water is scalding hot like a smack on my bare skin. Steam billows in my face. I switch to cold and when the level is past halfway, I turn the taps off and submerge.

The last time I had a bath rather than a shower was two days after we arrived in Vegas. Nick ran it for me on the morning of my eighteenth birthday. He'd scattered rose petals on the warm foamy water and told me it was my special day. He said he wanted me to feel like a princess. Breakfast was brought in on a trolley to the lounge-bar area of our penthouse suite at the Imperial Palace hotel. A waiter opened a bottle of champagne and poured two glasses. Two waitresses brought in platters of fruit freshly cut and displayed like jewels, warm sweet-smelling pastries, pancakes with maple syrup and a hot trolley of eggs, bacon, chipolata sausages, fried bread, hash browns and sides of thick white toast saturated with melted butter. I couldn't believe he had arranged all of this for me. No one had ever made me feel so special.

After breakfast, a hairdresser arrived and blow-dried and curled my hair. A manicurist shaped and painted my nails and Nick presented me with a pile of presents – a chic cream shift dress in shot silk, strappy heels to match and a single diamond on a gold chain.

'You look incredible,' he'd told me, taking my hand and spinning me round to see the full look. 'Are you ready to go?'

'Where are we going?' I'd laughed nervously wondering if we were going to an upmarket function where I'd have to hold serious grown-up conversations. If my friends could have seen me, they'd have been amazed at the transformation.

'I've got so many surprises planned for you today, are you excited?' The lift doors closed and we saw ourselves reflected back from the mirrored doors.

'Yes, of course, it's just that...'

Nick, almost half a head taller than me, had his arm around me, holding me close to him.

'What? Have I forgotten something?' He'd given that hangdog look I've come to know so well.

I wriggled away from him and looked at him full on.

'Could I have my phone, please, just for five minutes, so I can call my parents?'

'Oh Gemma, really? And spoil everything?'

'But they don't even know where I am. They'll be worried.' I concentrated on my shoes, not wanting to see his disappointment.

'How about later? This evening. Then you can tell them what an amazing day you've had. Assuming you do.' He smiled.

I pouted and pulled a face. He stroked my chin with one finger.

'I promise, okay?'

I nodded and let him lead me out of the lift. Waiting outside was a shiny white limo. The chauffeur climbed out and opened a door for us, his arm inviting us to get in. My eyes widened, not quite sure if this was a joke but when Nick nodded, grinning hard, I'd squealed with delight, clapping my hands together. This was for us? For me? This was incredible. Nick was incredible. He must love me so much. My friends and parents at home were forgotten in an instant. I'd fallen further under Nick's spell and no one had any idea where to find me.

The doorbell rings bringing me back. I look at the clock. It's almost two hours since Thomas was taken. I hear Nick speak in his friendly voice, inviting someone in. I pull the plug out and drag myself out of the bath. After a few moments, Nick's tapping on the bathroom door.

'Clean yourself up, the Liaison Officer is here,' he says in a low voice.

A few minutes later I come downstairs. I'm greeted by a man with a friendly face who shakes my hand and introduces himself as Greg Clark, Liaison Officer. Nick is noticeably shorter and older standing next to him. There are mugs of tea on a tray and a packet of Bourbon biscuits. There are 'New Baby' congratulations cards and flowers on every surface. But the house looks too tidy. Becca always says midwives can spot something isn't right when the mother seems to be concentrating on keeping the house in order instead of looking after the baby. In these circumstances, a woman would have noticed that.

'Please tell me there's news?' I say.

Chapter Twenty

Fourteen Days Before

Gemma

I arrive home at 8.45 p.m. This is the earliest I've been for a while. Georgio insisted on closing up for me tonight. Told me to get some rest because I look so tired.

Nick's in the shower. My dinner is in the fridge, a portion of lasagne I batch cooked and took out of the freezer this morning. Nick's already eaten by the look of the dirty plate in the sink. I've tried to encourage him to put things straight into the dishwasher, but he doesn't listen.

I check my phone while my food rotates in the microwave. The nasty messages seem to have stopped. Perhaps the person guessed I was going to report them. I sit at the kitchen table and reach around my bump. The baby is turning right over. It's the weirdest sensation, as though my body doesn't belong to me any more.

'You're back early,' Nick says. He's dressed in one of his smarter pairs of black jeans and a white T-shirt, a cloud of spicy cologne wafts towards me. I didn't know he was going out.

'Georgio insisted. Says I look tired.'

'You do, are you feeling all right?' His phone buzzes and lights up.

'I think so. Could probably do with an early night.' The microwave pings. I don't know if Nick heard me, he's looking at his phone. The tiniest hint of a smile passes his lips.

'I thought I might chill out in front of the soaps.' I click open the microwave door.

He looks up, stuffs his phone in his jeans pocket. 'Why don't you go up to bed after you've eaten?'

'Where are you going?'

'Meet the lads for a pint, so don't stay up.'

—

I settle in front of the TV with my dinner on a tray. Missy curls up next to me. I don't usually watch *MasterChef* but it's better than silence. My mind is whirring. There was something about that look on Nick's face when he read his phone. I can't put my finger on what it was exactly. I turn over to *Gogglebox* and try to push it out of my mind.

The thud of the front door closing wakes me up. I can't believe I drifted off on the sofa. I guess it's midnight if that's Nick just coming in. I check my watch. It's 9.40 p.m. It can't be. It must have stopped. Nick's clattering around in the kitchen. I press the remote control and the time on the TV says 9.41 p.m. He's only been gone forty minutes.

'Everything okay?' I ask, when he comes into the living room holding a large measure of whiskey in one hand and the bottle in the other. I can smell it from here. I twist my fingers together.

'Why are you still up?' He clonks the bottle on the table next to the tray with my dirty plate on. He drops down on the sofa opposite.

'I dozed off.' My one note of laughter is greeted by silence. Normally he'd laugh too, but he's frowning, his face like thunder. He drains his glass then tops it up with another generous measure.

'Has something happened?' I stroke my bump. The muscle in his cheek is twitching. He's not been like this for ages. I wish I'd stayed at work. My body has turned to jelly. I should get up, pretend Georgio has called and go and get in my car.

'Nothing that concerns you.' He leans forward and spits the words at me. A waft of cologne mixed with sweat catches in the back of my throat. He grabs the TV remote off the table and switches over to *Top Gear*. I daren't move. He keeps topping his glass up and eventually his eyes shut. I stand up as quietly as I can, but Missy jumps down, sending the Sky remote clattering to the floor. Nick's eyes flick open. He leaps off the sofa and grabs her tail. She hisses and scratches him. He grabs at her again, pushing over the coffee table. Everything crashes to the floor. I scream as the corner of the table catches my side, knocking me back onto the sofa. Missy dives away and out of the room.

He grumbles something to himself and picks the whiskey bottle off the floor and collapses back in his chair. I press my hand to my side and climb the stairs.

Chapter Twenty-One

22 July 2018
Scarlett

When I reach home after my lunchtime run the next day, a warm sweet smell welcomes me as I open the front door. Mum has whipped up a batch of fruit scones. Amy is already back from her shift, legs tucked under the table, buttering a thick layer on a huge stack cut in half, chatting away. For a few seconds they don't even notice me. Without thinking I snatch the half scone from Amy's hand and scoop a spoonful of jam from the jar, smearing it lavishly then take a bite. It's my job to spread jam and lick bowls. I feel ashamed of myself and the stab of jealousy in my chest. I should be more forgiving, learn to share, at least make the effort.

Mum's always made me feel special but has been sure to point out there are children less privileged than me who deserve all the good things I have. I'm never allowed to leave a scrap of food on my plate for this reason. Mum used to say she should have had another kid, then she wouldn't have spoilt me so much. There was no way that was ever going to happen. It would mean her actually committing to one of the blokes that comes round.

I've asked her why she didn't settle down and have one if she thought it was such a good idea, but she never gives me a straight answer. Maybe she secretly only wanted one child. Some people do so they can give all their love and attention to a single son or daughter, not a rabble of squabbling kids. Isn't that what parents moan about? And I've read that childbirth can be so traumatic that women can't bear the thought of going through it again. An image of Cole's heavily pregnant wife invades my head. It looks so uncomfortable and totally gross. I don't want kids for ages, until I'm in my thirties at least. And I want my children to have a dad that stays around. Not like mine. What if he chose to leave and wants nothing to do with me? Is that what Mum's protecting me from? When I find out where he lives, what's stopping him from slamming the door in my face? He might have another wife by now, other kids. He might not have told them about me. Deleted from his history. I could be his dirty little secret or he could deny he's anything to do with me at all.

'Shall I spread the rest of the jam?' I ask Mum, picking up the special wide knife so there's no doubt in anyone's mind that this is my job. I don't want Amy to think she can get one up on me, much as she's my bestie. For all her faults this is *my* mum.

It's always been me and her against the world. There's never been anyone who's come close to qualifying as a new dad. As far as I know. Much as she infuriates me, I love her to pieces. I just wish she'd be straight with me. I'm grown up now. Older than she was when she had me. There's a photo in the bookcase on the landing of Mum holding me as a newborn baby. She has this vacant look in her eyes like a startled rabbit looking up at a camera's flashing lights, baby bottle in one hand, me tucked awkwardly in the crook of her arm. I remember seeing the same kind of look on the face of a girl two years above me at school. She left when she had her first, at eighteen as well. The boy moved away with his parents. I don't think he told his family. Is this what happened to my dad? Seems crazily young to become a parent.

When I confided in Cole about it, he said that fathers are hard done by. He thinks society lumps them all together, calls them absent fathers, piling the blame on them, but often it's the mothers who've chucked them out. He says fathers have as much right as mothers to see their children. He encouraged me to go behind Mum's back and search for Dad. Said I should get in touch with Fathers 4 Justice, but I don't know, Mum seems so adamant that I shouldn't know who he is. Maybe there is something about him I'd be better off not knowing. I'm wary of digging around and upsetting her. Amy said if he's such a great dad, why hasn't he contacted me? Good point.

I try not to think about Cole. I finger the half-broken heart pendant around my neck and wonder if he's still wearing his. Wouldn't *she* ask him about it? He must have hidden it somewhere. I know he doesn't really love her. How can he when he loves me? He told me only last week at the hotel. It's not possible to love two people at once. Is it? Does him dumping me mean he's trying to do the right thing, standing by her because she's pushed him into a corner by insisting on keeping it? A tiny part of me does admire him for stepping up, but really, he doesn't need to have a relationship with her to see his own baby. They can share the childcare if that's what he wants. I don't even mind being a step mum. I think I'd be good at it. I'd be more like a friend than another parent.

If he thinks I'm going to walk away, he can think again. I'm not giving up.

'Have you thought any more about your birthday?' Mum picks up a broken corner of scone and eats it. 'I was thinking we could have a barbecue in the garden if it's still hot?'

'Can do.' She's just trying to be nice to me. Anyway, I can't think that far ahead while all this is going on.

'I want to do something. It's your 21st.'

I want to cry all the time, but it's easier to be angry.

'What's wrong?'

'Nothing.' She knows what I'd really like for my birthday, but if she's not willing to tell me anything about Dad, why should I bother?

'I'll do your hair and nails for you both.'

Cole told me right from the start that I'm his soul mate and no one will ever love me as much as he does – he said it's not possible. I could see the pain in his eyes when he finished with me. All because of her. Well, I'm going to stick around and be there for him when it all goes wrong as I know it will. They split up before, so they will again. This time for good. They just need a helping hand. I smack the spoon down hard on the counter and red jam splatters everywhere.

'Scarlett, what are you trying to do?' Mum slides two lattes across the table toward us, made with her new filter coffee machine. Amy and I lick jam seductively from our fingers. Mum tuts but smiles at the same time. We eat two scones each. Afterwards, I'm fit to burst. I stick my stomach out and Amy pats it flat. We catch each other's eye and start laughing even though I feel like crying.

Amy unashamedly scoffs one more scone. Mum doesn't eat any; she's trying to keep off the weight she's lost.

Upstairs, I check my Insta account.

'Ha, she's already blocked me.' I show her the screen.

'Fine, so now create a new account, find a new profile pic and post more comments.'

'So what else can we do?'

'Okay, so for the second part of our plan you're going to follow Cole and I'm going to follow his wife.'

'So what – we note down their movements, see if we can find out how happy they really are, if there's another bloke on the scene that could be the father?'

'Exactly, then find a way we can come between them, so they split up again.'

'For good this time. And I'll be ready and waiting for him to come back to me.'

We drop the idea of a poison pen letter because the police would be straight round. I only know this because the weirdo at number eleven sent a letter to the old woman at number eighteen, accusing her of snooping on him. He threatened to kill her cats because they shit all over his garden. The police were round to him like a shot. Even Mum got involved and had to answer a load of questions about what she was doing on such and such day and where Dad was and when would he be home? I'd listened closely at the door, even though I knew the answer I was hoping for a different one. She said he wasn't coming home ever. Does that mean he's dead? Wouldn't she tell me if he was? So, even if I find out his name, it might already be too late. I may never get my dad back.

Chapter Twenty-Two

The Liaison Officer, Greg Clarke, is holding a mug of tea in one hand, cradling it with his other. He has kind hazel eyes and lightly tanned skin. The sort of face that's used to showing empathy over endless cups of hot drinks and biscuits. I sit near him. I don't want to miss a word.

'How are you both holding up?' He looks at me, then Nick. Just his asking the question sets me off crying again. I dab my eyes with a tissue.

'I feel nauseous all the time, like something's stuck in my gullet.' I automatically rub the area of my chest below my neck. 'It's the waiting, not knowing and every moment keeps going around in my head, trying to sift through everything she said to me in case I missed a clue.'

'Keep going through it. You might come up with something. What about you, Nick?' Greg drinks a mouthful of tea. Nick walks round the room and shrugs.

'I can't believe Gemma gave Thomas to some girl she works with, who she hardly knows.' He stabs his finger in my direction, as though he's wishing he had a knife in his hand. 'I'm sorry,' he says quickly, and digs his hand in his pocket.

'I know this is difficult but that's not going to help you, Nick. If it is anyone's fault it's Rosie's.'

'I know, I know. I'm sorry. It's just that he's my son, my baby boy.'

87

'We're doing everything we can to find him.'

I stare at my lap. There's no point trying to explain to Nick how Rosie had become someone I could trust, who listened to me, was kind to me, because he won't listen. His way of coping is blaming me.

Greg drinks some tea and clears his throat. 'We've spoken to all the stallholders in the market today and to as many of the supermarket employees and shoppers as we could. A couple of people remember seeing Rosie pushing Thomas's pram, but none saw where they went or which direction.'

'None at all?'

'We're checking all the CCTV in the immediate area. We're hoping it will throw up some clues.'

'Hoping?' Nick is still standing, anger flashing in his eyes. I wince. 'I thought you'd have a bit more than that by now. Our son could be on a boat to France or a plane to the Middle East.'

I shudder at his suggestion.

'There's no indication that this is a child trafficking situation.' Greg's voice is quiet and calm. He pulls a notebook and pen out of his pocket.

'How can you be so sure about that?' Nick struts around the room, hands on hips. I grimace.

'It's not the way they normally operate.'

Nick is silent. He sits on the arm of the sofa nearest to me.

Greg flicks through his notebook. 'There's one thing, but we don't know for certain if it's significant yet.'

'Go on.' Nick folds his arms.

'The CCTV in the supermarket shows another girl acting suspiciously near the entrance, checking her phone, browsing through magazines but not appearing to really look at them. It could be the girl you told us about who followed you to work. When we inspected the footage of Rosie again, her head lifts slightly as she passes this girl. And when Gemma is looking around for Rosie outside, the girl seems to be watching her from the foyer. It's possible she is an accomplice.'

'And do you know who she could be?'

'Not yet, but we're pulling all our resources into this one, I promise you. I'm confident we'll find something soon.'

'It might be too late by then,' Nick grumbles, crossing his arms tighter.

'Unfortunately, because of all the tents up, no one saw if they took the escalator down to the underground car park or to the charity shops around the square.'

'Isn't there CCTV down there?'

'Only a few of the cameras seem to be working, but we're going to look at all the footage available.'

Nick shakes his head as though it's Greg's fault.

Greg turns a page.

'Like I said, we're covering all bases as fast as we can.'

I try to silence the niggling little voice in my head that's asking: *What if it's already too late?*

Chapter Twenty-Three

Eleven Days Before

Gemma

It's been a long evening, one of our busiest yet but I enjoy the buzz, the atmosphere. The good weather seems to bring out the best in everyone.

Nick calls in on his way back from watching a football match at the pub. He promised he wouldn't drink too much after last night. He promised to make it up to me with this weekend away.

He waits by the door. The moment I'm free I go over.

'I've had a text from Maggs saying she can't look after the bloody cat now.' He takes his phone out of his pocket.

'Oh no, did she say why?'

He reads the message. '*Called away, Dad's ill again, won't be back till next week.*'

'Who else can we ask at such short notice? Ben and Becca are away too, so are next door.'

'It'll be fine on its own, won't it? If it's hungry it'll catch something to eat.'

'Missy's domesticated. She relies on us feeding her.'

'Are you sure about that?' He grins. 'I think you'll find she's eating somewhere else too.'

'That doesn't mean we can abandon her. She's my responsibility.'

'Trust you to take in a needy rescue cat.'

'She is not needy.'

'Then let her fend for herself. It can't do her any harm. Leave a bit of dried food out for her in the kitchen and a bowl of water. The cat flap will be open so she can come and go as she pleases.'

'I can't do that. I promised the rescue centre I'd care for her properly. Anyway, she doesn't deserve that.'

'Well, you'd better sort something out because I'm not going to lose my deposit.'

'I'll think of something.' I look around for Rosie, but I can't see her. They're waiting for their coffees at table eight. 'You must meet our new girl.' I step away, looking around. Where's she gone?

'We're leaving first thing in the morning, okay?' Nick grabs my wrist. 'So, sort it out tonight because I'm not going to be late because of a bloody cat.'

'All right I will, I promise.' I lean in to kiss him, but he moves away before I can.

–

Later, after everyone's gone home, I change my clothes in the cloakroom and catch sight of the bruise in the mirror. It's so sore, especially when I touch it. If Becca knew she'd make me go straight to A&E. Nick was mortified when he saw it this morning. But he still wouldn't tell me where he'd been or why he was in such a bad mood last night. I think he's seeing someone. I sit on the bench and tears fill my eyes. If he is, then this is over for good and I'll have to bring Thomas up by myself.

There's a knock on the front door. Did I forget to put the 'Closed' sign up? Rosie is standing on the other side of the glass, miming something about her phone. I unbolt it and let her in.

'Thank God you're still here. I think I left my phone in the cloakroom.'

'Come in and have a look.' I wipe my eyes.

'Are you okay?' She looks at me surprised.

'I'll be fine, thanks, just the hormones kicking in, I expect.'

I follow her in, aware I'm walking awkwardly but the paracetamol has worn off. I carry on changing, pulling my top up to cover my head while she rummages in her apron. I turn away so she doesn't see the bruise on my side.

'How did you do that?' she asks, pointing right at it, wincing. I pull the top off. It crackles with static electricity.

'I walked into the corner of our kitchen table. Honestly, I'm clumsier than ever now I'm so big.'

'It looks really painful.'

'It's very sore, but not as bad as it was this morning.'

'If there's anything I can do that you need help with, just say, okay,' she says and pushes her phone into her back pocket.

'There is one thing I meant to ask you earlier. Our neighbour can't feed Missy while we're away. She promised she could, but she's been called away to look after her dad. I can't bear to go to London if we don't have someone going in to feed her and I was just wondering if perhaps you might be able to?' Rosie doesn't look convinced so I carry on. 'Especially as you love cats as much as I do and you're always so massively helpful around here. I'd pay you, of course. Do you think there's a chance you could do that for me?'

'Yeah, I can, but you don't need to pay me.'

'Really? Are you sure?' I can't believe she's agreed. I thought I wouldn't find anyone. It's such a relief.

'It's not a problem.'

'Oh my goodness, Rosie, you're a lifesaver.' I wipe my eyes.

'Honestly, I'm happy to help out.'

'I'll give you our address and spare key now, if that's okay? It's just that we leave first thing in the morning, so I won't have time to show you around, but I'll leave Missy's tins and bowl out. It'll be really straightforward, I promise. She's got a cat flap so if she doesn't turn up just leave her food down and she'll come and find it. Morning and evening if possible, whatever time is best for you.'

'What's your address?' She takes her notebook and pencil out of her apron and scribbles it down.

Chapter Twenty-Four

On Monday, I hang around outside Cole's house and follow him to the One-Stop shop at lunchtime then hide behind the bus stop. He's wearing knee-length denim shorts, a white T-shirt, and Vans. A few minutes later he comes out with a bottle of milk in a carrier bag and a single can of beer. Sitting on the bench further up the pavement, he cracks open the can and glugs it down. There's no mistaking how rough he looks. He might have been crying. I get a warm glow inside knowing how much he's missing me. It would be so easy to go and sit next to him, ask how it's going, but I need to make him suffer so that when he takes me back, he's grateful as hell.

After he's drained the very last drop of beer – and boy does he make sure he has – tipping it right upside down, he wipes his mouth on the back of his hand and chucks the can in the bin outside the library. Then he takes a tube of mints from the bag and pops one in his mouth. I wonder if he's got a large spliff lined up at home, or hasn't he told his wife about that either?

I keep out of sight and note everything down on my phone and discreetly take a photo of him.

It's late afternoon by the time Amy and I meet up at the park after her shift. I buy us both a 99 from Mr Softie and we take a swing each. The place is full of screaming kids and their ragged mums, already fed up with the school holidays. One mother who's tattooed up to her neck shoots us dirty looks but honestly, there's a load of other swings her kid can use.

'Come on then, what happened?' I bite half my Flake along with a mouthful of ice cream.

'His wife leaves the house at 5.55 a.m. drives into town and parks at the Harper Centre car park.'

'Where does she work?'

'I followed her to the restaurant on the corner of the high street and Embankment, by The Swan Hotel. She opened up, so maybe she's the manager.'

'Or head chef?'

'Could be. I hung around for a bit and more staff arrived.'

Amy shows me her notes and a couple of photos she took, then she pings them over to my phone. She takes her detective work very seriously. I tell her what I saw and noted and show her the photo of Cole on the bench.

'So what does he actually do all day? Doesn't he have a job?'

'He works for the council. Taken a few days off to decorate the nursery, apparently.'

'And getting drunk?' She seems shocked.

'I honestly think it's because he misses me.'

We crunch our way through a family size bag of chilli-flavoured crisps while I search on Google for Papa's Pizza but the website is under construction. I scroll through Instagram for updates from the latest *Love Island* celebs and leave a couple of comments. Then I switch to my other account and have a few things to say to @HappyWife.

'My guy wants to meet up,' Amy says, eyes fixed forward as she watches the kids in front of us kicking a ball.

'Are you going to?'

'Dunno.'

'How old is he?'

'Twenty-six.' She ties a knot in the crisp packet.

'What if he's fifty-six?'

'I've seen a picture of him.'

'You know that might be fake, right?'

She swivels in her swing, creaking the chain, so she's facing me and in a deadpan voice, she says, 'You sound like your mum.'

Her face cracks and we both laugh until we're hooting and snorting.

'Seriously, though,' I say at last, holding my stomach and sides, 'you should check him out first.' It wasn't so long ago that Amy would never have had the confidence to talk to a boy in a romantic sense. That time I found her on the school playing field surrounded by Chantelle and all her nasty little gang. Amy was being pinned to the ground by five girls. Chantelle, kneeling at her feet, had tipped out the contents of her bag and was going through her stuff, holding everything up one by one, including her sanitary towels. By the time I got there, Amy was in floods of tears and a whole crowd of kids had gathered in a circle. One of the younger ones had tipped off a teacher and, fortunately, I'd heard and sprinted over, pushing my way through the crowd, then shoving Chantelle in the back so hard her face hit the ground.

'Oh sorry, Chantelle, I didn't see you there,' I'd said. All her mates quickly let go of Amy and I'd helped her sit up by the time Miss Stevens had puffed her way over to us.

My phone buzzes.

> I need to see you.

It's Cole. I show the screen to Amy.

> When?

I text back.

> Today, 10 p.m. in the park. Come alone.

'Don't go,' Amy pleads, serious now.

I tip my head and pull a face that says, this is what I want.

'I don't trust him. You're making it too easy for him.'

'Are you calling me easy?' I give her a gentle nudge on her arm.

She shakes her head and grins. She knows me so well.

> See you there

I text back.

With any luck he's realized he's made a big mistake going back to his wife. A baby is not going to fix their relationship.

When we get home, Mum hands me a brown envelope. 'This came for you.' She crosses her arms. 'Must be something important.'

I take it and slide a look at Amy. Her eyes widen. I flick a look at the ceiling then back at her again.

'Maybe to do with my tax or National Insurance now I'm not working.' I'm tempted to tug the envelope open as I run up the stairs. I could burn it, then I'd never know, and I wouldn't be betraying Mum. Not really. But is she betraying me? It feels like I'm holding my golden ticket. I need to see this and I'm sorry if it hurts Mum but I've been waiting all my life to know my dad's name, who he is. It's time to find out why Mum's been keeping it from me.

I push my thumb under the flap and tear it open.

Chapter Twenty-Five

Monday 13 August 2018

Gemma

After Greg has gone, Nick grips the sides of his head and groans. 'Can't rely on any of these bloody pigs.'

I focus on a crack in the coffee table. A memory of the pain shoots through my side. Greg said he'll be back as soon as he can and to not go out because there are already reporters outside.

'I'm going to look for Thomas myself.' Nick grabs his keys and phone not looking at me when he speaks, and for both, I'm glad. There's no point in me trying to stop him. Greg will be furious.

The moment the front door thuds shut, relief floods through me. But the feeling is short-lived. Thomas should be here, curled in my arms, making little sucking sounds as he feeds or crying because he needs changing. My arms ache with emptiness and the cruel silence wraps around me so tightly I want to scream.

My mind fast forwards to days, weeks, months ahead from now, and he's still not been found. I stare into space at the void called the future. There'll be no first tooth, no first steps, no first day at nursery. There's so much I will miss out on. How will my life ever continue without my darling boy? I'd be left here alone with Nick and he'll probably want another baby straight away even though I'll say no, I'm not ready yet – I wasn't ready the first time. Could that be why something bad has happened to Thomas – because I didn't want to be a mum yet? But I *am* a mum now. It's still so hard to take in. My sore body, the milk in my breasts confirms it. I've been Thomas's mummy for almost a week. A title I'm proud of, so why couldn't I take better care of him? Is this really how it ends?

If we were a normal couple, I'd have offered to go with Nick because I'm desperate to search for Thomas too. I could go out in my own car, look in the park, around dustbins, in people's front lawns and behind bushes. I'd knock on their doors, rifle through sheds and rooms, but Greg would say that someone has to stay here by the house phone, just in case that call comes because Rosie knows where we live. She'd call my mobile, though, wouldn't she? Will she bring him back? Perhaps her face will be full of remorse. She'll explain how she was protecting Thomas, preventing him from ending up battered and bruised like me. But Nick would never hurt a baby, would he?

I take the walkabout phone, go upstairs to the nursery and sit in the rocking chair by the window. The draw of milk from the breast pump is uncomfortable but it gives me some relief from the swelling milk and at least I feel like I'm doing something. Thomas's babygro is still on the footstall where I changed him out of it this morning. I press the white cotton to my nose and inhale his powdery newness still lingering in the fabric. I was in such a hurry to get him changed and fed and out of the door. Why didn't I take the time to just hold him, feel his warm little body close to mine?

The phone rings and I grab it, fumbling with the buttons to answer it.

'Hello, is that Gemma? My name is Lorna Bolton and I'm calling from *Bedford Today*, I'd like to ask you about…'

I jab the keypad, ending the call.

The sound of a car's squealing brakes alerts me to the window. I stand briefly and watch a car pull up across the road, then another outside our house.

The doorbell rings. I ease the breast pump off my skin, fasten the flap of my bra and pull my top down. There's a grey shape of a person I don't recognize in the ripple of glass around the front door. I walk slowly down the stairs. It doesn't look like Nick or Greg. Not tall enough to be either. Who else could it be? Is it a plainclothes officer to tell me that Thomas has been found? My limbs become clumsy and wooden as I try to walk down the rest of the stairs. I'm desperate for news but what if it's to tell me they've found a body? A tiny cry escapes my lips.

When I open the door, a shower of flashing lights bombards me. Reporters surge towards me holding microphones, shouting my name, shouting a jumble of questions. I try to push the door shut but there's a pointed navy court shoe wedged over the threshold.

'Judith Smith from the *Bedford Echo* – how are you coping without your baby? Is it true Rosie works for you? Who do you think she really is?' I push the door, but her foot won't budge. It bounces open again just missing my face. A male reporter's hand is on it. Judith Smith carries on talking. 'Two minutes of your time, Gemma, that's all I ask, I really want to hear your side of the story.'

I frown at her. My side? Have I been accused of something?

Standing on tiptoes, I pretend to wave to someone behind her. It's enough to make them both half turn and step back. I slam the door shut and bolt it at the top and bottom. I'm strangely elated at my tiny victory. I stand with my back against the door, trying to steady my breathing. They knock and ring the bell. Judith Smith calls out for me to talk to her because she 'just wants' to ask me a few questions.

The truth is, I'm used to being trapped in my own home, just not like this.

I move away from the door. The letterbox swings open and a slither of the male reporter's face appears. One brown eye, a shiny long ginger fringe and beard whiskers.

'Does Rosie Symonds actually exist?' he bellows. 'Come on, tell us the truth. Have either you or your husband harmed your baby?'

I press my hands over my ears and step backwards, unable to believe what I'm hearing.

Chapter Twenty-Six

All the way home on the packed train, Nick is eyeing up a girl sitting opposite us. The more I glare at her, the more she makes eyes at him. I'm absolutely fuming by the time she gets off at Luton. I feel like shouting at her that she's a cheap tart in her ripped skinny jeans and low-cut top.

'What was all that for?' I ask him as soon as we get to Bedford station car park.

'What are you talking about?' Nick loads the car with our suitcase.

'You know what, that girl with black hair. You were flirting with each other all the way from St Pancras.'

'She was just mucking about, and I was going along with it.'

'Like you used to with me? Am I too old for you now?'

'Whoa? Is this your hormones talking?' He laughs and opens the passenger door for me.

'Of course not, but you've been eyeing up every female that walks under your radar all weekend.'

'Don't talk daft. I've only got eyes for you. Haven't we had a good time?' He leans over to kiss my cheek. I move so he can't reach me.

'I thought we had, but now you've spoilt it.'

'You're so bloody ungrateful, aren't you? I mean, have you looked at yourself in the mirror lately?' He starts the engine and pulls away.

'I can't believe you're saying I look fat. I'm pregnant, for God's sake. You wanted this baby.'

'I know I'm being selfish, but it's only because I fancy you so much. I can't wait until you get back into your size ten jeans. I love your shape, you know I do.'

'And until then you like everyone else's shape?' I'm pushing him into dangerous territory, but I have to tell him how it makes me feel. He can't treat me like I'm invisible. It was creepy how he was joking with that girl just like he used to with me, the same corny jokes that I found amusing once upon a time when I didn't know any better.

'You're getting really paranoid, do you know that? It's not even amusing any more.'

Tears sting my eyes. I so wanted him to think my pregnant body was beautiful and blooming. I feel ugly, unsightly and a turn-off.

Later I drive into work because I need to get away for a while, try and process what is going on with me and Nick.

'Didn't expect to see you tonight,' Rosie says as soon as I get in the door. 'Did you have a good time?'

'It was lovely, thank you. Thought I'd pop in to see how you're all getting on.'

'Everything's fine.' Rosie shoots a look across at Bonnie who nods too.

'Thanks so much for looking after Missy. Did she behave herself?'

'She did, but do you know you have a stray cat that comes in sniffing around?'

'I do and I don't know how to get rid of her.' I head straight out the back to the cloakroom and hang my bag on a hook and don't let go. I squeeze my eyes shut. What if he is seeing someone? I don't know what to do. This baby will be here any day now and it needs a mum and dad.

Chapter Twenty-Seven

23 July 2018

Scarlett

I shut my bedroom door and stand against it. Amy's by the window, biting the side of her thumb. I stare at my birth certificate but can't take in any of the words. I scan it slowly up and down, at my date and place of birth, my name, Mum's name and address. Some boxes are empty. Finally, my eyes land on the headings down the middle of the page: BIRTH, CHILD, FATHER, MOTHER, INFORMANT. But where my father's name, his place of birth and occupation should be, it's blank.

'It's not here, after all that.' I hurl the piece of paper across the room like it's a frisbee, hoping it will spin away, but after a few turns it lands on the floor. Amy picks it up and examines it.

'Different address, though.' She hands it back to me.

The address Mum's given as her 'usual address' is in Dunstable, not Brighton where I was born.

'That's odd, isn't it? I thought it would be a Brighton address.'

'Not if they were about to move house when you were due.' The certificate is dated almost a month after I was born.

'I suppose so. But why move so far and why has Mum never mentioned we lived there?'

'Why would she, it's part of Bedfordshire? They might have moved around a few times.'

'But I thought we'd been in this house since we left Brighton.'

'It might be a clue.'

'It's something else Mum has kept from me.'

'Or maybe…' Amy stops and puts a finger to her lips, a thing she does when she's on the brink of a smart idea.

'What?'

'Maybe she's not told you because that's when they split up?' She winces.

'Oh, yes.' We sit on my bed and look over the certificate again.

'See here, it's like mine, it only has your mum's signature as informant.'

I read the small text in Section 14 – *I certify that the particulars entered above are true to the best of my knowledge and belief.*

'It doesn't necessarily mean they'd split up already, though. He might not have been able to go with her to get you registered. It's just that…'

'What?'

'I remember feeling jealous seeing my cousin's birth certificate because her dad's details and signature were on it. If your parents are together and pleased they've had a baby, they'd both go to register the birth, wouldn't they?'

'He might have been working.'

'Yeah, but wouldn't he have taken the morning off to do that? My aunt always says that it was their first proper trip out with my cousin. It was special.'

'I don't know. I doubt if it's like that for everyone. Why don't we drive to Dunstable in the morning, once my car's had its MOT? See who lives at this address now. They might remember Mum, if she was with my dad when we lived there. And the neighbours could be the same ones. They might know something too.'

'It's worth a try.'

A breeze has picked up by the time we get back to the park after dinner. Amy waits for me behind the hedge, out of sight.

Cole is there, pacing up and down in the front of a park bench, hands deep in his jacket pockets, behind him the empty bandstand, a shadowy skeleton in the fading light.

I used to come here with Dad, I think, when I was about three years old. The Salvation Army brass band played every Sunday afternoon, and we'd sit with the crowd listening to crashing cymbals and rolling drums, my heart thudding louder and louder, faster and faster with each crescendo.

Like it is now, watching Cole agitated. I step towards him and when he sees me, his eyes go straight to my bare legs, up to my face and back down again. His hands grab mine and he rubs his thumbs in tiny circles on my palms. I inhale his Gio scent mixed with beer on his breath. I can't tell if he's happy or not because there's a puzzled look on his face, worry stacked up behind his eyes.

'How've you been?' he asks, as though it's been weeks instead of days since we last saw each other. He sits on the bench still holding my hands.

'Sad.' I kick up dust with my trainers.

We're silent for a while and then he tells me he's booked another week off. It's a bit of a random statement. Is he saying he's got time to see me after all? I don't want to unless he's leaving her. I'm not a home wrecker.

'What are you reading at the moment?'

'*Gone Girl*.' Surprise is etched on his face.

I shove his foot with mine. He smiles and strokes his stubbly chin. We sit in silence again. He's probably judging my choice.

'I miss you.' The words find their way out of my mouth all by themselves. *Shit*. I planned to be so cool.

'I do too, you're my special girl, but I had no choice, you know that, don't you?' He takes my hands again between his warm solid palms. 'But you have to stop following me. If someone saw you, it might get back, you know.'

I pull away from him as though he's cut me.

'And that friend of yours, the creepy one, tell her to keep away from my wife.' His voice is more accusing now. I frown and try to block the word wife from my head.

'Don't call Amy that.' My mouth twists.

'I mean it.'

'Okay.' I nod, as if I'm doing him a favour. Amy and I will have to be more discreet.

He pats my hand. I'm a problem dealt with. But he can't tell me what to do any more.

'So why didn't you tell me she was expecting?'

He looks surprised that I have the front to ask.

'Because I didn't know myself. She went away all those months ago and didn't tell me until she came back when it was pretty obvious. What was I supposed to do? Walk away from my own child?'

'I don't know. Did you have to go back to her?'

'Oh come on, Scarlett. I've got to give it a go, haven't I? For our child's sake if nothing else. I don't want to be one of those dads who's not around for his kid.'

'Like mine, you mean.'

'Well, yeah, sorry. You know exactly how it feels. At least my kid will know that I tried.' Sounds so half-hearted though, like he's only bothered about being seen to do the right thing. Makes me wonder if my own dad tried but gave up.

'You told me we were good together. That you two were over.' I'm convinced I can persuade him.

'And we were. You know how much I care about you.' He threads his fingers through mine, and together we gently move them backwards and forwards, skin on skin until our hands close together as one.

'Sometimes as a parent you have to make really hard decisions, put your own happiness second and just step up and do the right thing.'

I pull my hand away. I'm silent. I can't answer that because my dad never took that leap and put me first.

'I'm going to ask you something now, and I need an honest answer.' He takes his phone out and scrolls, but I'm not listening.

All those times he took me to beautiful hotels, treated me like a princess. Was it to keep me away from his house, so I didn't find out anything about his life? She could have been living there all this time for all I know. Why did I take his word for it? Has he been lying the whole time? He told me that as soon as he put a ring on her, she changed. Became demanding and petty. Withheld sex unless he did everything she'd asked him to do. How do I know if that's true?

'Are you listening?' He holds up the screen to me. 'Is this you?'

'What is it?'

He flashes up a short email I've never seen before. 'Did you send this?' He practically pushes the screen in my face.

> *I know your game, dipshit, whatever avatar you're hiding behind in those chatrooms. There's a name for people like you and only one option available. I'm here to rid the world of you.*
>
> *Experience points collected: 9,186*
> *Countdown: Four lives remaining.*

'Of course it's not from me. What's it even about?'

'Some weirdo threatening me, claiming to know some crap about me.'

'Like what?'

'I don't know. Websites I've been to, I guess, you know dodgy ones.'

'Porn sites?'

'Well, yeah. Show me a man who doesn't.'

'And you think I would send that?'

'I know you wouldn't, but I had to ask.' He tucks his phone in his shorts pocket and rubs his hands over his face. His tan has deepened and gives an aged look to his skin.

'Wait till I find the bastard behind this.'

'So, what happens about us?'

'My wife can't know about us, Scarlett. You and your mate can't follow us around any more, okay? I don't want her getting suspicious and asking me all sorts of awkward bloody questions.' His voice of authority again. He always goes back to it when he wants to reinforce that he's in charge.

His sea-green eyes fix on me, but instead of his usual dreamy expression, a hint of menace is seeping in around the edges.

I wonder how much it would take for him to lose his temper.

Chapter Twenty-Eight

I rush round the house closing all the curtains, ending in our bedroom. The chattering crowd below are blocking our quiet respectable road. This is madness. I cringe at what the neighbours must be saying. None of them will want to talk to us after this. We'll be forced to move away. I wish I had the nerve to open a window and shout at everyone to leave us alone.

A woman a few doors down is being interviewed on the pavement outside her house. I recognize her but can't recall her name. What is she saying about us? About me? Is she telling the journalist about the time Nick lost his temper at the Neighbourhood Watch meeting? Or when he shouted at a boy delivering the free newspaper?

My eyes narrow at number eleven directly opposite. Did the curtain move? I blink. Perhaps I imagined it. Becca won't say anything to the police or a reporter, will she? Only she knows why the ambulance came here last Christmas. Is she hiding behind her curtains watching everything? Or maybe she's in the throng below, already spilling our secrets to one of the tabloids. No, stop it. I pull at my hair. She's a friend. I can trust her. She said my secret was safe with her. Did she mean it, though? She might think Nick has something to do with Thomas's disappearance and feel duty bound to tell the police all she knows. *Everything.*

If the press get wind of all these 'incidents' it could add up and shape the public's opinion of us. Especially if they dredge up how we met. I shiver. And then what? Accusations? *Tarred with the same brush*, Dad would say. I couldn't bear it being splashed all over the papers.

Maybe Becca's not even home yet. I scroll through my phone and send her a text.

> Have you heard – Thomas has gone missing!! It's crazy outside, reporters everywhere. Could really do with a friend right now. Are you home yet?

I lie down on the bed. The room is stifling. But I can't open a window. They might start shouting up at me.

I text Nick asking when he's coming back. Where can he have gone? I pull up Mum and Dad's number. Is it too late to tell them about Thomas or is our appeal on the news already? I search the BBC website for the headlines. The story was filed over an hour ago.

> *Newborn Taken From Bedford Shopping Centre: Parents Appeal For Thomas's Safe Return.*

Too late. Another thing they'll hate me for. Perhaps it's too late to build bridges. I press the number and immediately end the call. How do I even begin?

The photo under the headline is of the other girl Greg mentioned. They're calling her Rosie's accomplice. I zoom in but I don't recognize her face.

I check my Instagram account. There are no new snide comments. That's one good thing. I'm glad Nick insisted on my using a handle otherwise I'd have hundreds of nutters commenting by now. People are so jealous. A few nice photos of your house and they think they know you, that you must be living the perfect life. If only they knew the truth.

My eyes rest on our wedding photo on the chest of drawers. Nick in his tuxedo, standing tall, a satisfied smile across his lips. Mum's voice pipes up in my head: *the cat that got the cream, more like*. His arm is securely through mine and I'm smiling as hard as I can because I didn't want the tears to break through and spoil the picture. The love of my life had married me, I couldn't believe my luck but there was a sour taste in the back of my mouth that wouldn't shift. I didn't understand exactly what it meant because I was so naïve, only eighteen years old.

The mobile rings in my lap making me jump. I expect it to be Nick but it's not.

'Gemma, is that you trying to call?' It's Dad's voice. Tears fill my eyes. I can't speak, trying to stop myself crying.

'Gemma, darling, we saw the news. Are you okay?'

'Dad. I'm so sorry.' I press the phone closer to my face.

'Darling, what are you sorry for?'

I take a breath. There are so many things, where do I begin?

'I didn't know she wouldn't bring him back.'

'Of course you didn't, sweetheart. You don't need to be sorry. It's not your fault.'

'But I trusted her.'

'She's the one at fault here, not you.'

'I just want my baby back.' Why is he being kind to me? It's only making it worse. I wish I could tell him everything.

'Of course you do.'

'Is Mum there?'

He hesitates and I picture her sitting in her armchair by the television, across the room from his. He's offering the phone to her and she's shaking her head.

'She's… a bit upset, love. Maybe another time.'

'I will bring Thomas to see you both, I promise. As soon as I get him back.'

'I know, love. It's okay, your mum will come round.'

He's in the kitchen now because he's talking over the kettle boiling, so Mum can't hear what he's saying. Why does he think

I don't know what he's up to when I've heard him do it scores of times before?

'Will she, though? Has she forgiven me?'

'I've got to go now, love. There's someone at the door.'

There is no one at the door. Another of his avoidance tactics. *I know them all, Dad*, I want to shout at him.

'Speak soon, love.'

'Bye, Dad.'

The line goes dead. I throw myself on the bed and cry.

Chapter Twenty-Nine

Five Days Before

Gemma

The midwife lays my baby onto my bare chest, cord still attached and covered in blood. His scrunched-up eyes gaze into mine for the first time, and I think my heart will burst with joy.

'Hello, Thomas, welcome to the world.' *I'll keep you safe little one, I promise.*

'You were amazing.' Nick kisses my head and neither of us can take our eyes off our beautiful baby boy. All that matters is us three here together right now. This is our world, our new family.

Once Thomas is cleaned up and checked, the midwife shows me how to latch him on to feed. Later when he's sleeping and wrapped up in a blanket, Nick holds him, so I can go and have a shower.

The skin on my belly is an empty sack. Will I ever shrink back to a size ten? I have a healthy baby and he's worth every single stretch mark. It's just Nick who will mind. My body has changed so much. Will he find me attractive again? I dry myself and look in the mirror. I'm a different person now. A mummy. My left eye has a bright red broken blood vessel near the inner corner. I hope Nick doesn't take any photos of me.

I wear my new nursing bra, comfortable knickers and a clean white nightdress. It's still so warm outside but I don't feel confident enough to wear shorts with this big sanitary pad. I towel dry my hair and put my slippers on.

Nick is still holding Thomas, looking down at him. The smile on his face is pure bliss. I really hope this is a new start for us, that he will be the good dad he never had and become a settled family man.

'Do you know where my phone is?' I ask. 'I need to text my parents.'

'Sssh.' He holds a finger to his lips and points at the rucksack in my hand. I take my mobile out and shove it in my pocket. He didn't object. Does that mean he wants me to tell them?

'Oh, there he is,' Becca whispers, appearing round the curtain in her nurse's uniform. 'He's gorgeous. And how are you guys doing?'

'Good, thanks,' Nick says.

'I'm fine, a bit sore.' I hug Becca, grateful she was around.

'You did so well, I hope you're proud of her, Nick.'

He smiles and nods still with that dreamy look on his face. I hope it doesn't change.

'Thomas looks a bit jaundiced,' she says peering over Nick's shoulder at him. 'I'll get someone to come and check, but he might need to go under the lamps for a day or so. Not in a rush to go home, are you?'

'Thank you.' We hug and she whispers "well done" in my ear. I'm happy to stay for another day. I'd rather make sure Thomas is completely well first.

Nick goes home to collect some more babygros and clothes for me. I feed Thomas again. Another nurse comes to check and agrees that Thomas's skin is looking a bit orange so does a blood test. She says she'll be back soon to put him under the lights.

While Thomas is sleeping, I take a moment to make myself a coffee in the kitchen next to the ward. The sun is blazing through the window. I'd almost forgotten that there's a whole world going on out there. I pick a chocolate digestive from the plate by the kettle. Life could be so happy every day if Nick stayed in a good mood. Maybe I should suggest anger management classes to him. If I say he needs to do it for Thomas's sake, maybe he will. I take my phone out and pull up my parents' number. I stare at it for a few moments. What will I say? I'll call them later. I open Instagram. I'm tagged in a series of sideways photos of a kitchen cupboard full of mugs. They look just like mine. But they can't be. I check the profile of the person who's posted it. @redgirl. The hashtags don't make sense: #mug #wife #perfect #lies #random. I don't understand. If this is in my house, who took these?

I finish my biscuit and carry my coffee. It's uncomfortable to walk so it's more of a waddle. Someone is standing by my bed.

'Hey, is that you, Rosie?' I'm frowning and smiling at her standing awkwardly by the baby's cot, half hiding behind a helium balloon she's holding which says, 'It's a Boy!' in enormous blue writing.

'I wasn't expecting to see you.' I thought only family were allowed. I smooth my hair down with my hand. I must look a mess. I grab my cotton dressing gown from the end of the bed and put it on, wrapping it tight. I'm not keen on an employee seeing me like this, without make-up and oh God, this red eye looks hideous.

'He's a big baby, isn't he?' She smiles. I think she's really taken with him.

'He is. Almost nine pounds.'

'What's his name?'

'We've called him Thomas.'

'That's nice. He was so still when I came in, I was scared. I thought for a second he wasn't breathing. Anyway, I forgot to give you this.'

'Ah thank you. That's good of you. Just put it on there.' She gives me our front door key. I'd forgotten she still had it.

'Anyway, I can't stop, I just wanted to make sure everything was okay.' She looks towards the door then hands me the balloon.

'Thank you, it's really kind of you.'

'I was so excited to hear the news.'

It's really sweet of her to come but thankfully, she doesn't stay long. Maybe I wasn't very welcoming, but I'm so tired. Perhaps Georgio sent her. I lie on the bed and shut my eyes.

Nick comes back a few minutes later with a sports bag of things from home. I unpack Thomas's babygros. All ones I've carefully selected from John Lewis and Debenhams. Soft good quality cotton. I take out another nursing bra and nipple cream and several pairs of knickers which are all tangled with static. I pull them apart. There's a dark green pair with black lace I've not seen before.

'What are these?' I pinch them between my thumb and forefinger.

'Huh?' Nick is sitting on the side of the bed staring at Thomas sleeping.

I sling them at him.

'What's wrong?' He stands up and examines them in his hands.

'What's wrong is they are not mine.' I glare at him.

'Whose are they then?'

'You tell me,' I sob.

'I don't know, do I?' He chucks them on the bed, an angry glint in his eye.

I want to ask him if he's been seeing someone, but I don't want to spoil this precious bonding time with our baby, so I bite my tongue.

Chapter Thirty

24 July 2018
Scarlett

We get up early the next morning and Mum's already on her way out for her first appointments at the salon. I make instant coffee and pour it into two ceramic travel mugs, grab a couple of pain au chocolate in their cellophane packets and we're straight out of the door.

It's a short walk to the local MOT garage and thank goodness there are no urgent advisories on it this time. I drive the scenic route to Dunstable via the A6 and skirt round Luton to avoid the morning traffic.

We drive into Dunstable high street and the sat nav takes us off Oldhill and around to Birchside, a cul-de-sac of neat terraced houses. Kids of all different ages are out playing on bikes and scooters.

I pull up outside number sixteen, a red front door and a tiny patch of grass on one side and a row of bins on the other. One of the two upstairs windows is wide open, not the whitest net curtain blowing in the breeze. Was one of those my bedroom? Did Dad look after me here as a baby or had they already split up by the time we moved?

'Are you okay?' Amy asks.

'Yeah, I was, but now I'm dead nervous.'

'We'll do this together. Unless you'd rather go alone?'

'Oh no, please come with me.'

We get out of the car and go and knock on the door, Amy right beside me. No one comes. I try the bell.

'Could be in the back garden on a day like this.' Amy walks along the pavement but there doesn't seem to be any access. I look through the letterbox. A waft of heat and stale cigarette smoke hits me.

'I'm coming,' a woman's voice shouts. She's shuffling towards the door using a frame.

'I'm sorry, I didn't know if you'd heard,' I call.

'Who are you?' she asks.

'My name's Scarlett. I'm looking for someone.'

The woman reaches the door and opens it a crack.

'I thought you were the Kleeneze...' She can barely speak she's so out of breath. '...lady.' Her arthritic hands grip the moulded handles, her knuckles white. Her face is flushed and she reeks of cigarette smoke. 'Who're you looking for then?'

'My dad. We lived here soon after I was born. Could you tell me how long you've been here?'

'A good ten years, I expect. I can't in all honesty remember.'

'You probably wouldn't have known them then. Thanks anyway. Sorry to have disturbed you.' I turn to go.

'Someone called Joan lived here before. On her own, like me.'

I turn back. 'That's very helpful, thank you.'

The door closes.

'That's disappointing.'

'It is nearly twenty-one years ago. Let's try the next-door neighbours. Left or right first?'

'Right.'

I ring the bell. A young family live there and only moved in six months ago. We try the other side. Similar story, retired couple with two chihuahuas have lived there for five years.

'What now?' Amy asks. 'Across the road or left and right?'

'Let's try left again.' I move out of the way to let a string of children scoot past.

'Shall I try right? Be a lot quicker.'

'Okay.'

There's an older man at number twelve. He's hard of hearing but he lives with his son who tells me they've been there fifteen years.

'Scarlett.' Amy waves me over. It's another elderly lady at number twenty. Smartly dressed in a tweed skirt, blouse, white ankle socks and lace-up shoes. Her hair is short and bouffant, as Mum calls it. She's got plenty of clients who still have that style.

'This is Mrs Weaver. She's lived here for twenty-five years.'

'Oh really. Nice to meet you, I'm Scarlett.' I hold out my hand and she takes it in both of hers, shaking it absentmindedly because she's staring at me like I'm her long-lost daughter.

'Is it really you?' Her Scottish accent is strong. 'That poor little baby?'

'Did you know my mum – Kelly?'

'No, no dear. Kept to herself. Joan looked after you both.'

I gently tug my hand away.

'Can you remember if my dad was living there too?'

'Oh goodness no, child. I shouldn't think she'd ever get over a thing like that.'

'Like what?'

The woman stares at me, like she's made a huge mistake and I'm not the person she thought I was. She shakes her head, mumbles 'sorry' and shuts the door.

'What just happened?' I ask Amy.

'I have no clue.'

I ring the bell and knock on the door a few times, but Mrs Weaver doesn't answer.

'That's so odd. She seemed perfectly fine talking to me and then it was like the shutters came down.'

'Do you or your mum know anyone called Joan?'

'No, but we used to receive a Christmas parcel from someone with that name every year when I was growing up. I think I asked Mum once who she was.' I unlock the car and we get in.

'And what did she say?'

'I don't remember, someone from work probably, or... I think it might have been someone Granny knew.'

'That doesn't really help us, does it?'

'No.' I start the engine and wait for an older boy on a bike to get out of the road.

'What do you think she was talking about when she said she didn't think your mum would ever get over a thing like that?'

'I have no idea. And I don't seem to be any closer to finding out who my dad is.'

Chapter Thirty-One

24 July 2018

Scarlett

We swing by Cole's house but his car isn't there, so we carry on to home. I drop him a message on Snapchat, but he doesn't reply. He must be really hacked off with me following him around.

'Ha ha, look at this reply on Insta.' I show Amy my phone and she cracks up. I scroll through my feed, liking a few new *Love Island* celeb beach poses. Cole hates me following them, but I told him loads of them have brains too, like that gorgeous Dr Alex.

Mum's out so we go searching for her address book. I want to find out if Mum's got a new address for Joan so I can go and ask her some questions. I don't remember the last time we had a Christmas card from her, though, but then I've not been checking.

We take a drawer each in the kitchen.

'It's red and slim with gold lettering that says "Addresses".' I can't think when I last saw it. Didn't she get a new address book for Christmas last year? Would she have transferred everything over and chucked the old one? I don't think so. Mum's a bit of a sentimental hoarder. It's probably got too many memories in it, like old boyfriends' numbers from back in the day before mobiles. She's kept all my birthday and Christmas cards from when I was born. Now there's a thought.

'Mum's got a box of my old birthday cards somewhere. She showed them to me once. I wonder if there are any from Joan.'

'Probably is if you lived with her, but it's not going to tell you anything about her, is it?'

'I suppose not. Unless she's written a message.'

'There's no address book in here.' Amy shuts the drawer.

'Come and help me then, it's a right mess in here. I think we need to take it all out, then put it back as we sift through.'

'How big is it exactly?'

'About a quarter of A4.' I grab all the papers in one go, tip them up, flick through, then hand them to Amy to put back.

'Not likely to miss it then, are we?'

'Let's face it, it's not here.' I slump down on a chair.

'Is there anyone she writes to? What I mean is, when's the last time she would have needed to look up an address?'

'Christmas, of course!'

'Bingo.'

'She keeps a shoebox of cards for next year and holds onto favourite ones from last year. There's a big tick list of who she sends a card to and who sent us one back. I'm sure Joan will be in there somewhere.'

'So where's this box?'

'I don't know. Maybe her bedroom?'

We both laugh. I can't help it, this is all so absurd. If Mum would tell me about Dad, I wouldn't need to go through her things behind her back. I hate lying to her, snooping round her stuff, but what choice do I have?

We stop for a cold glass of water and sit in the garden. I Snapchat Cole again, asking if he's still mad at me. Then I check through Instagram. His wife's blocked me again. I set up a new profile and add a new comment. Not getting away from me that easily.

We find the shoebox under Mum's bed. The list is there and the address book. I take it into my room and flick through every page, not knowing what Joan's surname is.

'Here it is. It's under Morris. Exactly the same address.'

'Not crossed out?'

'No, but there's tiny writing after the postcode – says "died, 2007" and she's drawn a teardrop.'

'That's it then, I suppose. Line of inquiry ended.'

'Who was she, though? That woman said Joan looked after "us" not just me.'

'Why don't you ask your mum?'

'Do you think I'll get a straight answer?'

'Probably not.'

'I'm not giving up. She cannot keep fobbing me off.' I slam the address book shut. 'Talking to Cole about him becoming a dad has got me thinking more about Father's Rights and mine too. Mum's wrong not telling me anything. I'm going to find out who my dad is, and she can't stop me.'

Chapter Thirty-Two

25 July 2018

Scarlett

'Why don't we go for a picnic along the canal this afternoon,' Mum says on Wednesday morning.

I was thinking of calling Cole and trying to arrange to meet him later except the mouse will probably be back from work. I Snapchat him anyway, saying I miss him.

'Can we?' Amy asks. She's been deprived of any kind of day trips growing up, so she jumps on any suggestion.

'Scarlett?'

I shrug. It's Mum's day off and she doesn't wait for my answer. It might be a good time to ask her who Joan is.

'I think it would be lovely to stroll down the towpath on a glorious day like this. I'll make us some sandwiches.'

I Snapchat Cole again that I want to see him, but he doesn't respond. That's decided then.

When we arrive, I help Mum lift the cool bag out of the back of her Mini. We find a shaded spot and spread out a blanket to sit on. Mum hands out the sandwiches: cheese or ham and pickle. We munch on them in silence. The air around us is thick with floating spores of pollen and tiny insects. I finish my sandwich and throw a tiny piece of crust into the water and watch the cascade of ripples.

Amy and I stand arm in arm at the grassy edge, our reflections dark outlines shimmering in the water.

'When are you going to ask her about Joan?' Amy whispers.

A waft of meadowsweet wafts towards us on a wisp of breeze. I search around and pick some of its tiny creamy-white flowers and crush them in my palms, the sweet smell changing to an antiseptic aroma.

'Mum, who was that woman who always used to send me a bar of chocolate every Christmas?'

'What made you think of that?'

'Don't know really – been having random little memories of when I was a kid, maybe because I'm going to be a proper grown-up when I turn twenty-one.'

'Twenty-one used to be when you came of age in my mum's day before they lowered it to eighteen.'

'What does that actually mean?'

'You couldn't vote or marry without consent then.'

'Wow, that's old.'

'Twenty-one is still celebrated as the big milestone, which is why we need to plan your party.'

'We can sit down and make lists when we get home.'

'Is a barbecue in the garden okay? There wasn't something else you had in mind was there?'

'What like jetting off to Ibiza with a bunch of my friends?'

'I wish I could afford that for you.'

'Don't be silly, I'm joking.'

'Ibiza in the back garden it is then. You'd better start writing your invitations. I've got a special guest coming to see you from America.'

'Oh. Not Joan, is it?'

'No, she died ten years ago.'

'That's a shame. It felt really special receiving a present from her every year. Did I ever meet her?'

'Lots of times, especially when you were a baby. We stayed with her for a while.'

'Do you mean we lived with her?'

'Well, yes, she really helped me after you were born.'

'So how did you know her?'

'She was one of my mum's best friends.'

'Is that because you'd split up with my dad?'

'I don't want to talk about this now, Scarlett,' Mum says over her shoulder. I turn away, rolling my eyes at Amy. I wish Cole were here. He should be with me now, kissing me all over. It's not fair that he's stuck with the mouse when it's me he wants.

I stand up and announce I am leaving. I march off in the wrong direction in a mist of tears. If I can't have him, I may as well be dead. I wipe my eyes on the back of my hand. Amy comes after me, but I don't feel like speaking to anyone, not even her.

'Is it about Cole?' she asks. 'He'll see what a big mistake he's made, I know he will.'

I stop abruptly and she almost crashes into me. I spin round to face her, arms crossed. 'How can you know any of that?'

'Why wouldn't he? He loves you. We just need to stick to the plan.'

'And what is the plan apart from trolling the mouse and following them around?'

'I'll think of something else, I promise.' She pauses. 'I've seen the way he looks at you.' Her eyes lift and she gazes into mine, beyond the surface, and I see for the first time that she's a little bit in love with me herself. I immediately forgive her for everything. There is no one as loyal to me as her. I know she'll help me get Cole back, but if he's going to stay mad at me, is that what I want? Maybe I should cut my losses and destroy him instead.

Chapter Thirty-Three

I curl up on the bed in a kind of twilight created by the closed curtains, waiting for news. I wish I could go to work but how would I be able to carry on as normal when my baby is missing? How could I concentrate? In my mind's eye, Thomas is crying until he's red in the face and suddenly I realize I'm leaking milk. *Where are you, baby? Are you safe? What have you done with him, Rosie?*

I need Mum but I don't know what I can do to win her back. She must be so disappointed in me, her only daughter. Will my parents ever have the chance of meeting Thomas? My younger brother will be on his school holidays. Out with his mates, completely embarrassed by his big sister. I check my phone hoping to see a message from Mum saying she knows we have different opinions, but what's happened to Thomas is terrible and she's thinking of me and prays he is found safe and well soon.

But there's nothing.

I try calling Nick but it goes straight to answerphone. Is he really looking for Thomas? I'm not sure I'd know where to start. They could be anywhere by now. I don't trust him. What's he up to?

The moment I put the phone face down on the bed, it pings. A text from Becca.

I haul myself off the bed, unbutton my skirt and let it slip to the floor. In the en-suite I peel off my cotton shirt and bra and drop the breast pads into the bin. Under the shower, I adjust the water to a cool light sprinkle as though I'm standing in the rain. Moments of my long labour flash through my head. The burning pain as Thomas was crowning, and later, the midwife saying the umbilical cord was wound around his neck. Nick shouting for her to get a doctor and me trying to stay in control breathing in gas and air.

As I dry myself off, I glance in the mirror at the bruise blooming on my arm. My eyes are drawn to the jagged scar on my leg, which never fails to make me shiver.

Once I'm dressed, I sit in the nursery, holding Thomas's soft toy Peter Rabbit. The pain of labour seemed to fade as soon as he was placed in my arms. Seeing my baby for the first time made everything I'd been through feel worth it. I'd done something right at last. Out of all the darkness, he was my beam of light into a possible brighter future. I believed everything could change for the better, including Nick. He seemed different the moment he became a dad, but after today I'm scared that he's worse than ever. He blames me for Thomas being taken. And he's right. I've lost the one thing that was going to bring us back together and give us a chance at normal family life. I rock backwards and forwards, sobs building in my throat. Tears spill onto the toy's soft fur. Nick will surely kill me if Thomas isn't found safe. How can my life have become so unbearable?

I'd had such high hopes that day on the plane to Las Vegas. I'd never been anywhere so far away. When I was growing up most of my trips abroad had been to European countries like France, Belgium and Germany. Always culture-driven holidays. Neither of my parents cared much for beaches so we visited museums, art galleries and national parks. Nick had borrowed my passport, pre-booked the tickets and only told me the day before that we were going on a mystery tour. I'd been beside myself with excitement to be flying away with him. When I found out we were going to America, I panicked and wanted to call my parents, but Nick reminded me of how little they thought of him and their opinion on our relationship. He didn't want them stopping me from doing what I wanted.

We arrived at lunchtime and by the afternoon I had a head-ache from the heat and jetlag and probably all the wine and liqueurs we drank on the plane, if I'm being truthful, so Nick had a doctor sent up to our room. I was lying in darkness when he arrived, the sun was too bright and made me feel sick. The doctor thought it was a migraine, so he signed a piece of paper and gave it to Nick, which I guessed was a prescription because Nick went out and came back with some strong painkillers which made me throw up.

He went out again for the rest of the afternoon, said he had some papers to sort out at the local authority office. I guessed it was something to do with his work. He wouldn't tell me exactly what it was about.

After sleeping off the migraine and jetlag, we spent the first two days lounging by the pool in the searing heat. Every now and again we swam across to the bar to order cocktails, usually a Pina Colada with a slice of pineapple for me. In the evenings we played a few slot machines in the hotel, and after dinner we strolled along The Strip with the zillions of other tourists, popping into a few of the other themed hotels like New York, New York and MGM Grand for a show or luxury shopping. It was a feast for the senses. Everywhere was as glitzy and dazzling as I'd seen it on TV. I couldn't get over how big everywhere was. All the hotels were like small villages with a variety of restaurants on every level. Casinos, bars and rows and rows of whirring bleeping slot machines stretched across the whole of the ground floor, further than it was possible to see.

Nick bought me loads of designer clothes, all hand-picked by him. Not things I would have necessarily chosen for myself, but he said that was the point, he was showing me how to be more grown-up and sophisticated. I liked my new quirky look; casual chinos, longer-line skirts, buttoned-up blouses and soft leather loafers. He said I looked beautiful, like a young Andie MacDowell in *Four Weddings and a Funeral*.

The following day was my eighteenth birthday. I wore the cream shift dress Nick had bought for me, had my hair and nails done, and there I was sat in a limo with the man of my dreams. I still hadn't worked out what he was up to. All I could think was how I'd never have guessed in a million years that I would celebrate becoming an adult in such style. Nick opened a bottle of champagne and poured me a glass. To control my nerves, he said, like it had on the plane. He kept smiling stupidly and wouldn't answer me when I asked him again and again where we were going.

The limo took us to the Little Garden Chapel. The driver opened the door for us. Nick got out first, then reached in and took my hand. I thought we were there for some friends of his, to surprise them on their special day.

It wasn't until we were inside and a woman in a pink blouse and smart trousers handed me a bouquet of twelve white roses that it finally dawned on me. I was speechless and he seemed to be too – he couldn't stop smiling.

'Is this for real?' I asked him, wondering if maybe we were at some crazy American make-believe place where you could try out your fantasies.

'This is what you wanted, isn't it? It's what I want.' A frown flickered across his brow. He'd clearly not expected this reaction from me.

'What about my parents?'

'What about them?' He took my hand between his. 'This is about you and me.'

'I always wanted them to be there for my special day.' I couldn't even bring myself to say the words 'wedding day' because it still seemed insane.

'But it's all been arranged.'

'When? You didn't say anything.'

'Because I wanted it to be a surprise for you, on your birthday.'

'I need to call my parents.' I laid the bouquet on the table and put my hand out for my phone.

'Don't spoil it, honey. We can celebrate with them when we get home.'

'But I want to at least tell them.'

'Call them after.' He held my hand up and kissed it then pulled me into his arms.

The registrar came back in and sat behind the desk which was decorated with tall vases of white lilies.

'Can I have your papers, please?' the woman asked eyeballing each of us, a smile fixed to her face.

Nick took out a folded form from his inside jacket pocket. He kept me tight to him, away from the desk.

'We want to be together, don't we?' He cupped my face with his hand and pleaded with me with those eyes of his. This was the man I loved. He looked heartbroken, probably wondering why I wasn't overjoyed after he'd made everything so special for me. Why was I complaining? Nick was always saying that I shouldn't live my life trying to please my parents, I had to start pleasing myself. Wasn't that why I was here? To break free from them, not to have to seek their approval. I'd prove that I could make decisions by myself. I didn't need them to okay everything for me.

Nick knelt down on one knee, took a box out of his pocket and opened it to a huge diamond solitaire ring.

'Gemma, will you marry me?'

There was only one answer for this kind, generous, gorgeous man.

'Yes, I will.'

And in those three little words, I'd put the seal on the biggest mistake of my life.

Chapter Thirty-Four

By the time we reach home from the canal walk, Amy's mum, Tina, has texted twenty times asking when we'll be back. She says she wants her daughter to go home with her tonight. I wonder what for. Maybe to clean the flat or cook dinner. It's usually something like that.

'When are you bringing her back?' Mum asks when Tina turns up on the doorstep. She lets her in, but Mum won't let Amy go until she knows.

'Sunday, Kelly. I'll bring her back Sunday. Is that all right with you?' Tina taps her long orange gel nails on the counter. I know how much they cost to get done. She could have bought Amy trainers instead. She could really do with a new pair.

I take Amy upstairs and help her collect her things together. We don't speak. Neither of us has anything good to say about her leaving.

'You can't keep treating her like a child.' Tina's voice suddenly bursts through the floor. Amy and I stop still, listening.

'How many times have I told you it's my decision, no one else's,' Mum loud whispers back.

'I cannot believe you sometimes.'

'I mean it, Tina.'

'You have to let her grow up.'

'So easy for you to say.'

'You can't protect her forever.'

'You don't understand.'

I switch Amy Winehouse on and try to drown their voices out. I can't even begin to decipher what they mean. What must I never know? I presume it's about me. Is it something to do with my dad? Does Tina know who he is?

'Come on Amy, time to go.' Tina bangs on the bannister.

There's a strange silence when we come downstairs. The air laden with everything that's been said and all the truths held back. Amy and I hug and quietly say goodbye. Mum and Tina don't say any more, they don't even look at each other.

After they've gone, it takes a while for the atmosphere to settle. I don't know what to do with myself. It's just me and Mum. How it's always been, the two of us against the world. She pats my shoulder and slinks off to the kitchen. I hear the glug of wine being poured. I want to ask her what they were arguing about, but I have a feeling now is not the best time.

I mooch upstairs and lie on the low bed, staring out of the window, up at the stars emerging as night falls. They always put my problems into perspective, knowing what a tiny dot I am in the universe. What's Amy doing right now? And Cole?

I hear giggling and pull my mattress up only to see Mum with Rob – is it Rob? – rolling about on her bed, the soft hypnotic sound of jazz coming from her old CD player. I didn't hear him come in. I wouldn't be surprised if one day she introduces me to one of these blokes as my long-lost dad. I just wish she could be honest with me about where he is now. Doesn't he want to know me? Aren't I grown up enough to accept whatever happened between them? My life feels like one of those sad puzzles that nobody wants to buy at a jumble sale because it has that one important piece missing which inevitably spoils the whole picture.

I check my phone. No new messages. I leave a couple of comments on the mouse's Insta page. She's not been posting up very much, but there's a new one of the newly decorated nursery, pale blue walls and wooden block letters on the window sill, spelling 'Thomas'. I take pictures of myself using bunny ear and devil horn filters on Snapchat and send them to Cole. Is it too late to drive there? I might catch a glimpse of him.

I'm there in six minutes. Barely any traffic at this time of night. I park a short distance away and walk by their house. There's a light on in the hall and a room upstairs. Someone's up there. I stand back, near the hedge over the road. They won't see me in these dark clothes and my hair is tucked up in a baseball cap. The door opens. Cole is wearing jogging bottoms and a faded REM T-shirt. The cat under his arm is struggling to break free. Cole's stubble is growing into a beard and his hair is thick and floppy already. It only makes him sexier in my eyes, although I can hear him laugh at that. He dumps the cat on the doorstep and pushes it with his bare foot then slams the door shut. The cat flicks its tail and struts off behind a bush. All I want is a message or a little heart or kiss emoji from him. No words needed when you feel like I do. Just *something*. He said he felt the same, but was he playing with me? *What if you're not the only girl?* I shake my head and scatter Amy's words that keep coming back to me. Something she said ages ago.

I drive back home and think of Amy in the tiny bed behind the curtain. What is her mother up to? Mum called Tina a bitch once. I want to know why they've fallen out this time. I hope it's not permanent, for Amy's sake and mine. But with Tina, anything's possible.

In the early morning, I dress and creep silently downstairs. Amy is not replying to my messages. Cole is ignoring me. I eat a banana and a glass of milk then pinch a tenner in one pound coins from the jar Mum hides behind the cereal packets. Then I'm out the back door, using the key to close it so it doesn't click.

The air is fresh but already edged with the warmth of the day to come. I drive to his house. The street is quiet except for the rumble of someone wheeling their bin out to the pavement.

I park across the road and check my watch: 5.40 a.m. His bedroom curtains are closed. His wife isn't due to leave for another fifteen minutes. I drive on to Amy's flat. My throat tightens as I turn the corner. There is a 'TO LET' sign planted in the front. I skid my car to a halt, jump out and run to the main door. The name 'Smith' in Amy's handwriting has been removed from the space next to the buzzer. I press the button anyway, holding it down until the flesh under my thumb splits away from the nail.

'No one's there,' a postman says, stopping by with his cart. I spin round.

'Do you know where they've gone, number twelve – Tina Smith and her daughter Amy?' I stare up at the block of flats, the stained cladding, washing hanging over the edge of a balcony in the flat below theirs.

'Nope. All I know is she never paid her rent. Mr Andrews owns this empire.' He taps the side of his nose as though this is top secret information.

'Aren't her letters going to a new address?'

'Not that I know of. Couldn't tell you if I did.' His sniffs.

'Thanks a bloody lot.' I stomp past him and get back in my car. He tuts to himself as he trundles away with his cart in the opposite direction.

It's all Tina's fault. Why didn't she pay the bloody rent? She's got a job. I imagine her dragging Amy out of her tiny bed, suitcase in hand and Amy screaming my name all the way down the road to the bus stop. There's only one person who'd have known about this and who'll know where they've gone – the same person who's been keeping secrets from me all my life – my mother.

Chapter Thirty-Five

26 July 2018
Scarlett

I drive as fast as I can all the way home. So much for going back to Cole's house to follow their movements. I can't do this without Amy.

Mum's tonging her hair when I burst in through the back door.

'Where is she?' I shout. Her smile is smooth as a knife slipping through butter, as though she doesn't know.

'You knew, didn't you?' I shout again, the words as rough as sandpaper on my throat, tears pushing behind my eyes.

She frowns at me and carries on twisting her hair around the tongs. Her dressing gown dips open as her arms come down. Sometimes I wish she'd cover herself up.

'Answer me, Mum. Where's Amy gone?' My thumb is throbbing from pressing their buzzer so hard and now my throat is sore from shouting.

'Tina's got a new place.' Mum turns her back on me and admires herself in the mirror. 'I'm sure I told you.'

'No, you didn't. Where is it?' I yank her arm to make her look at me, but she pulls away. Her flesh feels spongy, not firm like it used to be.

'She's Tina's daughter not mine. We don't have a say in where she lives, what she decides.'

'Tell me where they are.' My eyes sting, voice ragged.

Mum turns and grabs my shoulders. 'Calm down.'

'It's something bad, I know it is. Amy would have told me.'

'Look, they've had to go and stay in a B&B. Just for now. They're not far, not really and Amy can still come and stay again soon.' She meets my eyes, swollen with tears.

'Where?' I croak.

'Argyle Street.'

'Can we go there now?'

'Let them settle in for a bit. Maybe we can visit them this afternoon.'

After Mum's gone to work, I drive to Cole's place and park up. There's a transit van outside blocking my view. I back up a bit and watch two men deliver a cot and some other pieces of furniture – a rocking chair and footstall, changing table and chest of drawers. All matching no doubt. After the morning I've had, I'm not sure I can take this. I watch Cole sign for it and hand a black device back to the delivery man. Cole glances up but doesn't appear to see me. I'm parked where I was last night and I stand further back by the hedge, hiding behind the railing. I may as well be tied to them for all he cares. I drive off to the park. We spent some of our happiest times here. Hidden in the folly, me on his lap. Chatting and kissing for hours and hours. I was the one there for him when the mouse left. Has he forgotten that? It makes me wonder again if she had really gone. He said some of her stuff was still in the house, that she'd come back to collect it, but did she ever actually leave? He's going to wish he hadn't messed me around. I'm not going to let him get away with it.

Chapter Thirty-Six

Monday 13 August 2018
Gemma

Becca texts to say she'll be here in two minutes. I tell her to come through the back gate and I'll let her in. Greg the Liaison Officer is on his way over too with some news about a possible lead. I've no idea how long Nick's going to be, he's still not texted or called. It's not unusual for him to disappear for hours on end, but if he's really looking for Thomas, why doesn't he keep me updated? Does he know something about it that he's not telling me?

I try calling him, but it goes straight to answerphone. I don't leave a message. He won't like me telling him what to do, but he should have told Greg where he was going.

I unlock the back door and rapidly clicking cameras start up immediately. I shield my face with my arm and hurry to the gate. Several long-lens cameras are focused on me over the wall at the bottom of our medium-sized garden. The estate is so new there are no established trees to give us any privacy, but on the other hand the reporters have nowhere to hide. Fortunately, it's a high wall – about six feet – and the other side of it is a parking bay for the houses behind, so either they're on top of ladders or they're standing on residents' cars. I can only imagine how much stick we'll get for that at the next Neighbourhood Watch meeting. If we even survive that long.

I fumble the padlock keys, trying to ignore the questions being thrown at me. *How long have you lived here? How long have you and Nick been married? Do you plan to have lots of children? Have all your employees at your restaurant been questioned? Were any of them suspicious about Rosie?*

The tiny key goes in but then it won't budge either way. My hands are shaking. I want to scream at them to shut up and leave me alone.

What sort of employee was she? Could one of them have been Rosie's accomplice? Is it possible they were planning the kidnap of your baby right under your nose?

One of them calls my name and I automatically look over my shoulder. The flashes are an explosion of white light. I bury my head in my arm, blinded.

'I'm here.' It's Becca's voice calling.

'Hang on.' I take the key out then press it in again firmly. This time it turns, and I unbolt the gate. Becca squeezes in through the slimmest gap. Together we shove the gate closed against the reporters who try to push in with their microphones. We manage to bolt it and dash into the kitchen. I lock the door and fall into Becca's arms.

'Oh my God, you poor, poor thing. This is an actual living bloody nightmare. Is there any news at all about Thomas yet?'

I shake my head, crying into her shoulder. Deep racking sobs.

I don't know how long we stand there, but eventually Becca helps me into a chair and puts the kettle on.

'Where's Nick?' she whispers, glancing at the half-open door leading to the hall.

'It's okay, he's out. Searching for Thomas. They could be anywhere by now, though, couldn't they?' I grab some kitchen roll and wipe my eyes and nose.

'Do you think anyone else is involved? There's so much speculation on the net.'

'Maybe, I can't bring myself to think… she was such a nice girl, but they say she may have befriended me so I'd let her take Thomas without a fuss. I can't get my head round her doing that. I feel so stupid. What a useless mother I am.'

'Don't say that, it's not true. You're a wonderful, devoted mother. You love that boy so much.'

'What does she want him for? I can't bear to think about it.'

'Oh God, I know. You just have to try and hang on and believe he's going to be okay. Anyway, I'm not going to ask you 20 questions. You must be exhausted going through it all with the police.' She puts a mug of white coffee in front of me and sits down with hers. 'Is there anything I can do? Anyone you want me to call?'

'It's okay, thanks. Georgio is holding fort at the restaurant, but he's already messaged to say they've had reporters sniffing there too, so we may have to close up early. I can't have them bothering the customers.'

'I tell you what, though, it's crazy out there.'

'I rang my parents.'

'Oh God, did you? How was it?'

'Dad was actually really kind, but he did his usual thing of pretending he had to go. Mum was unavailable or something. Honestly, if she can't talk to me about what's happened today, I won't speak to her again.'

A text from Greg pings on my phone and a few moments later, the bell rings. Becca opens the door, making sure I'm standing behind her. It looks like Greg has had a word with the journalists as most have moved back allowing him to pass. One or two still shout for me to give them a comment and 'to have my say'.

'How are you doing, Gemma?' Greg asks.

'Surviving, just about. Any news?'

'One possible development – shall we go and sit down?'

'This is Becca by the way, she's my best friend and neighbour from across the road.'

Becca shakes hands with him then goes into the kitchen to make fresh coffee.

'Where's Nick?' Greg follows me into the living room.

'Went out looking for Thomas. I don't know where to. He's been ages. Any sightings of Rosie yet?'

141

'A few false leads – that green pram of yours is pretty popular. We're following everything up, though.'

'So can you tell me about this possible new development?'

'Let me say first that we're not a hundred per cent sure if this information is going to prove significant or not but,' he takes a deep breath, 'a couple of shoppers have come forward about a man they noticed waiting outside the supermarket. They said he seemed agitated, pacing up and down, clock watching, like he was waiting for someone. And when Rosie came out of the main doors pushing Thomas, he appeared to follow her.'

'Oh my God, what does that mean?' Chills run up and down my body.

'We don't know yet if it was a coincidence or misinterpretation of the couple that told us, but we're looking at the CCTV outside the shop right now. We're going to try and get a good shot of him and have it blown up. See if it's anyone you recognize.'

'Here we are, do you take sugar, Greg?' Becca comes in with a mug in each hand. Greg shakes his head and focuses back on me. Becca puts the mugs down.

'Oh sorry, have I come in at a bad moment?' She touches my shoulder. 'Do you want me to go?'

'No, no, stay, please.' I reach out for her hand and she takes it and sits next to me.

'Do you think he could be someone she knew?'

'I wouldn't want to even hazard a guess. He may be nothing to do with her at all.'

'But what if that man has put Rosie up to all this? He might be the one that made her keep Thomas from me. But why would anyone want my baby?'

'I know this is incredibly hard for you, but try and stay calm, Gemma. Like I said it could be a coincidence that they were going in the same direction. The couple didn't see if he continued following her because they didn't know at the time that it might be important. It's something that's occurred to them after they saw you on TV.'

I brush away my tears. Becca's arm goes round my shoulders.

'And that's the thing to focus on here, Gemma.' His hands thread together, fingers pointing at me. 'Your appeal is bringing in good quality leads and that's how we're going to find Thomas. And we will find him, okay?'

I nod and Becca passes me my 'Happiest Wife in the World' mug. I usually love the smell of fresh coffee but today it makes me nauseous because it reminds me of normal life and I'm not sure I'm ever going to get back there.

'When will you know if he's connected to Rosie?'

'I'm sorry, I'm not in a position to answer that at this moment in time.' Greg finishes his coffee. 'Now, Gemma, you said before that Rosie has a boyfriend. Did she give you any indication of his name, age, how tall he was, what he looked like?'

'I don't remember her mentioning any details, only that she wasn't keen on her mum finding out about him.'

'Which may indicate that he was a bad lad in trouble with the police, a married man – older than her mum would approve of – or all three.' Greg writes something down.

'I'm sorry, I don't remember her mentioning any of those things.'

'There's a possibility that he's our man outside the shop.'

'Oh God, really?'

'They could be trying to pass him off as their own child, which would make it harder to find him.'

My heart skitters. Thoughts rush through my mind one after the other. How could I have put so much trust in this girl? I picture Rosie with her arm around some man, strolling along with my baby, pretending it's theirs. She seemed so kind and caring, why would she do this to me?

'You mean, I might never see Thomas again – don't you?'

143

Chapter Thirty-Seven

26 July 2018
Scarlett

Mum and I sit in silence as we eat our cheese and pickle sandwiches for lunch. I've propped the back door open, hoping to catch a breeze in this searing heat. Mum puts our plates in the sink and gathers up her keys, handbag and a couple of Sainsbury's bags.

She drives us across Bedford to near the town centre, down a side road off a rundown housing estate full of betting shops and fried chicken takeaways that have plastic tables and chairs screwed to the floor. The smell of rancid cooking fat wafts onto the street.

'Not sure it's that safe to leave my car here, but still.' Mum locks it and tries one of the doors to check, looking around for any hoodies that might be waiting to jump us.

The cute-looking B&B is set back from the road. So out of place around here. The sort you see in old American films, with a low white picket fence and roses climbing the walls and around the door. Any minute now, Snow White will come out whistling a jolly tune, surrounded by bluebirds, bunnies and squirrels.

But close up the paintwork on the front door is cracked and lifting in places and there's a strong smell of drains. The wooded planter – from where a rose was growing – has split and rotted away. The buzzer is grimy-looking, Mum won't touch it, so she raps on the door with her knuckles.

'Can I help you?' An old woman answers, holding a small dog with a squat face under her arm like it's a rolled-up towel.

'We're looking for Tina and Amy Smith,' Mum says.

'Oh yes, come in.' She points to the stairs and says they're in room number five on the first floor.

We go up and Mum taps on the door. Tina opens it an inch.

'Amy, it's me,' I call. I spot her through the crack, sitting on the bed watching what sounds like *Home and Away* on a small-screen TV, a really old one that's a chunky great cube.

'You'd better come in.' Tina seems reluctant to open the door.

I slip under her arm through the widened gap and hug a bewildered Amy. She's wearing her old *Frozen* pyjamas and unicorn slippers. There are new scratches on her arm. I wish she wouldn't do that to herself. I hug her again, tears in my eyes. I'm so grateful to see her I could burst.

'What's it all about this time, Tina?' Mum sits uninvited on the end of the narrow bed, which is piled with clothes and bin liners of stuff spilling out. In the corner is a small sink with rusted taps and a dried-up piece of soap.

'They put the rent up, didn't they? No warning. I couldn't do it any more, so we got out of there as soon as.' Tina relights a half-smoked cigarette from a tin ashtray.

Amy leads me to a box room which was clearly part of the main room originally, but a partition wall now sections it off. It's not much bigger than a broom cupboard. A narrow bed is squeezed up against the wall. It's dim as there are no windows, but at least Amy has a bit of privacy.

'I told you to bring her to me,' Mum hisses, like we can't hear her through the flimsy wall. I put my arm around Amy, covering her ears, and rock backwards and forwards. She shouldn't have to hear this.

'Come back to ours,' I whisper.

'I don't know.' Amy stares at the worn carpet which has no underlay. The floorboards creak and clonk with every step. She's gone back to the quiet awkward girl she was at school. Hiding at the back of the library, curled up on the floor under the table with a book.

'You do what you like girl, you normally do,' Tina shouts through the wall.

Amy opens the door and stands there, toes pointed inwards, head down.

'Just till you get yourself sorted out,' Mum says to Tina. 'I mean, look at the state of this place. God knows what's died on this carpet.' Mum twists the toe of her slingback into the dark spot in front of her.

'You've got a nerve telling me what to do, how to bring up my own daughter.' Tina points her finger at Mum while looking sideways at me, lips pursed. If I wasn't here, she'd like to say a whole lot more about that. 'You get your own house in order first, that's all I'm saying.'

'It's not the best place for a growing girl, though, is it, Teen?' Mum tips her head on the side, seemingly unfazed by Tina's outburst. 'Let the poor girl come with us.'

'I didn't ask you to come here.' Tina crosses her arms and blows smoke up to the yellowed ceiling.

'I mean, what's she going to do here, eh?' Mum exaggerates looking round the tiny room, not much bigger than a cage at the zoo.

Tina stubs her cigarette out in a saucer until it's splayed out flat. She sits down heavily near Mum, her hand to her forehead. 'If you must know, I lost my job, okay? Happy now?'

Mum lifts the shopping bags she's brought with us onto the bed between them. 'Thought as much. Here, it's just a few bits I thought you might need. It's all right, you don't owe me anything. We've all been there, Teen. I only want to help.'

For once, Tina seems lost for words. She swallows then nods, her fingers pressed to her lips.

'Now let Amy come to us so you can start job hunting.'

Tina chucks Amy's rucksack across the bed. 'Go on then, before I change my mind.'

146

Amy and I grin at each other and hug. Now we can get back to reminding Cole that it's me he loves.

–

Tonight it's my turn on the floor. Amy and I chat in hushed voices, so Mum doesn't have to call out for us to keep it down. We share a bottle of beer I found in the fridge.

'Good to have you back.' I finish it off and chuck it in the bin under my desk.

Amy leans over the edge of the bed and gazes at me. 'Great to be back.'

I switch on my laptop. I need to find a new job. I've always wanted to be a travel writer, but I don't know if I can do it. I got my English A levels – it was always my strongest subject at school – but I'd need to build up a lot of money to pay for travelling and an English degree. My savings are dwindling now I'm not working.

Amy hugs her pillow. 'Do you think he'll come back to you?'

'I don't know. He told me – us – to stop following them.'

'I bet he misses you, though.'

'Said he does but now he's not answering my calls or texts.'

'I bet he wishes he hadn't got her knocked up, though. If it's even his. Did you suggest it might not be?'

'Not yet. I'll save it for when the time is right. He must have doubts too with her being away so long. Why go back to her?' I flop back on the bed and stare at the ceiling. I Snapchat Cole that I love him and send a selfie of me surrounded by lit-up hearts. 'How can I make him want to be with me again?'

'Tell him you can't live without him? That if you can't see him, you'll kill yourself?' She grins, her crooked teeth shine in the half-light. I give her a death stare.

I push myself up, onto my elbow, and search for new jobs in Bedford. I click on the first link for casual posts, stacking shelves, washing dishes or waitressing. 'I need him to notice me like it's the first time again. I mean, really know what he's lost, what he's given up for that mousy wife of his. He needs to understand that he doesn't have to sacrifice the rest of his life, his happiness.'

'Let's go to the market tomorrow and buy you the glitziest dress for your birthday.' Amy's practically drooling at the prospect of tarting me up.

I sit up fully, imagining Cole being dazzled by me.

Mum shouts up for us to quieten down. The doorbell rings followed by the faint hum of voices.

'Okay, we'll go shopping tomorrow. Lingerie first, got to be matching. You don't think he's back sleeping with her, do you?'

Amy shakes her head. 'With her looking like a barrel? Don't be daft. When he sees you, he'll be begging for it.'

Long after Amy has fallen asleep, I'm still awake flicking through Instagram, checking for any reactions to the comments I've left. The mouse has said nothing. Why hasn't she blocked me? Maybe she's onto me this time so I close that profile and start a new one. I comment on her latest post then look through my own feed at my favourite celebs and influencers, Kylie Jenner and Selena Gomez.

Every now and then giggles, shrieks and the low hum of soul music filter up from downstairs. I lift my pillow and spy through the hole in the floorboards. All I can see is the tanned hairy male shin at the end of Mum's bed. The man's foot is moving in slow circles. I cover the hole up and press my hands over my ears.

Chapter Thirty-Eight

27 July 2018

Scarlett

There's a lightness in my chest as we walk along the high street the next morning. Mum is chatting on about baking a beetroot chocolate cake and catching up on the soaps because she's staying in without company for a change. Amy's a good listener. I don't mind her doing that job for me now and again. If we were a few years younger Mum would probably be holding her hand.

I push between them and link my arm through Mum's so Amy is forced to take a step back and walk a bit behind us along the pavement. I feel guilty for doing that so I let go of Mum and twist round. But Amy isn't there. She's a few steps back and has stopped outside a restaurant. I wonder if she's so annoyed with me she can't bear to walk with us. I suggest to Mum to go on ahead, we'll catch up with her at home.

'Are you okay?' I ask, walking up to Amy. 'I'm sorry, I didn't mean to block you out.'

Amy grins and tips her head towards a piece of paper stuck to the restaurant window.

WAITRESS WANTED
★Bar Experience Necessary★
Please APPLY WITHIN or send CV to:
papaspizza.gemmaadams@hotmail.com

I do a double take then peer through the glass, cupping my eyes to block out the light. It's her all right, Cole's wife. She's standing by the till near the entrance, talking to a customer. Is she really in charge? I thought she was a subservient little mouse to Cole, the alpha lion. I haven't seen anything about this on her social media. I hug Amy. Sometimes she is so utterly brilliant, I think I'll burst with pride.

'Wait here. I'm going in to get this job.' I hand my shopping bags to her.

'What, now?' Amy's mouth stays open.

I frown. 'You think I should go home, email my CV and hope she picks me from a huge pile? No. I want to make a good impression. I need this job, don't I? And I need to know more about the enemy.'

'Good point. Go for it. Good luck.'

I blow Amy a kiss and push the heavy glass door open.

The man in front of me is being shown to a table. I step up to the podium the mouse is sitting behind. She's prodding a finger at the touch screen.

She looks up and smiles with heavily painted dolly eyes. 'Sorry, I didn't see you there. I'm Gemma, how can I help you today?'

'Hi, I'm really interested in the waitressing job you're advertising.' I point to the window.

'You're keen, I've literally just put that up there.'

I try not to let Cole push into my thoughts or allow my eyes to lower to her enormous bump. As it's before the lunchtime rush, she invites me to sit down for an informal chat over coffee. She eyes up the scratches on my hands and soon we're chatting and laughing about our love of cats and how they own us not the other way around.

I tell her about my experience working in bars and cafes in London's West End last summer and she seems suitably impressed.

'Excuse me a sec,' she says as one of the waitresses calls her to the back office. A minute later she's telling me that one of her waiters has called in sick and would I like to do a trial lunchtime shift right away?

I couldn't be more thrilled. After I've washed my hands out the back and tied up my hair, I text Amy an update and ask her to let Mum know that I won't be home for a couple of hours.

Gemma knocks and comes into the small cloakroom with my uniform.

'This is a bit embarrassing, but I didn't ask your name. Too busy talking about our cats!' She gives me a clipboard and pen with a sheet to fill out with my contact details and bank account.

'Oh yeah, that's okay. My name's Rosie,' I say, pinning on my biggest smile.

Chapter Thirty-Nine

Monday 13 August 2018
Gemma

'I'm not saying that, Gemma,' Greg says, 'it's just that it's going to be tricky to track this man and Rosie down if they look like any other couple with a new baby. They could have ditched your pram and changed Thomas's clothes, so it would be difficult to distinguish them. No disrespect, but one baby looks very much like another when they're so tiny, especially when they're tucked inside a pram.'

'So you're saying Thomas may not be found? I mean, we don't even know Rosie's real name yet, do we? She could have dyed her hair, had it cut short and taken him out of the country by now.'

'Let's think positive, shall we? It's very unlikely that she would have left the country without a passport for Thomas.' Greg's phone beeps.

'Easy enough to get one.'

'Not necessarily, plus all the ports and airports have been notified.' He takes his phone out of his trouser pocket.

Becca touches my arm. 'I know it's hard but please try not to tie yourself up in knots.'

'Here, take a look at this still from the CCTV. It's of the man waiting outside the shop. He's Caucasian, probably in his late forties, early fifties, five feet nine, medium build, dark hair with some flecks of white and tanned skin.' He hands his phone to me.

'Anyone you recognize?'

I squint at the picture, examining his face closely but the features are too blurred. I hold it at arm's length and it becomes a bit clearer but it's not anyone I know. 'Sorry.' I shake my head and hand it back to him.

I rest my head on Becca's shoulder. This heat is getting to me, as though it's pressing me down. Greg goes into the hall to take a call.

The sun is filtering through the gaps in the curtain, leaving wavy shapes of light across the carpet. I shut my eyes and I'm immediately transported back to the Little Chapel in Las Vegas and the sun beaming through the multicoloured windows almost whiting out my vision. The altar was a plastic wall covered in cascades of pink artificial flowers mixed with lengths of ivy. It had looked so pretty and impressive from the double doors. But the nearer we marched towards the pastor – me holding the small bouquet of roses, clinging to Nick's arm – the clearer they became. The leaves had painted-on veins and thin wire poked out of faded petals and matte plastic buds.

I'd tried to repeat the pastor's words without any mistakes, but I'd been so nervous and still in shock, that I had to wait for him to repeat each phrase again.

When the pastor pronounced us husband and wife, a woman to the left of us started to play 'Here Comes the Bride' on a synthesizer. Nick kissed my lips then led me back up the aisle and out of the double doors.

We stood in front of the same desk as before to sign the register. The lady who'd met us when we arrived stood up and clapped. She threw a handful of rose petals over us and said in an enthusiastic voice, 'Congratulations to the newlyweds, Mr and Mrs Adams.' Nick kissed me again.

Two of their employees were our witnesses. Next to Nick's full name was his age. I noticed they'd made a mistake, but I didn't like to say in case I embarrassed the lady. I thought Nick might point it out, but he didn't. Before we left, the pastor shook our hands again and wished us well in our new lives together. Nick handed an envelope to him, bulging with ten-dollar notes. How tacky and crass it all seemed. It was nothing like the stylish wedding I'd dreamed of as a little girl. I'd imagined choosing my own dress, something elegant and strapless with a sweetheart neckline, not the high-neck flouncy one Nick had picked for me. But he'd gone to so much trouble to surprise me, I didn't want to hurt his feelings. I tried not to feel ungrateful, but it was so hard to take in that this was it, this was my wedding. Over and done within a matter of minutes. I was grateful my parents weren't there, because they'd have hated it.

The next bride and groom, a middle-aged couple in cowboy gear had already arrived in the waiting room. The bride wore a red knee-length gown covered in silver rhinestones and lace, and matching cowgirl boots. She'd pulled a disapproving face at us then turned her back.

I hadn't thought it was possible to get married so quickly. Didn't these things have to be planned weeks ahead? But Nick had been prepared with all the papers ready from his inside jacket pocket when they asked for them. I didn't know how or when he'd organized it. But there we were, husband and wife.

'I have a bit more news for you,' Greg says, coming back in the living room. 'Security at the supermarket have checked their CCTV inside the store from the moment they opened this morning. Rosie has been identified as arriving this morning at nine and buying a small trolley full of supplies. Newborn's nappies, wipes, dummies, bottles of water and prepared formula in bottles with teats.'

'Oh my goodness,' Becca says. I can't even speak. My mind is numb.

'This proves pre-meditation without a doubt. And she wasn't alone either.'

'What?'

'The woman we suspected of being an accomplice was with her on this early morning shopping trip.'

'Two of them?'

'Here's a blown-up still of her.' He passes his phone to me. I don't recognize her face from the side view. Her hair is flat and short. She's wearing glasses and the picture is grainy.

'I don't know who she is. She could be anyone. But I don't understand why they've targeted me.' A thumping pain fills my head. All this time I had been convinced it was a mistake, that something had happened to Rosie to stop her bringing Thomas back to me. But these two girls planned to take my baby. A sob spills from my lips. 'What have they done with my boy?'

Chapter Forty

The next morning, Amy and I have a couple of hours before our shifts, so as soon as Mum has gone to work, we go up to her room and I tap lightly on the door. I open it carefully and peep round. There's no one there. I'm almost disappointed not to find a fit bloke asleep, tangled in her sheets.

Her bedroom is in its usual mess, clothes strewn across every surface except the dressing table which is immaculate. An ornate silver-backed brush is pride of place next to a matching dish containing her signature bright pink lipstick. All her other make-up is in a jute-lined basket. We check through each drawer but there's only fancy underwear, tights, stockings, tops and jumpers.

Amy checks under the bed while I wade through the stuffed-to-bursting wardrobe. Nothing. We both stand back and survey the room. Where would she keep private papers and what might she have kept of Dad's? Love letters? Divorce papers? Or has she really erased him completely from our lives?

'What about those boxes up there?' Amy points to a couple of hat boxes on top of the wardrobe, pushed right to the back.

'We'll never reach them.'

'All the more reason to try, I reckon. Have you got a ladder?'

'I don't think so, but there's the step-seat in the kitchen, do you think it'll be high enough?'

'Let's have a go.'

We take one end each of the metal steps and carry them upstairs. Amy's right, if there's something that far out of reach, it was put there for a reason. If I find out who Dad is, I may have the chance of meeting him one day. I just need one little clue.

'I'll do it,' I say, placing the steps close to the wardrobe, 'then if we get caught, I can take the blame.'

'You don't need to.'

'Yeah, I do. Anyway, I'm taller than you.'

Amy holds the steps steady while I climb up. I reach as far as I can but I'm nowhere near touching the boxes with my fingertips. I try again, on tiptoe. I touch the rough edge of one box but manage to push it further away.

'Go in the bathroom and look on the back of the door for Mum's backscratcher, it should be hanging from a ribbon.'

Amy comes back with the thin stick which has a curved hand shape at one end. I stretch up again and this time reach round the first box and pull it towards me. After a few more attempts it's near enough for me to lift down.

'I'm going to pass it to you – get your hands ready, I don't know how heavy it's going to be.' I pull the box towards me until it's next to my head, then bring it slowly down to my chest. It's not heavy thank God and I pass it into Amy's arms. She carries it over to the bed. I check the time. We should have another hour at least if we're lucky. I look out of the window. No sign of Mum's car yet.

'Pass me a tissue from the bedside table. I'm not going to dust the lid but I also don't want to leave our fingerprints.' I take the tissue from Amy and wipe a line where I've touched it. Then I carefully lift off the lid and put it on the bed the same way up. Inside under tissue paper is a pair of cream satin wedding shoes, lace-edged veil and gloves, and a diamante and pearl necklace. 'They're beautiful, aren't they? So delicate.'

'What's that underneath?' She points to a bundle of something, tied with a wide organza ribbon. I carefully lift everything out. It's a small bundle of photos but nothing else, no marriage certificate or any other documents.

'Have a look then, you can't chicken out now,' Amy says.

I untie the ribbon and pick up the first photo. It's of Mum when she was younger, maybe about my age now. She's linked arms with a slightly taller woman.

'They look a bit like sisters,' Amy says.

'They do look alike, don't they? But Mum doesn't have a sister so maybe it's a cousin or it could be her mum.'

A car door slams right outside and we both jump. I check out of the window.

'Quick, put everything away, Mum's back early!'

Chapter Forty-One

29 July 2018
Scarlett

I slip the photo into my pocket to look at again later and put the rest back, tying them up with ribbon as fast as I can. Amy slides the lid back on. 'Can you go down and make sure she doesn't come up, please? Offer to make her a drink or something, give me time to put this away.'

'Are you sure? I'll do it if you want, and you go down?'

'No, if she insists on coming up, I'd rather she caught me.'

Amy squeezes my arm and rushes out of the door. I take the box under one arm and climb the steps. My fingers don't quite reach all the way around its smooth surface and I start to lose my grip. I manage to push the box up and with the backscratcher, I slide it carefully back in place. Oh no, the steps are from the kitchen. Mum's bound to notice. I carry them up to my bedroom and leave them by my bookshelf to make it look like I've been re-arranging everything. I even take a stack down to show I haven't finished yet. Then I quickly hang the backscratcher on the bathroom door.

'There you are. What are you doing up here on your own?' Mum says as I come out of the bathroom. My heart is thumping hard, up into my ears.

'You're back early. Thought I'd tidy my room as my shift doesn't start for another hour.'

'Are you feeling all right?' Mum's eyebrows shoot up and she crosses her arms. I am the daughter who never tidies anything unless I'm made to do it.

'I'm sorting out my books.'

'Oh, I see, got too many, have you?'

'You can never have too many.'

She laughs because it's exactly what she always says. She runs her hand around the back of her neck. 'I think I'll have a shower. I'm so fed up with sweating all day every day. When's this heat going to break?'

'Shall I make a milkshake?'

'Would you? Although I think Amy's making me iced tea. I'd love a smoothie too, though. Just a small one. Banana and almond milk, please.' She glides off to her bedroom and my mind is darting all over the place, trying to think of everything we touched. Did I smooth down the bed cover? Although it was quite messy already. But if she notices a box-shaped imprint in the duvet, it'll give us away. Did I leave the box the right way round? Was there a right way? I can't bloody remember. I go up to my room and try to push the Velux window open wider, but it won't budge any further. The edge of the photo is poking into my leg. I take it out carefully and stare at it. Is it a cousin or could it be Gran? I turn it over. The date on the back is September 1995. Ten months before I was born. So Mum wasn't even pregnant yet. Gran died of a heart attack a month before. Mum and I stayed with Gran's friend Jean in Dunstable when I was a few weeks old. But where was Dad? Was he with us? I desperately want to ask Mum about it, but she won't tell me and then she'll know I've been snooping in her room.

I hide the photo in my old hardback copy of *The Railway Children* and carry the steps back downstairs.

Amy is in the kitchen making iced tea. 'Everything okay?' she whispers.

'Yeah, just about. I said I'd make Mum a milkshake, do you want one?'

'No thanks, I'll stick to tea.'

'Yeah, me too.'

I take the blender out and empty a glass full of almond milk into it, followed by a roughly broken-up banana. I switch it on and stand next to Amy, speaking close to her ear, 'Next time we'll try the other box too. There must be a clue there.'

I switch the machine off and we take our tea into the garden and sit on the grass, but it's as dry as a bristle brush. I drag a couple of cushions from the sun chairs for us to sit on.

'I think it's my Gran in that photo.'

'She looks really young.'

'She was only sixteen when she had Mum so would have been about thirty-three then and Mum would have been seventeen.'

A clatter against glass silences us. Mum comes out holding her drink, stirring with a long spoon, a hardback copy of Martina Cole's latest crime novel under the other arm. She's wearing her gold bikini and a new pair of pink glittery flip-flops.

'Mmm, delicious shake. Sure you don't want some? There's a bit left.' She peers at us over her sunglasses. 'You two are quiet, everything all right?'

'Just the heat getting to us. I think we're going to go out for a bit before work.' I stand up and finish my tea.

'What about your birthday barbecue? Is there anything special you'd like me to get?' Mum rests her drink on the table and leans back in the sun lounger, soaking up the sun's rays.

'Could we have a flamingo theme – bright and cheerful? Your usual would be perfect – ice tub of drinks, mixed salads to go with the burgers, sausages, etc, ice lollies and a good mix of music.'

'Okay, I'll pop everything in the shopping basket so have a look before I checkout, see if you want to add anything. Does that sound good?'

'Perfect, thanks.'

'Got any idea of numbers?'

'Say forty?' I look at Amy and she's nodding.

'Okay. I'll probably bring a few people too, like the neighbours. You okay with that?'

'Of course.' There's never been one year when she's not gone to town on my birthday celebrations and I'm more grateful than ever. Most of my friends' parents stopped throwing parties for them when they were about twelve years old.

'We'll see you after work, Mum. Bye.'

On the way into town, we stop near The Swan Hotel and sit by the river.

'Cole is still ignoring me.' I lean back on both arms and dangle my legs down.

'Why don't you send him something?'

'Like what? I need to meet up with him, keep the flame burning.'

'Something personal,' she taps her chin with her index finger, 'like your new pair of knickers.' She grins.

'You're a naughty girl, Amy.' I prod her arm playfully. 'I'd love to see what she'd make of that.' We roll towards each other, laughing.

'It'll really unnerve her,' she says in a low whispery voice, 'she'll question him but end up questioning herself when she realizes she can't believe a word he says. The evidence will be screaming the truth right there in front of her.'

'Will it be enough to make her leave him, though?'

She tips her head from side to side. 'Alternatively, I have another plan.' She pauses, her eyes alight, fingers steepled.

'Go on.'

'When you do see him again, how about I film it, or take photos? Then we can post them online.'

'Great idea. We could clone his Facebook page, if he's still not blocked you?'

Amy clicks on her phone and opens the app. 'I'm still in.'

'Good. So if he doesn't come back to me, we can invite all his friends to his new page to see what he's been up to.'

'I'll make a start on it tonight.' She checks her watch. 'I'd better get going.'

'Hang on a sec, what's this other idea you were going to tell me?'

Amy leans close to my ear. 'Why don't you tell Cole that *you're* pregnant too,' she whispers.

Chapter Forty-Two

Monday 13 August 2018
Gemma

'There's an update on the man outside the supermarket,' Greg says, looking up from his phone. 'He's come forward after seeing the CCTV still of himself on the news. He says he was waiting outside the store for his wife who went in to buy a newspaper and two bottles of cold water but got stuck in a queue.'

'So he has nothing to do with Rosie?' I ask.

'It seems not. His wife confirmed his story as did her receipt. The time matches up. When they checked the CCTV again, she can be seen walking behind him and stopping to look at a flower stall, that's why we'd not put them together.'

I sigh. 'So what does this mean now?'

'We're back to Thomas with Rosie and her accomplice. At least we can assume they are looking after him well, considering all the supplies they bought.'

'That doesn't mean they're going to bring him back, though, does it?'

'I'm afraid not. When did you say Nick was coming back?'

'He didn't tell me, why?'

'It looks like his Facebook page has been cloned.'

'When I last tried to call him his phone was switched off.'

'We need him back here as soon as possible so we can ask him if he knows anything about who might have done it.'

My phone beeps. It's Twitter alerting me I've been tagged in over fifty posts. I swipe through them, all have the hashtag #MissingBaby. I shouldn't read them, but I can't stop myself.

I don't believe a word they say. That poor baby!

Bet you anything they're the guilty ones. The father's right shifty.

Rosie can't be found because she doesn't exist – I reckon they made it all up to save themselves.

It's a cover up. They killed their own baby. Evil bastards!

Did you see the guilt all over their faces?!! Some people don't deserve to have kids.

What kind of mother kills her own flesh and blood? She should be locked up for life.

She's one of those selfish mothers who put their career first. They should be hanged for this.

'What on earth is going on?' I show my phone to Greg and Becca. Greg takes it from me I'm shaking so much.

Their shocked faces say it all.

I retch and run to the toilet.

I didn't think it was possible for this nightmare to get any worse.

But it just did.

Chapter Forty-Three

The next day I put my bikini on after breakfast and take a towel into the garden. My shift doesn't start until 2 p.m. so I can make the most of the morning. Amy hates 'getting her body out' as she calls it. She wears a long flowing cotton top, jeans and canvas slip-ons. She won't even wear flip-flops because she hates her feet. She must be roasting. Anyway, there's no point because she doesn't tan at all. Her skin is so pale it's see-through and turns pink if left in the sun for more than ten minutes.

Amy sits next to me on the grass without a towel. She doesn't mind the thought of ants or spiders running over her skin. Cockroaches are the main bug she has an issue with, especially because they were in her old flat. She says I'm welcome to be scared of everything else.

Pollen fills the air and the tiny spores float by on the breeze. My nose tingles. A motorbike buzzes somewhere in the distance. I swing my legs off the sun lounger.

'What do you think of my idea then?'

'I don't know, Amy. Do you really think he'll believe I'm having his baby?'

'Why not? It'll give him a good reason to leave the mouse.'

'I'll think about it. Fancy an ice cream?'

'Yes, please.'

Mum is home at lunchtime. She changes into her swimsuit and sun hat and joins us in the garden holding a large G&T.

Amy and I check the mouse's Insta page. There's a new arty one of a cappuccino with a stencil of a heart marked out with cinnamon on the froth, laid out on one of their rustic wooden tables with an open book. There's a selfie of her taken from the side, hand across her bump, except I'm not looking at the baby to be, my eyes are firmly on the rock on her finger. She never wears rings at work. The solitaire must be two carats at least. I zoom in. Even her wedding ring has diamonds in it. I would kill for an engagement ring like that. He must really love her to splash out that much. My stomach folds in on itself with jealousy. I leave a few choice words.

I stand up and Amy follows me indoors. I stop in the hall and keep my voice low. 'I'm going to see if he'll meet me. I've decided to tell him this bit of good news.' I touch my flat stomach.

We grin at each other and fist-pump.

I Snapchat Cole asking when we can meet because I have something important to tell him. I'm surprised when he texts back straight away.

> What is it? Are you OK?

> Not really. I can't tell you on here.

> Oh babe, don't do anything stupid.

> Can you meet me?

> I can come to the park – 9 p.m.?

I'll be waiting.

I hold the screen up to Amy before the message disappears and we high five each other. When Cole told me he loved me, that we could be together because he was divorcing his wife, he made a promise he can't break as far as I'm concerned. He's not been with her for the whole pregnancy according to him, so why get back with her now? I need to see him again, find out what's really going on and tell him I'm pregnant with his baby too, so what's he going to do about that? He needs to make up his mind.

Chapter Forty-Four

30 July 2018
Scarlett

It's a beautiful balmy evening with people chatting and drinking outside the pub on the embankment. Darkness is beginning to fall and the lights along the river are twinkling as couples stroll up and down, arm in arm. I hurry along to the park further down from there and wait on a bench tucked away from the main walkthrough. Amy is already there, hiding behind a bush near the litter bin. We decided it was safer if I arrive by myself in case Cole is checking out if I'm alone or not as we agreed. She left a good twenty minutes before I did, so as not to bump into him. We decided it would give her time to get into a comfortable position. All I have to do is try and keep him here so that she can record our conversation and try and take photos too.

He arrives dead on time. I throw my arms around him and he hugs me back, rubbing his hands up and down my body. Just the smell of him sends me into dizzy excitement and I have to remind myself what I'm here for. I kiss his lips but he pulls away, lets go of me.

'What is it you want to tell me?' he asks in such a formal way, it startles me. 'You sure it's not you sending me these bloody emails?'

'No, of course not.'

'See.' He shows me the message.

*Think you're so clever, don't you? But you haven't got
a clue what's coming to you.*

Experience points collected: 8,237

Countdown: Three lives remaining.

'What does it mean? Who's doing this?' He stuffs his phone in his pocket.

'I don't know.' I touch his arm. I can't help it, I will him to hold me again. 'When are you going to leave her?'

'I'm not, babe, I'm sorry, you know I can't… not now.' He cups my face and I lose myself in his serious eyes.

'Just because she's having a child?' I try not to sound whiny, but I can't help it.

'I'm going to be a dad any day now.' He blinks and his eyes redden. I am not the person he should be gushing to.

'You said you two were over, have you forgotten?' I fold my arms.

'I thought I made it clear.' He strokes my chin. 'In another life things could have been so different.' I push his hand away.

'You promised me.' The burn in my cheeks has gone up a notch. 'We were happy together. Why did you take her back?'

'Because I need to give being a dad my best shot. You must understand that? For the sake of my baby. He or she needs both parents.' He ends with a one-note laugh, like I've missed a private joke.

I don't comment and my silence unnerves him. He looks around, probably checking who might have noticed us. If I never speak again will he continue speaking for me? Deciding what I should and shouldn't do because it suits him?

'We had some fun together, though, didn't we?' He strokes my face with the back of his hand. 'You'll find someone new, I know you will. A beautiful, talented girl like you.'

'Someone my own age, you mean?'

'Yeah, why not? If that's what you want.' He digs his hand in his pocket, looks around as though he's worried someone will see us. Has he suddenly remembered that he's at least seventeen years older than me? A rustling comes from the bushes by the fence. I resist looking in Amy's direction and hope he doesn't think anything of it.

'You've not told anyone about us, have you?' He takes out a cigarette and lights it, blows the first drag of smoke at the ground. A man in luminous green shorts and T-shirt jogs towards us, rubbernecking as he goes past. Cole tuts loudly.

'Don't you love me any more?' Hot tears push at my eyes.

He takes my hand and his gaze slides over me as he constructs a suitable answer.

'Love between a man and his wife is… different to any other… it's deeper, enduring, more forgiving. Yes, I love you, of course I do, but we can stay friends, can't we?'

'Friends?' I push him in the chest. 'After everything we… we did together?'

He steps back, his eyes roving from side to side as though he fears someone is going to jump him any second.

'Maybe that was not the right word. Utterly wrong, in fact. The thing is, I care about you – you know in your heart I do, otherwise I wouldn't be here with you now, would I?'

'But you don't love me enough. You don't want me any more.'

'I have to try and do right by my wife and our unborn baby.' His voice is pleading but with the hint of a sharper edge. He's losing his patience. It's almost time for me to drop the bomb on him.

'You have to understand, I don't want to be like my dad.' He swallows and stares at the ground before he continues. 'He left when I was seven because my mum had an affair. He tried to win custody of me, but the law is so bent in the mother's favour, even though she's a heartless tart, he had no chance. I never saw him again and I've never forgiven her.'

'I'm really sorry that happened to you.'

'That's why I tried to encourage you to find your dad if he's still alive, no matter what story your mother spins. Whatever happened between them, he has the right to be in your life and you have the right to know him, have a relationship with him. It's not up to her.' He offers his hand to me, but I bat it away. 'He could be out there looking for you right now.' I don't want to talk about my dad.

'You said you wanted to marry me, and I believed you.' My voice is louder. I hope Amy captures it all. 'I *gave* myself to you believing this was the real thing.'

'I'm sorry, I shouldn't have let you think that. I genuinely thought at one point that my wife and I were over for good. You know we were separated when you and I got together, right? But when she told me she was pregnant and wanted to come back, I had to think again, give her one more chance.'

'You never said why she left you.' I search his eyes, but he looks away.

'We just weren't getting on. The pressure of both working long hours was too much. It happens to lots of couples.'

'But you don't have to stay with her. You'll still be able to see your child.'

'There's no alternative. I'm not going to take that risk. I cannot deal with only seeing my child every other weekend, if I'm lucky. And what if she met someone new? He'd see more of my kid than I would. I can't let that happen.' He shakes his head.

'How do you know it's definitely yours?'

'What?' His whole demeanour changes in a split second. His body straightens and he moves away from me. I may as well be holding a knife to him.

'You know for sure, do you, if she really was away all that time?' I cross my arms. 'Know where she went, do you?'

'That's not a very nice insinuation, Scarlett. My wife would never ever be unfaithful to me.'

Yet he betrayed her in a heartbeat. Does that mean he thinks of me in the same way he does his mother, a cheap tart?

'When you've calmed down, I think you'll understand why I can't abandon them. How cruel that would be.' He's gone into his teacher voice again. I've really pissed him off this time.

'When I've calmed down?' I shake my head. 'So, where does that leave me?'

'What do you mean?' He wipes sweat off his brow with the back of his hand.

'You can't walk away from me, not now.'

'Why not?'

He genuinely thinks this is it, all over, he can tidy me away and get back to his real life, like we never happened. I tut and turn my face up to gaze at him. He's not so gorgeous when he's being an arse. I make him wait and wonder for a few uncomfortable seconds. Then I hit him with it.

'Because I'm having your baby too.'

Chapter Forty-Five

30 July 2018
Scarlett

His face seems to move in slow motion – his eyes widen, mouth drops, his mind probably a muddle as to what to say to me. His eyelashes flutter and for a second I think he's going to pass out.

'You can't be?' he says at last, dragging his hand down his face, distorting his features.

'Well, I am.' How I'm enjoying this moment of victory.

'You told me you were on the pill,' he whispers.

'Is that what I should tell my mum you said?'

'Have you told her?'

The look on his face – as if I'm squeezing his balls with pliers.

'Not yet, but I'll have to at some point, won't I?'

'Are you absolutely a hundred per cent sure it's mine, I mean, if there's even remotely the chance it could be someone else's…'

I almost choke on my own tongue. 'You think I'm a slut, don't you? There's been no one except you.' So that's it, he thinks the mouse is purer than pure, because she'd never be unfaithful to him.

'Okay, I'm sorry, I had to ask.' He blinks at me, his eyes screwed up small like he's not sure who I am any more. 'How… how far gone?'

'About ten weeks.'

He presses his fingers to his eyes and a few moments later they open again. 'You'll have a termination, though, won't you?'

'Hang on, what about what I want?' I hold my hand up. He doesn't want me to mess up his little family.

'What about your future? I thought you were saving up to do a journalism course?'

'This is a human being we're talking about here.' I point to my stomach. Even I'm convinced I'm pregnant now. I flick my hair over my shoulder. He should be saying he's over the moon and that of course he'll leave the mouse and be with me. But he shakes his head, stares at his trainers. 'I'll give you money. Whatever it takes. You're such a talented girl, I don't want you to ruin your life.'

Jesus, he's really trying to wriggle out of it. 'I'm just a girl now, am I? Is that how you see me? Why would having our baby be ruining my life? You're only thinking about yourself. What if I want this baby?'

'No, of course you're not a girl. You're a sexy young woman. But please don't do this.' He walks round in a circle, hand to his head. 'You can't have this baby. You just can't.'

'Then leave her and we can be together.'

'How can I when she's about to give birth? Look, give me a few weeks. Once the baby's born I'll be able to think more clearly. I'll be ready to make a decision, I promise.' He covers his forehead with his palm.

'Do you really mean it?'

'Yes, of course I do. But I can't promise anything, okay?'

'Okay.' He thinks I'm stupid.

'You know you're my special girl, don't you?' He takes my hand and rubs my skin with his thumb like that first time he touched me in his classroom.

'In the meantime, what am I supposed to do?'

'Look after yourself. Do you feel well? Are you being sick?'

'Not yet.'

'Please don't tell your mum. I mean, there's no need yet, is there? We can work this out between us.'

'All right. But you better answer my messages straight away. Don't ignore me or I'll come and knock on your front door and tell her everything.'

He nods, looks me straight in the eye and pins a smile on his face but it's just hanging there. He's probably wondering how he can get rid of me. I grin back, imagining Amy as the Cheshire Cat, listening to us, recording every damning word.

He might think he's got the upper hand, but he'll never get rid of me that easily.

Chapter Forty-Six

Monday 13 August 2018

Gemma

Becca taps on the bathroom door. I struggle to push myself up, but I manage to stretch up to the bolt to unlock it.

'Oh, Gemma.' Becca kneels beside me next to the toilet. 'It's awful what those people are saying about you, but you mustn't take any notice, honestly, they're vicious trolls who don't know you.'

I lean against her shoulder and she gently rubs my arm. There are no words to describe how sick it makes me feel that people out there think I harmed my baby.

'Nick should be here. Where the hell is he? He's leaving me to deal with all of this on my own.' The anger balloons in my chest and a new determination to fight for Thomas rises inside me.

'Do you want me to try and call him?'

'Could you? Please.'

She helps me up and back to the living room where Greg is on the phone.

'I'll make tea and call him, okay?' Becca collects up the empties onto a tray and takes them into the kitchen. I rest my head back on the sofa.

'How are you feeling?' Greg asks, putting the phone on the table.

I shake my head. If I speak, I'll start crying again.

'The police are doing what they can to shut down the trolls. There's always a minority ready to feast on someone else's misery. Makes you wonder about the future of the human race, doesn't it?'

I nod and take a tissue from the box on the coffee table.

He takes another call. I shut my eyes and wish I could drift off to sleep but my mind keeps dragging me back to the call with Dad. How long is Mum going to ignore me for? Ever since I got together with Nick, I seem to be apologizing to them about something.

I'd left the wedding chapel with Nick in the limo and it had taken us to a quaint little restaurant on The Strip. We sat outside under the stars and ate seafood and steak and drank more champagne, except I couldn't eat very much because I was still going over and over in my mind how to tell my parents I'd just got hitched.

'Could I have my phone now?' I'd asked when dessert arrived. I'd wanted to call them as soon as we left the chapel, but I thought Nick would say it was rude to ask when we'd barely been married two minutes, so I tried to leave as polite an amount of time as possible.

'Do you have to, now?' He reached for my hand across the table and gazed at me with his mesmerizing eyes. They were hard to say no to. Sea-green like a jewel with a dark edge. I'd never seen eyes like his before. I'd searched the internet to see if there was a name for them. Limbal rings – *a dark border separating the iris from the whites of the eyes, they highlight the iris colour and make the whites look whiter.*

'Do you really want to let them ruin your special day?' he'd said.

I sipped my drink. The last thing I wanted to do was upset him. I hated him losing his temper, although it had only happened once in the three months we'd been together.

'You know the call will end in an argument.'

178

He'd made today so special and if Mum and Dad didn't like him, didn't accept our marriage, then I'd have to learn to live with that.

'Tell me I'm wrong?' He laid my phone on the table and gently pushed it towards me. 'I'm not stopping you, all I'm saying is do you want their disapproval to be your abiding memory?'

'You're right, it can wait.' I'd shaken my head of curls and tightened my lips. I pushed the phone back to him. It would spoil the whole day. Anyway, I'd had quite a lot to drink.

A tiny voice had piped up in my head saying that not telling them was tantamount to lying. But I'd brushed it aside, far away, out of my mind.

And look where lying to my parents has got me. That decision marked the end of my relationship with them. Now I'm utterly alone. I should have listened when they said he was too old for me, that we hadn't been together long enough to really know each other. I thought Mum was being nasty when she told me I sounded like a parrot, repeating everything Nick said, not having my own opinions like I used to. And Nick certainly made sure he isolated me from all the people who really care about me. Becca's the only one I see and that's because he keeps a close eye on us.

'I'm sorry, I can't get through,' Becca says, bringing in a trayful of fresh drinks.

I open my eyes.

'Oh sorry, were you having nap?'

'No, it's okay.' I rub my eyes.

'Maybe Nick's on his way back already?' Becca passes me a mug of tea.

'More bad news, I'm afraid.' Greg strides in switching his phone off. 'A rogue group have started combing the Dunstable Downs. The police are on their way to break it up.'

'You mean the Twitter trolls?' I can't believe it.

'It seems to have stemmed from them, yes.'

'What are they looking for?' Becca says, then immediately looks at me, mouth open aghast. 'I'm so, so sorry. I was being stupid.' She looks mortified.

A car horn makes us all jump and look towards the curtained window. A door slams hard. Someone is shouting and swearing. There's only one person who speaks like that, but he normally saves it for me. Voices are escalating. Greg pulls a curtain aside.

'Nick's back.'

Chapter Forty-Seven

30 July 2018
Scarlett

As soon as he's gone, Amy comes out from the bushes.

'He went for it then by the sound of it,' she laughs, her hair peppered with tiny flowers.

'Yep, completely.'

'Didn't ask for any proof, like a positive test. But he might.'

'Why would I be lying?' I grin.

'You can buy them online, so we'll need to order one.'

'Can you really?'

'You can get anything. Even fat suits to make you look pregnant.'

'That's crazy but if I have to do it, I will. As soon as he's left the mouse and has come back to me, I'll tragically miscarry. Tell him I'm not ready to try for another one. For a few years at least. I don't want to be saddled with a kid at my age.'

'Well, I've got everything recorded and I took a few snaps, but it was quite hard with all the leaves in the way. It was a nightmare trying not to make a sound.'

I laugh as I brush leaves and flowers from her hair. We stroll arm in arm over to the ice-cream hut and buy a lolly each, then sit under a tree and listen back to the whole conversation.

'That's brilliant, well done.' I hug her. I could not do any of this without her. 'Email it to me, then we've got a back-up copy. We need to keep all this evidence against him in one place in case it all goes pear-shaped.'

'I think you could ask him to do almost anything now. He'll be so scared of you turning up at his front door and speaking to his wife.' Amy's tongue is blue from licking her bubble-gum lolly.

'Please don't call her that.' I wrinkle my nose.

'Sorry, the mouse.'

'Hello, girls, what are you up to on this beautiful day?' Mrs Taylor, our old headmistress is standing at our feet wearing a long flowery dress and matching sun hat. Her ankles are as thick as her legs and she always wears tights no matter how hot it is.

'Oh you know, plotting murder and mayhem.' I turn over the piece of paper with Cole's name on it without looking down.

'Well, you know you were one of our star pupils, Scarlett, so I hope you're putting your time to good use. You can learn a lot from her, young Amy.'

'What are you doing this holiday, Mrs Taylor?' I ask.

'We came back from the South of France on Friday, now I'm back to working out details for next term. No rest for the wicked, eh?'

'No there isn't.' I side-eye Amy.

'Anyway, I'll say toodle-oo. Enjoy the rest of your summer, girls.'

We wave goodbye and as soon as she is out of sight our smiles drop away.

'Do you think she saw this?' I pick up the piece of paper with our plan on and Cole's name circled in the middle.

'I doubt it, honestly she must be so old I don't think her eyesight is that good.'

'As long as she didn't see Cole leaving. We need to be more careful.'

I gather up our papers and stuff them in my shoulder bag. We walk along the river, then over the bridge and back to my car parked at the Harpur Centre. Amy takes out the packet of Malted Milks she left in the glove compartment. She offers them to me. I take two, then she stuffs one in her mouth.

'Mmm.' I take a bite and nod. 'I'd forgotten how much I love these.' A moment later I'm in Dad's arms sitting in front of the telly with a glass of warm milk and one of these biscuits. Some old black-and-white film is on with grown-ups kissing and one of them has to go away. Dad is crying and I'm scared. I cuddle up closer to him, my head pressing against his chest. He says my name in minty breath mixed with tobacco.

But was it my dad or was it a boyfriend of Mum's?

Amy touches my arm and I'm suddenly back in the enclosed space of the car. 'Are you okay, you've gone really quiet?'

I start the engine. I must have only been about four when that happened. I don't remember him after that. If it even was him. I wish Mum would tell me why he went away.

'I'm okay, I just had a really vivid memory of my dad. At least I think it was him. Now I know why Mum doesn't buy these biscuits any more.'

'At least you believe you remember him. I can't recall a single thing about mine.'

'I know, I'm sorry.' I drop my token in the machine and the barrier goes up.

'Mum says it's the less painful option.'

'She's probably right, except I don't know why my dad's not in my life. Did he do something wrong or did Mum just fall out with him? Maybe she knocked him back so many times he didn't bother sticking around? He could be dead now for all I know.'

She pops out another biscuit and hands it to me. 'Your mum's really nice so I think he must have done something quite bad.'

'I don't know. Lately I've been wondering, what if he took his own life? That could be why she won't tell me because it's too painful for her.' I bite into the biscuit and queue behind two cars at the exit. 'Or maybe it's really straightforward and she just doesn't want him in our lives because it's easier for her. He probably wasn't paying maintenance and she didn't love him any more so why have him hanging around, turning up when he felt like it when he wasn't contributing? I know Mum wouldn't have put up with that.'

'Whatever the reason, even if it's hard for her, you should know.'

'She gets so upset or shuts down completely. I gave up asking years ago. But now it feels like there's this wedge between us – this thing I mustn't mention – a big secret I'm not allowed to know even though I'm grown up now. He could have been kidnapped when I was a baby and he's still not been found. What if no one knows where he is?'

'You really need to ask her again.' Amy bites a corner of biscuit and pulls a sad face.

'Cole blames his mum for his dad leaving when he was young. I think he's scared of the mouse not letting him see his baby if he breaks up with her. I would feel terrible if his kid grew up not having him there. I'd never stop him seeing his child.'

'Who knows what she would do. Whatever happens, don't feel bad because it's between them. They're the ones that need to do the right thing and let each other see the baby.'

'I suppose so.' I turn right at the lights opposite Wilko on the high street and head home. 'I'm going to ask Mum once more about my dad. Cole's always saying fathers should be able to see their children as much as mothers do, but kids have just as much right to see their dads. There's always been an empty space in my life no one else but my dad can fill. And now I'm almost an adult, I want to solve this final piece of the puzzle, so this time I'm not taking no for an answer.'

Chapter Forty-Eight

Monday 13 August 2018

Gemma

Nick barges in and flops down on the sofa, face ashen.

'Bloody mad lot out there. I thought they weren't going to let me in.' He runs one hand after the other through his hair, staring into space.

'Are you okay?' Greg asks.

'No luck, obviously.' He shows his palms, empty, where a baby should be. A pinch of sympathy trickles through me. I see now that he expected to be the hero, defeat the baddies and bring our son home safely, but he's failed. He doesn't like to fail.

'I take it there's no good news here?' Nick glances at me for the first time and I shake my head.

'Nothing concrete.' Greg fills him in on developments, none of which seem to be bringing us any closer to finding Thomas.

'It looks like your Facebook page has been cloned, Nick. I need to ask you something about it.' Greg taps the app on his phone and shows him. 'Do you know who might have done this?'

'No idea.'

'Someone you know, someone targeting you through work or completely random?'

'Where did they get all these photos of me?' He holds up a page to show me pictures of himself as a child, before he got his ears pinned. He scrolls through them. 'Have you got something to do with this?' His eyes narrow at me.

'No, of course not.' I frown at him and Greg, who looks puzzled.

'You're the only person who knows about these photos.' The muscle is pulsing in his cheek.

'Are you sure about that?' Greg asks. 'What about your parents, siblings or former school friends – wouldn't they have seen these too and possibly have their own photos of you from back then?'

'I suppose.' He carries on swiping through them without looking up.

'Perhaps you could make a list of those people for me. Are any of them likely to have a grudge against you.'

'All of them, probably.' He slaps the phone into Greg's hand.

'We need to assume this is linked to Thomas's abduction.'

'Why?' Nick pulls a face of disgust.

'Because a message has been posted up today, purporting to be from you.'

'Saying what?'

Greg swipes to the post and reads it out. '*Our baby is missing and it's my fault – do you think Gemma will ever forgive me?!*'

'What the fuck?' Nick grabs the phone from him. Greg glances at me. Maybe I should look surprised.

'Who would have written something like that?' I sit upright, frowning again.

'What do you think it means?' Greg asks Nick. 'Have you any idea why Thomas's abduction could be perceived as being your fault?'

'No, of course not. It must be from some nutter.'

'Could it be the same one?' I say to him.

'Same one as…?' Greg asks.

'As the emails I've been getting. Nasty emails.'

'And you haven't told us this because…?'

'I didn't think they were relevant. I assumed they were spam or some weirdo trying to attack council staff.'

'Has anyone else at work received similar emails?'

'Not recently that I'm aware of, but it's not unusual for staff to be targeted by the public because we've turned down their planning application for an extension or telling a landlord that we're sending an inspector to check an environmental hazard such as mould and damp that's been reported by one of their tenants.'

'Can you show me the emails?'

Nick takes his phone out and flicks through his mailbox. He shows Greg a couple of them.

'Can you forward them to me, please? We'll try and track them down. Have you had any, Gemma?'

'No, but I was getting horrible comments on Instagram. Actually, they seem to have stopped.'

'Have you mentioned them to us before? I don't think I was aware.'

'I'm sure I did. But it's hardly unusual being trolled on social media, is it?'

'No, but it could still be relevant.' Greg stands and holds both hands up. 'Okay, I want you both to think hard again about anyone who could wish harm on you or your family. If you have any enemies you think could have taken Thomas.'

Nick and I nod, like we've just been told off.

'And explain to me, Nick, because this could be relevant too – why do you go by the name Truman Fitzgerald on social media, why not your real name?'

Nick side-eyes me and for a second I think he's going to lie.

'Because I used to be a school teacher.'

Chapter Forty-Nine

31 July 2018
Scarlett

Mum makes us tuna pasta for lunch the following day. We carry the plates and bowls of food outside and sit round the table under the parasol. The low drone of a neighbour mowing his lawn is accompanied by the tinkle of next door's metal wind chimes hanging from her cherry tree.

'So what happened with Rob, I thought you liked him?' I ask, scraping my plate clean with a piece of garlic bread.

'I did but I think he was looking for a wife.'

'Isn't that what you want one day?'

'What for?' she snaps.

'I don't mean get married necessarily, just find a guy you really like, that you want to stay with.'

'I'm happy as I am, thanks. I don't need a man around telling me what to do.' She eyeballs me in case I want to dispute it.

'Were you ever happy with Dad?'

Her smile drops. She stands up and turns away from me.

'You had me, after all, so you must have liked him once.'

'I've told you I don't want to talk about him.' Her breathing quickens.

I wince and take a moment. 'Mum, I know you don't like me asking, but I do have a right to know who he is. Can you tell me his name at least?'

She glares at me. 'There's a damn good reason I haven't told you, so don't push me.'

I'm startled by her abruptness, but I try not to let it faze me. 'Which is what? Come on, tell me.'

'Drop it,' Mum shouts.

'I'm old enough to know the truth.' I stand up. She is shaking, but I won't leave it. Not again.

'Don't you understand, I'm trying to protect you? I've spent your whole life trying to keep you safe, I'm not about to let it all go.' She pushes her chair in, scraping the legs in an ear-splitting screech across the flagstones.

'And I'm really grateful, but I can look after myself now. I feel ready to find out where I come from, who I am.'

'You might think you are but believe me you're better off never knowing.'

She grabs her plate, the salad unfinished. 'I can't do this.' She heads inside. Moments later the front door slams shut.

Amy and I stare at each other.

'I think he must have had an affair. That's the sort of thing that's made my mum that mad.'

'I just want her to tell me!' I kick the table leg and everything wobbles.

'Carry on looking for him yourself, you don't have to tell her.'

'You're right, I don't.'

–

After we've tidied up, we go up to my bedroom. We've both got late shifts today, so another two hours to spare.

'Will you show me how to straighten my hair like yours?' Amy asks.

'Yeah, sure.' I suddenly feel like a diva. It's too hot upstairs so we take the straightening irons into the kitchen and open the back door wide. I place a chair in the middle of the room and give Amy a mirror to hold in front of herself.

'What can I do for you today, madam?' I say in an exaggerated polite accent, like Mum does in her salon.

'Oh, the usual please, nice and straight, no kinks.'

'Right you are, madam. Rest assured we don't do kinky here.' Amy laughs. I comb her hair through and separate a section with clips. 'Going anywhere nice on your holidays?'

'Oh yes, back to America for a grand tour. I really can't wait. I do love the yanks. What about you?'

'Probably Skeggy again. George does love a caravan holiday.'

Amy bursts out laughing and can't stop. I hold the straight-eners away so as not to burn her or myself.

I finish straightening her hair when we've both calmed down.

'Mum won't be back from work for ages yet. We could have another look in that box. Will you help me?' I show her the back of her hair in a mirror.

'That's lovely, thank you. Of course I'll help.'

'There might be a photo of him in that bundle.' I drain the last of my beer. Amy carries the steps upstairs behind me.

We have the box down in a few minutes. Amy keeps watch out of the window. I lift out the bundle of photos and start going through them. They're mostly of me, from when I was a baby through my toddler years up until about age seven. I've seen most of them before.

Then right at the bottom is one of them on their wedding day, cutting a three-tiered cake. And there's Dad, standing behind Mum, arms threaded around her waist. I peer as close as I can at him. His head is tipped back, mouth open, laughing. Big white teeth. Full lips. What is he laughing at? Has the photographer made a joke? Mum is smiling, head down, concentrating on cutting the cake. Her curls and veil have fallen forward. She looks so different, so young. Dad's fingers are firmly slotted over hers, hands entwined around the knife. They've made the first cut, deep into the cake. I examine their hands more closely. His fingers are long and slim, he's wearing a broad gold band. Hers are more delicate, the ring narrower but with the same rounded style. I crave more of his face, his features but that's it, except his long legs in straight black trousers and the tip of his shoe, shone to a high polish. I stare at his face, obscured as it is, until my eyes blur. *What's your name? Where are you? What happened between you and Mum?*

And then I see something odd.

'Look at this.'

'What is it?' Amy sits next to me on the bed. 'What am I looking at?'

'Mum's arm.' I shiver. 'What's that mark?'

Amy takes her glasses off and peers closer. 'I think it's a scar.'

'I don't remember noticing one on her.'

'I've not seen one either but they fade a lot, don't they?'

'Hang on,' she runs her finger over it, 'I think it's a scratch on the photo.'

I touch the surface. 'It could be.'

There's nothing else in the box that remotely indicates what my dad's name is. There's no wedding certificate, no wedding cards, letters or gift tags. Nothing with their names on. Has she really chucked everything else away to do with him?

'Let's try and get that other box down. I bet there's something important in it.' I have a quick look out of the window. It's quiet and still except for Pixi slinking across the road.

'I'll get it.' Amy climbs up the steps. I hand her the backscratcher and she eases the box towards her until it's at eye level. 'It's got a lock on it,' she says.

'Shit.'

'Do you want me to break into it?'

'Better not. I might ask Mum what's in it.' I hand it back up to Amy and she slides it into place next to the other one. 'I need to get ready for work.'

'Maybe you could order a copy of the marriage certificate online.'

'Without knowing both their names?'

'I don't know about that. You'd have to look into it.'

I'm burning to find out what Mum feels she needs to protect me from. Is it wrong to want to know if I'm like my dad? Why doesn't she want him to be a part of my life?

Chapter Fifty

31 July 2018

Scarlett

When I arrive at the restaurant, the mouse is already there at the front, showing a large group to their booth. I quietly go round the back and change into my uniform. The other waitress, Bonnie, is taking food orders. Her shift ends in fifteen minutes. She raises her pencil at me and smiles. I get on with clearing tables on the terrace.

The trellis is lit up with pink and yellow fairy lights and tealights at each table. It's another balmy night and there's a good vibe, an excited hum of conversations and laughter, the clink of glasses and cutlery on plates. 'Inner Smile' by Texas is playing softly in the background. I spray and wipe tables singing along, imagining Cole holding my hips from behind, the two of us swaying together as one.

There are lots of balloons set up on reserved tables which means we'll be helping people to celebrate birthdays and anniversaries in our usual way, encouraging all the customers to join in the singing. A lot of young families come here for that extra special service. Gemma spots me and smiles warmly. She runs a good business, I'll give her that.

I tidy the cleaning stuff away and grab a pencil. Another group arrives and she shows them to their table. I wince at the way she is walking, her bump sticking so far out her back seems to be caving in.

'You're early, Rosie,' she says, coming over, 'you must have a sixth sense. We're one man down again tonight and we're going to be packed out by seven. Bonnie is staying on an extra hour but that's all she can do. Could you blow up some more balloons after you've taken some food orders, please?'

'Sure. Are you okay? You look a bit… uncomfortable.'

'My back is killing, but the show must go on, hey?' She pats my arm as she goes over to greet another large party arriving.

The evening goes surprisingly well despite it being so busy. I've done everything I can to go above and beyond, helping the mouse out and making sure she notices too. I need to gain her trust so she knows she can rely on me. I'm about to make cappuccinos and lattes for the last few tables when I hear his voice. I daren't turn round in case he sees my face, but I can see them together reflected in the mirror above the bar. Gemma is talking to him just inside the door, then she tries to kiss his cheek, but he moves away. I could cheer. I sidestep to the end of the counter then dart forward into the cloakroom area tucked in the alcove. I peer out but Cole is still standing there. What the hell? Tables four and eight are waiting for their coffees, but I cannot possibly come out. Gemma seems to be looking around for me, so I dive into the ladies and lock the door. I'll have to tell her I was desperate for the loo, time of the month or something, because she'll wonder why I'm taking so long. I could blow all my hard work if she thinks I'm slacking off. How will I know when it's safe to come out? How long is he going to be here? I cannot let him see me. She knows me as Rosie, but he will expose me as Scarlett. His pregnant ex-girlfriend.

I wait a bit longer before flushing the toilet. I poke my head around the door. He's still there, his back to me now because he's leaving. Thank God.

'There you are, Rosie. I was looking for you.' Gemma is by my side a few moments later looking puzzled.

'Sorry, I had to dash to the loo. I'm just making coffees for four and eight.'

'Good, because they're looking a bit impatient. I was going to introduce you to my husband, Nick. Shame he missed meeting you.'

'Oh, is that his name?'

'He hates his name, Nicholas, says it makes him sound like a Russian tsar. Most of his friends call him Cole.' Her nose wrinkles in disapproval. 'Anyway, he's taking me away for a long weekend. Our last one before the baby arrives.'

'That's nice. Somewhere special?' I bite my lip. I don't want to know but I must sound polite and interested and not scowl.

'He won't tell me where, says it's a surprise, although I've got a feeling it's where we went when he first took me on a proper date.'

'Oh, and where's that?' My hand weakens and tips to the side so the milky foam I'm pouring spills over the edge of the cup. What a bloody mess. I start again, pouring semi skimmed milk into the metal jug and switching on the steam nozzle. Gemma doesn't bat an eyelid at my mistake.

'St James's Hotel in Mayfair. He said we're going to see a play first.'

'Sounds like fun,' I say in the best happy voice I can manage. I try not to picture them writhing around in a luxurious king-size bed of black satin sheets. My eye catches her hand touching her enormous bump and reminds me how impossible that would be right now. I smirk to myself: Nick, eh? Never told me wifey calls him that. He'll be craving our time together when he gets back.

'I really am lucky.' She stares into the distance. 'I used to go to the theatre a lot with my parents when I was growing up.' She wipes a tray down and passes it to me. 'Do you spend much time with yours?' She helps me stack the saucers and carefully place the cups of coffee without spilling any of them.

'With Mum, yes, because I'm still at home, but Dad's never been around.' I say it more sharply than I mean to, but it's hard holding in the bitterness sometimes. Saying it aloud makes the shame I've been holding in flood over me.

'I'm sorry to hear that, I hope I haven't triggered a difficult subject for you.'

'It's fine.' I do not want to overshare.

'It must be hard for you and tricky for your mum.'

'I suppose so. But she's told me absolutely zero about him, I'm not even joking.' I forget for a second who I'm talking to. Gemma's too bloody nice for her own good. But I guess that's what people are like who've never had anything bad happen to them. If she wasn't married to the man I love, we could be such good friends.

'Listen, if you ever want to talk about it… I mean, they say it can help confiding in someone who's not directly involved, don't they?'

I nod my thanks and carry the tray of coffees to table four, the image of her sympathetic face stays in my mind. It's the first time I've noticed a hint of sadness in her tone, in her eyes, behind all her fake glamour and her seemingly having it all insta-life. But I can't imagine what could be missing, unless she's aware of her husband cheating.

It's gone midnight by the time the last customers leave. Gemma doesn't like to hurry people and she doesn't seem to mind going home so late. She tells me to go, she'll lock up. As soon as I'm outside I realize I've left my phone. I tap on the door. It takes a good minute before she answers.

'I think I've left my phone in the cloakroom.'

'Come in.' She closes the door behind me, sniffing and dabbing her nose with the back of her hand.

'Are you okay?' I look right at her then. Her eyes are wet.

'Yeah, just the hormones kicking in, I guess.' I follow her to the cloakroom where my apron is hanging on the peg where I left it. I rummage around in the pocket and sure enough, my phone is tucked in there with a pen and orders pad. When I turn to go, Gemma has her back to me taking her work top off over her head, arms up in the air. Her face is covered for a few seconds in the dark material as I reach the door. I wait a moment to say goodbye, staring unashamedly at her protruding bump, the way the skin has stretched. As her head appears through the top, she turns and I catch sight of a blue–black bruise, the size of a child's hand. I shiver.

'How did you do that?' I wince and can't help pointing at it. As soon as I have, I kick myself, she's probably dead embarrassed.

'I walked straight into the corner of our kitchen table at home.' She grabs her floral top and pulls it over her head, her hair lifting and crackling, full of static electricity.

'Looks really painful.' No wonder she's been walking so awkwardly.

'It's very sore, but not as bad as it was.'

'If there's anything I can do that you need help with, just say, okay.' I push my phone into my back pocket, grateful that I'd switched it off. If Cole had texted and she'd seen it, it would have blown everything.

'There is one thing I meant to ask you earlier. Our neighbour can't feed Missy while we're away. She promised she could, but she's been called away to look after her dad. I can't bear to go to London if we don't have someone going in to feed her. Nick says she'll be fine on her own for one night. He doesn't want to lose his deposit, so I was just wondering if perhaps you might be able to?'

She barely takes a breath. I guess that's what she's upset about.

'Especially as you love cats as much as I do and you're always so massively helpful around here. I'd pay you, of course. Do you think there's a chance you could do that for me?'

'Yeah, I can, but you don't need to pay me.' I try and sound as casual as possible, but my brain is already buzzing at the possibilities this will give me. I've never been in his house before. He's been careful to keep me away. This is a perfect opportunity to find out more about their lives and ways I can split them up.

'Really? Are you sure?' She's grinning like I've promised to save the world which seems disproportionately over the top. I'll be feeding her cat, it's not a biggie.

'It's not a problem.'

'Oh my goodness, Rosie, you're literally a lifesaver.' She wipes her eyes. Maybe they had a big argument about it? It's so cruel to suggest leaving the cat on its own to fend for itself. I'm pretty shocked. But he'll be the sorry one now.

'Honestly, I'm happy to help out.'

'I'll give you our address and spare key now, if that's okay? It's just that he's insisting we leave first thing in the morning, so I won't have time to show you around, but I'll leave Missy's tins and bowl out. It'll be really straightforward, I promise. She's got a cat flap so if she doesn't turn up just leave her food down and she'll come and find it. Morning and evening if possible, whatever time is best for you.'

'Okay, what's your address?' I take my notebook and pencil out of my apron and scribble it down. Working here is even more useful than I expected.

Chapter Fifty-One

3 August 2018
Scarlett

On Friday morning we're up early to see them off. We crouch behind a couple of bins on the other side of the road and watch Cole load a suitcase into the boot of their car.

Mouse waddles down the path, one hand cupped under the bump and the other carrying her jacket and handbag. Her hair is tied up in a messy ponytail. She's wearing glittery flip-flops and her ankles are puffy and white, must be this heat. It doesn't look like she's had time to do her usual full spray tan. Probably can't wait to mask that horrendous bruise.

Cole rushes to open the passenger door for her. He takes her hand and helps her step down from the kerb then into the car. I presume she can't see her feet easily. He's being more attentive than I'd expect if he's thinking of leaving her. And why bother taking her to a swanky hotel?

'She looks like she's about to pop,' I whisper.

'He said in one post on Facebook that she's still got a few days to go.'

'Could happen any time, though, couldn't it? Mum says I was early. Took her by surprise.'

'I was too, at twenty-eight weeks. I only weighed a pound.'

Somehow, I'm not surprised, Amy is still scrawny now.

'Do you think they could be on their way to the hospital?'

'She'd have said if she was booked in to have a caesarean.' And she said he didn't want to lose his deposit. Could he really be that selfish?

'What, she's going to tell you?'

'Yeah, I think she would.'

'He's not said anything about it.' Amy taps her phone and starts scrolling through his Facebook page.

'Seems a bit crazy going away for the weekend so close to the birth.'

'No, nothing about it here if they are.'

They drive off and I'm left with a weird feeling that I've missed my chance to get him back by walking across the road and chatting to his wife right in front of him.

'Come on, let's go home. She'll have fed Missy this morning, so we'll come back later.' I touch the heart pendant around my neck. He gave it to me to celebrate our first month together. It's almost seven months ago. The mouse had left him and he was on his own. Maybe he really didn't know she was already pregnant. But I don't understand how he can turn his back on me like this. I won't let him.

It's 9 p.m. when we return to their house to feed their cat. There's no sign of Missy. It is almost dark but the yellow glow of light shines in one of the bedrooms. No movement downstairs. No kitchen or bathroom light. I guess the light must be on a timer, a burglar deterrent.

A couple of kids cycle past in labelled joggers and hoodies pulled over their heads. I grip the key tighter. They get a good look at us and vice versa. All up to no good or pretending not to be.

In the house on the right is a large noisy family. I lose count of how many kids they have. All their lights are on and the TV is blaring a game show so loud no wonder they have to shout at each other. On the left is an old couple, their faces lit up sitting so close to the TV screen in an otherwise dim room.

'Let's go in.' Even though Gemma has given me the key, I feel like an intruder. And I am I suppose. Intruding on her life.

Amy nods.

We eyeball each other but don't say a word. She scans up and down the street as I slot the key in the door. A cat meows somewhere nearby and something clatters to the ground making me jump. I nearly pull the key back out, but as I turn it and push, the door cracks from the heat of the day. We pause, then inch it wider. A second later and we're in. I shut the door quietly behind us.

We're statues frozen in the hallway. Something clicks and spits. I grip Amy's wrist. Is someone there? A strong artificial floral smell fills the air. Amy coughs and splutters. A white tower of plastic from the top of a shelf has squirted fragrance over us. We stretch our ears for any other noises. I close my eyes to concentrate harder, ears cocked and straining for any movement as we creep down the hallway. Nothing, except the ticking kitchen clock, its moon-face glowing in the dark. We know they're not here, but it still feels weird walking into their lives. This seems too easy. I half expect them to jump out, tell me the game is up, they know I'm pretending to be Rosie, befriending Gemma on false pretences.

The cat flap in the back door rattles and we practically jump into each other's arms. A black cat with a grey smudge on its head stalks towards us then stops. This is not their cat. Here we are, face to face with a fellow intruder.

I peer round the living-room door. It's tidy except for an empty mug on the coffee table. If it's warm, someone else has been here, someone to keep an eye on us. I reach out and touch it. Stone cold. Of course it is, I'm being paranoid. Amy stays close behind me, and I picture us looking like Daphne and Velma in an episode of *Scooby-Doo* and I almost give in to a fit of giggles. There are jumbo-sized canvas photos of Cole and Gemma on the main wall in nauseating poses, lounging against each other, cupping each other's faces. And a recent one, more cringeworthy than the rest, the one mouse posted on her Instagram page, showing her bump, her fingers resting on it in a heart shape and Cole on his knees kissing her taut bronzed skin.

The kitchen is immaculate as though it's never used. I open the fridge door. Prosecco, a pack of sliced cheddar and a bar of Dairy Milk. I feel peckish but on second thoughts, I shut the door.

Amy is opening cupboard after cupboard of neatly arranged tins, packets, pots and pans. She's taking pictures of everything. I wonder if I should stop her but she likes uploading random photos to Instagram and Snapchat. I peer out of the back-door window and scan the fence but there's no sign of Missy.

I find a calendar on the back of the larder door. I flick through it for the baby's due date – 8 August – five days' time. I take a picture of August, so I know their movements.

Amy shoos the intruder cat out and we put food down for Missy.

We creep upstairs, and I go on straight up to the room with the light on. As I thought, there's a standard lamp on a timer, next to an inviting easy chair. The walls are lined with books right up to the ceiling, all in colour co-ordinated order. I step back. Although I've seen it on her Instagram, I'm slightly creeped out. Who has time to do that to this many books? I'd love to stay and browse, maybe mess up the colour scheme, but I need to see what Amy is up to.

She's snooping in the wardrobes of their master bedroom. Nick's clothes are mostly the same, grouped together. Countless white T-shirts and black jeans. One dark navy suit, Armani. Three white shirts, Paul Smith. In one draw is a pile of polo neck tops. I've never seen him wear one. All his socks and boxers are designer too. Amy is flicking through the mouse's clothes. No order there. Clothes of different colours are packed in so tight it's hard to pull anything out. I rummage through her underwear drawer, nothing of any interest, no sexy underwear. I take my new pair out of my pocket and drop it in, then mix them all up.

Amy is on the floor, searching under their bed.

'Nothing there, not even a speck of dust,' she says.

I check out their reading material on their bedside tables. His is exceptional, of course: Proust, Marlowe, Atwood. Hers is a good selection of female writers: Maggie O'Farrell, Louise Doughty and Hilary Mantel, although nothing he would read, and it still makes me wonder why they're together.

We go into the third bedroom, which has a guest bed made up. Two large cupboards along one wall are full of vinyl records. It's mostly 80s and 90s albums, R.E.M, Culture Club, INXS, The Pet Shop Boys, stuff I've heard Mum play, but it's all so ancient.

The fourth bedroom is the nursery. All the new furniture has been put in place. The changing table has a mat to match the curtains, and the shelf underneath is already packed with newborn's nappies, Sudocrem and a pile of muslin cloths.

Large blue and green felt letters on bunting have been hung in the window, spelling 'NEW BABY'. Below on the window sill are the wooden blocks spelling 'Thomas' I've seen in her Insta posts. Next to it is a new baby cam monitor still in its box. Amy spots it at the same time as me and our smiles spread across our faces.

She picks the box up and pretends to read the back. 'From your very own smartphone in the comfort of your armchair, watch the darling little sprog sleep, even if he isn't yours.' Her head tips to one side and we both laugh. It's a bit creepy but we only want to keep an eye on them, hear what they say.

'Cole's nought per cent techie so chances are they won't even think to change the default password.'

'Perfect. Them and half the population.'

In the living room, Amy pulls the tab out from under their wireless router and takes a photo of the default password stuck on the piece of plastic. Missy comes in and eats her food. I stroke her and give her some clean water. We make sure we leave everything as it was.

We get back to mine around midnight and go straight up to my room. Mum's got Marvin Gaye on loud in the living room.

It sounds like she's having a bit of a party; I don't really want to know who with, and I don't really care. Mostly, I don't want her asking any questions about where we've been.

After a quick de-brief, Amy gets on with hacking into their router.

'Easy enough to get into, now we just have to wait for them to switch it on.' Amy pushes her glasses up. Her grin is wide like the Cheshire cat.

'Brilliant.' I push the window open wider. The heat of the day has yet to cool completely. Across the village are the skeletons of houses being built on a new part of the estate, their scaffolding bones shine eerily in the moonlight. The sky is red beyond them and the traffic on the M1 drones in the distance, whatever the hour. Amy goes to bed and is asleep in a few minutes.

Part of me is nervous about spying on them in their home. What if they really are planning to stay together? I'm not sure what I'll do if they are. I don't think I can handle being rejected again.

Chapter Fifty-Two

We go back to their house on Saturday evening. This time Missy comes to greet us with little cries. Her bushy tail flicks from side to side when I stroke her back, and she rewards me with a satisfied purr. I'm jumpy about staying too long, even though it's after 10 p.m. when most people are in front of the TV or tucked up in bed. I still wonder if Cole has got one of the neighbours to keep an eye on the place. He likes to be in control, so I don't think he'll be able to rely on Gemma organizing it, whatever he's told her. Perhaps it's the old couple next door. What if they have a key too? I don't want them seeing my face or Cole might recognize their description and how will I explain that?

Sure enough, there's a spoon on the draining board I'm sure wasn't there yesterday. The feeding bowl is near the cat flap still with food in. Maybe I'm imagining things.

'You sit near the top of the stairs in case someone comes. If you hear anything, run up and find me. I'm going to have a look at Cole's paperwork. We might be able to use some private info when we clone his Facebook page.'

'How about a few recent photos and some older ones, like from when he was at school or on holidays? I can copy and paste most of his personal stuff from his current page, where he went to school, jobs etc. But it would be good to add some embarrassing ones he wouldn't want to share.'

'Good idea, but something only those close to him would recognize and know is real.'

'Didn't you say he has a birthmark on the bottom of his foot?'

'Yeah.'

Amy sniggers. 'Any other intimate secrets you want to share about him?'

'Not the kind you're thinking.' I grin and go up, leaving her on the stairs.

I have my little torch with me this time. I don't want to chance putting on the lights. I go back to his reading room and check the drawers in the coffee table. There's nothing in them except pens and bookmarks. I hadn't realized how particular he was about his possessions.

I check their bedroom again. I can't quite believe it, but there's definitely nothing under the bed, even though it's a huge space and a prime storage area in our house. I suppose when your home is as big as this, you don't need it. By rights, I should be the one living here with him enjoying all this space, not her. I open both wardrobes. The bottom of hers is full of boxes of shoes and his contains nothing except a guitar and a football. I try the vinyl room. At last, I find something. The bottom drawer is a filing cabinet. I pull out mortgage papers, a personal loan for the car, bank statements, bills, but nothing personal to him alone.

I'm about to go downstairs when I stop and look back at the nursery.

'I think we should go in a minute,' Amy whispers behind me, 'I heard something outside.'

'Hang on a sec.' I creep into the nursery and pull open the bottom of the new chest of drawers. In there are two old photo albums. Bingo. I open one and flick through the crackling plastic pages. It's full of pictures of Cole as a little boy holding an ice cream, sitting on a steam train, riding a horse on a merry-go-round and building sandcastles on the beach. Same cheeky face but his ears really stick out like Prince Charles'. He must have had them pinned back because they are definitely not like that now. How cruel can I be? How angry am I? It depends whether he comes back to me or not.

There's a date on the back of one but it doesn't add up. I look at the photo of his fifth birthday again, blowing out candles on a batman cake. The date is 9 February 1977. It's definitely him, his name is on the cake – Nicholas. Cole. Nick. How can that date be right? That would make him forty-six. He told me he was thirty-eight. He's been lying. He's really old. More than twice my age. It shouldn't matter. It doesn't change him as a person. Except why did he need to lie to me? Maybe he's really sensitive about his age. I snap away with my phone camera, not really wanting to use these against him, but more as insurance if he pushes me too far.

Amy hisses, 'There's definitely someone outside. I can hear them talking. Can we go out the back?'

'I'm not sure I'll make it over the fence.' I tiptoe to the front window and peek round the edge of the curtain, trying not to disturb it too much. Who's out at this time of night? Two women are standing on the pavement by the bins they've just wheeled out. Shit, is it bin day? At the weekend? Gemma didn't say anything about that. One of them looks up, it feels like she's looking right at me. I move back, knocking over one of the books on the bedside table. It thuds to the floor. I'm sure they must have heard it outside. I look again. The other woman is pointing in my direction. I pick the book up, fumbling it in my hands. It's a copy of *The Great Gatsby*. A photo of me falls out of it. The one of me reading this novel on a beach in France when I was nineteen. I gave it to Cole when we met at a hotel in Tring for our first proper date. Does this mean he really does still want me? Why else would he keep my photo close to him? I put it all back carefully and dash to the stairs.

'Let's get out of here,' I say, my heart thudding with joy.

Amy is already waiting by the front door.

'I don't have a back-door key and all these new houses have security lights. Someone's bound to see us.'

'We'll have to sit it out until they've gone in.'

'How long's that going to be?'

'Let's wait ten more minutes. Come upstairs and have a look at some photos I found of Cole. It'll keep us busy.' I can see the problem clearer than ever. He thinks he needs to be a martyr, but I have to persuade him that he shouldn't stay with the mouse just because she's pregnant. They can split amicably and he can arrange to see his child every week if he wants to. Now I know for certain it's me he really loves, I'll do everything I can to help him leave her.

Chapter Fifty-Three

Monday 13 August 2018
Gemma

'The school advised the teachers not to use their own names on social media,' Nick says. 'Would be asking for trouble if pupils could see your photos and anything to do with your personal life.'

'Okay, I understand. So there's no chance a former pupil of yours could have guessed your handle and be targeting you?' Greg jots something in his notebook.

'Any of the brighter ones could have worked it out. It's not rocket science, to be honest. All my pupils were aware that Truman Capote and F. Scott Fitzgerald are two of my favourite writers.'

'You taught English then?'

'Of course, best subject there is. Reading, writing is like nectar from the gods, it's what sets humans apart from the animal kingdom.'

'Is that so? Why did you leave the profession to work at the local council if you feel so passionately about it?'

Nick side-eyes me again. I look the other way.

'I'd had enough of all the political correctness. Plus, I never seemed to have a free moment with all the lesson planning and the piles of marking. Everyone assumes you get weeks and weeks of free time in the holidays, but it never worked out like that.'

'I see. And how many years were you in teaching?'

'About twenty. It was very rewarding.' He smiles at me.

'Shall I make us all a fresh drink?' Becca stands up with the tray before anyone answers.

'Thanks, Becca.' Greg turns back to me. 'Any more thoughts about people who may have a grudge against you, Gemma?'

'I've been thinking more about Rosie. She came to see me at the hospital uninvited the day Thomas was born. It was so strange her turning up like that. The first day or two is for family usually, isn't it? It felt like she was intruding but I dismissed it as her being overly kind. But thinking back on it now, it was more like she was checking up on me.'

'You never told me this,' Nick snaps.

'What do you mean exactly, Gemma?' Greg writes in his notebook.

'She arrived when I was making a coffee so it was a shock to see her by the baby's cot. She said that when she arrived, she thought Thomas wasn't breathing and even wondered if he was dead, yet she didn't call for a nurse or try and find me. And then she was in a hurry to go as though she'd only really come to see if there was a baby. She was there barely five minutes.'

'I think we're building up a picture here of someone who'd planned this several days if not weeks ago. We just need to find the reason why she targeted you. I'm expecting some more CCTV pictures and hope we can get a positive ID on the second girl.'

Becca brings in a tray of cold drinks and a plate stacked with sandwiches. 'I know you won't feel like eating anything, Gemma, but just have half.'

Greg's phone pings. He clicks a few buttons and squints at the screen.

'Here we are. There's a good one here of both girls as they're walking towards the supermarket this morning.' He sits next to me and zooms in on their faces.

'They're much clearer pictures… I'm fairly sure that's the same girl I saw with Rosie. Can you zoom out again?'

Greg clicks back on the original image.

'Yes, she's the girl that followed me to work that day.'

'Are you sure?'

'Yes, because those are the yellow trainers she was wearing.'

'Let me see.' Nick holds out his hand and Greg gives him the phone. Nick zooms in on their faces. 'Is this one Rosie?'

'That's right,' Greg says, watching him closely.

Nick swallows hard. For once he's got nothing to say.

Chapter Fifty-Four

5 August 2018
Scarlett

On Sunday morning, Mum comes down later than us. Her hair is swept up in a messy knot and she's wearing a baggy T-shirt, off one shoulder.

'What are you girls up to on this lazy Sunday?' Mum nurses her coffee in both hands. Without make-up on, the brown patches of sun-damaged skin make her look so much older. Her eyes are small and red showing how tired she is. I've never known her go to bed early. She's suffered with insomnia ever since she had me. I think it's why she likes to have men round as company.

'Um, not sure yet.' I wink at Amy. We aren't about to tell her anything of our plans or she'd be sure to try and stop them. Amy's job this morning is to check to see if the baby monitor has been switched on. My job is to collect together all the information to finish the fake Facebook page in Cole's 'Truman Capote' name then, when the time is right, send friend requests to everyone on his list saying that his existing account has been hacked and to please join this new one and to ignore any warnings about it, because they were messages from the hackers. We're considering doing the same for the mouse. She's the one more likely to post news about the baby and what's going on in their lives, but at this point I need to know what he's thinking, what he's planning, if anything. I can keep an eye on her at work and on Instagram.

They are due home later this afternoon, so we rock up early and wait.

It had been silent when we left last night. I made sure I put all the photo albums back exactly as I'd found them. Amy and I had a laugh photographing all the best ones. His whole childhood was catalogued. There was even a snap of him at his first job, standing by the sign outside, pulling a silly grin and pointing to the name of a private grammar school. I remembered him telling me he was there for five years, but felt it had been time to move because his class were all so ridiculously talented he felt he could do more good at a comprehensive, find a talented pupil from a disadvantaged background. Someone just like me.

The first time I'd ever read a poem out was in his class. He persuaded me to do it. He stood up and clapped, encouraging the whole class to join in. I'd been so embarrassed but elated that he considered my work worthy of a standing ovation. No one had ever told me I was good at anything before, except Mum. He was only there for a year, covering maternity leave, but it felt like he'd plugged the gap in my life of not having a dad around to encourage and praise his little girl.

One day he'd asked me to stay behind for extra English lessons. He said he could help me reach the highest GCSE level, that he only ever cherry picked the best pupils for further tuition, the ones who showed real promise. He told me I was talented, special, not just brains but the whole package. It became a regular thing after school. He knew so much about books and writing and what sort of answers were expected in the exam, what I could work on to give me extra points, I soaked it all up.

'I'm thinking of organizing an extra-curricular trip to the theatre to see a production of *An Inspector Calls*,' he'd said one day in our session after school. 'Would you be interested in going? Do you think anyone else will be? It's on at a local theatre, we could go to a Friday matinee. I can get a good discount on a student group booking.' I'd stared at him speechless. It was breathtaking how there seemed to be so many books, plays and films we shared an interest in. I'd bought a copy of the play online and read it in less than a day. Mr Adams had waited for my answer, watching me, amused but not in a mocking way. The smile in his eyes, the way he gazed at me left me dizzy with desire for him.

'But I won't bother if my star pupil isn't interested, because chances are no one else in the class will be either.' He'd sat on the desk next to me, within touching distance.

'I am, I am,' I'd said earnestly, 'I don't know about everyone else, though.'

'Maybe you can help me persuade the rest of the class to join us?'

'I'll do my best.' I remembered glowing, self-satisfied at his praise and at him trusting me. Thinking I could galvanize the whole class to want to see it.

'Do you know, it's rare and wonderful to find such a gifted student as you.' He'd let his eyes rest on me for even longer than usual, as though he was really seeing me properly for the first time – as a young woman not just as his student. He was taking all of me in – my glossy blonde hair, peachy clear skin, long tanned legs, pert breasts. I was aware of how fortunate I was on the looks front. I could eat and drink whatever I wanted, and it didn't affect my waistline or my skin. But no one had known that all of it was hiding something ugly deep inside me – a cavernous hole in my heart, empty of love from not having a daddy. Instead, it was filled with resentment and jealousy. I knew all about consequences. I was living with whatever selfish or bad choices my mum and dad had made.

I'd reached for the next photo album and my stomach pinched as soon as I'd opened it. Cole and Gemma in silver lettering on the translucent first page, their wedding date underneath. Photo after photo of their wedding day on a beach somewhere exotic, four years ago. I flicked through windswept photos of her in a floaty cream dress, bare feet in the sand. Nothing original. Cole looking gorgeous in his white Armani jeans and half-open white linen shirt, hair streaked blond. She looked so young, so happy. I bet she couldn't believe her luck, bagging someone like Cole. I'd thumped my fist down on their faces. It should have been me.

We wait almost half an hour in our hiding place across the road before they finally arrive. The mouse is still enormous, so at least they hadn't sneaked off for a caesarean. Cole helps Gemma out of the car and, arm round her waist, walks her to the front door. On the step he says something to her and she stops and looks at him. He kisses her lips. Is this for real or is he putting on a show for me?

He carries the suitcase in just as the mother of the big family next door comes out in her slippers, arms crossed. I can tell he wants to get away, but she chats to them for a good ten minutes, pointing up to the window I'd been looking out of last night. Maybe she is only telling them that they'd left the curtains open. If she thought I was a burglar, she'd have called the police.

The urge to run over the road and throw my arms around Cole is almost too much. I want to let him know he doesn't have to be saddled with her and a baby. He can have a better life with me, like it was meant to be.

Chapter Fifty-Five

5 August 2018

Scarlett

The warm weather usually brings people out, loosens them up. Most want to enjoy dinner on the terrace, imagining they're on holiday in Italy or Greece. Georgio says Sundays are sometimes as busy as Saturdays but tonight it's barely half full.

'Didn't expect to see you tonight,' I say when Gemma comes in that evening. 'Did you have a good time?'

'It was lovely, thank you. Thought I'd pop in to see how you're all getting on.' I hope she doesn't feel the need to go into details.

'Everything's fine.' I shoot a look across at Bonnie who nods too.

Gemma heads straight out the back.

She's more subdued than I expected, like she's trying to give it a positive spin to convince herself. Probably dog tired.

'And thanks for feeding Missy, especially at such short notice,' She says when she comes back out.

'That's all right, she's really sweet. I've got your key in my bag, by the way. Do you want me to go and get it now?' I point to the cloakroom with my thumb.

'Later will be fine. No rush.'

'Did you know that another cat sneaks into your house? A female, I think, with a grey mark on its head.' I check the receipts on the side and start making the first order of coffees.

'I know, I can't get rid of her. She's often sniffing around Missy. I don't know what to do. I can't lock the cat flap in case she thinks we're locking her out.'

'I've no idea what to suggest. You look exhausted, by the way, if you don't mind me saying.'

She glances at me in surprise. 'I am actually. I'm not staying long. I just had to… I thought I'd check in, make sure everything was running okay. I knew we were going to be fairly busy tonight.'

'We'll manage if you want to get home? Up to you, of course, you're the boss.' I add a tiny wrapped biscotti to each saucer and lift the coffees and a pot of demerara sugar onto a tray.

She lets out a deep sigh. 'Nick can be… he likes to make all the decisions at home, but here I get to make them.'

I'm so close to asking her if they're splitting up but then I think of him wanting me to get an abortion. If he was intending to leave her, he wouldn't be so against my pregnancy.

'Did you know when you met him that this was the man you'd marry?' I hand the tray of coffees to Bonnie and start making the next order. The mouse hands me four clean cups. It's not like her to linger for a chat, but I get the feeling she needs to talk and I'm the perfect candidate to listen to her marriage woes.

'Does anyone ever know that, really? Soon after Nick and I got together, he whisked me off to Las Vegas. A couple of days later he took me to a chapel in a white limo, got down on one knee and proposed. He'd organized the wedding without telling me. I couldn't believe he'd sprung it on me. It was lovely and everything, but I couldn't exactly turn him down.'

'So you got married there?' But their wedding photos were on a beach.

'We did. I was very young. I hardly knew him really.'

'But you were madly in love with him, weren't you?'

'Maybe more flattered with his attention to start with, infatuated. But yes, he's easy to fall in love with. He's so charming.'

I realize I'm staring at her and I make myself look away. Without thinking I touch the hot steam nozzle with my fingertips. A jet of pain blasts through my skin.

'Sugar, sugar!' I try not to swear.

'Are you okay? Put your hand under cold water, I'll finish these.'

'I'll be fine.' I shake my hand.

'No, I insist.' She turns the cold tap on and holds my wrist, so my fingers are being drenched in icy water. I stand there while she makes three cappuccinos and two mochas. She carries on talking, almost to herself. 'I felt such an idiot for not guessing. He'd picked out a cream shift dress for me and matching heels and a hairdresser came to our room and styled my hair. He'd hired a tuxedo and looked every bit like James Bond. A bouquet of white roses was waiting for me at the chapel.'

'It sounds absolutely amazing.' I frown, bewildered. What about the wedding photos I found in their house? 'I've always dreamed of getting married on a beach one day,' I lie, 'but now I'm thinking Vegas is a much better option.'

'Funnily enough we did that too. After a few days honeymooning in Vegas, we flew to the Maldives. He said he wanted beautiful photos, so we dressed up and had a professional photographer take a whole shoot of us in a casual set of wedding clothes.'

'Wow. He really splashed out on you then.'

'He did. I know I'm very lucky.' She doesn't sound it, though. She glances at her rock of a ring, probably only just realizing she's forgotten to take it off.

'Trouble is I didn't have a chance to tell my parents or any of my friends, let alone invite any of them. I feel really sad about that. It's not how I imagined my wedding day to be.' She gazes down at her bump and touches it lightly. 'I'm sorry, I sound so ungrateful, don't I?' She pulls up a tray and lifts the coffees onto it.

'No, it's understandable. Almost every girl I know has a fantasy about their dream wedding. Were your parents okay with it once they'd got over the shock?'

She slowly shakes her head. 'They've not talked to me since.' Bonnie takes the tray from her. 'Anyway, sorry to dump all that on you. How are your fingers? A bit numb?'

'They're much better, thanks.' I switch the tap off and dry my hand.

'Thank you for listening to me.'

'That's all right. You can talk to me any time.'

'I've not told anyone half this stuff before. Nick doesn't like me sharing our personal lives, but sometimes it's a lot to carry around on my own.'

'They always say it's best to share.'

'A few months ago, I suspected Nick was seeing someone but of course he denied it.'

I blink once and freeze, waiting for her to scream blue murder at me, but she carries on talking.

'I was seriously considering leaving him. But then I found out I was pregnant. I didn't know what to do. I didn't tell him straight away but when I did he was overjoyed, insisted we work on our marriage.'

'So he wasn't seeing anyone and you didn't split up?'

'If he was, he must have ended it. He was at home more, being nicer. So no, we didn't separate.' She frowns at me probably wondering why I asked, but I have to know.

'That's good then.'

'He didn't see his dad after his parents divorced, so he's adamant we have to stick together because he won't let that happen to his child.'

'I can understand that.' I clench my teeth. I was so sure she'd got pregnant to entrap him. But despite him staying with her and wanting their baby, she's not happy with him. Why did he tell me they'd split up and were getting divorced? Why pretend he wanted to be with me? What is clear is that if Gemma is telling the truth, Cole has been lying to me from day one.

Chapter Fifty-Six

8 August 2018

Scarlett

I wave goodbye to Amy at 10 a.m. on the ground floor and take the lift up to the maternity ward. I bought one of those massive helium balloons from the shop by the entrance to hold in front of my face. My other hand is tightly balled up in my dress pocket. The maternity door has a security button, so I press it, not sure what will happen. A nurse comes and opens the door.

'Visiting Gemma Adams.' I wear my best smile.

'And you are?' The nurse's eyebrows are overplucked and too far apart.

'Her sister.'

'Up the top there, on the right.'

'Thanks.'

I walk silently along the corridor, glancing to one side then the other. Babies are being held up and admired by families while mothers lie in beds like war victims. Part of me wants to turn back, run away, but this bloody balloon keeps me moving forward as though it's pulling me along. I have to see the little shrimp with my own eyes.

The last bay on the right is quiet, the curtains drawn round each bed. I search for the name Adams on the board at the entrance. It's by the window. The curtain is half pulled to one side, but there's no one there. The bed is empty, the sheets crumpled and turned back. A clear box stands alongside it, next to the window. I peer in at the tightly wrapped bundle. It looks too big to be a newborn. When I went into work last night, Georgio told everyone the news.

The baby's golden thatch stands up on his head like a troll, eyes squeezed shut, fast asleep. He's like a doll with painted rosy cheeks and feathery eyelashes. Especially as there is no movement whatsoever. Is he even breathing? I lean in closer to his face and wonder if I should poke him. What if he's died and they don't know it yet. I should go in case they blame me. But then I detect a movement at the edge of the blanket, the tiniest flutter of fibres from the baby's breath.

'Hey, is that you, Rosie?' Gemma's voice is too loud as she hobbles towards me. I wince at her using my second name out loud.

'I wasn't expecting to see you.' She's wearing a white night-dress, the sort of thing I imagine they wore in Victorian asylums. 'Everything okay at work?' Her hair is unruly, neither completely up nor down and one of her eyes has a burst blood vessel I can't bear to look at.

'All fine. Just wanted to see how you both were.'

'Oh, well. That's really kind of you. And is this for me?'

'I hope you like it.' I pass her the balloon. It seems a stupid present now. Cole's bound to ask who it's from.

'He's a big baby, isn't he?' I try my hardest to appear inter-ested. I imagine Cole holding his son for the first time. Any thought of me erased from his mind.

'He is. Almost nine pounds.'

'What's his name?'

'We've called him Thomas.'

'That's nice. He was so still when I came in I was scared. I thought for a second he wasn't breathing.' Can't she tell that the wicked fairy has arrived to cast her spell? 'Anyway, I forgot to give you this.' I hand her the front-door key. It's been in my pocket. I could have let myself into their house any time.

'Ah thank you. That's good of you. Just put it on there.'

Mum spent weeks in hospital with me after I was born. She's never said why exactly. I guess the birth wasn't as straightforward as this one.

I wonder how long I've got before Cole comes back. When Amy and I arrived, I parked near his car and watched him return to it and drive away before I got out and came in. I don't think he spotted it amongst all the others. We ducked right down as he walked past.

'Anyway, I can't stop, I just wanted to make sure everything was okay.' I have one eye on the door. Cole could stroll back in any minute.

'Thank you, it's really kind of you.'

'I was so excited to hear the news.' I hope my sarcastic edge is subtle enough not to give me away. 'Are babies always so quiet?'

She turns to the cot. 'Not when he's hungry. Nothing wrong with his lungs, that's for sure. He kicks his little legs like mad when he cries.'

'I'd better leave you to it then.' I grin.

'Thanks for coming.' She eyes me up one last time and climbs into bed, immediately shutting her eyes. I head towards the door and hear the lift ping. I glance at a text from Amy warning me that Cole is back, only to see him coming towards me on the other side of the double doors holding a takeaway bag. I step into a side room and shut the door. I'm in a tiny kitchen area, holding my breath, hoping he didn't spot me. My phone buzzes in my pocket. I pray he can't hear it as he walks past. It's from him!

Come to the house. I'll be there this evening to collect a few things, check on the cat etc.

We must be only metres away from each other. How can he arrange to meet me when he's on his way to see his wife and new baby son?

Of course, what time? xx

Be there at 8 p.m.

What's your address?xx

I thought you knew it?

Er no??

49 Lansbury Road, near the park.

See you later xx

Has he guessed I've been in his house? I check the corridor is clear and walk briskly out of the ward, past the lifts and hurry down the stairs.

Amy strides towards me as soon as the lift doors open on the ground floor. I slump into her arms. She guides me out to my car. I'm glad to be away from the stagnant medical fug of the hospital. I don't say much at first, just follow the rhythm of our steps, letting the last twenty minutes sink in. I stop and cling to Amy's arm. Him becoming a dad is so huge, as though a crater has opened up between us at my feet.

Chapter Fifty-Seven

Monday 13 August 2018

Gemma

'Do you think you know Rosie, Nick?' Greg asks.

'I think she went to a school I taught at a few years ago. But her name wasn't Rosie. I can't think what it was. She was a nasty piece of work. Always bullying kids and slinging all sorts of accusations around at the teachers.'

'Such as?'

'Accused one teacher of touching her up and another of spying on her in the changing room showers. Right little trollop.'

'Please try and remember her name.' Greg sighs.

'Gemma let her in the house, gave her a key to come and feed our cat. She could have got up to all sorts here on her own.'

'When was this?'

'About three days before Thomas was born,' I say.

'Tell him what you found in the clothes I brought up to the hospital.'

'A pair of women's knickers that weren't mine.'

'Oh really? You said earlier that you didn't think a former pupil could be targeting you, but now do you think Rosie could be one?'

He shrugs. 'It does seem that way. Gemma wasn't to know what a psycho the girl is.'

'I thought the knickers were from someone he'd been seeing.' The words I'd been thinking pop out of my mouth.

'Don't be ridiculous,' Nick says.

'You stay out overnight without telling me where you are.' Becca lays her hand on my arm.

'Is there anything you want to tell us, Nick? Anything at all that could help us find your son, because now would be a good time.' Greg waits but Nick doesn't answer so he takes his phone into the kitchen and shuts the door.

'What did you tell him that for?' Nick shouts at me.

'Because it's true, isn't it?'

'I think it's time you left, Becca, don't you?' he says.

Becca looks at me and I nod. I mouth at her that I'll be okay, Greg's only in the other room.

Nick and I sit in silence, listening to the cameras clicking as Becca opens the front door, and the thud of it shutting after her. Reporters shout questions at her as she crosses the road.

'You're punishing me, aren't you?' I say. 'Because of Christmas.'

'You need to keep your trap shut. Get it?' He punches the sofa on the way out and stomps upstairs.

It's hard to know what are lies and what is the truth anymore.

The final thread of trust snapped on the plane home from the Maldives. We'd stayed for five days, a beach honeymoon and mini photo shoot so people could see for themselves how beautiful we were together, how wrong they'd been about us.

People had still been boarding the plane. We were sitting in our seats and Nick was taking our passports out of his shirt pocket. He unzipped the inside pocket of the rucksack to put them away.

'Let's see your photo.' I'd swiped the passports out of his hand.

'Give them back.' His tone had been flat. More a command than a request. I handed him mine and he tried to snatch his back. I held it in the air, stood up in the aisle to avoid his grasp. The man sitting next to him in the window seat was watching us, amused at the newlyweds. Nick tried to unlock his seatbelt but was fumbling in his haste. I'd already opened the passport to his photo.

'You look lovely. I don't know what you're worried about,' I'd said.

He looked so young and serious.

'I said, give it back.' He'd told me off, like one of his naughty children.

I glanced at the page then had to look again properly. His date of birth was the same as on the wedding register. It wasn't a mistake then. Nick really was forty-two. More than twice my age. He'd told me he was thirty-two which was still a big gap, but he'd said it didn't matter when it was true love.

I'd looked up at him and he'd snatched the passport from me, his face tight and burning with anger. He made me swap seats with him so I was sitting in the middle and wouldn't let me out until he was forced to because the man by the window needed the loo. All the way home he'd flirted with the woman seated in the aisle opposite. They'd shared two bottles of wine together and he'd barely spoken a word to me. I'd hardly been able to eat or drink a thing for the whole journey because of the tight knot of anxiety in my stomach. I wondered what my future would be like with a man who'd lied about his age and treated me with such contempt. I'd dreaded the thought of telling my parents we'd married in secret, knowing how strongly they would disapprove and how disappointed they would be in me.

Greg comes out of the kitchen. His face is drawn. He calls Nick down. My pulse spikes. Could there be news?

'Neither of you have been completely honest about who you are, have you?' He sounds weary and seriously pissed off.

'What do you mean?' I look to Nick to say something.

'Why didn't you tell us you were hopping from school to school as a supply teacher, Nick?' Greg leans against the wall.

'I didn't think it was important.'

'Just long enough to find your next girlfriend, was it?'

'I don't know what you mean.' Nick coughs.

'And you, Gemma, you failed to mention that you were his seventeen-year-old pupil.'

I look down at my lap. Shit, I bet Mum's been on to the police.

'You ran away together to get married,' Greg says.

'And why does that matter?'

'Apart from you abusing your position of trust, you mean?'

'You've got nothing on me.' Nick points a finger at Greg. 'I'd finished my contract.'

'Not exactly. Dismissed for inappropriate behaviour. Lucky for you the school chose not to prosecute, wasn't it?'

'What has any of this got to do with our baby son going missing?' Nick crosses his arms.

'Because we don't think Gemma was the only one.'

'Now what are you going on about?'

'We suspect that the woman who has taken your baby is another former pupil of yours. One you've been having a relationship with.'

Chapter Fifty-Eight

8 August 2018
Scarlett

'Perhaps I shouldn't have gone to see the baby. I feel so much worse now. I probably looked a right idiot turning up uninvited.' I open a can of Coke from the corner shop and take a long gulp, imagining the bubbles floating to my brain, carrying me away.

'No, you didn't. And anyway, if you hadn't gone, you'd have been driving yourself mad with curiosity,' Amy says, opening her can.

'True.' I want to be stronger, less affected but I can't help how I feel about him. Seeing their baby has left me weak and disarmed. I need to regroup.

'According to her they've never split up. Has he really been lying to me from the beginning?'

'She might be onto you and only saying that so you back off.'

'There's something about them that's not right. She wasn't exactly all glowy and gushing after their weekend away. When she came in the restaurant that night, she seemed glad to be away from him and even said he likes to be in charge at home.'

'I think you're reading too much into it. What man doesn't like to wear the trousers and make all the decisions?'

'I don't know.' I drink a mouthful of Coke.

'If he's anything like the blokes Mum goes out with, most of them think they can come in and take over.'

'Why does he want to see me, though? It's not because he's going to leave her, is it? More likely that he'll end it for good because he's scared of me telling her everything.'

We finish our cans and chuck them in the bin.

'Will you come with me tonight and wait outside his house in case I need you?' I ask Amy.

'Of course I will.'

'Thank you,' I say and we hug.

While I'm getting ready upstairs later, Amy changes into black clothes so she's not easily spotted.

'I was looking up online about other ways of finding out who your dad is,' Amy whispers, 'you can do a DNA test with a genealogy firm and see if they can match it with someone on their database.'

'Can you?'

'Even if it's not a match with your dad, someone related to him could be a match.'

'Do you know how much it costs?'

'No but I've made a list of firms that do it. I'll email them to you.'

I follow Cole's instructions and text him when I'm two minutes away. I leave Amy waiting by the neighbour's hedge.

Cole answers the door straight away. 'Come in,' he says, pulling my arm and looking around outside. I guess he doesn't want anyone to see me there.

He shuts the door. I can't read the look on his face but the usual joy at seeing me is missing. This is the first time we've been alone together for ages, but the atmosphere is brittle. I don't think throwing myself into his arms is going to fix it, but it doesn't stop me wanting to do it.

Without saying anything else, he turns on his heel towards the kitchen. My heartbeat spikes remembering the last time I was here, looking through his private things; finding out he's old enough to be my dad. He stands with his back to me for several long moments. It's as though I'm in his classroom, holding my breath not knowing if I'm about to be told off and given detention.

'When did you let yourself in?' His voice is low and menacing, his teeth grinding.

'What?' I try and feign astonishment. He can't know that for sure.

'I took some of Gemma's things to the hospital for her, tops, joggers, underwear, except when she unpacked them, there was a pair of knickers in there that weren't hers. How do you explain that?' His face twitches with impatience.

I try to hold in a nervous snigger, but my face gives me away.

'You think that's funny, do you? That she has accused me of having an affair?'

'No, but it makes it easier for you to leave her now, doesn't it, so we can be together at last?' I can't pretend I'm not glad she's found out. Does she know it's me?

'I'm lucky she's not kicking me out,' he shouts.

'But we could live together with our baby.' I touch my stomach.

'I'm not leaving her, Scarlett. You need to get that in your stupid head.' He jabs his temple with his index finger.

'But you said we were… that I only needed to wait a few weeks.' I try not to cry but hot tears sting my eyes.

'I only said I'd think about it, but that was before I held my baby in my arms.' He looks down at his open palms as though he can see his son there now. 'Seriously, Scarlett, how can I leave my wife and newborn child? What kind of father would that make me?'

'But what about our baby?' My voice is so small. Still I cling to this stupid lie. Why can't he be as passionate about having a baby with me?

'I don't want it. There, I've said it.' He wipes his forehead with the back of his hand, half turns away, then back again. 'I

231

know this sounds cruel, but you need to get rid of it, Scarlett. I'm serious. I'm not asking you anymore. I'm telling you. If Gemma finds out about this – about us – my life is over, do you understand me? You can't do this to me. I won't let you,' he shouts and thumps the counter making me jump back.

'What about me and our baby and how I feel?' My voice is gravelly like I'm the one who's been shouting. 'What about what I want?'

'It's best for you too, believe me.' He pours himself a whiskey and drinks it in one go.

'How can you be like this, after everything that's happened between us?' Tears are running down my face.

'It has to be done; we have no choice.' He grabs my arms, his fingers digging into my skin. 'If you saw my beautiful baby boy, you'd understand.' *But I have seen him*, I want to shout in his face.

'Don't you love me?' I whimper. He blinks slowly, his face a stone-cold mask. He is tired of me.

'Scarlett, babe, you know you'll always be my special girl.' He lets go of my arms and hugs me.

He pulls away quicker than I want him to, and he takes his wallet out of his back pocket. 'I got this for you, to help you sort it out.' He places a pile of fifty-pound notes on the counter.

I frown at them, then at him. 'I don't want your money, I want you and our baby.' My throat catches on the words. He won't look me in the eye. He won't answer. Instead, he digs around in his wallet and passes me a business card for a private clinic in London. 'This has to be over now, Scarlett. I'm sorry this has happened, but I had already ended it with you. You know I had no choice. This is a sad and unfortunate mistake.'

For a second, I truly believe I am pregnant with his baby because losing the man I love is so real and painful, as though I've stepped on a landmine and my whole life has blown up in my face.

'How can you call our child a mistake?' My voice is barely a croak.

'It's not technically a child yet, it's just a tiny dot of cells, which is why I'm imploring you to get it seen to as soon as you can.'

'Our cells, joined together.'

'Scarlett, come on. The sooner you get this fixed…'

'Fixed? Get it seen to? Is that what you think of me? And what if I don't?'

'I will be forced to have nothing to do with you. I may even have to move away.'

I'm stunned that he can be so cold.

'You never separated from your wife, did you?' I shake my head and back away.

'What?'

'You've lied to me from the moment we met.'

'Don't talk bullshit.'

'I'm right, though, aren't I?'

'You're upset, Scarlett.'

'All your friends down the pub knew. Why didn't they tell me?'

'You don't know what you're saying.'

'Then tell me you love me not her.'

'Stop it, okay?' He yells and thumps one of the cupboard doors. Something cracks. 'Now then,' he says in a taut voice, 'I don't know how you got my key from me, but I'll have it back, please.'

I'm shaking. I've never seen him like this.

'I don't have it.' I spit the words at him and lurch forward swiping my hand over the stack of money so it slides off the counter and flutters to the floor.

'If it wasn't you, then who was it?' he bellows.

I run out of the house, slamming the door as hard as I can.

Chapter Fifty-Nine

8 August 2018
Scarlett

Amy is waiting for me outside, behind the hedge. I stride past her and she trots along to catch up.

'What's happened?'

'He went mental. I've never seen him like that before. Bastard tried to give me money for an abortion. He was all set to leave her a few weeks ago.'

'Maybe she knows about you.'

'He found my knickers in her drawer and gave them to her at the hospital. So she's definitely worked out what he's been up to.'

'She probably threatened to move away so he can't see his son. Some women are ruthless like that. Emotional blackmail. Doesn't leave him much choice, does it?'

I stop dead and Amy almost walks into me. 'He denied lying to me about them splitting up. But I don't believe him. All the lovely things he's said to me, that he's promised me. It's all been a pack of lies.'

'We need to punish him for what he's put you through.'

'I'm going to make him sweat.' I cross my arms. 'Let him believe I'm still pregnant and might tell his wife about it at any time.'

'But what happens if he works out you were never pregnant in the first place?'

'Then we'll have to think of something else.' I walk towards the car leaving Amy standing in the middle of the pavement, her finger to her lips.

'All right then, how about this,' she calls and I turn back.

'What if their baby went missing? Just long enough to scare the shit out of him. Show him he can't treat you like his bit on the side.'

'Cole would never forgive me for doing something like that.'

'What else are you going to do?'

'I don't know.'

'Come on, he knows you wouldn't harm a baby. Anyway, it'll only be for a couple of hours, enough to put the frighteners on him. And it'll force him to tell the mouse about you.'

'Do you think we can get away with it?'

'Yeah, of course we can. You offer to take the baby for a little stroll. She'll probably be glad of the break – and she will be giving you permission to take him so it's not abduction. When you don't come back, he'll twig it's with you and he'll have to tell her everything.'

'I see what you mean. Gemma will know the baby is safe with me, so we'll only be hurting him for a little while. It could actually work.'

'She'll know you're looking after her baby because she trusts you, remember?'

I nod. 'I have to do something. He can't get away with what he's done to me. He's cheated his wife and me.' I wrinkle my nose. 'I believed everything he said. How could I have been so stupid?'

–

According to Gemma's Instagram page on Friday morning, she's coming home at lunchtime.

We hang around near their house to see them arrive with the baby. Cole looks crumpled and tired as he lifts the baby's car seat out. He stops a moment and kisses his son's forehead, then carries him into the house. The mouse gets out more slowly and waddles like she's holding something between her knees. Cole reaches into the boot for her holdall then he links his arm through hers and guides her inside.

As soon as we arrive home, Amy switches on her laptop and checks the baby monitor. At last it's been switched on. In moments we have a full-screen view of their nursery. Easy as anything. We don't have to wait long before Gemma carries the baby in and changes its nappy on the changing table. Fortunately, we only have a view of her back for that one, but we can hear everything she says to the baby, all the cooing and chat about this being his own special bedroom. She sits on the rocking chair afterwards, facing the window so we only have a side view of her feeding the baby. Soon after, Cole comes in with a mug of tea. He sits in the window seat opposite them and speaks quietly to her, but she doesn't look up once. Louder now, he tells her to listen to him when he speaks, but she shakes her head, looking down at the baby who seems to have dropped off to sleep. Cole catches her wrist in his hand and her pained face tips up to his until he lets go.

'What is he doing to her?' Amy points at the screen.

'Jesus. Is he for real? Why is he hurting her?' This isn't the same man I fell in love with.

'See, she knows that whoever owns those knickers has been in the house, probably in her bed. But he doesn't like her accusing him. He's not having any of it.'

'I'm going to invite him to my birthday barbecue tomorrow. If things are this bad at home, I think he might actually come.'

'Good because he's got a whole lot of shit coming his way.' Her lip curls in a snarl. We high five.

'I'll show him he can't chuck me away and get away with it. He'd better seriously watch out.'

Chapter Sixty

11 August 2018

Scarlett

I wake up early on Saturday and wonder what being twenty-one really means these days? There's not much I can do today that I couldn't do yesterday. Should I be climbing the career ladder by now or travelling the world like lots of my old school friends, according to their social media pages? All I want is to find out where I come from, who my dad is. Only then can I really work out what I want to do with my life.

Mum brings me in a cup of tea and a muffin. She sits on the bed and gives me a hug, holding me a bit longer than usual. She's always emotional on my birthday. I've never asked why, but I suspect it was a difficult birth and that's the real reason why I don't have any brothers or sisters.

'Thanks, Mum.'

I bite into the blueberry muffin, my favourite.

'You've turned into a beautiful young woman, do you know that?' she says stroking my hair. 'Ready to go out into the world on your own. I only wish…' She covers her mouth, swallows hard and stands up, goes across to the window. Outside, a spider in the top corner is busy spinning a fly in its silken web.

'What do you wish?'

'It's okay.' Whatever she was going to say has slipped down her throat. She glances at Amy on the floor bed, still fast asleep. 'Are you looking forward to your party tonight? Invited anyone special?'

'Not really.' I'm glad I've not told her anything about Cole. She'd be right to disapprove. 'I'm looking forward to it. Thank you.'

As she turns to leave, I call her back. 'Mum, you promised to tell me one thing about my dad, remember?'

There's a long pause before Mum speaks.

'Okay maybe, but not today.'

'I know you're trying to protect me, but I can handle it, whatever it is that went wrong between you.'

'I don't want to spoil your birthday. Please, let's just… enjoy it.' She swallows hard again.

'Okay. When?'

'Maybe tomorrow, or the day after that.' She looks down at the carpet.

'Did he leave you for someone else?'

She sighs. 'I wish you didn't have to know any of it.'

I still have the choice of living the rest of my life not knowing who he is, why they broke up. Lots of people don't know who their dads are and they're okay, aren't they? They get on with their lives. What makes me so special that I have to know? Maybe I will look back on today as the time before; when I was blissfully ignorant. Part of me wants to say, *Don't worry, I don't need to know*, but a worm of curiosity has burrowed so deep inside me, I need to feed it.

Amy wakes up as Mum closes my bedroom door. I tell her about our conversation in hushed whispers.

'I think it sounds like a bad break-up your mum has never got over. Maybe he ran off with someone she really trusted.'

'Yeah, that's what I'm worried about, digging it all up will upset her. Just the mention of him stresses her out. Maybe I should leave it.'

'Trouble is, there will never be a good time. Totally understandable if you decide not to find out. Sometimes it's better not knowing what went on. I used to think if my mum told me who my dad was, I'd be overjoyed, feel complete and I wouldn't care what he'd done, he's my dad and I'd love him whatever. But when she did tell me, I realized I couldn't erase it from my head. Robbing and killing an old woman in her own home is not something I can forgive or forget. I know I will carry it around with me for the rest of my life.'

'Yeah, I know you're right, but I can't help being curious. It's a piece of my life that's always been missing. I think I'd still like to know, even if it means I end up not wanting him in my life.'

'I'm just glad my mum doesn't want me to meet my dad or anything like that.'

We laugh at how bad that would be even though it's not funny at all.

'Anyway, happy birthday, I got this for you.' Amy takes a present wrapped in shiny paper out of her rucksack. There are creases in it where it has been used before, but it doesn't bother me. I rip the paper off and take out a book, *The Secret History* by Donna Tartt.

'I love it and I think you will too,' she says and gives me a hug.

'Thank you!' I hold the book to my chest and then I hug her back. She is more like a sister to me every day.

I text Cole to see if he can come to my party even though he'll probably say a flat no. He doesn't reply for ages, then an answer pings up on my screen.

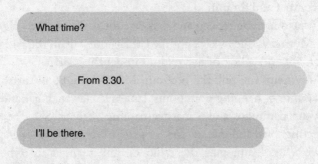

What time?

From 8.30.

I'll be there.

'Cole's coming.' I smile and high-five Amy.

239

Chapter Sixty-One

11 August 2018

Scarlett

Mum cooks us a full English. I suppose my birthday is a big deal for her, seeing her only child all grown up, hopefully moving out soon.

After breakfast, we help Mum unload the food delivery. She's really gone to town with drinks and nibbles and different varieties of barbecue meats and salads. We make layered jellies to go with the tubs of ice cream and a massive fruit trifle. I think of my birthday parties over the years – the trouble Mum has always gone to making cakes in the shape of my favourite cartoon characters, decorating the house with balloons and bunting, all to make it as fun and special as possible. She's always there for me, going way beyond my expectations. It makes me feel bad for pushing her so hard about who my dad is. Maybe there is a good reason for her not wanting me to know. Shouldn't I respect that and drop it?

'Why don't you two go and decorate the garden while I clear up?' Mum says once we've got the last layer of jelly in the fridge to set. 'There's a box of decorations under the stairs.'

Amy helps me pull the box out. Mum's bought all sorts of new bunting, hanging pom poms, lanterns, Hawaiian garlands, blow-up flamingos and a massive flamingo piñata. She's been collecting bits and pieces for a while. We carry it outside between us. Mum puts the radio on and turns it up when Queen sing, 'These Are the Days of Our Lives'. I go into the kitchen to get some string and a pair of scissors. Mum's standing by the radio, crying.

'Are you okay?' I put my head on her arm and she puts her arm around me, wiping her eyes with her fingers.

'It reminds me of someone very special.'

'Who's that?'

'I've never told you this, but I had a sister once.'

'Oh.' The photo we found pops up in my head.

'She died before you were born.' She stares ahead as though her eyes are fixed on a ghost. 'It was so sudden, and she was far too young.'

'I'm sorry, Mum.'

'I didn't get a chance to say goodbye to her.'

I want to ask how she died, but what if she was hit by a car? Instead I hug her back.

'I'm not sure I've ever got over it. It still hurts so much.'

'What was her name?'

'Jessica. We called her Jess. I wish she was here to celebrate with us, to see you.' She wipes her eyes. 'Anyway, I can't go around blubbing all day, we've got to get this party started.'

Back out in the garden, Amy has laid out the plates, plastic cups and serviettes on one of Mum's mosaic-topped tables.

'You'll never guess what?' I whisper. 'Mum's just told me that she had a sister who died before I was born. Maybe that was her sister's wedding in the photo.'

Amy wrinkles her nose. 'That would explain why your mum hasn't got that scar on her arm. And maybe your parents weren't married – that's why you can't find a marriage certificate.'

'And I think the woman in the photo who I thought might be my gran, was probably her sister.'

'Do you think her sister was the woman your dad ran off with?'

'Possible, isn't it? Mum's really sad she didn't get to say goodbye to her.' I take all the paper lanterns out of the box and pass some to Amy.

'Perhaps your mum had an argument with her just before she died, and they didn't have a chance to make up.'

I pin the paper handle of a lantern to a lime tree. 'We're back to square one.'

'I think your dad could still be out there somewhere. We could find out more about your aunt, see if that gives us any clues.'

'I'm beginning to believe my dad really was one of these boyfriends that turns up for a couple of days then disappears. Which means Mum may not even know who my dad is.'

Chapter Sixty-Two

In the sizzling heat we hang bunting from the garage wall to the fence, then to the side gate, and bright pink and orange pom poms on wire hooks along the clothesline. Amy fetches the steps and ties the flamingo piñata from the cedar tree and winds garlands around the trunk. Mum brings out a huge plastic tub for bottles of wine, beers, cans of lager and Coke. Later we'll fill it with ice. Mum has cleaned up the barbecue ready to go. By the time we've finished everything it's gone midday.

'Why don't you two go up and start getting ready? Have a real pamper afternoon. I'll straighten or curl your hair and paint your nails, how does that sound?'

'Perfect. Thanks, Mum.'

After our showers, we sit in our underwear and let our hair dry naturally. The day seems to be getting hotter. In the distance we hear shouting and clapping. The local fair is in town. Amy checks Cole's Facebook page. He's posted a photo of himself with the baby.

'Why doesn't he post one of Gemma as well?' I say, rubbing Factor 30 cream on my face and neck.

'I was wondering that too. I was also thinking that when we take the baby, we could make it look like she was being neglectful. Say we found the pram unattended. He'd go mad at her.'

'Won't he go mad at me when he finds out I was the one going off with his baby?'

'Not if we tell him his wife was nowhere to be seen. We just thought we were doing the right thing taking it with us.'

'I prefer your first idea about persuading her to let us take the baby out in the pram. It's him we're trying to get at now, not her.'

Mum looks round the door. 'You two ready to have your hair done?'

'Yes please, do you want to do Amy's first?'

'Oh, I don't know, you don't need to go to any trouble for me.' Amy tries to smooth down the frizziness.

'No, come on, let Mum straighten it for you, she's got some brilliant smoothing spray and the best tongs.'

'I'll go and get everything we need. Oh, actually, you may as well come into my bedroom. Everything's already set up, it'll be easier.'

Mum switches on the fan that sits on her dressing table and plugs in the straightening irons. Amy sits in front of the mirror first and Mum sprays her hair then sections it off. My eyes are drawn to the boxes on the wardrobe. I hold Amy's eye in the mirror.

'What's in those boxes up there, Mum?'

She pauses and looks up as though she hasn't seen them before. 'Oh, just bits and pieces I've collected over the years. Memories, I suppose.'

'What sort of memories?'

'You know, things close to my heart, that mean a lot to me.'

'Things to do with your sister?' I stand up. I can just about see the lock on the second box.

'Yeah, mostly.'

'I'd love to see a photo of her.'

'I'll have to dig one out to show you.' Mum pushes a window open wide.

'Were you good friends?'

'We were very close.'

'Why does that box have a lock on it? Is it full of the stuff you don't want to remember?'

Mum squeezes the irons on the next section of Amy's hair. 'Yes, there are some things in there I don't want to look at.'

Bullseye. 'Things to do with Dad?'

Mum bangs the irons down. 'What is this?'

'Sorry. You said you'd tell me something about him.'

'And I said not today.' She combs another section of Amy's hair.

'You do know who he is then?' I deserve a clout for being so cheeky, but I can't help myself.

Amy glares at me in the mirror, telling me to leave it. I always push too far.

'I'm not even going to answer that,' Mum says and continues in silence. A few minutes later she's finished.

'There we are, that's you done. Do you like it?'

'I love it, thank you. It's never felt this soft before or been this straight.' Amy smooths her hands down the shiny length of it.

We swap places. Mum plugs in the curling wand. None of us speak. Before long, my hair is transformed.

'Amy, why don't you go and get dressed?' She gives her a little wink.

As soon as she's gone, Mum opens a drawer of the dressing table and takes out a small gift box wrapped in glittery paper.

'Happy birthday, darling.' She kisses the top of my head. 'I hope you like it.'

'Thank you.' I open the paper carefully. Inside is a jewellery box.

'Go on, open it,' she says, her face filled with angst. Maybe she thinks I won't like it.

I pull back the lid and take out a ring with two diamonds set in a swirl of gold.

'It's so beautiful, Mum, thank you.' I slip it on my ring finger and it fits perfectly.

Mum nods, pressing her lips, unable to speak. She reaches out for me and pulls me in for a tight hug. 'I want you to enjoy your party, have the best night of your life. We'll talk tomorrow. I'll tell you about your dad, I promise. But today, please, just enjoy yourself.'

Chapter Sixty-Three

11 August 2018

Scarlett

Back in my bedroom, Amy is standing in front of my full–length mirror, adjusting her dark blue strappy dress.

'My God, Amy, you look amazing.'

'Do I?' She sounds genuinely surprised.

'Have you actually looked in the mirror?' I laugh.

'I haven't got my glasses on.'

'Why don't you get contact lenses?'

She slips her glasses in place. 'Does look okay, I suppose.'

'You look more than okay, silly.'

'What have you got there?'

'Mum gave it to me for my birthday.' I hold out my hand and Amy takes it, and inspects my ring.

'Wow, it's so sparkly.'

'Isn't it? I think they're real diamonds. I wasn't expecting anything like this. She's promised we're going to talk about my dad tomorrow, and she told me I should enjoy myself tonight. It feels more and more like the last supper.'

'It's not too late to say you'd rather not know.'

'Whatever happened is part of my history, isn't it? Once I know something about him – why they're not together anymore, why he hasn't stayed in touch – then I can deal with it, lock it away if necessary.' I tap my head although I'm not sure I really believe it's that simple.

I take my favourite emerald satin dress out of the wardrobe. It's strappy like Amy's but mine crosses at the back and has a low scoop. I slip on my favourite silver heels.

I'm spritzing on Daisy perfume when the doorbell rings. Mum hurries out of her bedroom and down the stairs in a red polka dot number.

'Someone's early.' I lean over the bannister. It's only 7.30. 'Who is it?'

'Someone I'd like you to meet,' Mum says as we follow her downstairs.

She opens the door to a smartly dressed man in beige chinos and a light blue polo top. He's holding a bottle of champagne with a ribbon around it. She hugs him and invites him in. He can't drag his eyes off her.

'Say hello,' Mum nudges me gently, smiling widely.

'Hi.' I've no idea why I'm blushing, but I feel like I know him from way back.

He holds me with a look of astonishment mixed with love that absolutely floors me. I guess he's about Mum's age and I don't mind admitting that he's dead handsome, for an old guy.

'This is Dan. Dan, this is Scarlett. We went to school together. He's come all the way from New York to see us.' Mum invites him in.

'Happy birthday, Scarlett.' He hands me the bottle, scanning my face. He looks at Mum then back at me and they both start choking up. They hug each other for what feels like ages. Dan pulls back, kisses Mum on both cheeks and they look full on at each other, their eyes flicking back and forth as though secret semaphore is passing between them.

'How've you been – I mean, really?' he asks quietly, stroking a curl back from her face.

'You know how it is, every day's a new start.'

He nods and hugs her again tightly and I think maybe I should slope away and leave them to it. But they move apart, and his eyes are on me again.

'Last time I saw you, you were a tiny tot running around the place.' He turns to Mum and she wraps her arms around him again, unable to hold her tears in this time. She's full on sobbing and I don't know where to look. I stretch my brain to remember his face, but I can't. He clearly knows me.

'Are you okay, Mum?' I don't know what else to say or do. Mum nods. Dan passes her a folded hanky from his pocket. Mum's eyes are a mess of make-up. Amy drags me by the hand up the stairs.

'What's all that about?' she whispers.

'I've no idea. Some old school friend of Mum's from New York.' I shut my bedroom door and we drop down on the bed.

'Do you think he could be your dad?' She pulls on my arm, smiling the biggest grin.

'I don't know. Do you think that's what the big secret is?' I put the bottle on the bedside table.

'I think it's what your mum's going to tell you. She's been waiting for him to arrive.'

'Wouldn't they have told me straight away?' I'm buzzing and tingling all over. Could it really be possible?

'Maybe they need to talk first then tell you together.'

'God, I hope so. He seems sooo nice. But why is he living in America and not here with us?'

'That could be the sticking point they have to talk through.'

She opens her laptop. 'Oh my God, look at this.' Cole and Gemma are in the nursery yelling at each other. She's pulling open drawer after drawer hunting through everything with her hands asking who it is he is seeing, while he stands by the door jogging the baby up and down, shouting at her to calm the fuck down and stop being paranoid.

'Is she looking for more underwear that's not hers?'

'I think so.'

'I hope this doesn't mean he won't come tonight.'

'He's not going to want to stay there, is he?'

'True.'

We go out to the garden where Mum is still talking to Dan. He smiles and gazes at me with a faraway look in his eyes. Mum hands him a beer straight from the tub and asks me and Amy to empty more bags of ice around the bottles of drink. Mum switches on some 90s pop music.

'So how long have you known Mum?' I ask Dan.

'Since the beginning of secondary school, wasn't it?' He turns to Mum and she nods then sips her glass of white wine. 'I was in the same year as your mum's sister. Six years older. We all went round together.'

'Dan dated Jess for three years.' Mum touches his arm and smiles affectionately.

'Oh, I thought maybe you two had been an item.'

Mum smooths her hair and glances sideways at Dan. He sticks his hands in his pockets and stares at the ground.

'There's someone at the door,' Amy says, and Mum rushes off to answer it. Dan takes a sudden interest in a red rose bush.

'Can I get you another drink or some food?' I offer him a paper plate. His eyes land on me again but it's more than a passing glance, he's really examining me.

'I'll grab myself a few bits, thanks.' He takes the plate and reaches for a biscuit. But it's not any old biscuit and I can't believe I didn't notice them earlier. Malted Milk. Why has Mum bought them today?

'So, can you remember how old I was when you last saw me?' My voice is all over the place.

'About two or three, I expect.'

'And you remember me well?'

'I'd never forget you. You were such a sweet happy child. You wore bunches in your hair and yellow ribbons and were always laughing.'

'Why didn't you stay?'

He's looking around for Mum pretending he hasn't heard my question. She arrives by his side.

'Some of your friends are here, Scarlett.'

Amy links her arm through mine, and I let her pull me away. I glance back at Dan for his answer, but he doesn't speak.

More of our neighbours and friends from school and the pub arrive and before long the garden is heaving with people. Mum stacks all my presents under the trestle table which is loaded with food. One of her male friends is manning the barbecue. I try and speak to everyone, making sure they've all got drinks and to thank them for coming. Amy stays close by, although she is mingling more than she ever would have before.

I check the time and look round the crowd hoping to see Cole. Perhaps he knows I'm on to him.

All my friends are dancing the Conga and keep pulling at me to join in, but I can't relax searching for a glimpse of him.

'Everything all right, Scarlett?' Mum asks, breaking away from the pack. How can I tell her that the man I love is a lying bastard who is married and has just had a kid? She'll expect me to be with someone nearer my own age. Another one of her boyfriends has arrived. She's been taken up with Dan most of the night. I wonder what they think of that. Is it possible one of them is my dad and she's going to spring it on me, announce it in front of everyone?

I wander through the house which Mum's decorated with different coloured fairy lights and tissue paper roses. There are couples curled up together in various dark corners of the living room and dining room. I reach the front door and my instinct is to open it. Cole is standing there, hand up, about to press the bell.

'I thought you weren't going to make it.'

'I said I would, didn't I? So here I am.'

He's not smiling or angry. Nothing. So why has he bothered coming?

Chapter Sixty-Four

Cole plucks a small package out of his back pocket and hands it to me. 'Happy birthday, Scarlett.' Now there's a menacing edge to his voice. He's either annoyed with me or it's because of his blow-up with Gemma earlier.

'Thank you.' I open it carefully. Inside is a small book of wisdom and a notebook with a mini pencil attached by a string. I imagine for a second that he's written 'All my love, Cole' on the inside page, but it is blank. I look into his eyes, but I can't read what he is thinking. I've never seen him so shut down.

'Come and have a drink.'

He follows me into the garden. The music is throbbing and the fairy lights are twinkling in the descending darkness.

'Cole.' Someone shouts and in moments he is surrounded by my friends who know him from school and the pub. I grab us a couple of beers swimming in the tub of grassy, melting ice. He takes one from me as he's drawn into the middle of the crowd.

'Are you okay?' Amy is at my side, hand on my elbow. 'I didn't know where you'd gone, I was worried.'

I nod, still watching him. 'I opened the front door and he was there, isn't that weird? It's as though we were drawn together at the same moment.' He's mid flow telling everyone all about his new son. I let them get on with it. I put my arm through Amy's, and she comes with me to the patio. We dance to ABBA's

'Dancing Queen'. I sense him watching me, looking over their heads and shoulders whenever he can.

When the song ends, Mum turns the sound right down and gathers everyone around the table. The alcohol kicks in and I sway, wishing I didn't feel so warm and nauseous. What is Mum going to say? She brings out the lit-up cake she's made in the shape of the number 21. Everyone sings 'Happy Birthday' at the tops of their voices. I catch Cole's eye at the back of the crowd. He's not singing. When the song ends everyone cheers then Mum waves her hands to quieten them down.

'I'd like to say a few words…' She rubs her hands together and smiles at me, misty-eyed.

I need to get out of here. I have a horrible feeling she's going to announce that one of these men is my dad. Or worse, she's going to embarrass me by saying what a wonderful daughter I am, when I'm not. She doesn't know the real me. Her sweet little girl having an affair with a married man. And everything I've been doing to take revenge on him. She'll be so ashamed.

'Sorry, need the loo.' My vision is sliding backwards and forwards. Amy offers to come with me, but I hold up my hand to stop her.

'Can't you wait a minute?' Mum holds my hand. 'I want to wish you a very happy 21st birthday and say how proud I am of you.'

I need to be on my own.

'Thanks, Mum,' I mumble and everyone cheers again.

'Are you okay?' she asks.

'I'll be fine.' I'm aware that my words are slurring. Mum looks surprised. I can't be the only one who is drunk. She's had quite a bit herself.

The crowd is beginning to thin out, and several people say their goodbyes to me as I navigate my way through the house to the only bathroom upstairs. Thankfully it's empty, and I'm relieved to lock the door behind me. I stand over the toilet, not sure if I'm going to be sick or not. The nausea passes. I fill a beaker with water and drink it down in one go. The local church bells chime midnight. Here I am, Cinderella. Except my prince has turned out to be the villain.

I open the bathroom door. Cole is waiting for me outside. He pulls me back into the room and presses me against the door, kissing me hard, one hand caressing my leg then lifting the hem of my dress.

'No!' I push him away.

'What do you mean, no?' He looks incredulous. 'What did you bring me here for then?' He cups my breasts.

'We're over.' I grab his wrists and fling them aside.

'I know we are. I told you three weeks ago she's my wife and I can't leave her.'

'So why are you here?'

'Thought you might like a farewell shag.'

'Are you joking? You lied to me!'

'Scarlett, come on.'

'You told me you loved me, but you've been playing me.'

He throws his head back and laughs. 'Oh Scarlett, you're so sweet when you're angry.'

'What about Gemma finding my knickers? She must know you're seeing someone.'

'You think a little thing like that will break us up?' He holds my chin with his finger and thumb pressing my skin against the bone. I twist my head away and he laughs in my face.

'I'll go to your house, tell her everything, then she'll leave you.' I back away.

He snatches my wrists and holds my hands together tight. 'She'll never leave me. You think she doesn't know about you and me already? You're more naïve than I thought. Dear, sweet Scarlett. I've told her everything about us, all the things you do for me that she won't. How exciting you are in bed compared to her.'

I cringe and shrink away from him. He tightens his grip. My skin burns.

'The trouble is, I'm bored with you now, Scarlett. You've become clingy and annoying, expecting too much from me.'

'What about our baby?' My voice is barely a whisper. I swallow, trying to hold the tears back, not wanting to show how much he's hurting me. 'I'll tell my mum.' I lurch towards the door.

He grunts and clasps my hair in one hand, yanking my head to one side. I gasp and shout at him to get off me. A smarmy smile spreads across his face. 'Is there really a baby?'

I so want to punch his face in.

'You've had a serious amount of alcohol tonight for someone who claims they're pregnant. And harming a foetus is not something you'd do, is it? So either you're telling little porkies to entrap me or you're doing your best to get rid of it. Whichever way, it's a win–win for me.' He jerks my head, pushing me away. I stagger and crash into the wall.

'And attacking me online isn't going to work either.' He takes his phone out.

'What?' I smooth my hair down and gauge how I can reach the door handle behind him.

'Signing me up for all sorts of dodgy sites, using my profile picture on dating websites for people into bondage and all sorts of bizarre shit, so I'm getting loads of messages from weirdos. Very clever.' He shows me one of the emails with a picture of a woman in a full leather outfit and whip.

> *Don't try and be clever with me, dipshit. Keep looking over your shoulder, because I'm there watching you, waiting for my moment.*
>   *Experience points collected: 7,145*
>   *Countdown: Two lives remaining.*

I try to hide my smirk.

'Oh yeah, think it's hilarious, do you?' He's breathing heavily. A strange grin emerges on his face, his eyes focusing on my bare legs as he reaches for his fly. I swing my arm back to slap him away from me, but he's too quick, grunting as he catches my wrist, his hot breath on my neck, he slams me against the wall. His hands are all over me and I cry out and manage to stab my knee upwards into his groin. He yelps and staggers back, both hands cupped between his legs. I yank the bathroom door handle, but it won't budge, he's slipped the lock across. I try again but he swipes a foot at me, misses and topples over still holding himself. I manage to unbolt the door and run out, smack into Amy.

'What's going on?' she shrieks, glancing behind me as she pulls me away.

'That bastard attacked me, I'm just a joke to him.'

He stumbles out still holding himself.

'Little bitch.' He scowls at me and makes for the stairs. Amy is ready to boot him in the back but breaking his neck won't fix this.

'Leave him,' I tell her. I want him to suffer the hard way.

Head down, he glances round at me with his sly wolf grin, his sheep's clothing well and truly removed.

'I'll make sure he knows where the front door is.' Amy shoves his shoulder. He holds on to the bannister with his free hand to stop himself falling.

'Hurry up or I'm calling the police.' She shoves him again and he stumbles. For a moment I think he's going down head-first, but he recovers his balance and moves faster, kicking the front door on his way out.

We sit on the bottom stair and Amy hugs me, rocking me back and forth. I can't even speak, let alone cry.

Mum finds us there some time later as she's ushering out the last of the stragglers. I don't know what to tell her when she asks what's wrong. We help her clear up some of the mess, the paper plates, empty bottles and cans. Once the barbecue is safely out, we decide to do the rest in the morning.

It's gone 2 a.m. by the time we're in bed. I finally tell Amy what happened in the bathroom. The more I recount what he said and did to me, the more her face swells with anger.

'Right, we are going live with his new Facebook page.' She sits up and drags her laptop onto the bed.

'I'm so tired, can we do it in the morning?' My heart is empty; he's sucked the life from me with his cruel words and lies.

'You go to sleep.' Amy pushes her glasses up, 'I'm going to do a bit of digging on Mr Nicholas Adams, see what else he's been lying about.'

Chapter Sixty-Five

Monday 13 August 2018

Gemma

'An intimate photo has been posted on your cloned Facebook page,' says Greg.

'What, of me in the nuddy?' Nick snorts a note of laughter.

'No, of you and a woman.'

'What woman? Show me,' he says holding his hand out.

Greg passes him his phone.

'Ha, I am topless then. Can't see who it is though, sorry. Her back's to the camera.'

'The side of her face is pretty clear though. It's a former pupil of yours, don't you recognize her?' Greg takes his phone back.

'Is it?'

Greg sits next to me. I don't want to see it, but he shows me anyway.

'Maybe you can see who it is, Gemma.'

In the photo Nick is lounging on a neatly trimmed lawn, sunglasses on, topless and tanned. Rosie is sitting sideways opposite him, wearing a tight neon pink top with spaghetti-straps. She does have her back to the camera, but it looks like someone has called her name and they've taken the photo just as she's turning to look over her shoulder. Her familiar blonde swathe of hair is caught in motion.

'It's Rosie,' I say quietly.

'Is it? That must have been years ago,' Nick says.

I blink at him and imagine cockroaches pouring out of his mouth every time he speaks.

'Are you sure about that?' Greg asks. 'Looks to me from the St George's flags and bunting in the background like June this year. I'd guess it was Monday 18th about 7 p.m., when most of us were busy watching England's first World Cup match against Tunisia.

'I can't in all honesty remember.'

'How about telling us her real name so we can try and find her and Thomas?' Greg takes out his notebook and pen.

'I'm not entirely sure.'

'You knew her all the time? Tell him! Tell the fucking truth for once in your life,' I scream and collapse back on the sofa.

Nick glares at me with steely eyes.

'Obstructing an investigation is a criminal offence,' Greg says, 'so do yourself a favour, Nick, and be straight with me. It'll help you in the long run.'

'All right. Both of you bloody nagging at me. It's Scarlett, okay?'

'Surname?'

Nick sighs deeply and sits down. 'Bates.'

'And when was she your pupil?'

'The year before I met Gemma, 2013.'

'School?'

'Priory Secondary.'

'When did your relationship with her start?'

'Last Christmas.'

How could he do that to me? He may as well be compiling a shopping list for all the regret he's showing. I'd told him I was pregnant not long before Christmas. Was this his revenge for me trying to leave?

'Until when?'

Nick purses his lips. *Bit late to pretend you care about my feelings*, I want to shout at him.

'About three weeks ago.'

I gasp. All that time, him and Rosie. That day he came into the restaurant and she miraculously disappeared. I trusted her with a key to our house when all along she was sleeping with my husband. She's bloody welcome to him.

Greg takes a call and minutes later he's telling us he's got to go out, an emergency has come up. He'll be back as soon as he can.

'Will you be okay?' Greg says to me. 'I can ask Becca to come and sit with you.'

I shake my head. I'm trembling but I don't think he's noticed.

'What, I'm not good enough to look after my own wife now?' Nick kicks the bottom of the curtain. There's a lull in activity outside.

Greg stands in the doorway and looks back at me. *Don't leave me*, I want to say. Instead, I raise my hand in farewell.

After Greg's gone, I stay sitting on the sofa in silence going over and over everything Nick's said. He's standing at the window spying round the curtain at the reporters. If I sit still enough, he might forget I'm here and go away.

Nick spins round. 'So you think you can shout at me like that in front of him, do you?' He strides across the room and stands over me.

'I'm so sick of your lies, Nick. How could you sleep with her when I'd just told you I was pregnant?'

'Oh, jealous now, are we?'

'Tell me when in December you started seeing her?' I brace myself for him to whack me, but I can't help it, I need to know.

'Don't worry, it was after you decided to leave me.'

'How long after?'

'Oh, let me think, about an hour to be precise.'

I shift along the sofa and stand up. 'Are you telling me you were with another woman, while I was bleeding…' I can't even bring myself to say it but an image of glass and blood on the kitchen floor flashes through my mind. If I'd not been able to knock the walkabout phone out of its cradle with the broom stick, I'd never have been able to call Becca. They said at the hospital that I could have bled to death from the deep cut in my leg.

'You didn't want to be with me so what are you complaining about?' He exaggerates a shrug.

'And you made damn sure I couldn't leave.'

'I gave you everything and you chucked it back in my face.'

'Because you're a bully.' I dart past him and dash to the hall but as I'm about to open the front door he grabs a handful of hair on the back of my head and tugs me sideways. I try and twist away but we crash into the coat stand and I scream, blood trickling down my face.

Chapter Sixty-Six

I wake up on Sunday to sunshine beating through the window. The air is thick with heat. A dog is barking relentlessly nearby. Amy is sitting in almost the same position she was in before I fell asleep.

'Morning,' she says.

'Have you slept?'

'Yeah, for a little while. You might want to have a look at what I've found out about Mr Adams. It took quite a bit of digging but guess what? He was dismissed from his job as a teacher.' She grins, triumphant.

'Really? I wondered why he was working for the local council.'

'He was a supply teacher in another secondary school after ours, around four years ago. Somewhere in Northampton.'

Suddenly, I'm wide awake.

'And he was sacked because…?'

'He was accused of having a relationship with a pupil.' She raises her eyebrows at me, as though I can guess the rest.

'Oh!' I sit upright.

'She was seventeen and her name was Gemma Brown.'

'You're fucking joking me?' I practically leap out of bed.

'Nope, I'm afraid not.'

'What year was that?'

'They met in winter 2014.'

'A few months after he left our school?'

'Yep. They started a relationship and fled to America on a long holiday in spring 2015. Las Vegas to be precise. It wasn't pursued because his contract ended and Gemma turned eighteen while they were away. They got married and came back to Bedford.'

'She's almost the same age as me? She never said.'

'She told you about this?'

'She said he whisked her off to Vegas and sprang the marriage on her. But I assumed she was almost thirty, I mean the way she dresses, long skirts, baggy tops.'

'Maybe he doesn't like her dressing her age.'

'Or he doesn't let her. So hang on, before he met her he was flirting with me when I was fifteen going on sixteen.'

'So it could have been you.'

'Shit. Makes you wonder what would have happened if he'd stayed at our school.'

'I think you had a lucky escape.'

'Now he's bored with me he's probably got some other girl in the picture.' I stand by the open window, but when I look down the ground is swimming. I stagger back a few steps. I take in a breath and let it out slowly and the light-headedness passes. Mum is in the garden sweeping up multicoloured streamers. I picture the moment everyone set them off with a bang last night, all at the same time. And now the mess that is left after that tiny moment of joy.

'Seventeen is still a child in the eyes of the law, especially as he was an adult in a position of trust.' I sit on the bed.

'But he got away with it because he was a supply teacher on a short contract. Away from the school she was a consenting adult.'

'Thinking back now, he was always friendly and flirty. I didn't do anything with him back then except a kiss. He must have moved onto her straight after me and taken it further. I could be in Gemma's position right now.'

I was flattered that he paid so much attention to me, always singling me out. I was desperate to please him and he must have known that. I started getting up earlier in the mornings, taking longer in the bathroom, doing my hair, making up my face in a natural way, emphasizing my eyes. I'd been out with a couple of the older boys, but Mr Adams, or Cole as he told me to call him, was so much more mature.

One day I got upset because of stuff going on at home. I confided in him that I didn't know who my dad was and that sometimes my mum drank a lot and went out. When she came home, it was with a different man every time. Cole had put his arms around my shoulders, and it felt natural for me to put my arms around him too.

'I'll always be here for you if you ever need to talk,' he'd said. I'd breathed in his Gio aftershave on his soft jumper. I felt so safe in his arms. I craved the protection and warmth he offered me when he held me like that. I was sorry when he pulled away, but he looked at me with those sea-green eyes that seemed to draw me in and wiped away my tears gently with his thumbs. He'd really seemed to care about me.

For ages after, there was an invisible barrier between us, as though neither of us intended anything to happen, but the tension in the air would have told you otherwise. I was the first to brush his hand with mine while reaching for a book. The feeling of touching his bare skin was electric, so much so my body jumped. He drew his hand away, but in the next moment, he stroked my cheek as his finger moved a strand of hair from my face. His hand was trembling ever so slightly, but in that second, I knew he fancied me as madly as I fancied him. I touched his leg and he leaned over to me and shut his eyes and ever so gently his lips landed on mine. Mr Newman saw us and banged on the window, coughing loudly. We sprang apart, pretending nothing had happened. But Mr Newman beckoned to Cole. I left the library walking on air, all the way home.

Cole texted me the next morning that he had to leave immediately. His mother was sick, he said. I knew Mr Newman must have told him to go before he got the sack. I didn't see him again after that. Until eight months ago.

I was underage, but he made sure his next victim wasn't.

Chapter Sixty-Seven

12 August 2018

Scarlett

I press my forehead with the heel of my hand. I wish I hadn't drunk so much last night. 'Let's go and help Mum finish clearing up, she's out there on her own.'

As we come downstairs, Tina arrives to take Amy back to the B&B.

'Hope you enjoyed your party.' She hugs me.

'It was fun, thanks.'

'What's the long face for then?'

Amy touches her forehead.

'Oh, I see. Hangover.' Tina laughs and hands me an envelope. 'It's not much, but I hope you like it.'

'Thank you.' I rip the paper off and take out a leather bookmark embossed with a rose. 'It's beautiful, thank you.'

Tina follows us out to the garden and helps Mum take down the bunting while Amy and I cook a late breakfast. Mum and Tina are chatting. I hope it's the beginning of them being friends again. It's weird them not getting along. When we were growing up, they used to share picking us up from pre-school then primary school. We spent so much time together, summer holidays to Devon and Wales, weekends away to Norfolk. We were like a family.

Amy switches the egg off and turns over the bacon and sausages.

'How many more times?' Mum suddenly shouts at Tina. 'I've said no and I mean no.'

Amy and I stop what we're doing and glance at each other. We can't quite hear what Tina says back but she's shaking her head, hands on hips. Neither of us wants to move nearer the window in case we interrupt them.

'I've told you before, she must never know. Promise me, Tina.' Mum's voice is shrill and pleading.

'It's her right, Kelly, and you damn well know it.' Tina kicks the plastic bucket that contained all the booze last night and marches into the kitchen. We pretend to be busy and unaware of them arguing.

'We're going, Amy, come on.'

'What about breakfast?' Amy looks longingly at the grill.

'I said, we're going. Now.' Tina is talking to Amy, but her eyes fix on me for a long moment. Then she shakes her head and drags her gaze away.

I nod at Amy that it's okay, even though she doesn't have to go because she's not a child, but I don't want to add fuel to Tina's fury.

The house is quiet when they've gone. Mum and I are left on our own with the radio on low in the background.

I dish up breakfast and we eat it slowly without speaking. I finish first and make filter coffee, all the time wondering what to say.

'You promised you'd tell me something about Dad today.' I stare into the empty mugs, waiting for her to bite my head off.

'Not you as well.' She puts away the butter and jam. 'I'll tell you one thing. Then don't pester me for more, okay?'

I sigh and sit down. She sits opposite me and takes my hands in hers.

'I'm sorry, but your dad did something I can never forgive.'

'Is that it? Is that the best you can do? I think I worked that out for myself.' I scrape my stool back, ready to stand up.

'He did a *terrible* thing. Can we leave it at that?'

'He's still my dad. Why is it up to you to decide what I should or shouldn't know? I'm not a kid any more. Is that what you were arguing about with Tina?'

'It's not going to do you any good knowing, believe me.'

'Don't you think I deserve the truth?'

'She thinks I should tell you. But sometimes the truth destroys lives.'

'Well, that's for me to judge. You need to tell me where he is because it's up to me if I want to see him, and you can't stop me.'

'No, I can't. But I'll tell you this much – he's in prison for what he did, and I hope he rots there.'

'What?' I tip back on my stool and almost fall off.

'This is why I didn't want to tell you anything.' She starts crying.

'You may as well. I'm going to do my best to find out anyway.'

'Please don't go digging. I've tried so hard to keep him out of our lives.'

'Is he in for a long time then?'

She raises her eyebrows but doesn't answer.

I wander upstairs and have a shower then sit on my bed in a towel. How has my life come to this? In less than twenty-four hours the two men in my life have let me down. They're both complete losers. If I have criminal blood in me, it's time to see where it can get me. I FaceTime Amy.

'Tomorrow's the day.'

Amy puts her mug down. A knowing smile sparks up her eyes.

'Cole is going to wish to God he hadn't crossed me.'

Chapter Sixty-Eight

13 August 2018

Scarlett

I'm so looking forward to making Cole suffer. We check the laptop for the goings on in the nursery. Gemma is in there feeding the baby. She told me before she left work that she's taking three weeks maternity leave then intends to go back to work part time for six months.

Amy and I go shopping for supplies first. I'm dressed in a plain T-shirt and jeans, my bank card in my back pocket, loaded with birthday money. We buy a sim-free pay-as-you-go mobile phone from Argos with enough credit for a week. I switch off our location. I want to be able to see what's going on in the world, but I don't want the world to find us. Amy will have to keep her laptop off but we can use my tablet. I stash everything in the boot of my car ready for later.

We check the nursery again and sure enough, Gemma has her shoes on and is dressing the baby in a T-shirt and terry-towelling shorts. I'm going to miss my shift this evening. I liked working there but I'll be fired after today. We make our way down to the shops. It's much busier than it normally is, which is good for us. Lots of kids running around with Peppa Pig or Paddington Bear helium balloons and a merry-go-round has been set up outside the library. A good distraction for mums and tots who otherwise might notice us. From our observations, Gemma seems to be a creature of habit, so we're banking on her sticking to her new routine.

First, she goes into the baker's and has a cup of tea. She sits in the same chair near the front and always dusts off her seat before she sits on it. If the baby is awake, she unstraps him from the buggy and cradles him across her knee. One of the waitresses brings over a small bowl of hot water. She sits the bottle in it for five minutes, then she feeds him. Next, she straps him back in the buggy and wanders a few doors along the high street to browse in the bookshop. By this time the baby is back to sleep, and it's her opportunity to go food shopping.

While we're waiting for Gemma to come back out, I text Mum to say I'm at a friend's house tonight.

> What friend?

Mum texts back.

> Rachel. She was at my party, but I don't think you met her. Amy's with me too.

> OK, let me know when you're coming back.

> Will do.

Except I won't because that phone will be switched off. Maybe I could send her a text from my new phone? Better not.

I'm the first to spot Gemma coming out of the bookshop. She's been browsing for ages. Amy stands up, walks around in circles, stabbing her finger at her phone. Gemma is carrying a paper bag full of books. She chucks it in the mesh basket under the pram.

I follow her round the supermarket and before long she's stressed out because the baby has woken up. By the time her basket is overflowing, the baby is full-on crying. Time to conveniently bump into her.

'Are you okay?' I touch her arm as she joins a long queue to the tills. She spins round and seems surprised but relieved to see me.

'Oh, hello, Rosie. Bit frazzled with this little one. Taking some getting used to.' She attempts to tidy her hair. Her face is pale without make-up and the circles under her eyes are purple, almost like bruises. I push aside the tiny tug at my heart and remember why I am doing this.

'I never seem to make it round the shop before he wakes up. He always cries when the buggy stops moving.'

'Poor little boy.' I lean over him and pull a smiley face then offer him my thumb which he grabs hold of with his hot little hand. For a moment he quietens down. The second I take my hand away his cries go up an octave as if I've hurt him.

The queue is not moving. Everyone tuts when the cashier presses the buzzer for help. Gemma jiggles the pram back and forth. Now's my chance.

'Looks like a spillage,' I say, leaning round the tall man in front.

'Oh no.' She looks at her basket of shopping then either side to see if there are any shorter queues.

'Can I help at all?'

She looks at me in a daze. I wonder if she's had any sleep.

'I could push him round for you, see if he dozes off? I can wait for you outside, just by that bench?'

'Oh God, could you? Do you mind?'

Not a moment's hesitation.

'Honestly, I'd love to. He's so adorable.'

'You're a lifesaver.' She smiles weakly and peels her handbag off the handle then watches me take hold of it, put my sunglasses back on and wheel him away. I turn round and wave and she waves back. My heart pitches at my deceit. I stroll towards the exit, aware that she'll still be watching me for as long as she can.

I pass Amy who pretends to be browsing the magazine stand. She will join me in a while, but she's going to stay and watch, see what Gemma does when she can't find me. If she tries to call my mobile, it will be switched off.

Moments later, I am out of the door and merging into the crowd in the precinct. Parents and children gathered around the merry-go-round are so taken up with the ride, they don't notice me disappear into the market. I take the opportunity to skirt round them and straight down the road to the multi-storey car park nearest the main shopping centre. Who knew taking a baby could be so easy?

Chapter Sixty-Nine

13 August 2018
Scarlett

'Did you see anyone look at you on the way out?' Amy asks when she meets me in the car park.

'No, I kept my head down. You know we'll be caught on CCTV, though.'

'Yes. but hopefully not for a while.' She climbs in the back seat next to baby Thomas, thankfully asleep in the pram car seat.

'Once they've gone through the whole tape for today, they'll realize it's us.'

'Cole will have confessed about me by then.'

For a moment we freeze at the sound of police sirens.

Hurriedly, I fold up the pram and lift it into the boot. I pass the bag of baby paraphernalia to Amy. As I join them in the back again, I check out of the windows. We're tucked away in a corner on the open roof level so there's hardly anyone around. The baby wakes up just as I shut the door with a gentle click. He lays there quietly staring up at us, occasionally kicking his feet and lifting his arms. I bend down and sniff the air around him. A strong urine smell knocks me back. I glance at Amy. I don't fancy changing him on my own. She pulls out the new pack of nappies, wipes and disposable changing mats, and between us we clean him up. Hopefully there will be as few cars as possible passing by and noticing us, especially on a Monday. As long as we don't have a screaming baby on our hands, I think we'll be okay.

Once Thomas is clean, I tear open the box of first baby milk. Six pre-sterilized ready-to-feed bottles of formula with six teats. I shake one up. Amy holds him in her arms and feeds him. He guzzles it down. I climb into the front and switch the radio on low. The clock beams the time at me. It's twenty-two minutes since I left the supermarket. My pulse is thudding in my head. Gemma will be frantic by now, searching up and down the high street for me and her precious boy, calling out, 'Where's my baby?' screaming my name, stopping anyone who has a pram to check it's not hers, panting breathlessly as she pulls and pushes these strangers when she can't find him, as though it's their fault he's gone missing. I try to block out these running images in my head and focus on why we're doing this. How crazed Cole will be when he finds out. He'll be forced to admit to his wife that he was in a relationship with me. I won't let him pretend it didn't happen, that I wasn't important to him.

'She'd have called Cole by now, wouldn't she?' I ask. 'He'll be panicking, trying to phone me. Sorry that he lied to me and treated me like dirt.'

'She was trying to call someone when I left. I guess it would have been you she tried first.'

I dread to think how many missed calls there will be from her. Nausea sweeps through me. This is so much harder than I imagined. Maybe I could drop her a quick message to say we got held up somewhere, just so she knows Thomas is okay?

I take out the new mobile and tap into someone's open WiFi signal. It's coming up to 3.29 p.m. I click on the BBC website and read:

New item filed two minutes ago: BABY SNATCHED FROM BEDFORD SUPERMARKET.

My heart crashes against my chest. I almost can't bear to scroll down, but I have to. The story is so new but completely over-blown in just a few sentences.

> *Gemma Adams, a new mother from Bedford, left her newborn baby in the care of her employee outside Sainsbury's supermarket this afternoon. Both employee and baby have since been reported missing. It is believed the young woman, Rosie Symonds, which is not believed to be her real name, offered to look after the crying infant while Gemma finished her shopping. Gemma maintains that Rosie is a kind and trustworthy individual who would not harm an infant.*
>
> *Baby Thomas, who went missing in his pram around 2.55 p.m., is just five days old. The girl, Rosie, agreed to mind Thomas and wait outside the supermarket with him, but when Gemma couldn't find them, she became distressed and passers-by helped her to look for them, but they could not be located. The police are concerned for the welfare of both baby Thomas and Rosie Symonds and are asking the public to come forward with any information that may lead to their whereabouts.*

I pass the phone to Amy. I didn't think they'd find out it's not my real name so quickly. The sun has moved round, it's even hotter than earlier in the day. A beam of light is shining through the front windscreen, a celestial finger pointing at us to let everyone know where we are. Thomas starts to grumble. Amy passes him to me so she can read the news on my tablet. I've never held a baby before. I turn the radio up and rock him in my arms. The movement settles him down so I carry on rocking him back and forth about fifty times until I think my arms will drop off.

'The police are after us.' Amy puts the tablet down and I hand Thomas back to her.

'But Gemma knows he's safe with me.' I check on Twitter and we watch the live news feed.

'*Police have released CCTV footage of Rosie Symonds walking at pace, pushing Thomas in the pram towards the exit and out of the supermarket. Detective Inspector Rachel Read is with me now. What can the public do to help?*

'"*Although we can't see her face clearly in the footage, partly because of the large sunglasses she's wearing, we're asking for anyone who recognizes anything about this woman to come forward. She is aged twenty-one, with mid-length blonde hair, slim build and approximately five feet seven tall. Any members of the public who saw this woman pushing a distinctive green BABYZEN pram should contact the police as soon as possible. Time is of the essence in cases such as this. We're in what we call 'the golden hour', the first hour after anyone goes missing, which is when we're most likely to find the person, child or in this case, baby, alive and well.*"

'*Thank you, Inspector Read. Let's go over live to our reporter who is outside the Adams' family home in Bedford.*'

'Oh God, we've only borrowed him! She said I could take him for a walk. She knows he's with me. I'm not going to hurt him.'

'Not how they see it, I suppose, because you didn't wait where you said you would.'

'Great. We need to sit tight.'

'Do you think Cole's been told yet?'

'I hope so. I only wanted him to suffer.'

I reach to the passenger seat for a two-litre bottle of water. Even though the window is open, the car is stuffy because there's no breeze. 'We need to save most of this, I'm not sure when it'll be safe to get out of here.'

Amy scrolls down the tablet and finds another news report. They're repeating the same information in every outlet, which means they don't have anything else to go on at the moment. Or if they do, they're not saying so. One reporter is outside Cole's house. I picture him strolling along the road with his bottle of wine in a plastic bag, not having a clue what's going on. I want them to show his reaction, I need to see him affected by this otherwise none of it is worth it.

Thomas starts crying again. I suggest another bottle, but Amy lifts him up and gently pats him on the back. He lets out a burp and soon after he closes his eyes.

'Where did you learn to do that?' I'm in awe.

We turn back to the news. '*The police spokesperson says the parents are distraught but will be making an appeal for Thomas's safe return in the next hour or so. They're asking for Rosie to come forward as soon as possible.*'

Amy and I look at each other. I wonder if Cole has named me as prime suspect yet. Will he have worked out that I'm the person who's been working for his wife? Who fed his cat while he was away? But he knows that as soon as he gives them my real name, they will start looking into why I've done this. He'll have to explain to Gemma and the police who I am and how he knows me. With any luck, it will ruin him.

Chapter Seventy

13 August 2018

Scarlett

'Hey, do you know what? They've still only got this down as one person being with Thomas. Why don't you go back to your mum's, then you'll be right out of it.' I check the rear-view mirror. There's no one around. We're only a short walk from Sainsbury's and I'm hoping they won't think of looking in car parks for a while as I was on foot.

'What – and leave you here to face this on your own?' Amy's face crumples.

'You've got time to get away. You don't need to get into trouble for me, you've done enough already.'

'No, I won't do that. We're in this together. You've always helped me.'

'But his beef is with me not you. Save yourself. It won't be long before they track us down.'

'No. I'm staying.'

I shake a new bottle of milk from the box, ready for when Thomas wakes up.

We wait for the next news bulletin. We'll need to go easy on how much we use the phone because there is no way of charging it up unless we start the car up and I don't want to draw attention to us. I have one battery pack as back-up, but it will only get us through a few hours at most.

Thomas wakes up crying, I chuck the throw over the back seat and Amy leans into it while she feeds him. I don't want her to get in trouble for me, but I am not going to lie, I'm grateful she's stayed. I'm not sure I'd cope with a baby on my own.

'It's gone 4 p.m., past their so-called golden hour.'

I switch on the pay-as-you-go mobile and wonder if Mum has listened to the news yet. She'll be one of those mothers pulled up close to the TV screen so as not to miss a word, tissue in hand. I wish I could tell her not to worry.

I click on a new update on Sky.

'*Was this woman delivering the baby into the hands of a man seen loitering outside the shop?*'

They show a CCTV clip of a man smoking a cigarette, leaning against a lamppost outside Sainsbury's. Then he's checking around him, moving position in the same spot as though waiting for someone. When I stride out of the shop pushing the pram, he appears to stub out his cigarette and go off in the same direction as me.

'Shit,' Amy says.

'What? It's good they're barking up the wrong tree.'

Amy shows me Cole's cloned Facebook page to see how many of his friends have liked it. Over fifty. Quite a few. There are loads of likes and funny comments for the photos of him as a kid. The baby has finished his feed and is wide awake and seems content.

'We could post something about the baby – him wondering why someone has targeted him. See if any of his friends can guess?'

'Have a look on his original page first, see if there's anything about it.'

He's posted in the last twenty minutes in large shouty text.

OUR NEWBORN BABY THOMAS WAS TAKEN FROM GEMMA THIS AFTERNOON WHILE SHE WAS IN THE SHOPS!!! CAN YOU FUCKING BELIEVE IT? PLEASE, IF ANY OF YOU KNOW WHO THIS WOMAN IS

– ROSIE SYMONDS – THEN PLEASE TELL
ME OR GEMMA OR THE POLICE AS SOON
AS POSSIBLE SO WE CAN GET THOMAS
BACK SAFELY. IF THIS SICKO IS READING
THIS MESSAGE, YOU'RE TEARING US UP
HERE, PLEASE BRING HIM BACK SAFE
AND SOUND. (Please share this message far and
wide. Link below to news story).

I type a new post on his cloned Facebook page:

Our baby is missing and it's all my fault – do you think
Gemma will ever forgive me?!

'Good one,' Amy says. I switch the phone off and rummage around in our bags for something to eat. Everything with chocolate in it has half melted. We open all the windows an inch or two, then lock the doors and settle down for a nap.

Amy and I sleep sitting up either side of Thomas in his car seat.

At ten minutes to five, the vibrating phone alarm wakes us. We move to the front seats without disturbing Thomas who remains asleep in the back. Someone in a car on the level below us is playing loud Bob Marley music. The beat to 'No Woman, No Cry' is both soothing and uplifting. Amy is being a proper mother hen checking on Thomas over her shoulder every few minutes. We decide that if he's not awake in half an hour, we'll gently rouse him for his next feed. The last thing we need is a screaming baby.

Amy switches on the tablet for the early evening news. The missing baby is the lead story. The reporter is at the news conference where Cole and Gemma sit behind a huge table looking haggard. My God, this has gone way too far. I didn't mean to hurt her like this. And he's acting like he doesn't know what's going on. They're not sitting that close or holding hands as I would have expected under these circumstances. Alongside them sits a very upright chief inspector in front of hordes of press. The camera flashes seem to disorientate Gemma. She holds her arm up in front of her face.

I remember when I was younger and hearing about the case of the toddler who went missing while on holiday with her parents. How the mother seemed stiff and emotionless. Far too controlled so that people pointed the finger at her. These journalists will be watching their every move just as carefully, waiting for one of them to put a foot wrong, gauging the possibility that one or both of them is guilty of harming their own baby, making out it's been abducted, when in reality there is no third party involved – it's all measured on a scale of how distraught they appear.

Gemma's eyes are small and red as though they've sunk into her head. She's clutching a small blue rabbit we've seen in Thomas's cot through the nursery monitor. Cole comes across as frosty, angry, shifty in his seat. He still hasn't shaved. The skin on his nose is a comical red, burnt and peeling from the sun.

The inspector runs through the facts of the case, his voice monotone, still only citing one woman as a possible suspect.

Gemma stands up, glances at Thomas's picture behind her, then takes a deep breath.

'*Our darling baby boy…*' Her voice breaks. She clears her throat and starts again. '*Our darling baby boy Thomas was taken from me…*' Her chin trembles, and she stares at the page. Nick touches her elbow and helps her sit down. He stands up and takes the piece of paper and starts reading.

'*Our son Thomas is out there somewhere with a girl called Rosie, except that's not her real name. I don't know why she tricked Gemma and didn't bring him back when she promised to. Gemma made the mistake of trusting her.*'

Gemma stands up again and nods at Nick who hands the paper back to her. She places it on the table and speaks without looking at it.

'*Wherever you are, Rosie, whatever the reason for taking our baby, please, please bring him back to us, please just bring him home, safe and… unharmed,*' she sobs, covering her mouth with the back of her hand. She glances down at the piece of paper then up at the journalists.

She takes a deep breath, tears running down her face.

'*I'm begging you, Rosie, please bring our baby back.*' Her voice is shrill now. '*We miss him so much. We love you, Thomas.*' She buries her face in her hands.

Nick stands again and links his arm through hers. He passes her a hanky from his pocket and they sit down together. A long moment passes before the inspector speaks. He points to the pixilated blown-up photo of me, my sunglasses obscuring my face. Fear shoots through my veins. I'm going to be in so much trouble.

Cole puts his arm around her shoulders. His other hand covers his eyes as he breaks down.

'Crocodile tears. He must know it's us.' Amy and I nod at each other, then fix back on the screen. One of the reporters asks if there's anyone that could wish them or their child any harm. If they have any enemies. They both shake their heads and say no. Cole is more hesitant. He looks right down the camera, as though he's looking straight at me like he did at my party, with the same lying eyes. I shiver. The camera cuts away.

Chapter Seventy-One

13 August 2018
Scarlett

It's stuffy in the car, even though the windows on both sides are open.

'Do you think the baby's okay? He's been asleep for ages.'

'I don't know.' I get up on my knees and lean between the two front seats. His eyes are shut, hair sweaty. It smells like his nappy is either full or has leaked. I touch one of his podgy legs. It's cold and clammy. That can't be right.

'He feels weird.'

'What do you mean, weird?' She clambers through to the back.

'Cool skin, but sweaty.'

She touches his forehead. 'His head is drenched.'

'Shouldn't we wake him up?'

'Some babies sleep a lot. It's really hot in here.'

'Gemma goes in the nursery every few hours to feed him. Maybe we've not fed him enough?'

'What, you've kept an eye on them at night?' Her eyes widen.

'Only if I couldn't sleep. I was curious.'

She hauls herself up and peers in the bag on the parcel shelf. 'He needs clean clothes and a clean sheet.'

'We haven't got any clean sheets.'

'A spare T-shirt or muslin cloth will do.'

I scratch around in our bag of stuff and pull out a spare muslin square.

Amy lifts Thomas up. He's floppy but his eyes are open. His cry is low and grizzly.

'I'll open some more milk.' I'm more than happy for her to take charge. I don't know the first thing about babies.

'Open that packet of baby wipes so I can freshen him up. He stinks.' She undresses him and wipes down his peachy skin all over then puts a nappy on him and drapes the clean muslin around his body. He's not looking his usual bright self.

'What's wrong with him?' I hand her the milk. He turns his head away at first, then roots around for the teat. Once he's found it, he guzzles like mad.

'Maybe he's a bit dehydrated.'

'He's not going to die, is he?' I press my thumping forehead. Amy smiles. 'He's a bit dozy, that's all.'

'We should take him back soon. He's such hard work.' Why anyone bothers having babies beats me. I bet I was a handful. No wonder Mum only had one. I pass Amy a breakfast bar and take one for myself. I think about switching my usual phone on. Mum will be expecting to hear from me by now. I hope she's not seen the grainy picture of me on the news. If anyone is going to guess who it is, it will be Mum, or Tina come to that.

I read as many papers as I've got access to online. I'm buzzing that the press vultures have already started digging the dirt on Cole, even lifting photos from his new Facebook page. One rogue digital publication has gone into detail about how Cole and Gemma met, outing them as 'the' notorious teacher and former pupil who ran away to Las Vegas to get married without telling her parents. I'm sure the other papers will soon pick up on it too, so when it goes mainstream he'll be reluctant to tell them about me because he'll know what's coming.

I click refresh and a news headline I've not seen pops up.

MAN OUTSIDE SUPERMARKET NOT BELIEVED TO BE CONNECTED WITH THE DISAPPEARANCE OF BABY THOMAS.

The man spotted on CCTV outside the supermarket where five-day-old baby Thomas Adams went missing this afternoon has come forward. He claims to have been waiting outside the store for his wife, who went in to buy a newspaper and two bottles of cold water, it has been confirmed. More CCTV footage of the girl, Rosie Symonds, walking along the high street pushing a pram has been shown on all the major news channels and social media. Images of her suspected accomplice have also been shared.

'Is it time to post up the picture of you and him?' Amy reads my mind. She opens his cloned Facebook account on the tablet.

'The selfie of us in the park, the one with his top off, me lying next to him, back half to the camera. That'll give him some explaining to do when his wife sees it.'

'And the police. They might just be interested in his intimate relationship with the woman who's supposedly abducted his baby.'

She selects the photo from the cloud and uploads it to his new page. We wait to see what the reaction is.

Public opinion is already shifting about them on Twitter. Some people seriously doubting the sincerity of Cole's plea at the press conference. Others blaming Gemma for leaving her baby with someone she didn't know that well. One single mother goes on a full-blown rant about how she manages to go shopping with her kids in tow, so what makes Gemma so special that she can't manage it with one tiny baby? A few people are beyond ruthless coming up with their own theories as to what's really happened, accusing them of killing their baby and attempting to cover it up by inventing a story of some woman taking him to hide their heinous crime.

It's strange how deliciously enjoyable revenge is. But it's disturbing how all these strangers feed on someone else's misfortune. We only have the luxury of enjoying Cole's discomfort because we know baby Thomas is safe and well. Gemma unfortunately is collateral damage. I do feel bad for her, but she has the man I wanted. I worshipped him. My use of the past tense saddens me, but it's true. We are so over.

There are already one or two people on Twitter who have picked up on the rogue news thread about Cole having been a teacher. One has moved on from their initial horror that a baby was left in the care of someone who then took him, to outrage that this man was allowed to continue a relationship with a former pupil, marry her and have a baby. A women's group have replied to the tweet, openly stating their concern for Gemma's welfare, questioning if she really wanted to stay in a relationship with a man they believe has shown signs of controlling behaviour. On the back of this, a couple of people wonder if Gemma's done something to the baby herself to get all this attention. As some kind of desperate plea for help. Some people are really sick.

'They've got a point about Cole, though.' Amy takes her glasses off and wipes her sweaty face with a baby wipe.

'Yeah. Bloody control freak. It was always him deciding when we should meet, what I should do. Everything was on his terms.'

'Then he was quick to turn on you when you made out you were pregnant because he wasn't in control any more.' Amy opens her door to try and get more air circulating.

'I thought it meant he really cared about me, that he was showing what a gent he was taking charge. Old-fashioned, isn't it? The man making all the decisions.'

'That's one way of looking at it.'

'He's more worldly wise than me, so it didn't feel strange to let him take the lead, to start with anyway.' I check over my shoulder. Thomas is still asleep, so I click on the tablet. 'Let's see if the baby cam is picking anything up.'

There's no one in the baby's room but the door is half open so we can see a small part of the stairs and the landing. I'm about to switch it off again when I hear a strange indistinguishable noise, a bit like a cat's wail. 'Was that Missy?'

'Don't know. It didn't sound good.' Amy turns up the volume.

'Maybe she's trapped somewhere.'

We strain to hear, but it's quiet again. Then a shout startles us and something clatters to the ground. Amy and I stare at each other open-mouthed. I hold the tablet closer, turn the volume up as high as it will go, trying to make out what's being said. I picture their hallway, was it the coat stand by the front door falling over? My pulse is pounding in my ears, I'm desperate to see what's going on. Amy glances at me but doesn't say a word.

'*Come here now, you stupid bitch.*' Cole's voice is guttural, vicious.

'*Get away from me,*' Gemma screams.

'*She's trying to get at me through you and Thomas. And you fell for it.*' There's a loud hard sound like a slap.

'Bastard, leave her alone,' I shout at the screen, but they can't hear me. Amy clicks the tablet's record button on.

'*I can't believe you actually gave her our baby.*' His words sound like a growl through his teeth.

'*I mean, what kind of imbecile does that? You, that's who. You're such a useless piece of shit.*'

Something smashes.

Footsteps pound up the stairs and Gemma bursts into the nursery. My heart stops. There's blood running down her cheek. Fear and panic are etched on her face. Cole leaps upstairs two at a time. She squeals as she tries to shut the door, but he is right behind her. His hand shoots out and pushes hard against the door. It opens wide, cracking against the wall. Gemma runs to the other side of the room screaming. Cole fills the whole doorway. He throws himself at her, punching and kicking her body, half off camera but there's no denying what he's doing to her. Gemma cries out, helpless she curls into a tight ball.

'Get off her!' I scream and amazingly he stops. He can hear me. He picks up the baby monitor, looks closely at it, right at us and switches it off.

'Jesus fucking Christ, how did he hear me?'

'I flicked the mic on,' Amy says.

'What about Gemma? We need to call the police.' I picture her left in a heap on the floor.

'What have we done?' I brush tears from my cheeks with the back of my hand. Amy passes me the pay-as-you-go-phone and I make an anonymous call, giving all the details of what happened, their names and address, then I quickly hang up.

Tears are pouring down my face. Amy and I hug. She is crying too. Guilt is burning a hole through my heart. What a stupid selfish child I've been. I had no idea he was capable of that. I'm sorrier than I ever thought possible that we've caused Gemma so much grief. I'm beginning to question whether she wanted to stay with him at all. What if he wouldn't let her leave? Did he make her marry him? She was only eighteen. I think of the bruise I saw on her side when she was pregnant. I shudder. And what would he have done to me in the bathroom if I hadn't got out? Maybe outing him for who he really is will help Gemma in the long run. Whatever my punishment turns out to be at the end of this, it will be worth it to see him taken down.

Chapter Seventy-Two

Monday 13 August 2018

Gemma

I open my eyes. I'm on the floor of the nursery, curled in a ball. I'm light-headed, woozy like I'm drunk. I can't seem to move very much. My stomach and sides are throbbing in pain. Where's Thomas? I want my baby. I groan and touch my face, force myself to look at my wet fingers. The blood is sticky, drying in places. I groan, recalling fragments of Nick's attack on me. How long have I been lying here? I need my phone. Did I have it with me when I ran upstairs? I pat the carpet in front of me and to the side, but I can't find it. My legs hurt but I manage to move them a bit. Am I going to die here, in Thomas's room and never see him again?

There was a voice, someone shouting. I must be imagining it. But no, because he stopped. Nick stopped hitting me.

What happened to the man I fell in love with? How has he become this monster? He doesn't love me. He doesn't care. I thought he was changing now we'd had a baby. But he was seeing Rosie. I can't believe it. All these months when I was pregnant, he was sleeping with her. His pupil. Before me. Before he came to my school and tipped my world upside down.

I'd been annoyed when he'd first arrived. The new supply teacher, Mr Adams. I liked Mrs Winston, but she'd been signed off by her doctor for three months. He could tell I wasn't overly pleased about him being there and in his very first class he picked on me to read Juliet's part to his Romeo. Then he chose Martin of all people to take over and read the balcony scene with me. It was embarrassing. I hated him immediately for doing that to me. The one boy in the class who had a major crush on me. Nick asked for me to stay behind after class.

'I can tell you're not going to be my biggest fan, am I right?' he'd said, packing his books back in his man-satchel, tipping his head down to look at me. There'd been a little smile of amusement on his lips and it was hard not to smile back.

'Of all people to pick, sir,' I'd said, rolling my eyes.

'Oh, I didn't know there was a problem? I guessed from the way he was gazing at you reading that you two are an item?'

'No, we are not and never will be.'

'Oh, I'm sorry. Not your type then.'

'He's so immature and he follows me around everywhere, and now you've probably made it worse, sir.'

'Well, I'm sorry about that. Do you want me to have a little word with him?'

'Could you? I've tried to tell him in a nice way.'

'I think I know what to say.' He'd picked up his bag and walked with me down the corridor and all the girls walking past us looked on enviously. He was the new teacher on the block, and he'd noticed me. After that, he'd chatted to me at the end of most English lessons. We talked about books and characters and I told him about wanting to write a book one day. He told me I was talented and he took the time to read my work and discuss it with me. Sometimes he'd offer me a lift home, but I didn't think my parents would approve. But one day it was raining so hard, I accepted. He'd pulled up outside my house and the rain was so heavy we couldn't see out, like sheets of iron closing us in. We were cocooned in our own world.

'You're very beautiful and special to me, Gemma.' He'd traced a finger down my face and neck then leaned over and kissed me, and I'd kissed him back. After that it became a regular thing. We'd meet in his car every day after school and park up somewhere quiet off a country lane. Once when he dropped me off at home, my parents insisted on meeting him. I didn't tell them he was my teacher, but they didn't approve anyway. They said he was too old for me.

When his contract was coming to an end after three months, he asked me to move in with him. But in his final week, Mr Birch caught us kissing in an empty classroom and Nick was dismissed with immediate effect. He said the only way we could be together was to run away. Only I'd not known he meant run away to America and get married on my eighteenth birthday.

All the lies and cheating and hurting. I'm so, so tired. All I want is my baby son safely back in my arms.

Someone bangs on the front door. I can't move. Greg is calling my name. Shrill sirens in the distance are getting louder and louder.

I shut my eyes.

Chapter Seventy-Three

13 August 2018
Scarlett

'Did you record all of it?'

Amy nods.

'Good, because we're posting it on his Facebook page right now.'

'I'm with you all the way on that.'

'We'll stay here a bit longer, it's probably safer.'

'The only problem is how hot it gets in here and the exhaust fumes. If we could just wheel Thomas around, let him get some fresher air…'

'We can't risk it. We don't know who might see us.' I click on Cole's new Facebook page. There are loads of messages of support from his friends. Sickening how they all feel sorry for him and question Gemma's judgement. It's really not fair on her. I tricked her. She trusted me.

Most of them seem to have switched over to the new page because when Amy goes into his original page, there are hardly any comments about the baby. Someone has written: *See you over on your new page. Thinking of you guys at this dreadful time.* We click back on his new page which we've left open to the public and someone with the name, May The Force Be With You, who has some weird profile picture of a cat with a lightsaber has commented: *I know what you've been up to with those schoolgirls. There's a word for people like you mate.*

Amy posts the video on his page of him beating Gemma up with the caption: '*This is what I do to my wife behind closed doors.*'

I go on Twitter and search for the same name. It comes up straight away, same picture. @MayTheForceBeWithYou has written the same message in a tweet, adding the hashtags #missingbaby #findthomas #uselessfather I'm tempted to contact him (is it a man?) and spill everything, but much as I like his comment, I don't know who it is. It could be a trap.

I turn to the news channel for the 6.30 p.m. bulletin and whack the volume up so we can both hear it.

'*The welfare of Rosie Symonds, 21, who disappeared with the infant, Thomas Adams, from a shopping centre in Bedford this afternoon, is cause for serious concern, said Detective Sergeant Helen Seymour leading this case. Rosie is thought to be Scarlett Bates, using her middle name in an attempt to disguise her true identity. Ms Bates is a former pupil of Priory Secondary School where the father of the missing baby, Nicholas Adams, was a supply English teacher four years ago. Gemma Adams, mother of the missing child doesn't believe Ms Bates intends to cause Thomas any harm. She is pleading with her to bring him home. It's now three hours since he went missing. In the studio, we have a midwife and a doctor from the borough of Bedfordshire to discuss how such a young baby may not cope well in this heat and the harm being separated from his mother at such a young age could cause…*'

I switch it off. 'Shit!' I smack the steering wheel. 'Where is all the dirt on Cole about his pupil bride? That he's beaten her up in her own home. Have they airbrushed that out because he's a man?'

'They know it's us. We may as well give ourselves up.'

We change channel. The two chattering monkeys that present it are going on about drinking enough water when it's this hot and not to overexert yourself because it can be dangerous. Like der… Before the break, the camera flashes over to our mums sitting nervously next to each other, clearly waiting to be grilled.

'What the hell are they doing there?' I throw myself backwards. 'They're completely betraying us.'

'We don't know that. They won't understand our reasons for doing this because you haven't told them about you and Cole.' Amy lifts Thomas onto her shoulder and he lets out a big burp. 'Good boy.'

After the break, the camera pans round to one end of the news desk where Mum and Tina are sitting, both with long, serious faces.

'This is completely weird seeing them, isn't it?' I say.

'I know. Hello, Mum!' We point and laugh nervously.

I wave at the screen. 'Come on, Mum, you know we wouldn't do anything to hurt a baby.' Although I suppose technically we have, simply by taking him away from his mummy.

'*The police think your daughters have abducted baby Thomas, is that right?*' The male presenter looks down his nose at them, crosses his arms.

'*We don't know that they have, though, do we?*' Mum and Tina shake their heads.

'*Do you think it's possible they were coerced into taking the baby away from its mum?*'

'*I believe so.*' Mum nods. I've never seen her so subdued. She looks properly cautious.

'*Our girls wouldn't do anything like this unless someone was threatening them.*' Tina points at him.

'*Where do you think the girls are? Do you believe someone is holding them somewhere against their will?*'

'*Something must have happened to them otherwise they'd have come home by now,*' Tina says.

'*And what would you say to your daughter if she was watching?*'

Tina blinks at him then turns to the camera. '*Amy, you need to come straight home. If someone is holding you against your will, threatening to hurt you, I want you to scream the place down. I want you to come home safe.*' Her hand flies up to cover her mouth.

'*I understand that Amy spends a lot of time at Scarlett's house, is that right?*'

294

Tina and Mum exchange a brief glance then nod.

'*I work nights, well, at least I did until I lost my job,*' Tina says.

'*In fact, Amy has been living at Scarlett's house all summer, isn't that right?*' he asks leaning forward.

They nod again, looking puzzled, like they're not sure where he's going with this.

'*Would you say it's a particularly close friendship?*' His voice goes up a key. What is this idiot getting at?

'*They're close, yes, they go everywhere together. We love having Amy stay over to help Tina out.*' Mum is being a bit too eager. Can't she see he's trying to trip her up?

'*But do you think they've spent an unhealthy amount of time together?*'

'*What do you mean?*' Mum snaps.

'*Do you think they are a bad influence on each other?*' He tips his head back a little. His tone is deceivingly gentle. I've watched him interview people before. When he steeples his fingers, it means he's about to go in for the kill.

'*They're like sisters, that's all.*' Mum cocks her head to the side as though she's not quite caught his meaning yet.

'*Do you think they're keeping secrets from you both?*' He gently rubs his chin, the smug grin growing.

'*If they are, then we wouldn't know, would we?*' She gives him a fake smile. '*I suppose all girls that age keep certain things from their mums and only confide in their closest friends.*' A nervous laugh escapes Mum's lips. '*We all have secrets, don't we?*'

'*I suppose we do,*' he smiles widely but he doesn't stop there, '*your daughter certainly does.*'

'*What do you mean?*' Mum straightens in her seat.

'*Are you aware of an affair your daughter has been having with a married man?*'

'*No, she isn't. You should get your facts right.*' Mum points at him.

'*Is her boyfriend's name Cole?*'

'*I don't know what you're trying to imply here.*' She rolls her shoulders back, feathers ruffled.

'*For a young woman to discover that she was in a false relationship might destroy her self-confidence, don't you think?*'

'*What is he going on about?*' Mum pulls a face at Tina, who shakes her head.

'*Finding out her love is based on lies and deceit might cloud her judgement, push her to do things she wouldn't normally dream of doing.*'

The female presenter is frowning at him too.

'*What would you say to Scarlett if she were watching this?*'

Mum swivels on her chair to face the camera.

'*Come home, darling. Whatever anyone has made you do, you know I'll forgive you.*' She turns back to the presenters. '*Now then, I want to know what else he thinks my daughter is hiding from me.*' Mum jabs her finger at him.

The female presenter gives her colleague a warning stare. She glances to the side as if looking for help.

'*Okay, if you're ready to know the truth. Our sources tell us that until very recently, your daughter was in a relationship with Nicholas Adams, who was her English teacher at school several years ago and as you know, he is the father of baby Thomas. What do you say to that?*' He crosses his arms.

Mum's lips pull in tight.

'*His wife is Gemma Adams, and your daughter has been working at her restaurant under an assumed name. Their baby boy, Thomas, suddenly goes missing. Coincidence? I think not. And let's not forget that he's got form. The woman he is married to was also a former pupil of his.*'

'*What the…?*' Tina's face scrunches up.

'*Nick Adams' wife was pregnant at the same time he was in a relationship with* your *daughter. So now do you think it's possible she has abducted the infant? Do you think Scarlett could be out for revenge because he hasn't left his wife as he promised to?*' He rocks back in his chair, a self-satisfied smirk on his face.

The presenter leans forward and adds, '*Has your daughter been in a secret relationship with Mr Adams since she was at school?*'

'*Don't be ridiculous! You can't make wild accusations about my daughter like that.*'

'*Well, again, and you're welcome to deny it, but according to our sources, Nicholas is being questioned by police as we speak.*' He fixes his eyes on her, a smug grin on his thin lips.

The programme cuts to an advert before Mum's expletives can be heard.

'What just happened there?' I jump forward in my seat. The jolt shakes the car and sets Thomas off. He lets out a screaming cry.

'Scarlett, you scared him!' Amy jogs him up and down in her lap. His cries are mournful.

'I'm so sorry, little boy.' I tickle his foot but it makes him cry more and kick his legs.

The programme comes back on. Mum is still sitting there red-faced. Thomas calms down and dozes off again.

'*We've had lots of comments from viewers coming in. One here from Norma saying,* lock Nicholas Adams up and throw away the key. I was a headmistress for forty years and if he'd been a teacher at my school I'd have… *okay, I can't read that bit out. Here's another one, this is from Lewis, he says he knows you, Kelly.*' He looks up at Mum to check her reaction. Her smile has dropped, face ashen. '*He's asking how his beautiful little princess is? Oh, is this Scarlett's dad?*'

Mum's eyes have glazed over. She's staring into space. Is that really from my dad? *Lewis.*

Chapter Seventy-Four

'*I take it from his comment he's not in contact with her?*' The presenter looks stupidly at his co-presenter who is watching Mum closely. Tina strokes Mum's hand which looks rigid.

My phone flashes up to tell me the battery is on ten per cent. I dig out the car charger and start the engine desperately trying to hear if Mum says anything about my dad.

'Shut the windows, I need to hear.' We press the buttons at the same time. Mum can't seem to speak. She is shaking, as though she's sitting in a bath of ice.

'*Come on, let's get you home.*' Tina puts her arm around Mum's shoulders and helps her stand up, but she dips awkwardly as though her legs can't hold her.

The presenter turns to his colleague, '*Was it something I said?*' And the camera cuts to the weather girl standing by a packed Brighton beach and surrounded by children in brightly coloured costumes, holding ice creams.

'Do you think Mum's okay? Was that man really my dad? Is Lewis his name?'

'I don't know. Are they allowed to phone from prison?'

'I have to call her. Where's my mobile?'

'You can't, they'll pick up your signal.'

I'm taken aback, Amy hardly ever questions my decisions. She stares blankly at my stunned face.

'I could text her, though, couldn't I?'

'You'll still be using a signal and they'll be able to track us down.'

'I have to risk it. You saw the state of her.'

'You should have told her about you and Cole.'

'Don't tell me off. If I'd told her that he used to be my teacher she would have made me end it.'

'And how would that have been a bad thing? We may as well give ourselves up now. We've been stuck in here over three hours.'

'They're not going to let us just walk away from this, are they?'

'Cole's the one who's going to be in the most trouble.'

'We can explain that we didn't abduct him; Gemma wanted me to look after him.'

'But we didn't take him back.'

'We'll return him now, call the police to say where he is.'

'We're not leaving him anywhere on his own.'

'Okay, but we're staying put until I've texted Mum first, make sure she's all right and let her know the baby is fine.' I search the glove compartment for my phone and switch it on. In a few moments I'm bombarded with notifications, mainly from Gemma hours ago, worrying where I am, if Thomas is okay, and from Mum asking me what I'm doing going off with someone's baby, and telling me to call her immediately. There are a couple of messages from Cole, mainly calling me a bitch. They still hurt.

I text Mum saying I'm sorry for what I've done and asking how she is. I say I need to know the truth about my dad. I ask her if it was really him contacting the TV programme?

Amy reads out a news headline from the pay-as-you-go phone:

'*Footage of Nicholas Adams attacking his wife, Gemma Adams, at their home in Bedford, has come to light on social media. Police are appealing for him to come forward for questioning as well as in connection to allegations made of a relationship with his former pupil, Scarlett Bates.*'

I sit up straight. 'How do we give Thomas back to Gemma?'

Amy strokes Thomas's sweaty hair. 'We could tell the police where we are.'

As if answering us, he wakes up crying. It's a different, gut-clenching cry I've not heard before.

'Are you sure he's all right? That noise can't be normal.' His face is pink and his body red and blotchy.

'He needs his mum. It's sweltering in here.' Amy jogs him up and down, offers him his bottle but he won't settle.

'The exhaust fumes could be making him sick.'

'What if he's ill? We won't know what to do.'

'Right, let's work out how to get him home safely. It's time everyone heard my side of things anyway. You'll back me up about Cole, won't you?'

'You know I will, why else am I here?' She rolls her eyes.

My phone rings. It's Mum's number. I pick up immediately.

'Scarlett! Where are you? Are you okay?'

I swallow but can't shift the lump in my throat. 'Can you help us?'

'Of course, where are you?'

'I'm at the top of River Street car park.'

'Okay, I'm on my way.'

A car pulls up in the space right next to us. A woman with wizened skin is driving. She looks across at us then gets out and slams her car door shut. We look the other way so she doesn't see our faces, but Thomas won't stop crying. She taps on the window and peers in. We eyeball her but don't speak.

'What are you doing to that baby?' She jabs her finger at the glass. 'Are you that girl they're looking for? You're wicked taking a baby away from its mother.' She takes her mobile out and starts prodding at it.

'Belt up, we're outta here,' I shout at Amy. She straps Thomas in and pulls her seatbelt across as I let off the handbrake and back the car out.

I head straight for the exit, leaving the woman standing there shouting and waving at us. A car whizzes up the ramp towards us and blocks our path. My heart leaps into my mouth. It's Cole.

Chapter Seventy-Five

Scarlett

'How did he know we're here?' I yell and change gear, reversing again, trying to spin round but the woman is standing behind us in the way.

Cole jumps out of his car and runs after us calling my name. He thumps on the bonnet, shouting at me to stop. Spit lands on my window, his angry face screwed up and swearing. The woman runs up to him ranting and pointing at us. It buys us a few seconds when he's not watching what we're doing.

We lift out the pram's detachable car seat with Thomas strapped in it. He's drifting off to sleep but the jolting wakes him, and he starts crying. Amy puts a dummy in his mouth and his eyes close again as he sucks it. I spot the door to the stairs and wonder if Amy can make it across to them. I whisper 'Sorry' to Thomas and wish him a good life, one where he won't know anything of the past few hours.

'Where is he?' Cole's shout is laced with menace as he comes after me in the other direction, towards the low railing surrounding the roof. 'I swear to God if you've hurt him…'

Amy has made it to the double doors, keeping Thomas safely tucked behind her.

'You think I'm capable of hurting a baby?' I shout at Cole as he runs after me.

'Who knows with you?' he growls, getting closer.

'Shows how much you really think of me, doesn't it?' I yell. 'You never loved me, did you?'

'Get over yourself, Scarlett.'

'How did you find us?'

Cole pauses to catch his breath and laughs. 'You switched your phone back on, didn't you? I knew you would.'

'What? How could you tell?'

'I installed a tracking device on your mobile. How else do you think I knew when you were following me and going into my house?'

'Your wife gave me the key to feed your cat.'

'She's too trusting.'

'We saw what you did to her, you piece of shit.'

'Yeah?'

'Yeah, Cole – or should I call you Nick? We know all about you. We've been watching you through your baby monitor.'

'Well, you're no better than me, are you? Taking an innocent baby.'

'Your wife gave him to me to look after. I wanted to make you suffer.' He's closing in, pushing me backwards to the corner of the rooftop.

'You little bitch,' he hisses.

I jump up on the narrow ledge and lean against the railings shouting, 'Fuck you,' at the top of my voice. 'One day your poor baby will grow up and find out what a shit his father is.' My heart aches for baby Thomas. A warm breeze blows my hair around. I look down and my head swims at the sheer drop.

'How dare you.' He strides towards me and takes a swipe, forcing my back to press against the railings. My stomach is in my mouth at the sight of the small crowd gathering below.

Sirens ring out and a policewoman with a loud hailer calls my name. A crowd of people are standing with her looking up, shielding their eyes against the evening sun. I imagine my dad sitting in prison watching me on the news. His bad blood running through my veins. I took a baby to get revenge on a despicable man. I would never have done something like this before. Does it make me as bad as him? Why couldn't I have a normal daddy, one to love and guide me? I grip the railings suddenly winded at my loss, the huge gap from not having him there.

'Please come down,' Amy shouts, standing in the shadows by the doors to the stairs, still guarding Thomas.

'There he is. Don't you move.' Cole points to Amy. He glares at me, vengeful, hate in his eyes. The once handsome face is grotesque, his bad core seeping through to the outside. I've seen the monster that he really is, attacking women. How could I have thought I was in love with him? Why didn't I see that he was using me? That one day he would turn on me too.

'I hope you go down for what you did to your wife,' I yell.

'You slut.' He thrusts his fist into me knocking me off balance. I let go of the railing. A gut-curdling scream fills the air.

Chapter Seventy-Six

I should be falling to the ground, but Amy has lunged forward and grabbed my T-shirt so hard she scratches my skin with her long nails. She pulls me to her, her other arm anchored around the top of the railing. I hold onto her and sob uncontrollably at the relief that I'm still alive.

Cole is running towards Mum who is by the stairs with Thomas, screaming at me hysterically.

'Scarlett, come down from there, please.' She's almost incoherent.

Three policemen storm through the doors. Cole does an about turn and tries to get in his car, but two of the policemen catch up and restrain him, arresting him on the spot. The other policeman takes charge of Thomas.

Amy draws me away from the railings and helps me climb over to safety. I am shaking so much she hugs me again and I whisper to her, 'thank you,' and tug her hand, and she squeezes back.

'He tried to push my daughter over the edge!' Mum tells the policemen as she runs towards me. I fling my arms around her, crying all over again.

Mum pulls Amy into our hug. Tina arrives and runs over to us. She kisses Amy's face and hugs her.

'I don't understand why you did this?' Mum says.

'I wanted Cole to confess to Gemma about me, but then I found out he'd been lying to both of us and I wanted to hurt him.'

'Well, he's in big trouble for what he's done to Gemma and you.'

'But now I've made things worse for her.'

Mum hugs me again. 'I only wish you could have told me about him.'

'I knew you'd be angry.'

'You have to tell the police everything that's happened between you to help your case and hers.'

For once I don't know what to feel except relief. I hope Gemma's okay. I'm glad for her and for myself. We are both rid of him.

Chapter Seventy-Seven

13 August 2018

Gemma

I wake up in hospital and the first thing I see when I open my eyes is Mum's smiling face.

'There you are. How are you feeling?' Mum strokes my hair away from my forehead. Her skin is cool and smells of tea tree and lavender.

'Hello, love, good to have you back.' Dad kisses my cheek.

'Thomas, where's Thomas?' I try to sit up, but Mum pats my arm and I lie back down.

'It's okay, he safe. He's right here with me.' Mum lifts him out of his pram and settles him on the bed under my arm. 'Here's your mummy, poppet.'

'Hello, little one. I've been so worried about you.' I kiss his head and my tears come hot and fast.

'Isn't he a handsome chap.' Dad's cheeks are pink, eyes watery.

'How are we doing here, Gemma?' a nurse asks, coming over. 'Oh, is this Thomas? Isn't he a heartbreaker.'

Just like his dad, I half expect one of them to say.

'Can I get you any painkillers?'

'Please. My chest hurts when I breathe and the pain in my side is going right through me.'

'That's because you've got five broken ribs, my darling. You're lucky one didn't puncture a lung.'

'Any other damage?' I daren't ask but I'm hurting all over.

'Black eye, cuts and bruises. You might want to avoid looking in the mirror for a few days.' She pats my hand.

'Greg's here,' Dad says, pulling up another chair. I cringe at the thought of him seeing me like this, but I can hardly tell him to go away.

'Hello, Greg,' Mum says, moving up so he can get nearer.

'How are you feeling, Gemma?' Greg towers over me, concern creasing his face. Dad offers him a chair.

'Okay, I guess.' Fresh tears squeeze out of the corners of my eyes. Is it possible to embarrass myself any more? 'Can you tell me what happened?'

Greg fills me in on the state he found me in. How Scarlett and her friend Amy saw what Nick did to me via the baby cam and shouted at Nick to stop.

'They called the police on Scarlett's phone, which had been switched off from the time she took Thomas. Nick found Scarlett before the police, in the Riverside multi-storey thanks to a tracking device he'd installed on her mobile. They kept the baby away from him, but he went after Scarlett and tried to push her off the car park roof. The police arrived and arrested him and found Thomas safe and well.'

'Thank God.' I kiss Thomas's forehead.

'Nick used his nickname Cole when he was with Scarlett. He'd told her at Christmas that you had left him, so she had no idea you were still together or pregnant. But when she found out, apparently she wanted to punish him.'

'Nick manipulated us both. I don't want to press any charges against either of the girls, only Nick.'

Chapter Seventy-Eight

The police question us, but they let us go because thankfully Gemma decides not to press charges. She tells them she gave me permission to look after Thomas and accepts our reasons for not bringing him back on time, given everything that has happened. I give the police all text and email conversations between Cole and me. He's being questioned for attempted murder, grooming me while in his care at school and for coercive behaviour and domestic violence towards Gemma.

Amy and I hug goodbye on the steps outside the police station. She goes with her mum back to their B&B.

When Mum and I get home, I go to bed exhausted. I sleep for twelve hours straight.

My tongue is rough from dehydration when I wake up. I have a shower and go down to the kitchen. Mum is there waiting for me with a pot of tea. I wonder how many pots she's made over the past few hours, hoping I'd wake up. We both know that without Amy, I wouldn't be here right now.

Mum and I sit in the kitchen for ages drinking tea, eating bacon sandwiches with brown sauce, enjoying the quiet, gentle routine. Pixi jumps on my lap, purring as I stroke her.

'How are you feeling today?' Mum asks.

'A bit stunned at everything that's happened. Grateful too. I hope Thomas and Gemma are doing well. I feel really bad about taking him, hurting her when she didn't deserve it.'

'It must have been traumatic for her when you didn't return her baby and she wasn't sure of your intention, but I think you may have saved her.'

'I was so angry with Cole. Why couldn't I see what he was really like?'

'Some people are good at hiding their true selves. He was cunning and manipulative. Don't blame yourself. People like that hook you in emotionally so they can get you to do what they want.'

'We looked after Thomas really well, at least Amy did most of it. She surprised me in so many ways.'

'I think the fact that you cared for him went in your favour with the police.'

'I hope so, we'd never have hurt him. He was actually quite sweet. I didn't know babies were such hard work, though – and I definitely don't want one.'

'Tell me about it.' A smile lifts her lips momentarily.

I stare into my cup of milky tea, trying to find a way to ask her about my dad.

'Was that man…'

'Yes,' she interrupts, reading my mind, 'your dad is the person who contacted the TV show. His name is Lewis.'

'Oh.'

'I didn't want you to ever know about him.' Her head dips and she curls both hands around her mug. 'I couldn't see how you'd benefit from it. But maybe I was wrong and Tina was right, I should have told you sooner.'

'It's okay, I know you were looking out for me.'

'Maybe I was too scared how you'd react.' Mum's eyes fill with tears.

'Why scared?'

She shakes her head.

'Do you have a photo of him?'

I follow Mum to her room and she lifts down the boxes from her wardrobe. She takes out the photos Amy and I looked at before. She sifts through them and places the photo of her sister and husband on their wedding day in front of me on the bed.

'This is your dad,' she says. I squint at it and frown at Mum.

'He was married to your sister?'

'Yes.'

I pick it up and examine their faces, how happy they were in this moment. 'What, so he had an affair with you?'

'No. Absolutely not.'

'You went out with him first?'

Mum shakes her head, balled-up fist to her lips.

'Then I… I don't understand.'

Mum takes both my hands in hers, tears falling down her cheeks. She swallows before she speaks.

'Jess was your real mum.'

Chapter Seventy-Nine

14 August 2018

Scarlett

I search Mum's face for some flicker of doubt but there is none. She's sobbing now, so it must be true. I can't get my head around what she's just said. That she's not my real mum. She pulls me to her and holds me tight.

'Are you sure?' is all I can think to say. It seems such a stupid question but I'm at a complete loss.

She pulls back, nodding, holding my hands. 'I'm so sorry. I told you Jess died young, didn't I?'

I nod. 'So what – you've been looking after me since then?'

'Yes. Since you were a baby.'

'Oh.' The floor seems to rush up to my eyes. My whole history has been altered.

'I've tried to do my best for you, Scarlett. It's not always been easy. And I know I've not been the greatest mum.'

'What are you talking about? Yes, you have. You'll always be my mum.' I hug her and she hugs me back. 'But I suppose Jess was my mum too.'

'Yes, she was. And I've wanted to tell you about her but it's been so hard, too risky.'

'I don't understand.' I pick up the wedding photo and try to find a connection with this woman who gave birth to me. 'I guess we do look alike, but so do you.'

'You really look like her. I'll dig out some more photos of when she was younger, then you'll see.'

'What was she like?'

'She was honestly the kindest, sweetest sister I could have wished for. Always thinking of others before herself. One time she bought me a Rick Astley single with her first pay packet from working as a cashier in Boots.'

'Did she like reading? What was her favourite music?'

'She adored reading, just like you. Her favourite song at the time was "Two Hearts" by Phil Collins.'

'How did she and my dad meet?'

'I was with her the moment they clapped eyes on each other. We were in Sweet, a nightclub where we lived in Brighton. He sent a glass of champagne over to our table for her. We didn't know who it was from at first. The barman pointed him out, said it was from a secret admirer. She didn't want to drink it. Left it on the table and went back to the dance floor. I drank it, though, and I saw him glaring at me from the bar. I had an uncomfortable feeling about him in that split second. They say always go with your gut instinct, don't they?'

'How did they get together?'

'He pursued her. Watched her dancing so she knew he had his eye on her, then danced near her and eventually when the slow dances came on, she couldn't say no to him because she was flattered by his attention. He was so handsome and knew it. She could hardly believe he'd singled her out. He told her he was shy and that's why he'd sent the drink over. There was nothing shy about him, so I knew he was playing a game. He sent her flowers the next day, wined and dined her and by the end of the first month it was hard to prise them apart. She stopped coming out with me and the girls and spent every moment with him. I'd catch his eye now and again and he'd have this smug look on his face as if to say, *I've got her now, she's mine*. And she wouldn't hear a bad word against him. He told her she was beautiful, yet he started to question who she was hanging around with, what music she listened to, what she was wearing. Little comments dropped here and there, always with a concerned face and a charming smile, so it was hard for her to disagree with him. *Isn't that a bit revealing? You wanna look classy, don't you? Only sluts dress like that.* He'd glance at me when he said it. *Are you trying to make me jealous? Do you want other men ogling at you?'*

'Didn't she realize what he was doing?' I think of Cole commenting on my clothes, always questioning the length of my skirts.

'She said she could see his side of it. That him being as jealous as he was showed how much he loved and needed her.'

'God, that's exactly what I thought about Cole.'

'You had a lucky escape then. Lewis told Jess a pack of lies about being brought up in a children's home so he had no one who loved him until she came along. I tried to tell her that he didn't own her and shouldn't say the things he did. But she was always trying to put herself in the other person's shoes to understand how they were feeling. She saw him as an injured bird that needed caring for. She was the sort of person who listened to people's stories of woe and would never make assumptions about them like some people do. And she really believed she was in love with him.'

'When did they get married?'

'Only about eight months after they first met. He planned it all. She thought it was sweet that he wanted to take control, told us he was a new man not expecting her to do it all. But by then he'd started to control everything she did.'

'That's what Cole did to Gemma. He sprung the wedding on her so she couldn't even tell her parents.'

'I think it takes a while to realize the person you love is taking over your life. Lewis insisted on seeing her wedding dress to make sure it was to his liking. She told him it was unlucky to see it before the big day and that he'd have to wait like everyone else.' Mum's voice catches in her throat. 'Sorry, it's just that she told me this from her hospital bed. The bruises on her body were horrific. She had a deep cut on her arm, but she insisted she cut it on a glass she dropped in the kitchen. Left a nasty scar. When I asked her outright, did he do this, she couldn't physically answer me, it was as though he was in the room with us holding his hands around her throat. She swore blind he didn't do it.'

'Bloody hell. Didn't the hospital ask questions?'

'She told them she'd fallen over. They had to accept that. I don't think there was much they could do if she didn't want to report it to the police.'

'Did you go to their wedding?'

'I did but only to try and talk her out of it. It had to be put back and rearranged because of her being in such a bad way, so in the end it was very low key, a registry office ceremony and buffet lunch at a pub afterwards with a few friends he'd selected. He'd got his way and seen the dress she chose. Too revealing for his liking, apparently, so he'd picked another one out for her. It didn't really suit her. Well, you've seen the photo. It wasn't the most flattering dress, high neck lace and ridiculous fishtail and flounces.'

'I must admit I did sneak a look in this box.'

'I guessed you had.'

'I assumed it was you when I first saw the wedding photo, but then I was puzzled about the mark on your arm.'

'We did look very alike. I've got some more photos in the other box up there. I can get it down if you're ready for more?'

'I think I am.'

Mum reaches the box with her fingertips. She slides it towards her and brings it down to the bed. The key is in a small dish on the window sill. She checks my face to see if I'm still okay with this. I nod.

'You've never said how Jess died.'

'No.' Mum turns away, fussing with unlocking the box.

'Please, I need to know.' I reach for her arm and she stands in front of me, taking my hands in hers again, but she looks everywhere except at me. Her skin is cool and smooth despite the heat. She takes in a deep breath, kisses both my palms. Then her hands grip mine tight, as though she's clinging to me over the edge of a mountain to save me from falling. My stomach flips.

'There's no easy way to say this. Your mum was murdered.'

Chapter Eighty

14 August 2018

Scarlett

'What, how?'

'Your dad killed her.' Mum sobs, eyes screwed up with instant tears.

My body jolts violently, as though the ground beneath me has cracked open and I'm tumbling down a dark hole. I drop to the floor and dig my nails into the carpet. My whole life is disintegrating in front of me. Everything I've ever known was constructed from this violent secret. It's all been a pack of lies.

'I'm so, so sorry.' Mum kneels next to me and wraps me in her arms, stroking my hair. 'I didn't want you to find out, ever. But I'm scared he knows your name now, what you look like.'

My head is floating. Nothing will ever be the same because now I know the truth: my dad killed my mum.

'Why?' I hear my voice, but it doesn't sound like me. Mum holds me tight and we rock backwards and forwards.

'We'll have to move away, start over again.'

'I thought he was in prison.'

'He's up for parole next year.'

My head is splitting open and a pain is stabbing the back of my eye. I'm grateful I didn't know before now so I could grow up happy and carefree. Ignorance really was bliss.

I take a deep breath and sit on the bed. 'Can you tell me how it happened?'

Mum sits next to me and lets out a sigh that sounds like she's been holding it in all my life, anticipating this moment.

'Jess's next-door neighbour found her lying on her side in the kitchen. Lewis had run out of the front door a few moments before, holding his hands up dripping with blood, screaming his head off at half one in the morning. Jess was trying to leave him. We had it all worked out. He said he was innocent. That he found her dead. But he'd stabbed her once with a kitchen knife.' She presses her hand to her mouth. I rub her arm. 'I tried so hard to help her get away from him, but he wouldn't let me near her. He took her phone away and was keeping her locked in the house.'

'That's crazy, she must have been so scared,' I sob and stare at myself in the dressing-table mirror, trying to imagine being Jess for a second, what it must have felt like living with someone so dangerous. I think of Gemma with Cole. Is that how it would have ended for them?

'What do you think made him do it?'

Mum cups my face and strokes my hair. 'It was because she threatened to leave him and he couldn't allow that. It's all about power, control. I helped her plan her escape. I found her a safe house to go to. They were all ready and waiting for her. I dropped a new mobile through her letterbox and some cash which she hid, but the night she planned to leave, he found them and worked out what she was up to. She'd just texted me to say she was on her way out of the back door. That was the last I heard from her. The next thing I knew, she was dead.'

'Jesus, and I guess you knew it was him straight away.'

'The women's refuge told us it's always dangerous when a victim tries to leave their abuser because they're losing control of them.'

'Do you really think they'll let him out? Can't we appeal against it?'

'I think it would be better to move.' She opens the box and lifts out more photos. 'I collected everything about the case, all the newspaper cuttings, court reports, interviews. I thought if you ever found out and wanted to know about it, it would all be here. I knew one day he'd be released and that you may be forced to deal with it. I've not looked in here for years, not since you were a baby.'

I sit on the bed and go through a small bundle of photos of Jessica and Lewis with each of their parents. She looks so small next to him. I search her face for some kind of recognition that this is my mum. I'm desperate to find a connection, but nothing comes and an ache spreads over me. To think what he did to her sickens me to the stomach. What kind of man does that? Beats a woman physically half his size and weaker than him. Presumably in front of me, his baby daughter. What a sick fucking bastard. Just like Cole. I should probably be grateful he didn't kill me too. I pick up a photo of Mum holding me at my christening, I didn't even know I'd been christened.

'Isn't there one of Jess holding me?'

'Erm, I don't think so.' She flicks through a few photos.

'She was religious, was she?'

'A bit. She got that from our gran. Our parents weren't regular churchgoers. Jess always had this dream of dressing you up in a beautiful christening gown, holding you in the church in front of the font. She loved traditional things, family values. He ripped all that apart.'

'Did she go to college or work?'

'When she met your dad, she was working in the big Debenhams in Brighton as manager of women's wear. She loved her job, but that was one of the first things he stopped her doing. Said she didn't need to work when he had such a good wage selling insurance. He told her it would be better for her to stay at home and look after the house and family. It seemed a luxury to her. But she wasn't one to sit around watching television or going to coffee mornings. She'd always talked about starting her own jewellery business and she thought it was the perfect opportunity, so she agreed to leave her job. But as soon as she did, he made her believe she wasn't good enough to be a businesswoman, that she was getting above herself to think she could design and make her own pieces of jewellery. "Who'd want this crap?" I heard him say to her once. He hardly gave her any money for food, and she'd have to beg him if she needed new shoes or underwear. But whenever I challenged her about it, she made excuses for him, saying they had to watch every penny. When I last saw her, there were holes in her clothes. If I tried to give her anything, he'd chuck it in the bin, tell her they didn't need hand-outs, that I was trying to embarrass him, make her think he couldn't provide for her. He had an answer for bloody everything.'

I flick through each photo in turn then go through them all again.

'What are you looking for?' Mum gives a little cough into her balled-up fist, a thing she does when she's nervous about something.

'I can't find *any* of me with them.'

Mum blinks rapidly, knots her fingers together.

'You must have another box somewhere with ones of me with Jessica?' I scan the room for where they could be – some secret hiding place I've missed. 'You haven't thrown them away, have you?' I desperately want to see one. It will help solidify in my mind that I had another mother who gave birth to me, who loved me because I was her little girl.

Mum tidies up the photos and tucks them back in the box.

'Mu-um?' It dawns on me that she's never mentioned exactly *when* Jess died, which seems odd as it's often one of the first things people tell you about a loved one who has passed away as anniversaries are such a special time to remember them.

'How old did you say I was when Jessica died?'

'I don't think I did.' Her tone is flat.

'So when was it exactly, can you tell me the date?' I'm uncomfortable pushing the point, but there's something she's not saying.

Mum takes in a breath and exhales slowly, focusing on the box, stroking the lid. She looks up and locks eyes with me for a moment, then quickly looks away.

'Your mum died on the day you were born.'

Her words are a hot poker prodded in my heart. 'Oh. But there must be photos of me with her straight after I was born?' I think of Gemma with baby Thomas, their first photos together. Gemma beaming at her beautiful newborn son, proudly displayed on her Facebook page despite her exhaustion and the blood-stained sheets.

'I'm sorry, there aren't any.'

'Why not? There must be one.'

'Well, there aren't,' Mum snaps. She sits heavily on the bed, hand to her forehead. 'I'm sorry.'

I frown, trying to work out what could have happened. Perhaps the birth was a difficult one and Jess was in surgery afterwards. But no, Mum said my dad killed Jess at home. Perhaps she left hospital before anyone had a chance to take a photo. She went home and tried to leave him that night. I might have been in my carrycot near her and seen the whole thing.

'Please can you tell me why?' I brace myself for her to shout at me to stop pestering. Instead she is stony-faced for what seems like minutes but maybe it's only seconds. 'Hang on, didn't you tell me your sister died before I was born?'

She brushes her hair away from her face. Her hand is trembling.

'How is that possible if she gave birth to me?'

'Jess was still pregnant with you when your dad stabbed her to death.'

Chapter Eighty-One

14 August 2018

Scarlett

I stare at Mum in utter shock and hope this is a nightmare I'll wake up from, but she doesn't stop there.

'Jess died and you had to be delivered at the scene. You spent your first few days in hospital because of the lack of oxygen. You were so weak but thankfully you grew stronger and were able to come home. You're lucky to be alive.'

Come home? I had no home without a mother or father. *Lucky to be alive.* I stumble towards Mum and I collapse into her arms. She kisses my hair, whispers that she loves me, and everything will be okay because we have each other. I picture her as she would have been then, a frightened eighteen-year-old girl who'd lost her sister in the most horrific way and suddenly she had the responsibility of bringing up her niece from the moment she was born. Delivered from my dead mother's body. At last I understand the photo of mum holding me as a tiny baby. It captures the anguish, fear and love in her eyes, in the very fabric of her face. It's not surprising she never trusted a man enough to marry him, and never had children of her own.

She rummages around in the box, digging to the bottom and pulls out a folder of newspaper cuttings. I flip open the cover then immediately slam it shut. I can't face seeing the pictures. It's too much to take in.

All the wonderful parties each year for my birthday flutter one after another through my mind. Never realizing it was the day my mother died. Each year without fail Mum cried and I assumed she was being soppy. But she was crying for her sister missing out on seeing her baby grow up, crying for Jess never seeing me, never holding me, and for never having the chance to be my mummy. Maybe she was crying a little for herself too, for everything she'd sacrificed for me.

'Why did she stay with him?'

'At first, I suppose because she loved him and couldn't see that she was being controlled.'

'Did she want to have me?'

'She really wanted a baby, but probably not straight away. I guess his plan was to keep her occupied and reliant on him by looking after children. He wanted her to have a whole lot more so she'd be vulnerable and dependent. She became too scared to leave but she'd plucked up the courage. I tried so hard to help but I failed.'

'It's not your fault.'

She nods once and looks away.

'Do you know if she wanted more children?'

'Yes… she did. She lost one a couple of months before falling with you. She believed that if she could build a family, he would mellow out. She never said how or why she miscarried; she was about four months gone. I always wondered if he hurt her in some way. When she got pregnant with you, she started to accept he wasn't going to change. Our mum died suddenly of a heart attack a few weeks before you were due and he wouldn't let her go to the funeral. She pleaded with him, but he ripped up all her photos of Mum and Dad and said he was her family now, she didn't need anyone else. That's when she asked me to help her plan how to leave him.'

My chest weighs heavily with grief for the mother I never knew. Ripped from her dead body where I grew, where she nurtured me. The place I was supposed to be safest in the world.

'Jess would have wanted you to have this.' Mum hands me a small jewellery box. I open it. Inside is a gold star pendant.

'She always wore it because she believed in hope. Right up to the end she had this amazing belief that things would improve, that deep down he loved her enough to want to change. Maybe he did in his own twisted way. I hope he's living with that pain every day of his miserable life.'

I take it from her and examine it in my palm. There's a tiny stone in the centre. 'It's an aquamarine, her birthstone.' Mum does the clasp up for me. I kiss the star wishing she could be with me. What would she think of me taking someone's baby? I'm so ashamed.

'You don't think I take after Lewis in any way, do you?' The words fall from my mouth. I'm not sure I really want to know.

'Maybe his temper a little, but you're not cruel like him. You're more like Jess, kind and bright and thoughtful.'

It feels weird having parents I've never met – one alive but in prison and the other dead.

I spot a notebook tucked down one side of the box.

'What's that?'

Mum takes it out and hands it to me. 'Diary 1996-7' is written on the front in gold letters. I glance up at Mum and she nods. I open the cover and inside is 'Jessica', written in beautiful loopy handwriting, a bit like my own. I run the tip of my finger along it. Mum sniffs back tears. 'See, you and Jess are so alike.'

'Can I read this?' I ask.

'Of course. Be warned, though, it was her secret diary so it goes into detail about the things Lewis did to her. She'd hidden it at the back of a cupboard in the kitchen. I found it when I was clearing her stuff out after he was sentenced.'

I flick through the pages, she's dated each at the top.

> *16 October 1996 – Found out today I'm five weeks pregnant! Lewis is so happy. This is what I've been hoping for. Something for us to focus on, a baby we've made together that we can love.*

14 April 1997 – I'm getting so big already. Lewis makes fun of me not fitting in my clothes. I worry that he's more interested in other women, like Alka who works at the corner shop.

5 June 1997 – I'm so uncomfortable but not long until I meet my little baby girl. We found out the sex at the last scan. Thought it would be nice and easier to plan the nursery. I hope with all my heart that this baby brings Lewis back to me. A nicer, kinder Lewis, like when we first met.

30 June 1997 – We've decided we're going to name her Scarlett after Scarlett O'Hara in Gone with the Wind because she's going to be beautiful, resilient and strong.

3 July 1997 – I didn't realize what was happening at first, but then the scales fell from my eyes. Things have gradually got worse. He criticizes and questions everything I say and do. He blatantly puts me down in front of others, then he either denies it or tells me I'm overreacting. He's never been a great talker, but now he's stopped all communication with me. He's grumpy with me all the time but in front of others, he becomes his usual charming self. I put it down to work stress and that his mother's breast cancer has come back.

Could he be depressed or having an affair? I don't know, I'm constantly trying to find a solid reason for his behaviour towards me. It seems that the more I let him get away with, the worse he becomes. So often I've argued back, demanded that he treat me with respect but he shifts the blame back to me, takes no responsibility for anything. He denies things I accuse him of with such conviction, it scares me. It always ends up with him telling me I'm mad and me apologizing to him just to end the argument. It's *easier not to point out his bad behaviour just to avoid rowing.*

It feels like he hates me, he's so against me in everything I do.

12 July 1997 – Last night we went out for dinner and it seemed to have gone really well. We were in the car and I don't know exactly what I said to irritate him, but we were coming into the drive and he slammed on the brakes. The atmosphere froze solid, as though all the air had been sucked away. I moved to get out of the car but he got out first and came round to my side. I thought he was being gentlemanly for a change, but he grabbed my hair and slammed my head on the side of the car, then he strolled up to the front door and walked in, leaving me there. When I went in he'd gone to bed. I was in shock that he could do that to me. I sat on the sofa, stunned. If he could do that so casually, he could do anything. I sat there all night, fearing for my life. I didn't know how I was going to hide the bruising on my face.

When it started to get light outside, I made myself get up and go to the downstairs loo. I didn't flush because I didn't want to wake him. I peered in the mirror. The whole side of my face and my ear were swollen. He came down soon after and I was sitting in the kitchen with a hot cup of tea but I was shaking all over. There were tears in his eyes. 'I'm so, so sorry. It was an awful thing to do. I was so stressed about work. Please forgive me?' He knelt in front of me and cupped my hands in his. And I forgave him because I love him and I truly believe he loves me too. He has a temper that he can't control but it doesn't stop his love for me and the bump. I honestly think that he's shocked by what he did. Perhaps he'll think before he loses it. Maybe it's me? Do I say things to press the wrong buttons in him?

14 July 1997 – Every day I think about leaving him. What kind of wife am I? I should stick it out. Anyway, I can't go anywhere. I have no money. We don't have a joint account. He owns everything, including the house. I have absolutely nothing. But it's hard to imagine life without him. I'm ashamed and embarrassed to tell anyone, even Kelly. She looks up to me. She thinks we have a happy marriage and are just having a few difficulties. I thought I did too.

I put the diary down. I can't read any more. I'll have to come back to it bit by bit. I pick up one of the newspaper cuttings, but I can't stomach the details.

'Why didn't she leave him sooner?'

'It's the nature of coercive abuse. Living like that had become normal to her. She couldn't make any decisions without him because he'd taken away all her confidence. Chipped at it bit by bit. He pushed her family and friends away, controlled everything she did, everything she wore. In the end she had no free will. I tried texting and emailing her but every time the messages bounced back or failed to be delivered. He'd taken her phone and laptop away from her. Stripped out any contacts. He locked the front door when he went out and took the key with him, so she was a prisoner in her own home. He had all these weird rules she had to follow, like not opening the curtains during the day, not sitting at the table to eat with him at the same time. God, I wish I'd known sooner. I wish I'd asked more questions, made more fuss, but on the other hand, he made her suffer when I did turn up unannounced. He'd think she'd contacted me somehow, even though she had no means of doing so. I remember calling back the very next day when I knew he was at work, but she couldn't open the door. I saw her through the letterbox, the bruises on her arms. She was so scared she could barely speak and of course it was so much worse once she was pregnant with you. She had to protect her bump and herself.'

I think about Gemma and wonder how far down this line she was with Cole. How long would it have been before he'd lost control and killed her?

I shudder at the thought of Lewis knowing my name, knowing who I am, sending a message to Mum on live TV.

'Will we really have to move away because of him?'

'I can't see another way. I don't have the money to appeal. Anyway, he knows who you are now, what town we live in.'

I pick up Jess's driving licence and passport. She was a beautiful woman. This was my real mother. It's going to take a while to get used to that.

'I kept these for you too. I know she'd have wanted you to have them.' She hands me a jewellery box with lots of colourful pieces inside. A scan photo. My first booties and the tiny wrist bands with my birth date written on underneath: 'Baby girl of Jessica Gordon.'

'I ordered a copy of my full birth certificate, but it has your name on it.'

'I'm sorry. I panicked after you were born. I packed up and moved us to Bedfordshire when you were only a few weeks old. My mum's friend Jean took us in and looked after us for the first few months until I felt ready to find my own place. I needed a fresh start where nobody knew us. I registered your birth when we arrived. Putting my name as your mother seemed the best solution at the time. Jean was a midwife and wrote up some discharge papers in my name. I didn't want Lewis having any claim over you.'

'Where is Jess buried?'

'She was cremated. I scattered her ashes off the end of Brighton Pier. It's somewhere she always enjoyed going when we were kids. It was hard to know what to do. We'd never talked about what we wanted if one of us died. Being the eldest, she was the one I always turned to for advice.'

'Could we do something together, a little ceremony in her memory?'

'Yes, of course, that would be lovely.'

We hug each other.

'So what happens now with you and me?' I ask. 'Can I still call you Mum?'

'Of course you can, if you're happy to. I'd be honoured.'

'Where does Dan fit into all this? You said he dated Jess.'

'They were serious for three years. I thought and hoped they'd get married, but they broke up when she met Lewis. Dan regrets not being able to save her but there wasn't much he could do. Lewis threatened him to keep away. Jess was dazzled by Lewis, that's the bottom line. I think she really loved him.'

'I thought he might be my dad.'

'Definitely not, but he was like a dad to you when you were a toddler. He emigrated to America straight after Jess died. I think it was too much for him. But he came back to see us a couple of times. He used to take you to the park and watch kids' programmes with you.'

'Oh I see. So the memories I've had which I thought were with my dad were with him? Did he used to give me Malted Milk biscuits?'

'That's right, his favourite. He was so good with you. I wanted him to stay. We grew close but neither of us could take it further. Too many reminders of Jess.'

'He seemed really nice. I wish you could have met someone special.'

'I wasn't going to say anything yet, but he's invited us to go with him to America.'

'Mum, that would be amazing! Do you really like him?'

'I do, but tell me, what do you think?'

'I'd love to go there on holiday.'

'I'm not talking about a holiday, I mean to live.'

'What? I can't leave Amy.'

'I told you, we need to get away as soon as possible. He's offered us this chance.'

'What about the house?'

'I've already given the landlord our notice. We have to be out of here in two weeks.'

'Mum! Why haven't you said a word to me about this?'

'Because I knew you'd find some excuse to stay. Do you realize what a brilliant opportunity it is?'

'I'll think about it, okay?' I go to the door. Perhaps she'll settle with Dan, he'll be good for her. But I don't think I want to go.

'By the way, the ring I gave you on your birthday was your mum's engagement ring. She'd have wanted you to have it for your 21st.'

I gaze at my finger, the diamonds sparkling a spectrum of colours as it catches the light. I lift it up to my lips and kiss it. Knowing that it was something my mother wore when presumably she was happy and hopeful for the future, instantly makes it my most precious possession.

Mum comes up to me and touches my face then holds me close. All this time she's kept me safe.

We go downstairs. I call Amy and wait for her to arrive. I stand at the patio doors with a glass of water. The grass is yellow, dried out and brittle from the long hot summer. Rain is forecast for next week. Some things never seem to change. But my whole world has tipped on its axis.

I think back to the day Cole finished with me. I was such a child still really, not thinking what I was doing, what *he* was doing to me, manipulating me. I was lost in a blissful bubble that wasn't real. I was so stupid to believe he would leave his wife and baby for me. Our lives together had seemed within touching distance, but I'd have been walking into the same trap as my mother had found herself in – loving a jealous, controlling man.

Tina drops Amy off and Mum persuades her to join us for a coffee. I give Amy the biggest hug ever. Tina tells Mum she's decided not to work nights any more. She's seen a job as a receptionist in a gym that she's going for. She wants to be around more for Amy.

Mum makes us a mango and banana smoothie. She's just heard from the police who've told her they traced the threatening emails Cole was claiming to be getting from me and Amy. They confirmed they were from Cole's teenage son. He had a baby with a woman seventeen years ago. He was knocking her about too, but she managed to run away with their baby. The boy was getting his revenge on his dad for what he did to them. Cole had such a skewed view of fathers not having rights to see their children. Sometimes there's a good reason.

Amy and I sit in the garden sipping our drinks in silence. The weather is nowhere near as hot as it was. I suppose summer is almost over. A torn red piece of piñata raffia flutters in the rose bush. I tell her everything Mum told me about my parents and that we're moving to America in case Dad finds us when he's released. I hold Amy's hand and we both cry.

Mum lets me take Amy upstairs to see the contents of the box we couldn't get into. I lift open the lid. There's his face again. I pick the photo up and stare at it for ages. I wonder if he was like Cole; charming, complimentary, persuasive, authoritative and clever with words. It's a grainy picture but it's clear how handsome he was then. How easy it must have been for Jess to fall in love with him.

Chapter Eighty-Two

I meet Gemma for coffee at her restaurant. She's surprisingly welcoming considering what I did.

'Come and sit down,' she says, leading the way to a table near the coffee maker.

'I'm really grateful you didn't press charges, Gemma.' I look her in the eye then hang my head in shame. 'I'm sorry for what I did. I really wish I'd known how he was treating you. All the signs were there but I didn't quite join the dots.'

'You saved me, Scarlett, and I'm so grateful.' She blinks, getting teary and I do too, thinking about what he did to her, seeing him turn into an animal. I think about my mum, going through something like this too.

'I never thought to tell anyone about him when I was at school,' I say. 'I didn't imagine he'd go on to do what he did.'

'How were we to know what was going on in that sick head of his? You should count yourself lucky you got away.' She brings over two cappuccinos.

I wish my mum had got away. I wish she'd stayed with Dan. What a good life they'd have had. Maybe living here or in America. But I'd never have been born.

'Your job's still here if you want it.'

'Thanks, but we're moving away, starting afresh.'

'Somewhere nice?'

'America.'

'That's a big move. Good luck. Would be good to keep in touch.'

'Yeah, I'd like that.'

—

Later, I pack my last few things and vacuum my bedroom. It looks strange, empty. We've had some good times here. Most of our stuff is in storage. We'll get it shipped out later, but for now we're only taking essentials.

It's been hard deciding to go with Mum and Dan to New York, but Amy persuaded me it was an opportunity I couldn't pass up. If I really hate it, I'm coming back. That's our agreement.

'Dan says he'll be here in about ten minutes, Scarlett. Are you ready?' Mum calls up the stairs.

'Yes, all packed.'

'I'd better go.' Amy hugs me one last time. 'You promise to FaceTime me every day, okay?'

'I promise. And you have to come and visit.'

'I will. I've started saving up already. Mum's keen too.' She picks up a rucksack of my old things I've given her. She's going to ebay them and make a bit of cash.

I follow her downstairs. She waves to Mum who's still on the phone to Dan. I see her out. Neither of us wants to prolong the agony with a long goodbye.

As I'm turning to go back upstairs, there's a knock on the front door. Amy must have forgotten something. I open it and a tall man with dark blonde and grey hair is standing there grinning at me. He looks familiar.

'Hello?' I wonder what's so amusing to him.

'Hello, Scarlett.'

'Do I know you?' I tilt my head.

'I don't think so, but I'd like to get to know you,' he says, putting his foot up on the step, 'because I'm your dad.'

Chapter Eighty-Three

Scarlett

'Go away, I don't want to see you,' I scream and try to shut the door, but his shoe is in the way.

'Who's that?' Mum rushes out of the kitchen, phone in her hand. 'What the hell? Hurry, Lewis is here.' She shouts down the phone.

'How are you, Kelly?' Dad pushes the door wide, steps into the house and shuts it quietly behind him.

'I'm calling the police, do you hear me?' Mum shouts, her hands shaking.

'I wouldn't do that if I were you.' He strides towards her and takes her phone clean out of her hand.

'You can't barge in here,' she says, 'give that back.'

I run ahead of him and stand in front of Mum, arms out, blocking him so he can't get to her.

'Scarlett, stop that. Get behind me.' Mum tries to pull me out of her way.

'I've come to see my daughter, no law against that, is there?' He stops and smiles down at us.

'She doesn't want to see you, didn't you hear her?' Mum backs up, stumbles into the kitchen.

'I thought you were in prison?' I stand by Mum, glancing at the back door, trying to work out if it's locked.

'Got out a month ago.'

'Did you know this, Mum?' The key is in the door, so it's probably unlocked.

Mum glares at him with such hatred, then she slowly nods.

'Why didn't you tell me?' He must have been watching the news, finding out all sorts about me including what school I went to, where we live, where I work.

'I didn't want you to be scared. I tried to get us away before he found us, I'm sorry.' She clasps my hand in hers.

'I'm a changed man, Scarlett.' He holds his palms up.

'But you killed my mother.' I look at him disgusted and pull away from Mum as he comes towards me. I feel my back press into the counter. My pulse is thundering in my temples. There's nowhere else for me to go.

He shakes his head. 'No, I didn't.'

'What?' I look at Mum, frowning. 'Why would he say that?'

'He's lying, Scarlett. He was found guilty.' Mum reaches out to me but he's in the way. I'm cornered.

'Doesn't mean I did it. You know that. Remember the Birmingham Six, Kelly? All innocent men. Banged up for life. All false convictions. Happens all the time.'

'So if you didn't do it, then who did?'

He is silent as though waiting for something.

The back gate rattles open. Lewis steps past Mum and opens the back door.

'Right on cue. Hello, Danny boy. Still sneaking in through people's back doors, are we?' Dad eases a length of lead pipe out of Dan's fists and thuds the heel of his hand into his chest. Dan falls backwards, down the two steps.

'Still trying to play with the big boys, aren't you?' Lewis kicks Dan's heels.

'What are you doing?' Mum screams and pulls at Dad's jacket but he gently swots her away.

'And you should tighten up the security on your phone. I can read and hear all your calls.' He twiddles her phone around in his fingers and chucks it back to her.

'Tell them what you did, Danny boy.' Lewis leans on the kitchen counter.

Dan rubs the back of his head, looking bewildered.

'I'll tell them for you then, shall I? The night Jess was going to leave me, Dan here tried to be the big hero. He let himself in through the back door into our kitchen where Jess was getting ready to leave. Except he wasn't supposed to be there, it wasn't part of the plan, was it, Kelly?'

Mum's eyes are wide. She shakes her head.

'You see, Kelly made the mistake of telling Dan her plan to get Jess to walk out on me – leave the back door open and sneak out in the middle of the night.'

Mum frowns at Dan, but neither of them says a word.

'Trouble is, while he was there, he thought he'd have a go at getting rid of me by stabbing me. So guess what? He took a big carving knife out of the block on the counter but Jess tried to stop him going upstairs to find me, and he dodged out her way. Except that made her lunge towards him to try and take the knife off him, but the fucking idiot was holding it out and stabbed her to death.'

'You're lying,' Mum screams.

'He dropped the knife, ran out the back door and left me to find her. I came down to see what all the noise was about and found her on the kitchen floor. I knelt over her but I couldn't find a pulse, she was already dead. I was covered in her blood when I went out the front to shout for help.'

'You killed her, you did it.' Mum points at Dad. 'Tell him he's wrong, Danny.'

Dan doesn't move or speak.

'Why do you think he snuck off to America? And he's been sending you money for Scarlett every year, hasn't he? Guilt money.'

'Dan, tell me he's lying.' Mum kneels next to him, pleading with him. I hold her arm trying to calm her down.

Dan shakes his head, eyes to the ground.

'What? Don't let him do this?' Mum stands up.

'Don't let me do what, Kelly? Isn't it enough that I've spent the last twenty years at Her Majesty's pleasure for something I didn't do?'

'It doesn't mean you weren't guilty of hurting Jess, intimidating her, making her life hell. Dan was trying to protect her from you.'

Dad turns to me, hands out. 'I've been on a DVPP rehabilitation programme. I know I treated your mum badly and it was wrong. But I did not kill her.'

'Is it true, Dan? Did you kill my mother?'

'I didn't mean to – it was an accident. Just like he said.'

'How does he know all this?' Mum crosses her arms, still determined to prove this is all a lie.

'I went to see Lewis in prison.' Dan finally pushes himself off the ground.

'You what?' Mum's face creases in disgust.

'You have to understand, the guilt was eating me away. I couldn't live with myself. Jess was in contact with so few people, I knew he'd work out that, apart from you, I was the only person who could have been there that night.'

'I can't believe I'm hearing this.'

'We talked and came to a deal,' Dan says.

'What sort of deal?'

'I make sure Scarlett is financially secure for the rest of her life and he doesn't tell the police it was me.' Dan stands up.

'There's no point another man doing time for this. He's suffered too. He killed the woman he loved,' Dad says.

'Did you love her?' I ask.

Dad turns to me. 'I did, but I didn't know how to love her. She was frightened of me. I hate that, but I was so insecure and scared of her leaving me. The only way I knew of keeping her with me was by controlling her. I understand that now. I have changed, Scarlett. I promise you. I'm working with the prison service as a counsellor, helping men learn to control their anger, recognize where that deep-rooted insecurity comes from that makes them want to control women.'

'So come on then, prove it,' Mum says.

'Erm, how about the simple fact that Danny boy is still breathing? And after everything I've been through, do you think I'd give up the chance of spending time with my daughter? If she wants to, of course.'

Mum doesn't have an answer for once. And I don't know what to say either. My head is spinning. I have my dad at last, but he's hardly how I imagined him to be. There's so much I need to get my head around. All three men have left my life in a complete mess. At least Gemma can enjoy being a mum to Thomas now, without fear and threats. I only wish Jess had been as fortunate.

I reach for Mum's hand and she smiles at me. Whatever happens next, I'm lucky to have her.

A letter from Ruby

Dear Reader,

Thank you for reading my fourth novel, *The Face at the Window*. I hope you enjoyed it! If you did, I'd be grateful if you could leave a quick review on Amazon, Kobo or Goodreads.

This novel was difficult to write for many reasons but mainly because of the subject matter. I've not been in an abusive relationship myself, but I've had a taste of it from a 'wrong' boyfriend and have known women who have been victims. When I was a teenager, I worked with a girl who showed me bruises on her legs and told me how her boyfriend held her face down in a sink of water. I think I asked her why she didn't leave him. I didn't understand why she stayed. I didn't understand that perhaps she was too scared to leave. Maybe we're all guilty of doing nothing, or not doing enough, but I've never forgotten my mistake.

In *The Face at the Window*, I wanted to explore the aftermath of domestic abuse in one family and the escalating abuse in another. One situation mirroring the next. How the nature of coercive control means the victim may not be strong enough to walk away because the perpetrator has worn down their confidence, taken over their finances, locked them in. Although there is a twist at the end of my novel, I wanted to show how my characters Lewis and Nick, were both capable of extreme violence.

I've watched several programmes on domestic abuse over the last few years and closely followed the case of Sally Challen, who was convicted of murdering her abusive husband in 2010.

Maybe not so well known is the case of Natalie Queiroz. I came across Natalie's story quite by chance online. I felt I needed to understand from a first-person account how such a violent act could come about. Natalie bravely and eloquently tells her story in her book, *Still Standing*. Fortunately, Natalie and her child survived.

Women's Aid reports that the Covid-19 pandemic escalated abuse and closed down routes to safety for women to escape. Child survivors have not had the respite of school or nursery. A few celebrities have shared their personal stories of surviving domestic abuse, including singers Mel B and Brenda Edwards. Talking about their experiences helps to bring this difficult subject into our conversations.

When I was growing up, domestic violence wasn't talked about at all. The police wouldn't interfere in a 'domestic'. Perhaps my ignorance and naivete are the reasons why I didn't know how to help the girl I worked with. I believe the more we talk about it, the more we can help those in need before they become another tragic statistic.

Warmest wishes,

Ruby x

Website/blog: rubyspeechley.com
Twitter: @rubyspeechley
Facebook: Ruby Speechley Author
Instagram: @rubyjtspeechley

Domestic Abuse Helplines and websites:

If you are in immediate danger call 999. If you cannot talk, dial 55 and the operator will respond.
National Domestic Violence Helpline: 0808 2000 247, open 24-hours a day, free and in confidence.
Nationaldahelpline.org.uk
Refuge.org.uk
Womensaid.org.uk

helpline@womensaid.org.uk
Men's advice helpline: 0808 8010327
Mensadviceline.org.uk

Acknowledgements

I wrote the messy zero draft of this novel via NaNoWriMo.org (write a novel in a month). It has changed a lot since then, but this writing tool helped me to get the words down quickly from my ideas and notes.

I would like to thank my husband and children for giving me the time and space to write during the national lockdown and a house move.

Thank you to all my friends and writers on social media and in real life for keeping me sane while working through such trying circumstances. I am incredibly grateful to be able to continue doing the job I love.

Once again, sincere thanks to my brilliant agent, Jo Bell for her expert advice and guidance, and to all the team at Bell Lomax Moreton for their support and enthusiasm.

Special thanks to my talented publishers at Hera Books, Keshini and Lindsey, for bringing this fourth novel to readers. Their dedication to their authors and to readers is so impressive. Thank you again to Keshini for being the best editor I could wish for.

Thank you to the many resources online including Refuge.org.uk, and to Graham Bartlett for his advice on crime and police matters in this story.

I've taken the liberty of merging Sainsbury's at Kempston with Bedford's main shopping centre. Any other changes or errors are entirely my own.

DVPP – Domestic Violence Perpetrator Programme is run by Cafcass.gov.uk "It aims to help people who have been abusive towards their partners and ex-partners to change their behaviour and develop respectful and non-abusive relationships."

Finally, thank you to all those working tirelessly every day to help and support victims and their families of domestic abuse.